C.E. Ricketts

❧❧❧

The Ship

Centuries in the future humanity has moved beyond the solar system into the farthest reaches of the galaxy.

Existing in-between the massive corporations that act as defacto governments in the frigid expanses, are independent ship captains plying their trade. Despite the innate risks of space travel, most eke out a decent, if boring, existence punctuated with engine troubles, transit delays, and the occasional pirate run-in.

Run-ins that are typically more irksome than dangerous.

Except for when they're not.

To Nicole

For Everything

one

emory, Sam thought, was a hell of a thing.

Sometimes, she couldn't remember where she'd put her comm unit thirty seconds after she'd last used it. Or the name of a contact she'd spoken to dozens of times would tickle on the tip of her tongue.

But sometimes it was as if the memory was an image file that had been burned into the hard drive of her brain.

Take, for instance, the bar station she was currently in. If she could download the picture in her head onto her tablet, she would wager a tidy sum that the rickety chairs and chipped tables, the dark corners, and the worn faces of the clientele would all match her recollection, despite it having been over fifteen years since her last visit.

Even the frail, ancient-looking man all but hanging off the end of the stained and dented bar looked the same.

She squinted, certain it was the same man. And there was a good chance he was dead. A shriveled corpse near the front entrance of his bar was just the kind of message Miles Floodwater would leave—

Oh, he moved. Not dead then.

Absently, she checked the multi-unit on her right wrist, but the black screen reminded her it was either uncharged or broken, which was incredibly relatable. She tried to recall the last time she hadn't felt exhausted and thought it might have been during that previous visit.

God, she'd been young. Twenty-one, eager, and absolutely desperate to get off the satellite she had lived on her entire life. She had wanted the freedom a ship promised so badly that she'd ignored the reputation of the bar and the man behind it. All that had mattered was fulfilling that want. That need.

Well, she figured she'd more than paid for that mistake.

You hadn't been alone then, though, her mind helpfully reminded her, as a pinch twisted in her chest. *It wasn't just you filled with youthful vigor dropping down into one of those chairs, foot tapping incessantly.*

Hey, stop jittering.

Sorry, I'm nervous.

Yeah, everyone in here can tell. Get a drink or something if you need it.

Fingers, still stiff and shaky from the cryo-chamber of the last job, punched in an order on the cracked screen of the table console. Whiskey dispensed from the table spigot into a spotted glass before being snatched up by a grease-stained hand.

Sam blinked and reached for the squat jar of slightly cloudy water in front of her. She sipped delicately, tasting a faint metallic tang, and wondered how much longer Floodwater was going to make her wait. Who would have thought that being an intergalactic criminal and all-around shit heel made one so busy.

It wasn't like she had anything better to do but, you know, there was always sleeping.

Yeah, because that comes so easy to you these days, her brain taunted.

The glass of water was halfway to her lips again when she noticed the first sign of trouble brewing. *Brewing* wasn't the right word; rather, trouble slid in almost silently. There were a few little things that tipped Sam off about the stranger: the simple jeans, dark shirt, and blue jacket were similar enough to the almost uniform threads of the bar's occupants, save for their pristine state. The gray scarf wrapped carelessly around her neck was not uncommon, but the silky fabric was hardly practical as a shield against dust swarms. The healthy, warm tone of her umber-colored skin was a marked contrast to the dull complexions around her; someone with access to better than substandard UV.

More so though, it was the openness of the woman's face that outed her—everyone else who came through Floodwater's front door on the regular looked as if they had something to hide.

The shift of tension in the room was subtle, and Sam knew she was not the only one to take note of the newcomer. She dropped the glass of water back down to the table even before the voice in her mind warned, *don't get involved.*

Despite her internal admonishment, her gaze lifted a second later. The room's flickering lights caught in vivid, coppery curls, drawing Sam's awareness again. The unknown woman was surveying the room, making no attempt to hide it. Sam leaned back in her chair, unconsciously pushing further into the shadows. She was sure she had nothing the woman wanted, but neither was she interested in clarifying that with a conversation.

As Sam watched, confusion and frustration clouded the stranger's face, as if what she saw was not what she had expected. Sam tried to imagine what could have brought her there. She looked neither desperate nor in despair, two of Floodwater's most typical visitors. And she didn't appear stoically resigned, which was the camp Sam placed herself in.

Otherwise known as "tired of this shit."

Sam was terrible at guessing ages, but the woman was either determined or reckless enough to make up her mind quickly. Twenties? But even as the sharp lines of her jaw set and she approached a table occupied by two men, there was a wariness in her step that hinted at caution—or control. Sam revised her estimate—mid-thirties? From that distance, it was hard to tell if the lines around her eyes were from age or stress.

The men might have been long haulers, judging by the rumpled state of their flight suits, plus the collection of mugs and shot glasses littering their table. Chances were they were either recently returned from inter-system travel or preparing to leave for a run into the outer reaches, where decent booze could be in short supply.

Wincing, Sam took another sip of her water to distract herself from the scene she suspected would unfold. She couldn't hear the conversation but knew what was being said. Her gaze drifted back in time to see the disbelief as it streaked across the woman's face, followed by anger and disgust in equal, warring measure.

Don't get involved, Sam reminded herself.

The woman stalked off, avoiding one of the men's arms with considerable agility. Methodically and with what had to be inhuman patience (*late thirties?*), she made her way around the room to every occupied table or booth and each interaction lasted about as long and went about as well as the first.

Don't get involved. The stranger drew closer, and Sam felt the hairs on the back of her neck prickle. She was seated deep in the corner, as far away from the bar as possible. Easily overlooked. Yet even as the woman seemed to scan every inch of the room except Sam's table, her feet brought her closer and closer.

Don't get in-

Two men stepped in front of the woman, blocking Sam's view. Their dark suits distinguished them from the clientele, but it meant a new, far more dangerous party had taken notice of the newcomer. On the table, Sam's fingers involuntarily curled into her palms.

Thanks to their proximity, a few snippets of conversation reached her ears.

"...with us."

"...don't ... go anywhere with..."

"...wouldn't ... make a scene..."

"Back off, assholes."

As soon as the curse left her lips, the woman bolted for the door, moving faster than Sam had expected. The two men looked equally surprised—Sam thought maybe it was too fast for them to want to bother chasing her—

Nope. They always chase.

The woman knocked over a chair, leaving it tumbling in her wake, before darting outside. Her pursuers avoided it easily but became tangled up near the door before they managed to push through.

Before she fully realized it, Sam was halfway to her feet.

What are you gonna do Sam?

She could hear him, so clearly that she squeezed her eyes shut, certain that if she looked, he'd be there. Sprawled out in the chair beside her.

You gonna rescue her like you rescued us?

"Fuck," Sam muttered, and when she opened her eyes, she realized she was still halfway up from her seat, still staring at the door swinging with the force of three expulsions.

Glancing about, no one else appeared interested in the display. Conversations continued, both hushed and raucous, and attentions remained fixed within their respective spaces. Sam lowered herself back into her chair, her heart knocking against her chest. Fingers reached for the ordering console, hovered over the screen. Then they curled into a fist and drew back until they brushed the side of the glass of water.

Her hand steady, she lifted it to her lips and drank.

Don't. Get. Involved.

Yeah, yeah, she thought darkly, her stare nearly boring a hole in the table. She focused on the scratched surface, and the dark, water-spotted screen reminded her of something else. Something colder.

Like you rescued us?

Thirty minutes later, the men returned, wet and disheveled. Sam had pulled indifference to her, as tightly as the jacket she had zipped all the way up to her chin. They shoved through the door, their complaints about the weather pushing ahead of them. As they passed her table, she couldn't help but note the disappointment radiating from them and felt a small twist in her gut she tried to ignore. Either their prey had gotten away or—

"Can you believe that?"

"Mad as hell. First I've ever seen it."

Out of the corner of her eye, Sam watched the men huddle a few feet away, outside the entrance to a back hallway no one had entered or exited all evening. The men took up places on either side of it, sodden guardians. Hands wiped at rugged, brutish faces that were forgettable save for the tendrils of a tattoo sneaking up the side of one's jaw.

Unconsciously, her head tilted in their direction.

"I mean, right over the edge! Full speed into the pit! And then—" the lackey made a long, whistling noise. Sam's brow crinkled.

"Think she could have survived it?"

A grunt. "Hell, no. That main shaft's gotta be more than three miles down. Maybe four."

"Could be flooded?"

She could almost hear the head shake. "Wouldn't matter. From that height? She's dead."

"Well, shit. What are we supposed to do now?"

"Tell the Boss the woman he was asking about took a header into the old mine."

"He'll be pissed."

"Shit. He can go down there himself if he wants her so badly."

"You gonna tell him that?"

"No way! Look, we'll just—"

Sam didn't hear the rest. An argument broke out near the bar, drowning out the conversation. She tried to welcome the chaos of the distraction. But despite her fervent desire to remain uninvolved, she had been hoping for the woman's escape. Just not... not like that. She glared at her glass of water and gave a quick shake of her head, as if she could jostle loose the unidentified stirrings that threatened to rise. There were already enough ghosts to mourn without adding some stranger she'd only gotten a fleeting look at.

Don't get involved.

It was just... *odd.*

The way the men spoke, it sounded as if there had been no hesitation on the woman's part. Only a few words and Sam could picture the scene. The woman's form, racing across the rusted grates of scaffolding, the men closing in. Then the edge of the railing, a thin separation between land and deep, empty darkness, an easy placement of one hand, legs swung over and... gone.

Strange. Maybe the void had seemed a better choice than what had been behind her, literally *and* figuratively. Could have just been looking to self-terminate. It certainly wouldn't be the first life the old mine had taken.

But then, what had she been doing in the bar? What about the determination that had been all over her face?

Sam told herself there was nothing she could do. It was over. With any luck, some thick-skulled minion was a few minutes away from dragging her from the table so she could get her own goddamn business concluded.

She managed five long seconds before she got to her feet.

Shit.

Shouldn't be there. *Stupid to get involved.*

The thought repeated as Sam eased the immense bulk of her quad-engine space cruiser down into the massive crater of the abandoned iron mine. Surrounded by a sprawling set of industrial ruins, the pit was a colossal hole in the earth, gaping wide like a yawning mouth with a throat that descended, if the assholes she had overheard at the bar were right, over three miles.

Sam could not, for any reason, understand why the woman she had watched be chased out of that same bar, had gone *there*. Nor could Sam, despite numerous attempts in the last five minutes, comprehend why *she* was *following* said woman. If Sam had even a drop of the self-preservation she had so often prided herself on in the past, she would be back at Floodwater's bar, nursing her glass of water, and waiting patiently for the meeting she had taken such pains to set up. Instead, she was there, engaging in an act of... Heroics? Insanity? What do you even call it if you don't know if the person you're going after is even alive? And really, what did it matter if there was one more body lost to the depths of the old quarry? Who would even care? Even if Sam did find it, what exactly was she going to do with it—her? She knew nothing about the woman other than she was reckless enough to go down into the Floods after dark. For something.

Oh, and she dove into abandoned pits.

Hope she at least has some ID on her, Sam thought sourly. *Stupid. Just because you think you saw—*

What? What could she have possibly seen in a handful of glances?

Something, her brain supplied, in a familiar voice that sounded suspiciously like her own.

"Well, that's a help," she grumbled. Reaching up, Sam clicked the lever for the outer search lights. When they blinked on, they illuminated only tiny droplets of rain cascading into a well of blackness.

Great. God, Jonah would be laughing at her right now. *Oh boy, Sam, what do you think you're gonna do?*

This time there was no bitterness, just the easy-going tone that had once filled the room. She had to pause to take a deep breath, pushing out against the pain in her chest. There was a blur of motion to her left and she glanced over in time to see a slightly chubby gray tabby cat land silently on the tiny side panel. A small metal disc swung from around its neck, the letters "NATA" engraved in white against a black background. The cat kneaded its paws into the dark canvas jacket Sam had tossed there earlier, blinked its large yellow eyes twice in her direction, and then curled up, benign and seemingly content.

Sam knew better. Exhaling slowly, she eased the control wheel forward into descent and gave the overhead monitors a routine check of flight status.

Out of the ship's viewport she could see the underside of the mine's upper walkway and the woman clinging to one of the stringers.

Sam's fingers tightened on the controls, as if it could somehow help steady what must have been a failing grip around cold, wet steel. Without any further attention to the warnings going off in her brain, she maneuvered the ship until the emergency hatch on the roof was as close as safety would allow. She hit the hover lock, twice to make sure it stuck, and pushed up out of the chair. Her hip gave a groan of protest when it smacked the corner of the console; she barely noticed. She jabbed a finger in Nata's direction.

"Don't touch anything."

He gave zero indication that he heard her.

It felt like ages to get from the bridge to the hatch with her rigid right leg hampering her movement. She hustled along the main corridor, one ear cocked for the sound of something striking the hull, though the likelihood of the sound penetrating was slim. When she finally reached the emergency hatch tunnel, she stepped onto the elevator plate and hit the lift controls with the side of her fist.

Nothing happened.

Sam punched it again, with a little more force than was probably necessary.

Still nothing.

"Of course," she growled, tipping her head back to look up the length of the tube. She turned, grabbed hold of the emergency ladder, and began hauling herself up. The coarse metal dug into her palms, but it barely registered through thick calluses. It was the weakness in her right grip that reminded her she was too tired for this kind of shit.

She paused, halfway up, and laughed quietly to herself. Zeroed in on the empty space between her index and pinky fingers. Too tired.

Too broken.

As if to second the opinion, a sharp pain pinched in her knee. Gritting her teeth, Sam forced herself to start moving again. If she stayed too long in one spot, all her aches were likely to awaken and then there'd be two bodies at the bottom of the mine shaft, plus one very expensive space vehicle.

By the time she reached the hatch, the back of her shirt was damp, and her right hand was threatening to cramp. She glared at the *open* button near the hatch. "You better fucking—" she threatened as she struck it.

There was a *hum* followed by a *pop*, like the first release of a top to a jar of foodstuffs. The hatch sluggishly rose up and to the side. Rain drizzled down and a rush of cool air blew in, stealing the heat generated from her climb. It chilled Sam enough to have her wishing she had grabbed her jacket, but there was no going back down for it now. She climbed out onto the top of the ship, setting her boots carefully on the slick surface.

At least the hover thrusters were—for the moment—steady. She wasn't in the mood for mid-air acrobatics. Lifting a hand to shield her eyes from the rain, she squinted, searching for the figure she'd seen in the lights.

The under railings were empty. As were the struts and support beams. Had the woman already fallen? Or had Sam misjudged the area? She inched forward, peering further down past where the lights of the ship illuminated, and felt a sudden pressure in the middle of her back.

Well. It just freaking figured.

Sam slowly lifted her arms until her hands were even with her shoulders. She cocked her head and could see a fragment of the figure standing behind her. Blue jacket sleeve, the hint of a gray scarf. Twisting ever so slightly, Sam could feel the edges of the weapon through her shirt. Not sharp or pointed. So, not a knife. Could have been the barrel of a gun but...

"Who are you? What are you doing here?"

The voice was quiet but full, easily audible over the thrum of the ship's engines. The accent was heavy in the regional tone. Sam had been planetside long enough to know it was terrestrial.

When Sam didn't immediately respond, the tip of the weapon pressed in a bit more firmly and she could feel the trembling of the woman's hand through it. It might have just been from the engines but ...

Hmmm, Sam thought.

With a great deal less fluidity than she was hoping for, Sam spun, her left hand shooting down and her right arm pushing up. Her fingers caught the end of the pipe, wrenching it free as she shoved her elbow into the vicinity of her assailant's throat.

Sam expected her to counter or flail in defense, but she simply stood there, her chin tilted back from the slight pressure of Sam's forearm. Their eyes met and held. Sam was caught off guard by the golden brown, and even more so by the lack of fear, in the other woman's stare.

Dropping her arm back to her side, Sam threw the pipe over the side of the ship. The woman's eyes widened but she said nothing, made no move.

Nodding her head in the direction of the hatch, Sam wiped rain from her face and declared, "Let's discuss this inside. It's fucking raining out here."

Sometimes when you fall, it's into something better than you expected.

And sometimes it's much, *much* worse.

Kate wasn't sure how to feel about her current situation. She wasn't lying broken at the bottom of a three-mile-deep quarry shaft. Nor was she imprisoned, tortured, or whatever it was those two thugs had been planning on making her. So, good there.

Instead, she was in the galley of a spaceship that appeared approximately five minutes from self-destruct, with a stranger who looked like the last thing she wanted to be doing was standing there, pouring her a drink. Strange, sure, but not necessarily *bad*.

None of those options had been part of her *Plan*, which, in hindsight, had not been the best laid. She wasn't oblivious to the fact that one of those options was remarkably better than the other.

Plus, there was a cat. What kind of homicidal maniac would have a cat?

"Thank you," she said with total sincerity.

The woman paused with a tall metal thermos tipped against the rim of a sturdy mug. After that brief hesitation, she lifted it and steaming water poured forth. When the mug was full, she shifted the thermos to a second one, taller and far worse for the wear than the first.

"The support cable I'd been standing on gave way. I wasn't sure how much longer I could have held on," Kate continued, watching as she set the thermos aside and dropped two dark cubes into each mug.

Wordlessly, the woman held out the sturdier cup and, for the first time in ten minutes, looked at her. Kate thought it had been a mixture of the rain, the night, and the wash from the search lights, but in the clear glow of the ship's lighting, the woman's irises really were a pale gray. Like puddled water.

They were also flat, matching her expression. A marked difference from the mixture of irritation and resignation that had crossed her face after she'd torn away the pipe Kate had mindlessly grabbed for protection.

It was hardly an unusual face; long and thin, a bit sunken around the eyes, as if she hadn't slept well in a while. Her skin was only a few shades lighter than the tea she provided, with a hint of sallowness that suggested the sunlights on the ship needed adjusting. Narrow lips pressed into a permanent straight line, with a hint of a dip below the right cheek as if to suggest yes, occasionally she did smile. It was a face that did not necessarily speak to kindness or compassion, and yet there she was, having offered both.

The sides of her head were shaved close in a manner that made Kate think military, but the top of her hair was tousled tufts that didn't exactly scream regulation. They looked more like the result of fingers constantly running through them.

Kate took the mug, her own fingers warmed by the heat seeping through the ceramic. The sudden contrast made her realize her clothes were soaked through. There was a dry chill in the air, like the inside of a refrigerator. She lifted the cup to her lips to try and hide the shivers that raced over her skin.

The tea smelled of vanilla and tasted the same.

"How'd you know there would be a support cable?"

Outside in the rain, the woman's voice had sounded sharp and authoritative. Inside, without the competition of the engine or the elements, it was softer and almost flippant.

"What?" Kate asked.

Motioning with her cup, the woman eased back against the counter. "When you jumped," she clarified, one eyebrow quirked, "how did you know there'd be a support cable underneath you?"

The back of Kate's neck flushed, either from the warmth of the tea or being caught off guard.

The woman sipped from her mug and waited.

"Ah... it's a standard feature on class-B mining structures built after 2230. They're marked on the railing with a digger's box."

"You a miner? Or just know a lot about mining equipment?"

The flush crept up into her face. "I like to read."

"About mining regulations?"

"It's more interesting than it sounds," Kate mumbled and as her mind whirled back to the rusted walkway, she felt her stomach pitch abruptly. The nerves she had been fighting down all evening erupted inside her chest, and she found herself babbling out,

"I didn't—I can't believe I just jumped—I thought it would be closer but then it was way further out because I think part of the causeway snapped at some point because it definitely wasn't there—and I really, really expected it to be there and—"

She could *hear* the panic in her voice and bore down hard, sucking in a deep breath to cut herself off. The cat, which had been sinuously weaving itself in and around the other woman's legs, padded its way over to her, butting its head against her shins, perhaps in search of the adoration its owner had not seemed interested in giving. Reaching down with a free hand, Kate ran her fingers over soft fur. Feeling some semblance of balance return, she drank again and cleared her throat. "Look. I very much appreciate your help and I'm sorry about the pipe but there were these two men—"

"I saw them."

"—chasing… okay. Okay." The interruption threw Kate off and she tried to realign her thoughts. "Okay. So then, what are we doing here?" she asked.

A slight shrug. "This is where the tea was."

Kate wondered if this was an advanced interrogation technique designed to instill confusion in the hopes of gaining intel. She had to admit, she felt more inclined to give answers if it would lead to any kind of understanding of *what was going on*. Because nothing else currently made sense, she continued to stroke the cat and heard the quiet rumbling of its purrs drift up from the floor.

Seemingly unaware of her own enigmatic emanations, the woman set her mug down on the counter behind her and straightened.

"You got a name?"

Surprised by the normalcy of the question, Kate didn't even consider going with anything but the truth.

"Kate."

Nodding, the woman slipped her hands into the front pockets of her dark pants. "All right, Kate. You have a place to go?"

Even as Kate's mind began to flip through addresses, the woman added, "Whatever you were thinking, it was a terrible idea. Maybe give yourself another day to think it through."

Though she bristled at the chiding rebuke, Kate knew she was right. She was exhausted and nothing had gone the way she had expected; had *planned*. She thought of stark white walls and empty rooms and sighed.

"Yeah. Yeah, I have a place." And getting back to it was going to be a pain in the ass; four transfers and an air shuttle, since there was construction on the outgoing line. She barely remembered the long trip in; her worries had been an easy distraction. Now she would have all that time to think about how badly—

Kate noticed the woman was looking at her expectantly. "What?" she asked, irritation creeping into her voice.

"Can't go anywhere if I don't have the coordinates," was the patient reply.

Kate's lips parted; she shook her head. "You don't—I mean, it's not—"

The woman held up a hand and Kate closed her mouth. "It'd be unfortunate to save your ass only to have you end up getting mugged on the way home."

Kate might not have *appreciated* the way it was put, but it made sense. Plus, a kraken (which Kate was pretty sure was the ship's classification), even one as beat up as this one seemed to be, could get across the city in a quarter of the time it would take on public transport. *And with a hell of a lot less weirdoes.*

"Doesn't need to be door to door; I can drop you off in your quadrant," the woman continued, shifting on her feet. The wince passed over her face almost too quickly for Kate to catch, except she had grown accustomed to the stealth of pain.

Kate rattled off her address; quadrant, street, unit number.

There was recognition in the woman's expression, so Kate didn't bother to wonder how a ship that size would navigate the landing zones.

The woman pointed to the cup still in her hand. "Finished with that?"

Kate glanced down and saw she had drained the mug; she hadn't even realized it. She held it out.

"So. Do you have a name?" she asked as the woman took hold of it. There was a moment when both their hands were on the cup; hers on the handle, the other woman's on the bottom. With an easy movement, the woman transferred it to a small sink in the counter.

"Come on," the woman stated, turning and jerking a thumb toward one of two exits. She trudged through it without looking back, clearly expecting Kate to follow. With no other option, Kate trailed along, half her attention on the layout of the ship and half on her still nameless rescuer.

From that angle the woman's limp was obvious, a clear hitch in her stride despite confidence in the motion. An old injury. Something she'd had years to grow accustomed to.

Kate had just enough time to wonder if it made getting around a ship difficult when the woman pulled up in front of a door. She lightly punched a palm plate on the wall and the door slid open with a *thunk*.

"There's a drying tube in there you can use. Can't promise it'll last a full cycle, but it should get the worst of the wet out," the woman declared.

Curious, Kate poked her head in and saw a mixture of storage unit and living quarters. At least a dozen crates were stacked atop one another near the center of the room. A bunk hung from one wall, stripped of sheets. Near the far wall was a tall cylinder she assumed was the drying unit. It looked about ten years out of date.

There was a quiet *chink* and when she turned, she saw the woman standing beside a set of lockers built into the hull. From one, she pulled a bundle of folded green fabric and from another, a small white box. She tossed the fabric on top of a stack of crates.

"If you want, you can change into that. Should only be about two full clicks to your quadrant. Might take a little longer to find a place to burn." She held out the box. "And you'll probably want to make use of this."

There was a faded red cross on the lid. Kate frowned at it. "What for?"

"Your hands."

Kate noticed that her palms were scratched and spotted with drying blood. The faint pattern of the cable she had been hanging onto was stippled into her skin. Gingerly, she curled her fingers into fists and hissed at the sharp sting that followed.

"Yeah, probably a good idea," she agreed, taking the kit. As the woman drew her hand back, Kate noticed the missing middle and ring fingers.

The woman gave a brief nod and shuffled to the door. She stopped halfway through the portal, glancing over her shoulder.

"It's Sam."

"What?"

The corner of the woman's mouth tipped up, barely. "My name's Sam." She made a vague motion with her left hand—no digits missing there. "You can come up to the bridge when you're done."

And then she was gone.

two

*Y*ou can come up to the bridge when you're done.

That would be fine.

That is, if Kate could figure out how to get to the bridge.

After Sam (not quite the name she had been expecting. Soft and short, unlike the woman herself) had left the room, it had taken Kate less than ten seconds to decide her need for dry clothes outweighed the smarting in her hands. She inspected the bundle of cloth Sam had offered: a simple flight suit. Did it belong to Sam? Because if it did, it would be a good four to five inches long on her.

Last resort, she thought, setting it aside. Things seemed neutral between them, but she did not think she was currently up to sharing clothes.

That left the drying unit, which she approached cautiously. It was old but appeared serviceable, capable of calibration for skin, cloth, or both. Considering its age, she had a feeling it would probably do better with either or, but she sure as hell wasn't going to stand around naked in a strange ship, even for the five minutes it was programmed to take. She stepped in and slid the door shut. It took a moment for a fuzzy menu to display on the frosted glass. Kate swiped in her choices and heard the subtle *click* of the door lock, followed by a gentle humming and the sudden rush of warm air.

Sam had been right in her prediction—the tube shut off after three minutes, twelve seconds rather than the full five-minute cycle—but it was an improvement. Kate caught sight of herself in a mirror to the right of the tube. Her clothes were heavily wrinkled, but no longer wet. The tips of her hair curled toward her chin, the red shiny under the lights. There was color in her cheeks, and her eyes looked less wild than she felt. Not as crazed as she had feared. As far as first impressions went, it could have been worse.

Getting the first aid kit open had taken some muscle. It looked as if it hadn't been used in years—or possibly ever. Inside were several rows of disinfectant, ointment, and healing strips. She used all three and felt relief when the sharp stinging faded to a minor burn and then a cooling ache. Not certain of its proper place, she returned all the items to the kit and set it on top of one of the stacks of crates. And though she'd been tempted to rummage through them she'd managed to keep her curiosity in check.

Okay, so she had peeked into *one*. It had been half-filled with medical text discs. Odd interest for a ship captain but—she thought of the limp and the missing fingers—probably useful knowledge to have.

After that, she had left, not wanting to invade her host's privacy further.

Then she got stuck.

Because even though there seemed to be a single hallway looping throughout the entire ship and theoretically *had* to lead to the bridge, Kate could not *find* it.

On her third pass of what she was calling the main hall, she stopped in front of a wide door that, no matter how close she got to it or how many times she tapped the hand plate, failed to open. An old speaker box hung on the wall next to it. It didn't look at all functional, but then again, neither had many of the other things she'd seen on her self-imposed tour. There were three buttons near the bottom, but only two still had their outer casings. Exposed wiring snaked out from behind a burnished, smooth metal tab that might have once been the third button, and there was absolutely no way she was going to touch that.

The other two were marked "Call" and "Cancel." Kate reached out and pressed the call button.

Nothing. And then:

"Hey."

She jumped a little at the sound of Sam's voice, far clearer than she had thought possible, considering the visual state of the speaker.

"That thing doesn't work," Sam's voice continued.

Frowning, Kate looked at the box and then over her shoulder in either direction into the emptiness of the hallway.

"Then where—"

"Up here."

Lifting her chin, Kate saw what she had failed to notice the first two times she had passed that way: an opening just large enough for a person to fit through in the ceiling. She could see the bottom part of Sam's profile.

"How do I—"

"Use the ladder."

Kate stared at the wall underneath the opening until several narrow ruts vaguely took shape. Halfway up, there was a small section of railing that *might*, in a very loose sense, have been considered a hand hold. She thought of her palms, freshly bandaged, and sighed before setting her right foot on the first step and reaching up.

It took her two tries to boost up enough to grab hold of the rail and traverse the wall into what she assumed Sam meant by "the bridge."

It was small, barely large enough to fit them both. Kate found herself taking up nearly all the remaining available space. Sam occupied a sloped pilot's chair crammed in front of a wide console and control wheel. A narrow rectangular window was the only physical view out into the world the ship was shuttling through. Several displays flanked the console, though all but one were dark. The cat was bathing itself on a jacket draped over a small input of some sort.

"This is the bridge?" Kate asked, because really, it couldn't be. Sam remained fixated on the control board in front of her.

"Auxiliary bridge, actually."

"Auxiliary?"

"Yeah. Main bridge is below, behind the door."

Kate waited a moment. "Why don't you use the main bridge?" she probed when Sam didn't elaborate.

"Door's stuck."

"The door... is stuck."

"Haven't gotten around to fixing it."

A pause. "Why not?"

"It's beyond my current mechanical abilities."

"Shouldn't you—" Kate stopped, because the answer was obvious. Yes, of course the door should be fixed. But she knew perfectly well that some things that should be fixed sometimes *couldn't* be.

Maybe that was a little too deep for the current situation.

She shifted her thinking. "How long have you had it?"

"Had what?"

"The ship?" Kate replied, though it came out less of a statement than she planned. There was a long moment of silence as Sam, Kate assumed, counted out the time frame in her head.

"A while," was Sam's response.

Biting down slightly on her bottom lip, Kate felt her back stiffen.

"What do you do with it?" she asked, trying a different tack.

"With what?"

"With the—" Kate swallowed back the sudden rush of irritation that reminded her of late afternoon phone conferences with vendors who refused to do basic things like *read contract stipulations* or *follow directions*. Sam had saved her life; snapping in frustration would hardly be appropriate, no matter how clipped or vague the woman's responses were.

"With the ship. What sort of work do you do?"

Without so much as a glance, Sam replied, "Shipping and transport."

Kate relaxed a bit at the common thread. Finally, something she was acutely familiar with.

"I work as a receiver and dispatcher for RSM Service and Freight. What cargo are you rated to carry?"

"Most of it."

Sam was splitting focus between the screen and the controls she sat in front of. Kate searched the lines of her face for any hint of humor, of jest, of any indication that the woman was simply fucking with her, because... *seriously*?

Sam's expression was placid, with only a ripple of concentration between her brows.

"Are you always this chatty?" Kate finally quipped.

There was that faint twitch of a smile, passing quicker than before.

"Not with strange women who jump into open pits in the middle of the night and require rescuing."

Kate inclined her head and counted off on her fingers.

"I think that's the longest sentence you've said so far," she pointed out.

No response.

Determined to gain footing in the truncated conversation, Kate leaned forward so one elbow rested against the edge of the pilot console. "What about women who don't need rescuing?" she teased, though she wasn't entirely sure why. Maybe she just felt compelled to get some reaction.

Again, Sam didn't reply. But to Kate's amazement, a flush of red crept up the captain's neck. Feeling as if she had just scored a point in an unspoken game, Kate shifted further into Sam's space.

"Would you—"

"Hold on," Sam interrupted, leaning forward to peer at one of the monitors on the panel. Absently, she patted the neck of her shirt then glanced around the controls, her head lifting and lowering as she checked each section, then snatched a pair of glasses from atop the console, slipped them on, and hunched over again. Kate blinked in surprise, both at the sight of the unusual accessory and the poor fit. The oversized thin metal frames almost wobbled where they perched on Sam's nose. She tried to remember the last time she had seen someone wearing a pair.

"What's your authorization code for the building?"

"You're parking at my building?" Kate asked, wincing at the note of suspicion she couldn't keep out of her voice.

Sam did not seem to notice; she remained preoccupied with the screen as she replied, "Technically I'm parking in the old service station on the platform next to your building. I still need authorization to be in the area."

Made sense. Yet Kate couldn't quite bring herself to answer, more shaken by the night's events than she had realized. It was only now occurring to her that maybe it hadn't been the best idea to give a stranger her address. Unease began to gather in her stomach; how many bad decisions could she make in one evening?

Either Sam was more perceptive than she appeared or else Kate's uncertainty was plain on her face, because the other woman sat back in the chair and motioned to one of several keypads.

"I promise not to look," she said.

Sighing, Kate shook her head and reached out. What would be the point for Sam to have pulled her out of the mine if she intended to do her harm? The captain could have fished her body out and taken the ID off her corpse if she wanted it so badly. Not that a mid-range project manager's identification was in high demand.

Or so she imagined.

And anyway, there was only one of her, and she limped. If Sam tried something fishy, Kate was certain she could at least outrun the captain, nifty little disarming move aside.

She's the only one you know about.

 Kate ignored the thought that bubbled up. Her brain was what had gotten her into the situation in the first place, so clearly it wasn't dispensing useful advice. As she keyed in the first digit, she noticed Sam had pointedly stared away at the ceiling. It wasn't necessary, but she appreciated the gesture.

Once the last keystroke was entered, a short series of beeps sounded, and Sam sat up to take hold of the control wheel. A few subtle movements of her arms later and there was the jostle of landing, enough to rock Kate back on her heels. With one hand still on the stick, Sam clicked a series of levers and buttons with speed and ease that spoke of countless repetitions. The ship gave a firmer jolt and went still. Atop its perch, the cat gave a big yawn and wiggled in place, looking as if it were about to jump down into Sam's lap.

Turning sharply in the chair so that her left arm slipped over the back, Sam pointed at the cat and snapped her fingers toward the floor. The cat yawned again and shifted its course easily, slipping down through the opening.

"Are you allergic?" Kate asked, bemused by the behavior.

"To what?"

"To cats?"

Sam frowned and reclined in the seat. "Don't know. I've never eaten one before. I didn't think you were supposed to."

Kate felt her jaw drop, just a bit. "You're … not? Some people are allergic to their saliva. Makes them sneeze or gives them rashes."

"Oh." Sam narrowed her eyes in the direction of the cat's departure. "Well, it hasn't spit at me. Yet."

The last part came out with such barely disguised distrust that Kate couldn't help but ask, "Why do you even have it? You don't seem to like it very much."

A tension that hadn't been there seemed to flow through Sam's entire form. Her voice was chilled when she replied, "It isn't mine."

Abort! the logical part of her brain shouted while the impulsive part, the one that had started this whole mess, tried to guess where another person was hiding on the ship.

"Oh, who else is on the—"

"This is your stop. Probably best if you use one of the single exits in the cargo bay. Can't miss them. Says 'exit' right on the doors."

Only half in jest, Kate asked, "Any of them stuck?"

Sam's face remained closed off. "Push hard."

Kate tried to decide if Sam was attempting to return her humor or just being honest. Could be both. She was directing entirely too much effort and energy toward understanding a person she would, in all likelihood, never see again. But when she stopped thinking about *Sam's* odd behavior she started thinking about *her own* and—

Suddenly, Kate felt exhausted and wanted nothing more than to be back in the semi-familiar place she had abandoned only hours before. Even if it was crawling with memories she hadn't wanted to deal with.

"Okay. Then I guess I'll... just..." she trailed off, feeling an uncomfortable itch between her shoulder blades that increased as Sam looked on, the barest hint of impatience starting to cross the captain's face. Kate couldn't blame her. She also felt a bit irritated by her own reluctance to leave. Well. Not *reluctance* per se, as she certainly wouldn't mind being somewhere more comfortable. It was more... anticlimactic.

"Right," she murmured. Clearly, she was still shaken by her near miss, not to mention everything that had happened in the last couple days, weeks, *months*. She was going to go back to her living quarters and go to sleep.

It would be better in the morning.

Shaking her head (whether to get herself moving or in doubt of her last thought), she crouched and started back down the sorry excuse for a ladder. It sure as hell wasn't up to Intergalactic Disability standards.

When her face was level with the floor, Kate paused.

Sam continued to watch her, the index finger of one hand drumming lightly against the console. Maybe she was completely wrong, but Kate got the sense Sam was more than a bit anxious for her to leave, and she didn't know why the idea chafed. Neither could she stop the next words that came out of her mouth—*nor* the borderline flirtatious tone accompanying them.

"Aren't you going to walk me to my unit?"

Sam actually looked startled by the suggestion. "What?"

Kate let her lips pull back in a faint grin. "Would be a shame if I got mugged ten feet from my door, wouldn't it?"

Halfway between the ship and the walkway that connected the service platform to the building housing Kate's unit, it began to rain again—a light, teasing mist. The two women hurriedly crossed the lot, the only things moving in the darkness. When they reached the walkway's opening, with water dripping down the collar of her jacket, Sam thought:

This is far enough.

And yet, she followed Kate through the passage, out of the wind and precipitation. They trudged through the dimly lit corridor, the open expanse of the city visible all around behind lofty, clear windows. At the end, in front of two sliding doors which led into the apartment building, Sam thought again:

This is far enough.

It was as if the words went no further than her brain because her feet stubbornly persisted to fall upon the path Kate led her on. Each time they came to a stop, a pause, an opportunity to turn around, Sam found herself stepping forward instead of back.

Until finally they were standing side by side in a rising lift and Sam had resigned herself to the fact that returning immediately to the ship was not an option. The elevator gave a quiet *ding* and the doors *whooshed* open to a short hall with a single door. Kate exited first, a keycard already in one hand. Sam jammed her fists into the pockets of her thick canvas jacket and trailed along behind.

It took a swipe from the keycard, an input code, and a palm print screen before the door released. With a casual push, Kate nudged it open and motioned for Sam to enter.

"Come in," she said.

Twisting her shoulders, careful not to let any part of her brush against Kate, Sam sidled through the doorway. She didn't understand the look currently gracing Kate's face, but then she also didn't understand what she was doing there.

Shouldn't have gotten involved. Stupid.

Bit late for that.

The room expanded into a much larger area than she had been expecting. She couldn't remember the last time she'd been in an on-planet living unit. Four, five years? There were only vague recollections of cramped spaces, cluttered and restrictive.

This space stretched backward to a wide window looking out into the night. A pair of doors interrupted the left wall; a staircase in the corner spiraled up to a second floor.

Along the right wall, a few feet from the entrance, was a kitchen. The only item of furniture in the room was a couch, pressed back underneath the window. Everything was a clean, stark white.

Sam tried to imagine it as the inside of a ship; all that white would have been gray in a day.

"It's... nice," she offered.

Kate closed the door. She fidgeted, looking almost as uncomfortable in the space as Sam. Their eyes met and Kate turned to a small panel by the side of the door.

"Thanks," she replied, her back to Sam as she fiddled with something. "I actually just moved in last week. That's why it's a little... bare."

The lights flared; Sam squeezed her eyes shut in response. Kate muttered a "sorry" and the room dimmed. Sam blinked the spots from her vision. Despite her desire to return to the ship, she felt compelled to stroll over to the window. On the sill was a holo stand with a frozen image of Kate, beaming, under the arm of an older man, also smiling. Beside it, a box of tissues. The hairs at the nape of her neck prickled and when she glanced back, she caught Kate watching her.

"Roommate?" she surmised, nodding to the image while her eyes cast about quickly for any hints of another individual nearby, speculating if she had walked blindly into a setup. Maybe she was the idiot about to be missing some organs.

A throat cleared and when Sam's gaze returned to Kate, there was a gloss of wetness over the other woman's eyes that made the brown glitter in the low light.

"My dad actually."

Momentarily assuaged as to the safety of her person, Sam took a closer look, thought she could see the resemblance in the shape of the eyes, the smile.

"How'd he die?" she asked, raising her eyes to the window and peering out. It only took seconds to realize that rather than a view to the outside, it was a holo-screen set to an image of the night sky. The subtle pulse of stars, even fake ones, was a comfort. She felt some of the stiffness leave her shoulders.

Then she realized her question hadn't been answered. She turned around completely and saw Kate frowning. Sam replayed the question in her head. Right. Shit.

"Sorry, that probably wasn't—"

Kate shook her head and Sam paused her fumbling apology.

"It's fine. He was… sick. For a while. And then…" Kate let out a trembling exhale as she explained, "it was quick."

Sam rubbed the back of her neck, the skin hot under her fingertips. "Sorry," she repeated. Discomfort made her tone harsh, and the single word fell heavy between them. Across the room, Kate sagged against a small island in the kitchen, hands twisting together in front of her.

"Have you ever lost anyone?" she asked.

Feeling like she was in an airlock rapidly being pressurized past the optimal point, Sam's shoulders hunched inside her jacket, pushing the stiff collar into her jaw. "Sure," she gritted out around an ache in her throat. She added, somewhat testily, "Hasn't everyone?"

It was late, she was tired, and she felt the stirrings of ghosts she did not want to disturb.

The snip did not appear to deter Kate. "Why did you follow me out of the bar?"

There was none of the accusation or suspicion Sam expected to see in Kate's face. Just perplexity and a bit of bafflement. Sam could understand that. She was perplexed and baffled as to the whole thing herself.

"You were in the bar. I remember now. I saw you, all the way in the corner. You were the only one alone," Kate continued.

Sam shrugged. "I like to be alone."

Kate made a derisive noise. "No one likes to be alone."

"I do."

There came a sniff of resigned mirth. "Fine. So? Why did you come after me? Or are you going to tell me that you just like to cruise around abandoned spaces in your free time?"

Silence returned. Sam kept her hands balled inside her pockets and tipped her head back to stare up at the ceiling. It was aggravating that she couldn't put a finger on the reason behind her own actions, couldn't put a name to the tug in her gut. Maybe because it was too close to what she'd spent the last six months trying to bury.

"I don't know."

The words slipped quietly from her.

Kate smiled faintly. "Well, whatever your reason, I'm glad you did." She stopped and wet her lips before running a hand through her hair, pushing it back from her face. "I thought... I mean, for a moment, out on that cable..."

"You didn't."

"I know. Thanks."

"Said that already."

A genuine laugh burst from Kate, and for the first time, Sam got a full look at her smile. And being able to see it... helped, she supposed.

"You are so..." Shaking her head once more, Kate refrained from finishing the thought, though the smile stayed in place. She lifted her hands briefly. "I guess I shouldn't keep you any longer. You probably want to get back to your ship."

Yes. Absolutely. The words flashed in Sam's brain, but she didn't think it would be a good idea to voice them. Instead, she gave a noncommittal bob of her head. And since that seemed okay, she ambled toward the door, idly wondering if she was supposed to wait for Kate to open it or if it would be fine to handle that detail herself.

"Sam?"

She had reached the door when her name was called. Glancing over, she saw Kate was still in the kitchen, still leaning back against the counter, still watching her.

Still smiling.

Sam stopped and waited. Those short hairs at the top of her spine tingled again.

"I feel like you should have a reward. You did save my life."

Sam felt her brows rise. "Reward?" She hadn't even considered it.

Kate nodded and her smile went a little sly, reminding Sam of the charged banter they had shared on the ship. She hadn't imagined it. "Yes. Any… requests?"

A little jolt ran through her, like a spark from static electricity. It was mildly disorienting and… strange. She nearly shook her head no, of course she didn't need a reward, but—

There was one thing. One thing she had gone some time without. Just thinking about it stretched her lips back in a way she hadn't felt in quite a while. Feeling a quiver of anticipation, Sam sauntered back toward the kitchen. She stopped a foot or so in front of Kate and let her eyes drift over the cabinets.

"Got any chocolate chip cookies?"

three

Kate didn't think she would sleep. With the adrenaline of a close call lingering and the unsettling newness of the apartment surrounding her, she didn't expect exhaustion to have much pull. But her eyes were gritty with fatigue and her body protesting, so she stretched out over the barely used white sheets.

She dropped off almost immediately.

And fell into dreams.

Running through endless tunnels, chased by something unseen but close—horrifyingly close. Back of the neck close. Leaping into darkness so black it was like being swallowed by the night. Feeling the snap of the cable beneath her feet and tumbling down, nothing left to grab hold of. Falling. The ground miles below, invisible, but rushing up fast. Falling, falling, fall—

She jerked awake, heart pounding. Her first ragged breath was not nearly enough to fill her lungs. Staring at the ceiling, Kate listened to her own shuddering gasps until, slowly, they evened out. Turning her head, she checked the clock on the table beside the bed.

6:58.

Sitting up, she swung her legs over the side of the bed and pressed her face into her hands. She wasn't sure if it had been the dreams, the sleep she had been sorely lacking, the distance morning brought, or a combination of all three, but even at two minutes to seven, it was abundantly clear that her thinking last night had been...

Not great. Less than brilliant. The plan that had seemed so well thought out revealed itself to be three bad ideas in a trench coat.

Had she really gone alone to a station on the outskirts hoping to secure a spot on one of the long-haul transport ships? Did she really think a stint as a manual laborer and the space of a couple hundred lightyears was the best way to deal with loss and stagnation? What bad book had she stolen *that* plot line from?

Maybe there was such a thing as reading too much.

Looking back, she couldn't even reconstruct her reasoning from the day before. Yes, she'd been feeling smothered by grief, still fresh. Yes, she'd been feeling stuck and suffocated for far longer, months before. Maybe even years. Yes, she'd suddenly wanted to be a million miles from the empty, but somehow claustrophobic, rooms of her new home. A home with no memories of her father, and yet he seemed to be everywhere, an overwhelming presence despite his absence.

None of those things necessitated a trip into the seedy underbelly looking for—

God, she just used the words *seedy underbelly*. Obvious proof of what a terrible idea it had been. Why hadn't she just booked a flight on one of the public transports to the nearest entertainment satellite? She could have taken a week's vacation, sat on an artificial beach, and drank colorful drinks until the feelings had all faded. And if the colorful drinks hadn't worked, well, there were plenty of other distractions on an entertainment satellite that might have done the trick.

Except she hadn't wanted a vacation. She hadn't wanted a brief break from everything—she'd wanted an *escape*. She hadn't wanted to spend another minute at work, behind that stupid desk, doing those stupid monotonous tasks that had once seemed so important. She hadn't wanted to know that in a week she'd be back at it and stuck having to wait for the next stretch of time she could take off.

Kate rubbed her face and stood up. It was seven o'clock in the morning; she needed caffeine in an amount that could wake a small city. On legs that burned, a reminder of the previous night's exertion, she strode out into the living room and over to the kitchen. A healthy enjoyment of coffee had been something she and her father had shared. He used to keep a surplus of three canisters, a throwback to a time in his younger days when there had been massive droughts on the planet, and the dark grounds had been strictly rationed to preserve water.

"*Can't be caught without it,*" he'd say, whenever one can was empty. "*Otherwise, what would there be to drink?*"

"*Water?*" she'd suggest. And her father would pat her arm and shake his head.

"*Never heard of it.*"

The memory made her smile even as her throat constricted. She couldn't seem to decide if she wanted to linger on the reflection or push past it. Actually, now that she was thinking of him, it was probably her father who had put the idea of transport hopping into her brain. He'd told her the story of his brief stint in cargo shipping before meeting her mother. The expanse of space. The freedom of it.

Really, you're just being dramatic, she scolded herself as she measured out the grounds and programmed her first mug. *You've been feeling bored and under challenged for a while and with everything happening so quickly with dad, you're just...*

Spiraling? her mind helpfully suggested.

Kate pushed a wisp of hair out of her view. *It'll get better*, she told herself. *It's hard now, but it'll get better.*

Taking the mug from the dispenser, she tried to convince herself that the phrase sounded more meaningful than she thought. Looking down at the black liquid, she could anticipate the sharp, bitter, familiar taste. She paused, the cup halfway to her lips. After a moment of consideration, she set it on the counter and rooted through one of the drawers, pushing aside various tins and shakers until she found a petite, opaque bottle. Twisting off the cap, she poured a tiny splash of amber liquid into the coffee. When she lifted the mug to her mouth again, the scent of vanilla tickled her nose.

Leaning against the counter, she noticed the package of cookies she had pulled out the night before and smiled. Not everything about the night had been terrible, though it wasn't easy to say exactly what Sam was.

Interesting. Aloof. Probably not bored with her day job, considering she operated a kraken class spaceship.

Did it belong to her or did she only captained it?

Not *friendly* per say but considerate. Rescuing her in the first place, offering tea and dry clothes, a ride home. Taking nothing in return but a sleeve of cookies.

Asking for them with a grin; quick and coy, with charm Kate never would have expected. She'd been dangerously close to becoming a cliché in one of those books where the damsel fell for the tall, dark, mysterious stranger.

And underneath it all, a heaviness. Like she was dragging some weight along behind her.

Or maybe Kate was projecting. Maybe Sam had just been tired and not at all interested in a woman who displayed terrible decision-making powers.

Kate blew out a breath. Well, she'd left. Was mostly likely already off planet, engaged in whatever transport kept her ship running. Or mostly running, Kate mused as she remembered the sad state of the drying unit.

Wandering to the window, she pondered where the crew was. While she wouldn't call herself an expert in the complex mechanics of spaceflight, Kate knew a ship that big would have been difficult to operate long term without at least a couple of other hands. She thought about the stuck door to the main bridge and Sam's wry confession about her skill set. Kate clicked off the holo-screen, switching to the actual view outside the window. The apartment unit was high enough in the building to offer a clear line of sight to the old service station they had landed in. She could still see the way the kraken had taken up nearly all the available space on the landing pad.

Kate blinked.

She *could* still see it. Because it was still there. A laugh of disbelief escaped her. It was almost like—

A hand lifted to her mouth as a new plan formed.

Kate went over it in her head as she moved methodically around the unit, pushing a mixture of clothes and a few other things she thought she'd need into a travel bag. Her practical side tried to point out that she couldn't possibly have any idea what she might need, but Kate ignored the quiet, rapidly weakening voice.

She considered it further as she stood impatiently in the elevator, the bag slung over one shoulder. Above her the numbers counted down. It wasn't nearly as foolhardy or rash as her previous plan had been. At least it wouldn't involve strangers.

Well, not *total* strangers.

She searched for the potential pitfalls as she walked through the tunnel toward the platform. There were many, and they all began with convincing Sam, but Kate sidestepped them with an *I'll figure it out later*.

The ship loomed monumental and still; Kate half expected the massive engines to fire and for it to take off as she approached. She kept her steps even and measured, resisting the urge to race onwards. If the ship flew off before she could get to it, then that would be that. She'd turn around, go back to the apartment, and rescind the resignation letter she had scheduled to go out in three hours.

But if it didn't… maybe she'd take that as the sign she'd been looking for.

Kate strode out of the passageway and onto the platform. With each step she took, she felt giddiness bubble within her. She was going to do it. She was actually going to do it.

The ramp that had extended the night before to allow them to exit was gone, and the wide bay door it had led from was closed. Searching, she wandered around and beneath each section, from the modestly angled nose to the tendril-like wings.

She should have spent more time in the maintenance and service department at work rather than up in processing. As it were, she usually only saw the ships belonging to her vendors as names on a manifest, not up close and personal.

Well, eventually she'd know this ship like the back of her hand, she promised herself.

It was back near the engines that she found what she was looking for: a ladder built into the hull that reminded her of the one she'd climbed to get into the auxiliary bridge. This one led up to a hatch that released with a few hard twists and a lock bar. She crawled inside.

And clambered into what might have been… a service tunnel? A maintenance shaft? Whatever it was, it was a compact and uninviting space. Hunching, she crept further in until the ceiling opened into a larger room, filled with enormous machinery she vaguely recognized from her father's work. He had spent his life tinkering with all types of engines; she'd seen those same kinds of tubes and funnels rendered on his imaging console. Taking in the maze of circuitry and pipes, she wished she had asked him more questions. And felt the pinch of grief anew.

Kate paused, awed by the sheer size, which was difficult to sense from a model image. Nearby the sound of music drifted, light and echoing, unlike the steady pulsing beats currently broadcast on planet. She followed it, skirting around the engine casings.

There came a tinkering crash, a stark interruption of the quiet melody, followed by a terse, "Shit," in Sam's low, flat voice.

Followed immediately by, "What the fuck is *that* supposed to be?"

And then, "Jonah, you asshole, could you have tightened this POS any further for fuck's sake?"

Kate had a good idea of what she was going to see even before she came around the corner.

A large panel had been removed from one of the engine walls, exposing the inner workings. Sam was deep inside so that only her legs from the knees down stuck out. A short grunt was followed by a frustrated clanking noise that might have come from striking metal against metal. There was no sign of the cat.

Too bad; she could have used the support.

"Having trouble?" Kate asked, as if this second meeting were as random as their previous one. It was hard to tell how well it came across, what with the music still trilling and the way the surrounding metal seemed to dull sound.

Still, she had the sense that Sam heard her, even without any outward sign of it. The legs didn't jump, there was no clatter of dropped tools, no sudden withdrawal from the engine housing. There was another grunt, followed by a *pop* and a faint grinding. Then the grinding ceased, the legs shifted, and Sam sat up, her head and shoulders coming into view. A pair of dark-tinted safety googles obscured her face, the magnification attachment engaged, and she held an octagonal piece of metal in one hand. A long beat of silence stretched out between them.

"Forget something?" Sam asked finally, turning the piece in her hand.

Kate shook her head and drew closer until she could peek up into the encasement. "How come you're still here?" she inquired. She tried to gauge Sam's reaction to her presence, but the woman's face was smooth, and with her eyes hidden behind the goggles, it was impossible to have any window into what she was thinking.

Sam studied her and Kate had to wonder how magnified she currently was. Pushing the googles onto her forehead, Sam gave a few long blinks, eyes refocusing. They were tinged red, as if she'd been rubbing at them. As Kate watched, she did just that and then squeezed the bridge of her nose.

"Got a significant power drain. Not enough juice for the engines to fire," Sam explained. She brought the piece of metal in her hand up close to glare at it accusingly; it looked like a cap or end piece.

Still peering into the engine hold, Kate noticed a tablet balanced on part of the drive, blueprints and instructional text displayed on it. She chuckled, careful to swallow the noise.

"Any ideas?" Kate asked as mildly as possible. Another length of silence. She met Sam's gaze again, watched the frown twist the captain's lips.

"No. This isn't exactly my forte."

Lifting her brows, Kate turned back to the engine. "You have a ship and you don't know how to fix the engine?"

She practically felt the glare transfer to her. "Do you know how to fix your toaster?"

Kate started to pull back, some inane half-formed quip traveling between her brain and mouth, when she spied a familiar sight. She bent closer. Yes, that was—and there was—probably overloaded the—

Straightening, she grinned at Sam. "Your primary and secondary power lines are braided together." She was almost positive that was what the two thick cables were.

Almost.

Sam didn't even look in the direction she pointed. Instead, she rubbed the side of her neck. "And that's... bad," she surmised.

Kate quipped, "If you want the ship to go, yes."

Suspicion darkened Sam's eyes. "You an engineer?"

Shaking her head, Kate set her hands on her hips. "Nope. I'm a project manager. But I do know that those two cables definitely shouldn't be wired together."

"Let me guess: you read something about it?"

"Something like that."

Sam's fingers moved to worry the skin at the base of her throat. Some internal argument was going on in her head; Kate could all but see the dueling thought bubbles rising from the tips of her hair.

"Can you fix it?" Sam asked, a mixture of reluctance and caution coloring the request. Leaning back into the core space, Kate inspected the cables. Doubt churned in her stomach as she gazed into the inner workings of a complicated piece of machinery she probably didn't have any business putting her hands on.

It could be yet another really bad idea.

But she had the memory of sitting beside her father, watching him lay out varying lengths and sizes of wiring. She heard him explaining the differences, the uses, and the dangers in his steady voice.

"Some hotshot will tell you that you can wire the primary and secondary together to get a boost in power, in acceleration. But it's only temporary, and you run the risk of overloading the stabilizer. Besides, there are better ways to get moving in space."

"Yeah," Kate heard herself confirm. She nodded, not sure if the extra affirmation was for herself or for Sam. "Yeah, I think so." Crawling further in, she hunkered down in front of the cables and rubbed at her chin. "Do you have a splicer and some proto-casing?"

The ship felt different with someone else aboard it in a way it hadn't the night before. Maybe because that had just been about transportation, easy and simple enough. Passengers never made themselves part of the ship; they were shuttled from Point A to Point B with potentially a few stops in between. They did not climb into the engine housing and begin rewiring the power transfer lines.

Sam scratched at the base of her skull; the concept really should have caused her more concern than it did. She had a stranger messing around with the inner guts of her ship's primary engine. On the spectacularly reassuring declaration of, "I think so."

When anxiety failed to rise in her, she shrugged. Probably couldn't do any worse than if she continued to muck around with it herself. Jonah hadn't often required help with repairs, so visits to the engine room had been rare.

"You said we'd be up and running in an hour. It's been three."

"No, actually, what I said was 'I think we'll be up and running in an hour.' It took a long time to get the coil to sit right. Now I have to make sure the others are aligned correctly to it."

"Jonah? How much longer?"

A shrug and a shit-eating grin. "An hour?"

"Jonah."

"Probably. Maybe more. Probably not more than three."

"This is not a good place for us to be dead in the water."

"We're not dead; just resting."

"Sam?"

Sam blinked her eyes open. She didn't remember closing them. Her hand scrubbed down over her face; her throat was dry. It took all her willpower to keep her fingers from shaking. For a second, she could see him there, that stupid smug smile stretched across his face, even when there had been absolutely nothing to smile about. Then, he abruptly morphed into the woman she had pulled from the mineshaft the night before.

Kate waited, watching with more than curiosity. Sam braced for the questions, felt herself flinch even before Kate started to speak.

"I'm all finished. I think it should be fine now."

Without responding, Sam turned and stalked over to the engine room console set into the nearby wall. Hitting the screen a bit aggressively, she brought the diagnostic script online. As she programed the initial run, she was careful to keep her back to the room in the hope it would give her a little space.

It didn't help; she could feel the weight of Kate's stare in between her shoulder blades.

Onscreen, the program cycled through its tests, different sections of the engine flaring in a color-coded sequence. Some of the stats displayed were basically gibberish to her, but she picked out the key numbers easily enough. She wasn't concerned with efficiencies and benchmarks; she simply wanted to go.

When the script finished its run, a relieved breath released at the displayed status. It took another two deliberate exhalations before she felt settled enough to turn back around.

Of course, now something had to be said. Kate was sitting there, half inside the engine, not looking expectant, but the moment was expecting and goddamn it, something was supposed to be said after—

"Thanks," Sam spit out with more gusto than she intended when the word finally came to her. "I guess we're even now," she added because thanks didn't seem like enough, but hell if she was going to try for something deeper. An itch was starting to creep along her skin, and she barely resisted rubbing her hands together. *Time to get off planet*, she thought.

Except off planet wasn't where she had been planning on going. *Shit*.

It was odd, though. There had been no communications about the missed meeting the night before. She would have expected at least half a dozen messages on her—she looked down at the blank screen of her wrist unit. *Right. Should get that fixed.*

She'd never missed a meeting with Floodwater before but it

wasn't like there weren't other ways he could get in contact with her if he wanted.

Meanwhile, a wide smile was spreading across Kate's face. Sam recognized the caginess in it and had a feeling she wasn't going to like what came next.

"Technically, I already rewarded you for saving my life," Kate pointed out, sounding more pleased with herself than Sam thought was warranted.

Sam's mouth fell open and then snapped shut. What the hell was she—

Her mind rewound to the apartment the night before. Right. Chocolate chip cookies. An entire sleeve of which she had feverishly devoured despite her intention to ration them. Somehow *just one more* had repeated until the entire packet had been laid bare.

Oh well. Worth it.

Folding her arms across her chest, Sam nodded in reluctant agreement. "All right. So, then what? I owe you a favor?" she asked, only a third serious. Half at most.

Kate's grin widened and she pointed a finger straight at Sam. "I'm so glad you think so."

"Actually, that was a quest—"

"Yes, you owe me a favor now."

With her bottom lip between her teeth, Sam stared down at the other woman, trying to get a sense of what she was about to step into. But there was only the smile, bright and a little mesmerizing around the edges.

"What can I do for you?" she heard herself ask, slowly, as if each extra second of time could better help her prepare for the response.

"Take me with you."

Nope. Not prepared. Not prepared at all.

Maybe she misheard. "Take you where?"

"Wherever it is you're going. I want to come along."

"What makes you think I'm going somewhere?"

Kate's head tipped to one side as if questioning Sam's intelligence. Sam might have been offended, only she didn't exactly feel like her brain had been firing on all cylinders lately, either.

"You have a spaceship. And it works now. Why the hell *wouldn't* you be going somewhere?" Kate reasoned.

Sam turned from the longing and enthusiasm she felt radiating from Kate and zeroed in on the screen, blinking the ready status of the engines. *Why?* How could she articulate her reasons to a woman she barely knew when she couldn't explain them to herself? Hadn't she sat down at the station bar and asked herself *what the hell am I doing?*

When Sam looked back at Kate, Jonah was there again. He stood behind her, resting as casually against the engine casing, his curly brown hair spilling out the back of a red bandana. She was afraid to look past him, afraid she'd see Triss, with her wild red waves, or Ollie in his neatly buttoned shirt. All ghosts and memories burned into the hull of the ship. For the past six months she had been drowning, and it had gotten to the point where it felt like she had to let go or risk being dragged down by them.

Now, suddenly, it was like she was throwing away the only possibility of keeping her neck above water. *What do you think you're gonna do?*

She shook her head. "Look, you don't even know me," she began, intent on cutting the crazy notion off before it could take root.

Kate rolled her eyes. "Did you know every single passenger you ever carried?"

"Yeah well, in case you didn't notice, I don't have a crew."

"So, you'll hire one. Isn't that what you were doing at the station?"

That was a joke, right? But from the expression on Kate's face, it did not, in fact, appear to be a joke. Sam rubbed at her temple.

"Hire a crew from the Floods? Did last night not give you an accurate overview of the clientele there?" Sam retorted.

"So, then what *were* you doing there?" Kate challenged. Sam had enough presence of mind not to wince.

Walked into that one. Hell, it wasn't like it was some big secret.

Strangely, though, she almost enjoyed the argument—though not enough to actively consider changing her mind.

"I was supposed to be meeting a buyer. For the ship," she admitted, slipping her hands into the pockets of her pants.

Kate's forehead furrowed tightly as she processed this news, and the ensuing look of disappointment that flooded her face was borderline comical.

"You're selling it?" she asked, slumping further against the engine hold.

Sam nodded and firmly told herself the feelings of guilt poking at her were completely unreasonable and in bad taste.

"Yep," Sam confirmed.

Seconds clicked by, stretched and awkward. How long was long enough to let someone recover from having their dreams crushed? A minute? Two? Would it be bad if Sam suggested Kate wait down in the main bay, closer to the doors? There were a few more sequences she had to run through before the engines would be heated enough to take off, and if she was lucky, Floodwater wouldn't be too irritated about her missing their meeting the night before.

Of course, his station wasn't open for business until the sun went down. Which meant she needed to find something to do in the in-between hours. There were one or two other repairs she could attempt in the meantime: little fixes she was fairly confident she wouldn't muck up. She started to turn back to the console, looking once more at Kate, still unmoving.

Still disappointed.

Shit. Right. Something to say...

"Is your life really so bad here?" As the words left her mouth, Sam thought she could have said that a little nicer. Or maybe not at all.

To her surprise, Kate laughed. It was short and less *ha, ha, ha* and *more damn, this sucks*, but it was a laugh nonetheless.

"No," she answered, shaking her head. "It's actually not bad at all. I just..." she sighed. "Haven't you ever wanted to go somewhere else? Do… something else? Just. Get away?" She laughed again, the same mirthless chuckle. "It's stupid. Stupid idea."

Hard not to agree; it was stupid to trade safety and stability on a whim. Space wasn't some great utopia—it was cold, dark, and dangerous—and the kind of work she dealt in was, for the most part, boring. Hauling freight, small payloads, or persons between systems. She did it because it was simple, steady, and had the side benefit of rarely requiring conversations with actual people, other than crew members.

On the other hand… she got it, maybe better than she wanted to admit. She'd taken that last job, even though it had smoked around the edges, because the thought of another steady run had felt smothering. She'd picked it, going against her head, because her gut had been pulling at her for *something different*. Hell, isn't that why she bought the ship in the first place?

Sam thought about the sterile white walls and the nearly empty space that barely looked lived in. How the woman who had stood there, in that room, had run and leapt into darkness as an escape.

Yeah, she understood. Not enough to necessarily do anything about it, but—

The open engine casing gaped at her. It was funny. What were the odds she would rescue a total stranger who happened to know how to diagnose and fix a problem she didn't even know the ship had? Must have been some astronomical number.

Jonah would have called it fate.

Sam would have laughed at him. *What are you gonna do?*

Shit.

"We'll have to go to Icarus 3," she murmured, loud enough for Kate to hear. When the other woman raised her head, Sam lifted her shoulders with forced nonchalance. "It's the closet place to pick up a couple of crew members, good crew, and a job."

Kate moved to speak. Sam made a curt motion with her right index finger to cut her off.

"One job," she warned. "That's it. And as of now, you're crew, which means you listen to and agree with every single decision I make. Got it?"

Grinning, Kate gave a quick salute. "Does this mean I get paid?"

Sam tamped down on the smile that wanted to spread across her own face, schooling her features into something more serious. "Be thankful I don't charge you passage."

Snorting lightly, Kate straightened, and all signs of disappointment were gone. In its place was an almost contagious excitement that burned in her eyes. Sam deliberately looked away so as not to catch it. But she couldn't quite deny the prickling along her spine.

"So, what next?" Kate asked.

Sam gave a moment's consideration.

"Any chance you can get the door to the bridge open?"

four

aving worked in the transportation sector for nearly fifteen years, Kate was aware of the multiple dueling factions found within the industry. The rivalry between on- and off-planet transporters played out in advertisements, job bids, and even regulatory laws that routinely came up at local commerce meetings. On-planet shippers regarded their off-planet counterparts as reckless and borderline deranged. After all, why would anyone in their right mind agree to shoot themselves out into the cold endless void of space, where the chance of rescue was slim to none?

Space haulers, on the other hand, thought of terran freighters as boring and lacking any sense of adventure. Also, didn't they know the accident statistics for ground shipping were astronomically high? Space transports were lost maybe one in a thousand. The last on-planet convoy accident had been the previous *Tuesday*.

Kate assumed this was why Sam insisted they travel to Icarus 3 to find a crew. She didn't necessarily *agree*—there were more than enough transport depots on planet from which to hire able and willing bodies.

In fact, Kate probably *could* have just finessed one of the dozen or so small jobs her company declined every week, not to mention get a few solid recommendations for crew members with a couple phone calls to familiar vendors. Sam's expression when she had voiced *that* suggestion had been... not positive.

She reminded herself that it was not her ship, and if Sam had certain notions regarding potential hires, well then, Kate would keep her opinion to herself. Sam *was* doing her a favor, power coupling restoration aside.

Instead, Kate stared out of the small view window of the auxiliary bridge (the main bridge door had, despite her best efforts, been beyond her capabilities) and, as the ship drew closer to the massive construct, reviewed everything she knew about Icarus 3.

It was classified as an entertainment satellite, the larger of two orbiting the planet. "Entertainment" being a broad category meant the satellite was home to a dizzying array of amusements intended to drive away all thoughts of work or responsibility, along with hotels and lodges designed for those who could afford to spend more than a day away. Kate had heard enough tales around the office from co-workers who had visited to know there was a sprawling gambling sector, a perpetual club section, an unrivaled selection of holo and gaming stations, and an artificial white sand beach where awed visitors could swim under constant starlight, only a thin barrier keeping them from drifting off into space.

Kate thought the effect lost something when one learned it was just a hologram projected onto the thick hull of the station.

Despite having lived her entire life with the satellite passing hourly high overhead, Kate had never stepped foot on its surface. It had been on the wish list of family trips growing up, a "someday" that never happened. And when she was older, when it was just her and dad, she remembered promises and intentions, but something always came up.

Maybe it had something to do with the fact that neither you nor your father wanted to shoot yourselves into the void of space where the chance of rescue is slim to none just for the sake of some holo-games?

*Which is why, if you stopped to **think** about it, this entire idea is completely—*

"Shut up," she murmured to herself.

"What?"

Kate looked over to where Sam was once more sitting behind the navigation console; the captain hadn't glanced up from the dash. Those dark-framed glasses teetered on her nose and Kate could see the reflection of coordinate maps in the lenses. She wanted to ask the other woman about them but couldn't figure out a way that wouldn't come across like *how come you don't get your eyes fixed?*

Because, you know. Rude.

Instead she asked, trying to keep any sense of impatience out of her voice, "How much longer until we dock?"

"Depends on how many other ships are docking. We'll have to join the queue."

Peering back out the view window, Kate noted several shapes occupying the space between them and the station. How many were ships and how many were smaller satellites or jettisoned junk? It was hard to see the difference or have any sense of how far away or how big the objects were. She hoped whatever Sam was glaring at on the console gave a better picture.

Kate's leg bounced with nervous energy. "Well... is there anything I can do or help with?"

Over the top of her frames, Sam's pale eyes were tinted green with the light from the screen.

"Yes. You can sit there quietly. That would be very helpful."

Rolling her eyes and folding her arms across her chest, Kate bit down on the inside of her cheek.

Right. Icarus 3. It wasn't *only* an entertainment satellite. Due to its location and the sheer volume of goods and people passing through it every hour, it was also the largest shipping hub in the sector. Anything and anyone who needed to go somewhere in the solar system went through Icarus 3's transfer station. Ideal place to hire experienced crew members and peruse the job postings. Not to mention it had a thriving market, which would be helpful in securing any supplies they might need. Considering the current on-planet economic conditions, Icarus 3 probably had a better selection of goods at better buy or barter rates.

Frowning, Kate set her back to the window as a thought suddenly occurred to her.

"You said you were in that bar station because you were going to sell your ship, right?"

"I am going to sell the ship. One job, remember?"

Kate pushed past that reminder. "But why that station? Why wouldn't you do it at one of the auction sites or shipyards?"

"I told you, I have a buyer already."

Kate shook her head. "No one in that sector could afford a kraken class spaceship. No one in that sector could afford to travel on a kraken without offering partial employment and a lot of extended credit. And you don't seem like the type to accept credit."

"No? What type of currency do I seem like I *do* accept?"

Kate pursed her lips. "Secrets."

Sam tipped her head thoughtfully. "I like that. Not at all practical, yet oddly alluring. Involves way too much conversation, though."

"What's their name?"

"Whose?"

But Kate was familiar with the game now. "The buyer's," she pressed determinedly. When no answer came, she prodded, "What, did you have a confidentiality agreement or something?"

Sam sat back from the console and Kate had the captain's full focus. A long, unblinking stare that felt like it read the thoughts in Kate's head as easily as the console screen. It distracted Kate enough so that she nearly missed the next words out of Sam's mouth.

"Guy by the name of Floodwater."

Kate stared, certain she had heard incorrectly. There wasn't any way that Sam had actually said— "*Miles* Floodwater?" she asked, drawing out the first name like the impossibility it was.

Sam raised one eyebrow in a manner that did not at all speak to the terror or concern it *should* have. "Didn't realize you were acquainted."

Kate shook her head vehemently, her stomach suddenly ricocheting around like a pinball. "No. No way. Definitely not. But *everybody* knows who Miles Floodwater is. The Fisher King. He runs the Floods—he *is* the Floods. He owns half the businesses there, and the other half pays him protection money so his goons don't burn them out. They say he's responsible for nearly two thirds of the crime on planet and that nothing and no one moves without his permission."

Looking amused, Sam had set her chin on one hand as she watched her rattle off statistics. When Kate paused to take a breath, she made a *tsking* sound with her tongue.

"Really? All that? So then why were *you* in *his* station last night?"

Kate's stomach fell away completely. "That was his station?"

"Yep."

"God." Kate could literally feel the blood drain from her face. Her hands went cold and she rubbed them together for warmth. "That means the boss those two meatheads were talking about—"

"Definitely Floodwater."

"God," Kate repeated, sinking down into the seat behind her. "Oh my god."

"He's not actually all that bad."

Kate straightened up. "Really?" she asked, hopefully.

"No, he's a total monster. One time I wouldn't hand over some cargo to him and his goons, so he took these instead," Sam replied, pointing to her missing middle and ring fingers with her thumb. At Kate's stricken expression, she laughed. *Laughed.* "Don't worry. He's got other things on his mind besides some unknown woman who refused his summons. Hell, I stood him up."

"Is that what you would call it? A summons?"

"It's the politest word I can think for it."

There were many thoughts racing through Kate's head, and she tried to shuffle them into some reasonable order. One minute, Sam had been a begrudgingly compassionate, reticent, but still interesting transporter and now—

"You set up a deal with a *space mobster*," Kate hissed. "You broke a deal with the *Fisher King*. He's probably pissed."

"Yeah," Sam agreed, still appearing less than concerned. At the sound of distress that escaped Kate, Sam chuckled and shook her head. "It's not a big deal, trust me. He probably didn't even notice. And don't call him a space mobster. That sounds ridiculous. He—"

Whatever she was about to add dropped away as static crackled over the communications line, followed by a curt voice demanding something like *identification codes*. Sam snatched an earpiece from off the dash, fitted it into her ear, and flicked several switches before rattling off a series of numbers. She paused, one finger resting on the earpiece, and then verbalized a second set of numbers and letters.

"Yes. Yes. Bay 12. Confirmed."

Pulling the com from her ear, Sam tossed it back onto the dashboard. Her fingers flew across the rows of buttons and knobs in a sequence Kate couldn't follow. The fact that Sam's right hand was missing two digits barely affected her motions, save for when she needed to reach over with her left to punch more than three buttons at a time.

The ship lurched and Kate's head shot up to the viewing window. Icarus 3 did not appear any closer than it had before. Sam stood up from the control board, pulled her glasses off, and set them down near one of the monitors.

"They've locked on to us," she said, as explanation. "Come on. I'll walk you through the docking procedure," she added, swinging down onto the ladder and disappearing through the floor.

Kate wasn't sure what she had expected; she had an average interest in space for a planet dweller and an above average knowledge of it due to her current—or former—employment. Added together, she figured it meant that while she enjoyed science fiction as a genre, she knew better than most that what you saw in the movies and on your in-home screen was far from reality.

Yet the sheer *boredom* of the last couple of hours surprised her. So far, space travel had entailed long periods of waiting, followed by a very brief flurry of activity—handled almost entirely by Sam—and then more waiting. It wasn't much different from what Kate had done every day for the past fifteen years, only with a big piece of extremely expensive equipment rather than random action items, doled out daily via a digital board. Only with the digital board she was allowed to give actual input.

So really, space travel was like if she had gone into work and stared at her console while someone else did all the tasks—

someone who also occasionally barked out the order to "move out of the way" or "press the button—no, not that one, the big one— never mind, I'll get it."

If she hadn't been so annoyed by Sam's obvious impatience at her unfamiliarity with the docking sequence of a kraken spaceship (and seriously "the button" is not enough of a descriptor in an area with at least half a dozen "buttons"), Kate would have been impressed by the easy rhythm of Sam's movements. Despite a limp, and the fact the docking procedures almost *demanded* two people, she cruised between the engine room and cargo space—hitting switches, inputting scripts, and calling out orders that she barely gave Kate enough time to *comprehend* let alone *carry out*—hardly breaking a sweat.

Figuratively speaking. Physically, there was a thin bead of perspiration running down the side of her neck, dampening the collar of her t-shirt by the time the ship gave its final shudder.

Even with the flush of exertion reddening her cheeks, Sam grabbed her jacket before shuffling toward the main exit doors.

"It's always chilly on satellite," she explained, and Kate nodded, grabbing her own coat from next to the engine housing before following close behind.

That had been nearly an hour ago. Again, she wasn't exactly certain of what she had been expecting to see once they trudged down the cargo plank into the docking bay, but commercials for Icarus 3 strongly suggested there would at least be some other people around, If not the frolicking, exuberant tourists shown enjoying the satellite's many offerings. They walked across the enormous bay, past nearly two dozen ships of vastly different sizes and shapes, and into the small receiving office, and Kate hadn't seen a single other soul.

That is, except for the tired, thin man hunched over a screen in a skinny booth, but Kate didn't know for sure if he was a person or one of the newer models of androids; he hadn't spoken more than two words since they entered. She thought human was more likely since they usually programmed androids to be *helpful* and *communicative*.

If she hadn't watched the ship being pulled into the belly of the satellite, Kate might have assumed they were in any random waiting room on planet, being dicked around by some employee who really didn't like his job. The only indication that it was Icarus 3 was a faded sign above the exit door that read *HEXOR Energy & Propulsion Welcomes You to Icarus 3.*

She glanced at Sam, who stood with her hands jammed into the pockets of her jacket. The captain's form held no sign of irritation at the long wait, which amazed Kate. She would not have thought waiting to be one of Sam's mysterious skills, but maybe in space, you could only move as fast as a quad core engine could take you?

Kate's frown deepened. *That's not the right metaphor.*

She hummed quietly in her throat, and when Sam looked to her, she motioned with her head toward the sign. "I thought the UNE passed a law against the ownership of public satellites by private corporations?"

Sam's eyes ventured to the sign and then back, her amusement clear. "There aren't a lot of missives from Earth Prime that make it all the way out here. And it's not like they ever send anyone out to check."

"Aren't there Peacekeepers stationed on planet?"

Sam scratched the back of her head. "Yeah, and that'd be like using explosives to remove a screw. Anyway, it could be worse. I was at a station once that was part of the AF Corporation and it was… unpleasant."

"The reach of these corporations is—" Kate paused and looked around, as if a black-suited representative would be hulking in the corner. "—unethical," she finished, quietly.

One of Sam's eyebrows lifted. "Someone had to fund the great space search. The UNE certainly couldn't come up with the money."

"That was four, maybe five hundred years ago." Kate waved her arms back toward the hangar and beyond, out into the expanse of space. "It's pretty well funded now! Meanwhile, the major corporations act like their own private governments with their own rules. It's dangerous."

"Well, you can always try leaving a detailed customer service complaint."

"Doesn't it bother you? That they can just do whatever they want?"

Sam stood against the nearby wall. "I've got a lot of other things on my mind at the moment."

"Like what?"

"Like hiring a crew and finding a job. That is, if we don't grow old and die inside this office first."

The unsubtle cut made Kate smile; she tried not to read too much into the fact that she found a slightly aggravated Sam easier to be around.

"What do you think is taking so long?" she asked, pointing with her chin to the booth.

"He's checking the ship's current setup against its last official registration. Also running it against any warrants or OI searches."

"OI?"

"Of interest. Plus, I think he's technically finishing his lunch break."

Now that Sam mentioned it, she could see the wrappers and packets spread out on the desk that the clerk reached into every so often, even as he remained glued to his screen.

"What is he checking the registration for?"

"To make sure any modifications have been properly logged."

Kate's brows drew together. "Ah. For identification, right?" she guessed, and Sam nodded.

"Yeah and—"

"Here it is!" The man in the booth declared, success breathing animation into his face. "Kraken, freighter class, registration MCV-09890-1B." He looked at Sam over the top of his screen. "No ship name?"

Approaching the window, Sam cleared her throat and shook her head. "No."

"Quad engine?"

"Yes."

"Two auxiliary shuttles?"

Kate thought she saw Sam's face pale, but it might have been the poor lighting in the office.

"One. Primary shuttle was lost." The words seemed to creak out of Sam's throat, and she coughed lightly, as if they had been sharp.

The clerk didn't notice or didn't care; he merely made a notation on his screen. "Intent to replace?"

Sam did not reply. She stood stock still, as if something in those three words had paralyzed her. The only sounds in the room were a whining from the machines behind the clerk's window, the buzzing of the lights overhead, and a sudden uptick in Sam's breathing.

Not sure what else to do, Kate gently brushed against Sam's arm and felt the captain jump under the touch. Sam's gaze lingered on the point of contact between them and then rose to meet Kate's; something dark and haunted was reflected in her pale irises. Then she looked back at the man in the booth, who was awaiting an answer.

"Do you intend to replace the unit?" he repeated, slightly slower and louder than before, his tone conveying his confusion over a lack of answer to a basic question.

Sam shook her head. "No, not at this time." Her shoulders hunched so that the collar of her jacket all but swallowed her neck and pressed up against her chin.

The clerk made several more motions on his screen and looked up with a poor attempt at a cheerful expression.

"You have successfully been logged in. Docking privileges are extended for 24 station hours. If you need additional time, you'll need to purchase an extended visa," he droned, repeating the mantra he probably said dozens of times a day.

"Twenty-four is plenty," Sam stated, snatching up the electronic pass the clerk slipped through the pickup window. Without hesitating, she pushed out of the office, leaving Kate to scramble along behind her.

Beyond the threshold of the door, the world was completely different. The relatively empty office gave way immediately to a mammoth space packed with people, crates, equipment, products, maintenance crews and debris, lighted signs—the volume and variety was blinding, and Kate lifted a hand to shield her view. She lost sight of Sam as the other woman was instantly swallowed up by the horde of things that hadn't been there a second before. Kate gave serious thought to ducking back inside the office where dull and quiet boredom beckoned.

Instead, she took a deep breath as if about to dive into water and pushed into the throng, shifting and sliding past bodies and baggage, trying to ride the current of movement as best she could while scanning the mass of faces.

The absolute impossibility of picking Sam's mug out of the surging crowd was just occurring to Kate when a strong hand curled around her upper arm and tugged her sideways. Stumbling and bouncing off a number of irritated souls, she finally came to a stop against a wall. Kate turned and saw it was Sam who had pulled her out of the way of the heavier foot traffic.

Foot and cart traffic, she amended as she watched with amazement as a small vehicle zipped its way through the stream of people at a questionable speed.

"Shift change," Sam stated.

The captain evaluated the slow-moving crush of bodies with an expression of distaste. Kate didn't blame her; she felt the same way every morning when she had to ride the commuter rail into the office. The press of humanity at its finest and most aromatic. She wrinkled her nose in remembrance.

"All these people work on the satellite?" she asked with fascination. Sure, the station had seemed big on approach but still— she was having trouble believing every person there had a role to play in its upkeep.

Sam glanced at the unit on her wrist then shook her head, annoyance settling more firmly into her features. "Check out time, too, probably." She craned her neck, looking out over the throng, clearly searching for something. "Come on. Let's go this way."

She shouldered them through the crowds to a discreet door marked "service" and shoved through. The wide avenue funneled to a narrow tunnel, significantly less crowded and a good deal quieter once the door banged shut behind them. Dull orange lights ran along the top of the corridor, a far cry from the bright illumination of the main thoroughfare. The muffled din of the crowds mixed with the steady thrum of machinery and the echoey murmurs of hushed conversations from the few individuals they passed.

Kate had to hustle to keep up with Sam's long, determined strides.

"Where exactly are we going?" she questioned as they stepped around two workers with "MAINTENANCE" blocked in white across their bodies bent over an exposed section of the wall, pointing and nodding at a spot within that Kate hoped was not a serious issue.

Sam didn't look concerned. "The stationmaster's office. Best place to get a lead on a job," she replied, her tone short. The alley was darker than either the office or the main walkway had been, but Kate could see a lingering pallor to Sam's skin.

"Hey, are you—"

"Fine," Sam snapped, cutting off the question. She tugged the zipper of her jacket down, as if overwarm.

Kate bit back the rest of her question, though it was painfully apparent Sam was not *fine*, that something was bothering her. It hadn't been tedium that had put the deep, faraway look into her eyes and the shadow of grief onto her face.

But Kate had learned several things in 24 hours: never visit a station in the Floods; space travel involved a lot of waiting; and Sam—whatever her last name was—was not one for conversation. Particularly if it involved information about herself.

It was none of her business. Kate had absolutely no problem with that. It was more than enough that Sam had acquiesced to her request to take her along. There was no requirement the woman also provide her entire life story as well.

Kate just wished that life story didn't hint so much at being *fascinating*. Where and when had she first gotten the ship? What happened to her leg? How well did she know Floodwater? Why was one of the shuttles missing? How long had she been without a crew?

What was the *attachment* to that jacket? She wore it like a suit of armor, as if the thick material could ward off blows. Or like some magical cape that could shield her from view.

Okay, that might be a bit fanciful.

Worrying the side of her cheek with her teeth again, Kate tried to keep her curiosity under wraps. Sam's hurried pace garnered more than a couple looks thrown their way, but the woman didn't appear to notice. She was fixated straight ahead, as if she had a destination in mind and no plans to deviate from her chosen course. Though her jaw was tight, the rigidness of her shoulders had loosened, and Kate thought maybe she could risk asking one little thing.

"You didn't name your ship," she voiced, and then added, "Isn't that bad luck?"

For a second, Sam gave no indication she had even heard the question. Then, she abruptly slowed her steps and glanced over with a roll of her eyes.

"Why bother when MCV-09890-1B rolls so nicely off the tongue," she deadpanned.

Okay, so not superstitious. "How long did it take you to memorize that?"

"Fucking forever."

Their shoulders bumped and Kate placed a hand on Sam's arm to steady herself, felt the other woman, again, tense at the contact. Pretending not to notice, Kate let her hand drop.

"So why not go for something easier?" she reasoned, shifting so there was space between them once more.

Sam's shoulders jumped. "I haven't ever thought of anything that seemed to fit."

"You could always name it after your cat," Kate suggested, hoping to prolong the levity.

It didn't work; instead, there was a long, resentful pause. "I told you, it's not my cat."

"Right." Kate chewed her lip briefly. The weight was back, an awkward and uncomfortable heaviness to the air around them.

It occurred to Kate that maybe this was a bad idea, too. Was it really fair of her to ask Sam, this stranger who had already saved her life, to put aside the decisions she had made or been in the process of making before Kate had, literally, fallen into her life? Kate felt like she was infringing in a space much more complicated than she had considered.

She *hadn't* really considered, Kate realized and sighed, ready to declare they should forget the whole thing and she could just grab the next planet-side shuttle. And Sam could go back to ... what sounded like early retirement?

Before she could get a word out, Sam gave a full body shake, like a dog flicking off water. "The sooner we get a job, the sooner we'll know what kind of crew we'll need," she stated, her manner reverting to its natural state—mildly irritated.

And like that, the tension was gone. A bit off-kilter, Kate fumbled as she tried to adjust to the shifts in moods.

"Wh-Where do you plan on picking up a crew? Are there any guild outposts on station?" she prompted, in an attempt to catch the tail of the new topic.

"Yeah, there's one."

The reluctance in Sam's voice was as thick as engine sludge. "But?"

"But I've run into some... problems with them before, so I'd like to avoid dealing with them if possible."

Kate didn't bother asking the question; she knew she wouldn't get an answer. But the spark of curiosity inside of her flared that much brighter. "So where else can we go to find the people we need?"

"The most important thing is a good engineer; the rest will depend on the job. Lots of engineers hang out in the holo-stations. I don't imagine it will be too hard to find someone willing to take on short work."

"And if it is?"

"Well, then your great space adventure might be over before it begins. Watch your step," Sam added just as Kate had been about to set her foot down in a pool of unidentified liquid seeping from a seam in the wall. Kate eyed the leak warily as she stepped over it. Sam hadn't even given it a first look.

"Shouldn't someone be fixing that?"

"Hmm?" At Kate's nod back the way they came, Sam said, "Not my job."

Kate slowed, looking from the walls to the floors and back, every single space disaster she had ever read about abruptly flooding back into her brain. She remembered, *acutely*, why she had never made the trip before. "People *pay* to come here?"

It was both a statement and a question.

Sam paused at a small intersection where others were huddled in a loose group. One was curved over his com unit, thumbs tapping the screen while his companions amused themselves by slapping at each other's hands. The captain ignored them and squinted down each offshoot. "Nothing in space stays new," she replied, as if that excused everything.

"How about just 'intact'?" Kate wanted to know. She took an unconscious step closer to Sam while trying to inspect, without making it *seem* like she was inspecting, the surrounding structure, searching for fissures or fractures. Mostly, she was getting a weird pain in the middle of her forehead and a bit of disorientation each time her eyes inadvertently crossed.

Her gaze slid unconsciously toward the group, as if tugged by an invisible string, in time to catch a dark-haired woman giving Sam a pointed twice-over before passing Kate what might have been a congratulatory wink.

Kate felt her ears burn and was immediately grateful when Sam turned down the right alley, leaving the little cluster behind them.

"Relax. If there was a problem, there'd be lights and sirens going off," Sam threw over her shoulder, once more picking up her pace. Kate hurried to stay in step.

"Not necessarily. The crew of the *Trident Research Station* had no warning when the fuel pod exploded. It took out all the emergency sensors."

"And yet the crew still survived."

The casualness of the statement was at odds with the dark

expression on Sam's face but hell if Kate had any idea where either had come from.

"Well yeah, thanks to their commander. And he didn't make it—"

Sam halted in the middle of the tunnel and pinched the bridge of her nose. "Look, if I promise to throw myself like an idiot on an imploding hatch so you can escape, will you quit worrying?"

Kate frowned at the description of Commander Jack Hero's final actions. "No need to be dramatic about it."

Sam gave her a look. "You're the one imagining the demise of a functional satellite and I'm dramatic?"

Flushing slightly, Kate trained her eyes ahead and kept moving. "It's a perfectly legitimate concern. How much further to the stationmaster's office?"

"It's just up ahead."

They walked in silence for a few seconds.

"You wouldn't throw yourself on a faulty hatch," Kate began.

"It would be pretty stupid."

"Swooping in, *dramatically*, with your kraken to rescue everyone just in time is more your style, isn't it?" she finished, teasing.

She expected a grumpy retort but out of the corner of her eye she saw Sam flinch as if struck. The sharpness of her reply took Kate by surprise.

"It's perfectly fucking safe here for crying out—"

Her words cut off as a fist shot out from nowhere, slamming like a shuttle train into Sam's jaw. The captain spun in the direction the fist had been traveling, sprawling against the far wall.

Before Kate could even think to scream something came down over her head, plunging her into darkness. She heard a heavy *smack* and felt a tightening around her throat. Her fingernails dug into soft flesh, but the pressure remained until consciousness slipped out of reach.

five

She wasn't supposed to be there.

It was 8:57 a.m., which meant she was supposed to be in, or heading into, classroom A, all the way on the other side of the satellite, so there was no way she'd be able to make it on time. And if she was going to be in trouble for being late, then she might as well skip the entire day.

She'd had the nightmare last night. The one—the same one. The clock beside her bed had read 4:31. Though her eyes had been gritty and heavy, returning to sleep was never an option; it would just put her right back into the dream to start all over again. She had gotten up, dressed, and left the tiny room that was hers. Not everyone got their own room, but she did. She didn't know why but thought maybe it was because of the nightmares. Nobody wanted to be woken up early. Stephen Rand, who probably was in classroom A right then, said it was because of her dad, but she didn't see how that was possible since he was dead. Her mom, too, but no one ever said anything about her mother.

So, instead of classroom A, she was slipping into a holo-station, one of the out-of-the-way ones that did without the loud music and flashing lights of the popular spots. Kids were not supposed to be in a station without an adult, but Link was on door duty and as soon as they saw her, they shifted to block the overhead camera just as she ducked under the employee pass. She didn't look back to grin her thanks—the dream was too fresh in her mind. Instead, she hurried around the larger machines and set-ups, her eyelids half closed with exhaustion, until she got to the back of the station where the antique games resided. A handful of ancient computers stuck inside colorful cabinets, operated by physical inputs—buttons or joysticks—rather than direct mindlinks or holo-rooms. She slid into one machine that was shaped like the inside of a cockpit and, accessing a side panel that stated in bold red letters it was for employee use only, punched in a code that would offer her free play. She hoped it hadn't been changed since the last time.

The machine lit up, and she was treated to a scrolling, slightly fuzzy screen explaining how her help was desperately needed to defend against the Intergalactic Empire.

And for hours, she blasted her way methodically through the Empire's hordes, waiting for the tightness in her chest to pass.

So focused was she on the targets zipping across the screen that she didn't notice the figure standing beside her until she swung her ship about and brought the last two cruisers into target range, where she promptly zapped them.

"Yeah! Blast those suckers!"

She jumped—if she hadn't been harnessed into the machine, she might have fallen out—and her head jerked to the right. Her heart clutched; for a second, she was sure it was one of the guardian droids come to escort her over to the school. But then, a droid wouldn't be celebrating her gaming skills.

It was a boy somewhere around her age, which was 12 years and 32 days. She kept an exact count because once she was exactly eighteen, she'd be able to go wherever and do whatever she wanted. Even though she didn't know where or what it was that she wanted to be doing, she already knew it was somewhere other than where she was.

He had messy brown hair that hung over his forehead, slightly chubby cheeks, and bright brown eyes that crinkled at the corners, squished by the stretch of his grin.

"What is this game? Is it fun? Can I play?" The words tumbled from his mouth in a cascade of enthusiasm.

She looked back at the screen; it was waiting for her input before progressing to the next level. The last level before the final battle with the Empire's massive war ship, a fight she'd only gotten to attempt twice before, both ending in defeat. If she died now, she'd have to start all the way back at the beginning.

She turned to the boy, intent on telling him to bug off. "Yeah, okay," she said instead as she removed the pilot belt and climbed out of the machine. The boy gave a whoop and jumped into her place. Then he stared at the multitudes of levers and buttons.

"What's all this stuff? How do you use it?" he asked her, still grinning broadly. Despite the fact that patient or *thoughtful were the last words any of her instructors would have used to describe her, she leaned in and carefully explained what each piece controlled, when and how to use it, and especially how he had to be careful with the throttle lever because sometimes it got stuck if you pushed it too hard, and that always made the ship crash. He nodded vehemently after nearly every word, and when she finished, he gave a big thumbs up before grabbing the control stick with both hands.*

"All right! Let's blast some alien scum!"

"It's the Empire."

His nose scrunched and his head tilted. "Huh?"

She tapped the side of the machine where the words 'Intergalactic Empire' were scrawled in bright red. "You're fighting the Empire."

His head bobbed up and down so quickly it made her a little dizzy. "Oh. Right. Let's blast some Empire scum!" he corrected himself with even more zeal than before. Feeling her lips twitch, she bent forward again and pushed the start button so the level would progress. After all, the sooner he started, the sooner she could get back to playing.

"Hey."

She looked over at him; he was scanning the text appearing on screen. In some corner of her mind, she recognized that the constriction in her chest had finally eased, and the lingering remnants of the nightmare had been pushed aside for another day.

"My name's Jonah. What's yours?"

"Sam."

"Sam? Wake up Sam."

The voice was distant but familiar, like a tune she could remember but couldn't quite recall the words to. She knew she had heard it before, somewhere, though it was hard to think over a heavy, incessant buzzing noise.

"Sammy. Come on, Sammy. Wake up."

Sammy? No one called her Sammy. And good god, what was that noise? Had she fallen asleep in the engine core? Was there a parade going by? When was it going to stop?

"Jeez, Sammy. You're gonna get me in trouble."

Sam made what she thought was an inquisitive sound and

barely heard it over the steady pounding in her ears. Whoever was speaking seemed pleased by the response.

"Oh good. Okay. Now, come on, open your eyes."

Sam was confused, because she thought she already *had*, had assumed that wherever she was, was simply dark as hell. Then she blinked, slowly, and light came rushing in with a piercing swipe, momentarily blinding her. The rolling drumming reached a fever pitch, and she abruptly realized the clamor was all going on inside her head, which felt like one gentle breeze would send it rolling off her shoulders. The right side of her face was stiff and chilled; with a very cold weight pressed against it.

It ached like a *sonofabitch*.

Sam winced as her vision adjusted. Both the world and the pain came into sharp clarity. Directly in front of her was a ruddy-cheeked, moon-shaped face she had really hoped to never see again. Watery green eyes stared out at her from beneath dark bushy eyebrows and were set off by a big, gap-toothed smile.

"Hey Sammy. You're awake. That's good. That's real good."

Her gaze drifted to either side of him as she tried to get some sense of where she was. There were walls of dark windows stretching from floor to ceiling. On the other side of them were scores of people strolled past; the tint of the glass told her they likely saw nothing but their own reflections. She could see a shadow of herself with a bright light highlighting her face. Further behind her were other, darker shapes, but the light didn't reach all the way back, and she couldn't make out any of their details.

She was in a chair with a high back that curled over her head and thin metal arms that felt cold when she set her hands on them. When she sat forward, the chair shifted with her until the soles of her boots rested against the floor. The words *Intergalactic Empire* flashed in her brain, and she shook her head to dislodge the image. She immediately regretted the motion as her vision swam and her stomach pitched.

The floor was black and polished. Her outline was dimly reproduced in its surface. Breathing deep, she waited for the rolling nausea to pass; whoever the floor's owner was, she figured they wouldn't appreciate her throwing up on it. It gave her some time to order her thoughts—her immediate concern was Kate. She couldn't tell if the other woman was nearby, and on the off chance they hadn't taken her, Sam didn't want to give any indication she had been with someone.

"Boss wants to talk to you, Sammy. Sorry about it, but the Boss said to bring you, so I brought you. Your face okay?"

Actual worry was etched into the saggy folds of the face hovering in front of her. She reached up, touched her fingers to her right cheek, and felt the smooth edges of a cold pack stuck to it. The gentle brush sent a lance of pain directly into her temple like a laser zap. Her brain kindly connected all the loose dots.

"Jesus, Benny, what the hell did you hit me for?" she groaned.

Benny's apprehension melted into confusion, his usual expression. "Boss said to bring you. So I brought you."

Her fingers grazed against the pack again, and this time, the pain shivered down her spine. "Yeah, well, you could have brought me without hitting me," she pointed out, even though she knew it was useless. Not even a live puppet show production could explain the concept of non-violence to Benny.

"Sadly, that is a construct that Benny seems unable to grasp.'"

From behind the chair came another voice, thin and sour. She had no trouble placing it. Sam walked her fingers carefully over her nose, pressing lightly. It seemed okay, at least.

"You could have sent me a comm message. No need to set the goons after me," she groused, not bothering to try and spin the chair toward the speaker. He'd show himself soon enough, and anyway, she remembered what he looked like.

"If you had deigned to keep our arranged meeting the other night, it would not have been necessary to contact you." There was a snip to the words that had Sam fighting not to roll her eyes. With the way her head was throbbing, she wasn't sure she would get them back.

"Well, Miles, maybe I got tired of sitting around waiting for you to remember that we *had* a meeting. It wasn't exactly ladies' night at the station." She hadn't expected this from him, not this level of retribution for a missed appointment for fucksake. Her right hand flexed involuntarily, and phantom pain flared briefly to rival the throb in her head.

She probably should have.

"Oh? And here I was assuming you had gotten distracted by this charming new addition to your crew."

What followed was a curse that definitely came from Kate. Sam pulled herself up in the chair and bore down on the swell of panic. No place for it now. She forced a calm into her voice and tried not to resent the fact it was such a struggle. No time for *that* now either.

"Look, something came up. I've decided not to sell the ship just yet. If that pisses you off, okay. Take it out on me. She's got nothing to do with it," she stated, her mouth dry. The soft sounds of scuffling continued behind her, but turning her head would be too much of a tell.

A chuckle seemed to come from nowhere. "Oh, Sam. You've known me long enough to know that doesn't matter. But first, I do want to get this other little matter cleared up."

Out of the corner of her eye, she caught movement and then, suddenly, there he was, stepping out from behind the chair and continuing past Benny to stand before the windows. It must have been more than five years since she last saw him, but he looked more or less as she remembered. A small man who made himself appear taller with a ruthlessly straight posture. His hair had more silver in it now and it weaved through the dark curls in a deceptively distinguished manner.

He wore a cream-colored suit; even with his back to her, she knew the shirt would be the same and buttoned all the way up to his throat. His hands were covered in matching smooth gloves so that the only glimpse of his sepia-colored skin was his face. In his right hand he carried a simple, thin walking stick. Most might see it as a weapon of convenience or an affectation, but Sam could tell by the way he leaned into it that it was more than that. One tired body recognized another.

He stood at the windows for a long, silent moment, watching the passersby. His shoulders rose as he drew in the breath to speak.

"Where is it?"

It took a moment for the words, softly spoken as they were, to register. When they did, they didn't make much sense. Sam felt her forehead scrunch and the ache radiated across her cheeks.

"Where's what? The ship? It's in dock 12 for the next 24."

Floodwater turned, and Sam was taken aback by the anger twisting the features of his face. Even with their current distance, she could see his eyes almost glowing in the light; they were green but not at all like Benny's guileless gaze. Usually they were cold and clear, like frozen absinthe. Impenetrable. But now they were wide and wild, brimming with imminent violence.

The sudden transformation appeared to take him off-guard as well, and he pivoted toward the glass, hiding his face. Tendrils of that seething rage shook his voice, however, as he spit out a single:

"Benny."

The goon grabbed hold of Sam's right wrist with one massive hand and tugged it up above her head. Her body went completely motionless, and she had to wonder if it was preservation or muscle memory. Maybe both. Behind her, Sam heard a shaky increase in Kate's breathing. At least, she figured it was Kate. Couldn't imagine any other allies in that room.

Sam waited for Floodwater to speak again, kept her sight trained on his back even as the blood drained from her hand and the cold prickling of numbness climbed into her fingers. Her shoulder grew tired, her back ached, and still she waited. Benny's grip was like a band of steel squeezing flesh and muscle against bone.

Finally, Floodwater sighed and walked back toward her with short, deliberate steps. Seemingly with little interest, he glanced down at the hand upheld to him in forced supplication. The walking stick lifted, shifting in his grip so that the golden top hovered over her missing digits.

"Do you recall losing those two?" he asked, his tone mild. Controlled once more. His rage locked away, as if it had never been set loose.

"Vaguely," she replied, stretching the syllables of the word.

He smiled, a faint pull of his lips, and that did nothing to soften the lines of his face. "I would be more than happy to refresh the memory for you." A pause. "Now I'll ask you again; where is it?"

Sam concentrated on not moving an inch. The fury might have been gone from his face, but she saw it shaking in his frame. His leather gloves creaked as his fingers clenched the head of the walking stick. The air in the room felt volatile, as if one twitch were all it would take to set off an explosion.

She certainly *wasn't* interested in losing any more fingers.

"You're going to have to give me more than that, Miles," she ventured cautiously. She thought she remembered hearing somewhere that using a person's name helped build empathy with them. *Really hope that's not just screen bullshit.* "I don't know what you're talking about." Green ice threatened to shatter, and she saw the snap working its way along his jaw. Sam lifted her free hand up and out as quickly as she dared. "Look, I just got smashed in the face by the flesh equivalent of a brick," she reasoned, hoping to stave off the flashpoint. "Tell me more about what it is you want, and I'll tell you everything I know. I swear it."

His face rippled as if more than anger lurked beneath his flesh. "The package," he ground out through clenched teeth. "*My* parcel. Where. Is. It."

Sam sat back as much as she could with Benny gripping her arm; she couldn't help the motion because the bewilderment that punched into her was too heavy to bear upright. She couldn't keep it out of her voice either.

"What package? I've never done a job for you. You know that," she stated, though maybe now wasn't the best time to point out their already non-working relationship.

But to her shock and relief, the reminder placated him. His face resumed its smooth plasticity, his lips hinting once more at a smile.

"That is true, yes. Yes. You have always disregarded my overtures. Of course, the same cannot be said of your crewmates. In particular, your friend Jonah. Oh, that does remind me. I am terribly sorry for your loss."

Sam, caught on the word *overtures*, reared back at the mention of Jonah, feeling like she had been struck again, like all the air had been pushed from her lungs.

"Jonah would never have taken a job from you," she refuted, forcing the words past the lump in her throat.

An emotion akin to delight, only a great deal harsher, animated his face. His smile widened, turned smug, and managed to be devoid of anything remotely pleasant. She really wanted to wipe it from his face.

"Ah, I see now that he didn't tell you. What an... amusing, if somewhat troublesome development. I assure you, though, he most certainly did take a job from me. He was even successful at it, according to the last transmission I received." He reached into his breast pocket and produced a thin tablet. His thumb swiped across the screen and a voice she hadn't heard in six months filled the room.

"I've got your parcel, Floodwater. We're on a run that'll take us into Sector Six, and then we'll be heading back to Icarus 3. A week, maybe a little more. And then you better hold up your end of the deal you son—"

Jonah's voice cut off and Floodwater chuckled. "Ah, no need to recount his colorful term for me." He tucked the piece of tech back into his suit. "I trust this is adequate proof of our arrangement."

She barely heard him as her own breaths labored painfully loud in her ears. It felt impossible to drag in enough air. Sam wasn't sure what was worse: hearing Jonah's voice again knowing he was gone or finding out he had gone behind her back to work for the one devil they had sworn never to take a job with.

"It's quite clear that he did not disclose our deal with you," Miles repeated, ostensibly without sparing her a glance. She knew better. He was enjoying every ripple that played across her face. "And so that changes things, ever so slightly."

"Great, so you're gonna let us go now?" Kate's voice rang out clear, strong, and *pissed*. Sam would have been impressed by the *go-fuck-yourself* tone if her mind weren't reeling in so many directions.

He did nothing more than slowly shake his head. "I'm afraid there is still the matter of my parcel."

"So, search the damn ship," Sam rasped, bringing his notice back to her. Clearing her throat, she twitched a shoulder, making sure not to jostle the hand that was in Benny's firm grip. "Have your men go through the whole thing, take your fucking *parcel*, and leave me the hell alone."

His eyes narrowed and he bent closer until his face was inches from hers. She could feel a clammy chill radiate from his skin and a pungent medicinal smell filled her nose.

"I've already had your ship searched, on planet and again after you docked here."

"What?" Sam demanded, lunging forward without thinking. Benny's response was swift, and she bit back a yelp as he wrenched her wrist. "Goddammit, Benny," she cursed, holding herself rigid again.

Benny was immovable and Sam thought he might twist her hand completely off. Floodwater made a small motion with his fingers and, despite never looking away from Sam, the large man released his hold. Drawing her hand into her chest, Sam returned to the chair, briefly entertaining the idea of grabbing it and smashing it over Benny's head.

Probably wouldn't even feel it, she thought darkly.

"Here is what is going to happen," Floodwater began, in an even, measured tone. "You are going to find the items that your friend agreed to deliver, and you are going to bring them to me. And then, if they are in a condition that pleases me, our business will be concluded." The corners of his mouth pulled back. "I will even consider a monetary reward for your... assistance."

Sam swallowed down the automatic response that came to her lips and focused instead on the beginning of his demand. Because fuck if she was going to— "If it's not on the ship, then how the hell am I supposed to find it? It could be anywhere in the damn universe," she argued. She thought of the mess that had been Jonah's living quarters, the quagmire of junk she had thrown into boxes that ham handed goons had already been through. It's not like there were any hidden residences or lockboxes. There had been no secrets between them.

Except for this, her mind supplied. *If this, then what else?*

He lifted a gloved finger and she stewed silently. "I think not. After all, he claimed to have it prior to your run into Sector Six. That means you should only need to check the stops you made between the time of his transmission and his unfortunate demise," he reasoned, as if anything about the situation was reasonable.

Folding her hands together, she pressed her knuckles against her chin. She didn't even bother to consider refusing, because she had a solid idea what his next move would be if she tried.

And it wouldn't be *her* fingers that he took.

"What is it that I'm looking for?" she bit out, everything inside of her tight and twisted.

He nodded, looking pleased, as if it were exactly the question he had been expecting her to ask. She imagined driving her fist into the center of his forehead.

"You will receive a transmission with the same description that was provided to Jonah. Expect it upon your return to your ship." He looked down his long nose at her. "I imagine you don't intend to stay on satellite for too long?"

She heard the subtle warning in the question and shook her head. "Just need to pick up an engineer. Maybe a medic. Grunt might be useful."

He waved at the words. "Yes, replacements." Sam tasted blood in her mouth at the term. "Shouldn't be too difficult for you. Well, we won't keep you any longer then."

Benny stood, pulling back so that he loomed. Two other figures came from behind Sam, moving swiftly to flank their boss on either side.

Floodwater started to turn back toward the windows and paused midway. "Oh. And one more thing. Just in case you were entertaining any thoughts of simply blasting off to some other sector where you think my reach might not extend, one of my associates will be joining your crew." He held out one hand, palm up, as if offering a gift. "Consider your grunt acquired."

Sam sure as hell didn't want to consider or accept it but understood it wasn't a choice. She exhaled sharply, unable to mask the rumble in her throat. The idea of sharing any space with one of his hired thugs made her hackles rise. "It better not be Benny."

He laughed, a high, stilted, gasping sound that sent needle pricks through her. Beside him, Benny looked between them as if unaware of the joke. It was an uncomfortable few moments before the laughter died away.

"No, I'm afraid I require Benny's presence. But I'm sure you'll find the help more than adequate."

She pushed herself up from the chair and tugged the bottom of her jacket down. "Miles?"

"Hmmm?" His back was to her, as he watched the crowds once more.

"What was the deal you had with Jonah?" His head tipped to suggested his was listening. "What did he want from you?" she clarified, struggling to convey nothing more than mild curiosity.

Without even seeing his face, she knew she had failed.

"It occurs to me that I could withhold that information from you, leaving you to forever wonder as to the reasoning behind your friend's actions, which you consider so heinous. And I admit, the idea is appealing, especially considering your past impudence toward me."

Sam pushed her hands into her coat pockets, scraping against the fabric, and waited.

"But, as a show of goodwill, I will have the recording of our last meeting included in the transmission. You should find it most illuminating."

She was already moving before the last word was spoken. As she rounded the chair, the rest of the room was revealed: an ornate desk to the left with another high-backed chair, shelves made of glass, and low cabinets of gleaming metal. An office in the midst of the most popular destination satellite in the system. No wonder he hadn't met her in the back room of a rotting on-planet station.

Kate stood only steps behind the chair with arms folded, as if being taken hostage by a complete nutcase was an everyday occurrence. Maybe it was. It wasn't like Sam knew a whole lot about her. The other woman started to open her mouth, but Sam gave a sharp shake of her head.

She knew Kate had some unfathomable depth of questions—hell, *she* had questions, and she hated questions.

But not now. Not *here*.

On the wall behind Kate was a door, solid dark wood strangely out of place, set into gunmetal gray walls. Sam wanted to kick it, briefly considered doing so, until she reached it and realized it swung inward. She settled for grabbing hold of the bright brass handle and jerking it open, not caring at all if Floodwater could see her anger. Asshole probably wasn't even looking at her.

The door led to a spacious waiting area, complete with another desk and a suited individual behind it. Several cushioned chairs were occupied with neatly dressed people who looked up as Sam stormed in. She froze at the sudden juxtaposition of scenes and felt Kate bump into her back.

The young man behind the desk half rose from his seat. "Would you like to make another appointment with Mr. Floodwater?" he called out, as if that could be the reason for her confusion.

Sam stared at him, taking in the trim, dark suit, the unlined face, and the ten long fingers that rested atop the desk.

"No. I think one was enough."

She strode forward again, pushing through another door until finally one of the satellite's crowded streets was in front of her. And then she pushed some more, shoving through people and bags until she reached a patch of uninterrupted space at the corner of a building beside a nearly overflowing trash bin with an odor that warded away all.

Sam rested a hand against the building and dragged air into her lungs, willing back the shudders that wanted to shake through her. She knew Kate was behind her and waited for the questions to come.

But there was only silence. The center of her burned. It spread slowly outwards, running down into her stomach, into her legs, out along her arms, her fingers, like the spark sprinting along the fuse of an explosive. She suddenly spun and, the move barely registering, drove her foot into the side of the garbage unit. It spun off with a screech, spilling trash and widening the area of emptiness as those nearby scurried to avoid airborne rubbish.

And finally, the silence was broken.

"So, what do we do now?" There was the slightest catch in Kate's voice, but when Sam turned to face her, it was nowhere to be seen in her face. Her neck was lined with red, blotchy marks where someone had gripped tight. The heat in Sam's chest flared again, though not the same as before. She jammed her hands into her coat and pushed the feeling down, where she wouldn't have to think about it.

"Now we go find a fucking engineer."

Sam was angry. Even without the waste bin field goal display, Kate would have figured that much out. She wasn't sure if anyone could have come out of that experience calm and collected but the depth of Sam's reaction *was* unexpected, since up until that point the captain's most evident emotional state had been vague annoyance. Mild irritation when Kate had voiced her desire to join her non-existent crew.

Given how terrifying it had been to be dragged by persons unknown into a surprisingly well decorated room and threatened by a man far more frightening than his appearance implied, Kate found some comfort in Sam's fury. Even if it, too, had been a little scary.

Kate was relieved to be free from the confines of—had that been Floodwater's *office*? She'd expected something more... sinister. They joined the meandering crowd as the mass of bodies shuffled along the pre-laid paths to entertainment and delight. The holo-stations were all located near the satellite's central ring, Sam had explained before falling silent, her face fixed in a blank mask that suggested a scowl was lurking beneath the surface.

She would have looked incredibly intimidating, if not for the oversized compress stuck to the side of her face, where that giant goon Benny had cold cocked her. Even with the med-pack, the dark purplish bloom of bruising was starting to peek out around the clean white edges.

Kate had questions; *of course* she had questions. Literally millions of questions, these on top of the ones she had from before. Who was Jonah? How many dealings had Sam had with Floodwater? Why wouldn't she do any jobs for him? And if she refused to do any work for the man, why had she been planning on selling her ship to him? Had that punch hurt as much as it looked like it did?

She swallowed every one of them down for two reasons. The first, because she was certain Sam wouldn't answer any of them. (And *maybe* one or two were inappropriate to ask.) The second, and more important, was because there was something else that was of far greater concern to her. The further they got from that opulent room, the more space that concern took up in her brain, pushing all the other questions to the side. She ran through possible arguments and likely scenarios in her head as she waited for Sam to suggest it. Each extra minute of muteness gave her more time to perfect her case, and she fully intended to be able to refute any possible angle.

They paused, the street traffic ahead of them jammed with people trying to lumber past each other. Sam turned, the muscles in her face shifting, and Kate set her feet and her jaw and declared hotly:

"I'm not going back."

Sam closed her mouth with a snap. She frowned.

"What?" she asked, bewilderment flooding her face.

Kate folded her arms, determined to hold her ground. "I'm not going back to the planet," she repeated.

One of Sam's brows lifted. "Okay," she replied in a long drawl. "Who said that you were?"

Kate dropped her hands to her waist. "Please. Don't tell me that you weren't just about to say how this is all way too dangerous, not what I signed up for, and how I should go back on planet where I'll be safe while you swagger off and risk your neck tracking down that asshole's goodie bag."

By the time Kate had run out of steam, Sam's other eyebrow had risen. "That's not what I was going to say," was her response.

Huh. Wary, Kate straightened and her arms uncurled. "What were you going to say?"

"That we should keep Floodwater's involvement between us. His name has a habit of making people skittish, and we don't have a lot of time to find someone who fits."

Oh. Biting the inside of her check lightly, Kate nodded and then rolled her eyes when Sam continued to stare expectantly at her. "Yeah, okay. I won't mention him or the fact that he's forcing us to go on a scavenger hunt for him with the threat of bodily harm and/or death."

One corner of Sam's mouth twitched. "Yes. Best not to mention that. Also, I do not swagger."

"Yes, you do."

"Whatever."

"You really weren't going to tell me to go back to the planet?" Kate asked, unable to hide her doubt.

Sam met her gaze squarely. "Floodwater's base of operations is on planet. Trust me, that's the last place you would be safe."

Kate grinned. "So, you are worried about my safety," she quipped, not totally sure what that information meant, but glad she had it.

The response was a thinning of lips and a long, drawn-out exhale. Looking over, Kate thought she saw the faint hint of a blush coloring the tiny strip of skin between Sam's chin and the collar of her coat.

six

The inner rings of Icarus 3 were a sharp contrast to the outer utilitarian sectors where offices, storage, and transpo bays were located. Here the crowds could open up and wander in all directions; they were encouraged to do so with winding paths and bold, flashing advertisements promising anything and everything. Entertainments of all kinds were available wherever one walked, looked, or stood.

Sam had almost forgotten how much she *hated* the inner core. Whenever jobs or job hunts had previously taken her to Icarus, she usually managed to avoid it. A large percentage of her clients had been busy folks and happy enough to talk specifics over a comm meeting. Forays into the amusement sections had been reserved for fishing Jonah out of whatever social tank he had dunked himself into.

"Not everyone enjoys the icy quiet of space as much as you, Sam."

Well, no one had enjoyed the company of others more than Jonah, Sam thought while glaring at the back of the head of a slow-walking tourist. So, everyone had their faults.

As she and Kate pushed their way through the meandering bodies, ignoring the ad droids that changed targets—and pitches—with blazing speed, Sam realized she had a completely new reason to despise the loud, obnoxious, hedonistic space.

Everywhere she looked, she saw Floodwater. Not the man himself, but his potential influence. Every station guard, resort worker—even those seemingly oblivious tourists—any and all of them might be under his thumb. His eyes and ears. Carrying out his whims and desires. Was the doorman of that bar keeping tabs on them, even after they passed? And the middle-aged guy that kept "accidentally" bumping shoulders with her? Just someone who couldn't keep track of his personal space or one of Floodwater's lackeys trying to herd her into another ambush?

She wasn't sure even after he mumbled an apology and nearly sprinted off—though she suspected his retreat had to do with her frustrated snarl when he'd nudged her again.

How was she going to find someone she could trust with the very heart of her ship in a place that could be lousy with his agents? He had already saddled her with one of his goons. The last thing she wanted was a fucking infestation.

They passed by countless doorways and open stalls. There were stations on top of stations. Bars, dance, holo and gaming halls, all stacked over each other with no discernible pattern. Sam wondered if the people stuffed inside each of them even knew what kind of enjoyment they were supposed to be having. Maybe it didn't matter.

Beside her, Kate was silent. With every establishment they passed, Sam could feel the other woman's attention shift to her. Probably wondering where the hell they were going. It was a question Sam was having trouble answering, what with her newfound sense of suspicion screwing with her brain. Between that, the way it made her take note of the people around her (something she typically took pains to *avoid*), and the gut-punched feeling from Jonah's betrayal, there was a simmering feeling within her that made it difficult to hone in on the best next steps.

She wanted something to be *easy*. When was the last time something had been easy?

"Sam?"

Here we go, Sam thought as she lifted her head. They were halted in front of an advertisement screen flashing a broadcast. Kate motioned to it by tapping the text ribbon scrolling along the bottom. *Big Five to become Big Four? TISAD Group and Chestor Holdings in merger talks.*

"What do you think about the merger talks?"

The banality of the question was unexpected. A short huff managed to escape Sam, and a small measure of tension released. She looked to Kate, whose face was perfectly innocent, as if she wanted nothing more than to know Sam's thoughts on a matter of intergalactic business.

"I think it'll never happen," Sam replied, walking away from the screen. She took in her surroundings, the signs and store fronts. Her feet picked up the path even as her mind was still forming it.

"But what if it does?" Kate pressed, falling into step beside her again. "Independent shipping in this quadrant would be decimated."

"Well, it won't matter to me. I'm retiring, remember?"

"Ah. I figured you might be reconsidering, you know, considering..."

"I'm sure as hell reconsidering my buyer," Sam muttered darkly. She'd sell the ship for scrap metal before she'd take Floodwater's money for it now. Why she hadn't just done that to begin with—

You know why.

"So why don't you think it'll happen? The last big merger was over a hundred years ago, and they still talk about how successful that one was."

"Yeah, tell that to the mining companies that got shafted. Oh wait, they all went out of business and the price of iron went astronomically high."

"Some of them got bought out."

"I'm sure they were delighted to sell. It won't happen because it's too much power in too few hands. The other corps won't accept it."

"It's not like the other corps could do anything about it. They're not the government."

"Out here they might as well be."

Sam stopped and looked up to see where her feet had taken her. A building front not dissimilar to all the others they had passed. A single sign attached to the façade with marquee lights so bright that Sam could barely read the name blocked out on it. *Palace of Adventure.*

Back to the beginning apparently.

The building was just as it had been in the memory Benny had knocked her into. Save for one small addition in neon purple and pink script: *Link's*.

"Are we going in here?" Kate asked, craning forward, as if trying to peer through the glass doors.

"Yeah." What the hell. She could use someone she… mostly trusted right about now. "Yeah, we're going in."

"So, what should I expect when we get in there? Is it going to be dangerous? On a scale of one to ten, how concerned should I be for my life? Okay, I don't understand what that look is supposed to mean."

Sam shook her head and pressed two fingers to the crinkle between her eyebrows. "It's a holo-station on a major entertainment satellite. There'll be a bunch of nerds playing games and drinking sugary alcoholic beverages. I don't think you have much to worry about."

"Yeah, you also didn't think Miles Floodwater would be upset about you ditching a meeting with him," Kate pointed out.

There was a long beat, followed by Sam's audible inhale. "In my defense, I don't really think the meeting is what he was upset about."

"We'll have to agree to disagree. But considering our predicament, you can understand why I'd like a little more heads up about potential dens of infamy we may be walking into?"

Sam's mouth moved as she silently repeated the words *dens of infamy* to herself. "Honestly, I don't know. I haven't been to this station since I was a kid. I—I met Jonah here." The admission fell out before she could stop it. She jerked a shoulder and continued, reaching for nonchalance. "I have no idea what it's like now."

Kate frowned and her hands lifted. "But then why did we come here?"

"No idea," Sam repeated, her eyes narrowing on the marquee, then lowering to the door. "Just a feeling I had. But we're here now. Might as well go in."

She pushed on, taking a place in line behind several other

patrons waiting to step through the entrance. Kate followed suit, pressing in a little closer when more people crowded in behind her.

Walking through the doors was at once a familiar and unfamiliar action; Sam half expected to step back in time, to see Jonah rushing in. She deliberately stared ahead, not ready, or willing to imagine such a scene.

It hardly took more than a glance to realize there was no danger of reminiscence overwhelming her. The inside of the station was completely transformed from the dull, serviceable space it had once been. Bright, bland lightning had been replaced with dark, muted colors that swirled and pulsed in a way that made her head swim. A heavy beat pounded through the air and echoed within her skull, reinvigorating the throb in her face. And the bodies crowded around tables and along the walls, dressed in slick and flashy fashions, looked nothing like the plain, tired strangers she remembered.

The only thing that propelled her forward was the knowledge that Kate was behind her, probably staring at everything in wide-eyed wonder, just waiting to ask a dozen or so questions about everything. There was no way Sam would admit she'd rather have Floodwater remove the rest of her fingers than wade into... whatever the gyrating mass in front of them was. That would have been an easy indicator that she had been wrong, and she knew it was entirely too early for her to be *that* wrong about *anything*.

Kate's question rolled insistently through her head. *Why did we come here?*

Just a feeling. Poetic. Nostalgia.

Maybe she should go back to the ship and run a scan for brain fever.

What had she been *thinking*?

The trouble was, she hadn't been. Ever since she had stepped on satellite—no, way before then—Sam had been trying not to think, not to remember, not to picture those three faces. She'd been mostly successful; two out of three wasn't bad, right? But then Jonah had always been different. He had dug in deeper than the others. Despite all her efforts, she'd somehow managed to drag herself back into the past anyway. Or into a past that no longer resembled the past. Or—what the hell was she trying to get at?

Was she *high*?

Sam ran a hand through her short hair, wondering if the station was pumping some kind of enhancement into the air that was jumbling her thoughts.

"So, engineers really hang out here?"

Glancing over at the terse tone, Sam noted it wasn't exactly wonderment on Kate's face. Instead, the other woman's expression was dour, as if she were looking at somewhere she'd rather not be. The tightness in Sam's shoulders eased.

Maybe there was a way out of this.

An excuse was starting to form on her lips, when a pair of massive hands gripped her shoulders, swung her around, and lifted her up against the nearby wall. Her back hit with a thud, but it was the jostle to her face that hurt more than anything.

"Well, well, well, what do we have here?" a low voice growled loud enough to be heard over the music. Sam felt a disorienting mixture of fear and exasperation, because who the fuck else had she pissed off and how much deeper shit was she going to be in?

But then she recognized the voice and knew that the knowing feeling she'd had in her stomach when she'd looked at the name scrawled out in lights had been correct.

"Put me down, Link," she snapped, glaring at the sharp-faced figure dangling her nearly two feet off the ground. Their answering smile was more vicious than Benny's, thanks to the jagged scar interrupting it, but the hands that brought her back to the floor were far gentler. As was the elegant finger that brushed the skin below the compress stuck on her cheek.

"Why is it that I only see you after you've been in some kind of trouble?" they asked, their words whistling lightly between their teeth. Their other hand drifted along a trim mustache and down into a neatly pointed goatee.

Sam considered pulling the ice pack off; it was hardly even cold anymore. "I don't know what you're talking about. Last time I saw you—"

"Was just after you and Jonah nearly got martialed for shipping contraband," Link finished.

"That wasn't my fault."

"Mmmhmm, so you said. Where is that good looking shadow of yours?" Still scratching thoughtfully at the hair on their chin, their eyes slid past her to give Kate a slow once over. "You trade him in for a new model?" they asked, reaching out to bump Sam's arm.

Pulling back, Sam ground down on her irritation and tugged at the edges of the pack, wincing at the pull of the adhesive. Something solid struck her shoulder; when she looked over, Kate was motioning to the compress.

"Leave it on."

Link watched them with amusement in eyes that glowed gold in the odd mixture of light. Sam nodded her head toward the thrum of music and bodies.

"What happened here?" she asked instead, hoping to distract them. The smirk that came to their lips let her know they were well aware of the attempt, even as they followed the cue.

"Times change. Gotta change with them."

"This is your place now?" Sam inquired, to confirm.

They lifted a slim eyebrow, smile unwavering. "That's my name over the door, isn't it?"

"Is it just your place?" Sam pressed, with an edge sinking into her tone. She resented the question but couldn't stop from asking it. It was vague, but speaking Floodwater's name felt like the first step to summoning him.

Link's smirk fell off and was replaced by a thin, firm line. "I got an interest in it."

Setting her right index finger against the side of her face, Sam set her chin into the space where her middle and ring finger would have been. "Anyone else got an interest in it?" Their eyes cut away and she knew. "Shit," she hissed, running a hand through her hair. "How deep are you in?"

Link chuckled and looked apologetic. Mirroring her movement, they rubbed their palm over the smooth skin of their head. The lights shimmered over glittering lightning bolts tattooed on tawny skin. "He gets a cut, a substantial one. All he seemed to be interested in."

"For now."

"For now," Link agreed, lifting their big shoulders. "Fact is, you aren't going to find any station on satellite that doesn't share interest. They might claim otherwise, but he has his fingers in everybody's pockets. Better the devil you know, right?"

At that point, Sam thought she might prefer the actual Devil.

"Are there any devils you don't know?" came Kate's clipped question. Link's head fell back, and laughter roared out over the music.

"Well, well, Captain Sam has got herself a—"

"A problem," Sam interrupted, rolling her own shoulders, and putting her hand down. "Look, is there someplace quiet we could talk?" she added when they continued to simply smile.

Link shook their head. "No," they noted, but turned and pushed their way along the edge of the room, splitting through huddled groups like a spear. Sam and Kate followed in the wake left clear by their broad footprint. Height alone made them an easy beacon, and the hot pink and purple color of the short-sleeved jacket they wore helped as well. Tucked away in a corner, a discreet lift took them all up a short flight to a private bar occupied by an inebriated couple.

Whatever protest the couple might have been about to offer was dispelled by a quick jerk of Link's chin. Without bothering to collect glasses half full of smoking liquid, the pair dispersed, disappearing down the lift.

Slipping behind the bar, Link motioned for them both to sit. As she settled onto a cushioned bench, Sam noticed the music grew marginally quieter after Link made a few motions with their hands.

"So. What are you doing here?" Link prompted, setting their elbows down on the bar. Jagged bolts of lightning crawled up both forearms.

"Looking for an engineer. Preferably one that can handle a quad engine and doesn't flinch at a bit of distance."

Link's eyes narrowed; out of the strobing lights from the previous level, they were an ordinary, if skeptical, brown. "An engineer, why would you—" they stopped, and she watched the realization hit. Sam felt her jaw clench. The pain in her cheekbone flared.

"Triss?" they asked quietly. "Ollie?"

Sam shook her head silently. She was acutely aware of Kate beside her, listening, and tried not to feel resentful. Tried not to feel like a private part of her life was being cracked open and inspected.

"Shit."

"Yeah."

The look they gave her now was full of pity; something wanted to claw out of her chest. "When?"

She focused on the glossy glass bottles lining the wall behind him. "Six months ago."

They let out a hiss, followed by "Christ, Sam."

"That's space." She gave a shrug, trying for casual, for the illusion that shit happens and who cares? It was an attitude that had once fit like a second skin—or so she had thought.

She had been wrong about a lot of things.

Link did not seem willing to bite. "So, what? You're just looking for a new crew?" they pressed, with evident disbelief. The incredulity mixed with concern in their voice had resentment burning up from her stomach. She didn't want to talk about that— she wasn't going to talk about it. Struggling to hide her irritation, she pushed back at the memories trying to rise to the forefront and shook her head.

"No. I'm out. Just have one last job to finish and then I'm out."

She had to believe it.

"Who's the job for?"

It was almost funny. "The Devil."

They stared at her for a painfully long moment before their eyes closed. "Shit."

"Come on, Link. Can you help me or not?" She didn't even attempt a smile. "I need someone who can make sure there's no trouble with the systems. Hell, there's at least half a dozen repairs that need to be made before I can sell it anyway." Sam figured the last part was mostly true; she should at least get the main bridge doors open.

When their eyes opened, Sam watched some kind of war play out behind them and then spill out across their face. She waited for the next objection or straight refusal, but instead, Link looked to the bartop. A quick swipe of their hand over the surface had a screen underneath springing to life; a series of video feeds showing various sections of the station. As they slid one long finger left or right, different views slipped into or out of place. They muttered to themselves as they sorted through them.

"Clarke and Issacs are both off satellite. Clarke on a run. Issacs might be on pla—no. He joined up with the new survey expedition. Won't be back for two years. Jonesy? You hate that bitch. Dougie? Hate him, too. Fuck, I hate that POS."

The list of people Sam *didn't* hate was remarkably short. But Dougie was a POS. If she had to, she figured she could work with Jonesy. The fight must have been five, six years ago. Bygones could be bygones. She was about to interrupt Link to suggest it when her shoulder twinged. Rubbing at it, she recalled the sharp flare when it had popped from its socket.

Suddenly, she remembered the fight a little more clearly. Maybe six years wasn't quite long enough.

Link's mouth pursed as they continued to flip through the feeds. Their hand paused, hovering over a view. They gave the surface two quick taps and the screen zoomed in. Sam tried to see what had caught their interest, but she'd never been good at looking at things upside down.

Link didn't keep her waiting. "This one just came in a few days ago. Don't know much about her though. Came in on a deep space gas capture vessel. Two years out. Ship left yesterday. She didn't. Obviously. Her file's clean; got good recs."

Sam scratched her chin, considering. Just back from deep space could work in her favor. Might be open to something short term. Not likely to balk at going past the outer edges.

Then again, most deep space divers she'd ever known preferred long-term contracts. Bigger paydays. Maybe the fact she hadn't gone back out with her ship meant she didn't want to go back out at all. Happened all the time. Space fatigue—or worse, the tempers.

Probably wouldn't be out of quarantine if it were the tempers, Sam reasoned.

She glanced up to find both Link and Kate watching her, nearly identical expressions of expectation and sympathy on their faces.

"That all you got for me?" she asked, pushing back from both the compassion and the bar.

They tapped a finger lightly against their full lips. "That's it for straight e-hands. If it doesn't work out, I might have a couple of mech heads I can recommend that could probably handle your bird."

Sam frowned at the suggestion. "I hate mech heads," she complained.

Link's look turned pained. "Sam, you hate everyone. It's a character flaw."

"So, who and where...?" she asked, making a swirling motion with her index finger toward the rest of the station.

Link swiped quickly again over the video feed, bringing up a text display.

"She's on level two, in the Puzzle Sim section. Name's Adelaide. Adelaide Brisbane." They squinted at the screen, their tongue sliding between their teeth as they made a *tsk* sound. "Now why does something about that name tickle my brain?"

Sam didn't give a shit what her name was. "Maybe it's time for a parasite scan. That thing tell you her guild level?"

They nodded. "Six."

Sam tipped her head and calculated. Clucked her own tongue. "Shit. That's going to hurt."

"Speaking of which." They ran a finger under their own right eye and pointed to her. "You want another compress for that? The one you got on is looking spent."

"No," Sam said firmly as Kate answered, just as firmly, "Yes."

Sam scowled.

"Yes," Kate repeated, ignoring her.

Link looked back and forth between the two. They held up one hand. "I'll be just a minute."

"Was that necessary?" Sam complained once they had disappeared through a cleverly concealed door behind the bar.

"Very. You're not the one that has to look at your face."

"Am I not pretty anymore?"

"Yours is a rugged sort of handsomeness."

"I don't know what that means."

"Look," Kate's hands spread out in front of her, as if they could better help explain her point, "I get it. You're a hard ass. But I'm not Floodwater. I don't need you to suffer for me."

Sam touched the side of her face, flinching at the tenderness. It felt significantly less swollen. And the drumbeats had thankfully quieted, though the thumping of the station's music wasn't helping much. She felt her shoulders start to hunch and deliberately straightened her back and made sure all the annoyance she was feeling was properly displayed across her face.

"I'm not suffering," she noted crossly. She dropped her hand. "But if it'll make you feel better."

Kate stroked a hand over the front of her neck. The red marks from earlier had faded. "It will."

Link chose that moment to return, a small white package in their hand. Sam reached out, but Kate beat her to it, snatching the compress before Link had even offered it.

"Seriously?" Sam grumbled.

"You can't even see your face," Kate reasoned. With a sharp twist of her wrists, she broke open the package, then raised one hand to Sam's jaw. Sam flinched back, but Kate managed to catch hold of the edge of the spent compress. "Don't move," she warned.

Resigned, Sam held her head still while the other woman peeled off the seal of binding and tossed it on the bar top. Link swiped it away with a pass of one hand while watching with undisguised delight.

Because she figured the best way to pretend the entire thing wasn't happening was to ignore the goings on in front of her, Sam stared out over the level below. On the far side of the crowd of mingling personas were a mix of old, traditional-style card games and their more modern updates.

She smelled the sharp sting of antiseptic a second before she felt the spread of gel over her cheek bone and the numbing rush as the chemicals reacted.

A few of the tables had actual dealers; most were holograms or droids with only a passing human facsimile.

There was the light press of the compress against her skin, the chill of which she could barely feel over the numbness.

Sam had never really understood the appeal of card games; numbers were bad enough when you had to calculate them for navigational or accounting purposes. Why the hell would you stare at them for fun?

A gentle touch around the edges of the compress drew her back to Kate in time to see her hand withdraw.

"How does that feel?" Kate asked, setting the empty kit on the bar where Link once again swiftly disposed of it.

Like a compress has just been stuck to my face, is what Sam started to say, but she caught the look Link was shooting her, which clearly read, *Do Not Say the Words You Are Currently Thinking*.

So instead, she answered with, "Great." And after a moment's pause added, "Can we go talk to an engineer now?"

In response, Kate turned to Link and gave a bright grin. Brighter than was necessary, Sam thought, annoyed. "It was nice to meet you, Link."

They flashed their own grin in response and Sam nearly bit down on her tongue with impatience. "Likewise."

Shifting back to Sam, Kate motioned for her to lead. Without so much as a goodbye glance in Link's direction, Sam strode off. In her mind she continued to see the layout of the station as it had been, and it vexed her to have to look up for the section signs as they made their way toward level two. She was even more frustrated when she realized not only had they shifted the entire floorplan; they had also reordered the floors themselves. Instead of being the floor above them, level two was two flights down, which didn't make any sense. The nonsensical aggravation was a flick on an already exposed nerve.

"You know, you didn't actually meet them," she grumbled as they stepped onto a descending open glide.

Kate set one hand on the railing, and the subdued, pulsating green light shifted to a purplish hue. "I think what you mean is you didn't introduce me to them," she corrected.

An unexpected chuckle bubbled up in Sam's throat and she swallowed it. It made an odd little grunting sound as it went down, and Kate's smirk was a touch satisfied.

The Puzzle Simulation section was thankfully only a few steps beyond the bottom of the glide and, as it was almost completely empty, it took very little effort to locate Adelaide Brisbane. The guild level six engineer sat in one of the first booths, a dark-haired woman with thick-rimmed goggles; Sam recognized the detail magnifiers, since she had a similar pair.

The engineer was employing the holo feature of the booth she was in rather than the tabletop screen, and what looked like a circuit board hovered in the air in front of her. One finger cut through the image and trails of yellow followed, as if she were tracing a path. Her concentration didn't shift as Sam and Kate approached.

Others might have waited until the engineer had finished whatever she was doing, but Sam didn't see the point. Plus, they were on a bit of a time crunch. She stepped up to the table opposite from where the woman was seated.

"Adelaide Brisbane?" she checked, just in case. "Do you—"

"Addy," the engineer replied without looking up.

"—mind if—what?" Sam fumbled a bit with the interruption.

"Addy," the engineer repeated. "Call me Addy."

Sam glanced at Kate. "Okay. Addy. Do you mind if I—"

Kate cleared her throat.

"—if we join you?"

Adelaide—Addy—continued to fiddle with the lines on the hologram. "As long as you don't mind being quiet for five more minutes," she answered absently.

And Sam *did* mind, but since her only other option at that point was a mech head, she reluctantly sat, jerking her head to signal for Kate to do the same.

Five minutes was a long time to stare at someone who was ignoring you. Impatience pooled in the base of Sam's spine and she consciously tried to loosen the clench of her jaw.

Finally, the hologram flashed, a long, winding yellow path lighting up through the entire schematic. Then it abruptly winked out and there was no longer anything separating the three women.

Pulling the magnifiers down so that they hung around her neck, Addy folded her hands atop one another on the table and met Sam's stare. Her eyes were almond shaped and a speckled mixture of green and brown. Without the blue wash of the game cast over her, her skin was a russet, reddish brown that reminded Sam of Jonah.

"Tell me about the ship."

Some of Sam's annoyance receded. Clear and direct: that was something she could work with. And nothing like Jonah. She leaned forward in her seat, setting one arm against the edge of the tabletop. Before she could start, Kate jumped in.

"Don't you want to know our names? Or what it is we want?"

Addy said matter-of-factly, "I'm an engineer. You're on the largest hub satellite in the system. You have a ship and you want me to work it. So, tell me about the ship first, then the job. We'll see about the rest."

Sam nodded, because *finally*, someone who made sense.

"It's a kraken; quad engine, Bosen containment, standard configuration. Modified core. FNG information system."

The engineer's face remained passive, but interest sparked in her gaze. "What's the modification?"

Sam flipped a hand, palm up, before resting it back down. "I have the complete specs if you'd like to review."

That received a short nod of confirmation, and Addy reached into a holster strapped to the front of her shoulder. She pulled out a slim tablet.

"Repairs or known issues?" she asked, her gaze dropping to the small screen.

"There's some general maintenance needed. Cooling system should be flushed and rebooted. Power cores were braided," Sam cataloged.

Addy glanced up. "Were?" she asked, and Sam found herself looking to Kate again, slouched in her chair. The other woman straightened at the question.

"I fixed that," she stated, with more than a hint of bravado. "You should probably still look at it," she concluded, no hint of resentment in her tone. *Jonah would have flipped if anyone had wanted to check his work*, Sam thought and then wished she hadn't. It was too easy to picture.

"The doors to the main bridge are stuck," Sam added quickly, hoping to keep from taking any more potential trips down memory lane.

Addy's fingers dragged over the tablet screen, tapping every so often. After a moment, she gave another nod.

"And the job?"

Sam took a moment to plot her response. Some of the details were ultimately more important than others; they needed to find an item and deliver it back to the station. The trip would most likely take them into the outer sectors of the system. Less important were the facts that they were being forced to look for the item by a space mobster and didn't exactly know where or even what it was. So really, the trick was to highlight the important bits and completely neglect to mention the others.

"Recovery. Client needs us to find a parcel and return it here to the station," she explained.

"And where is the pickup location?"

It had been too much to hope she wouldn't ask. "Near the outer borders," Sam replied, shooting for indifferent and unconcerned.

She must not have managed, because Addy's expression went from vaguely interested to guarded.

"That's Secession Territory," the engineer pointed out warily.

Sam shrugged. "Don't plan on being there long," she replied because they didn't *actually* have anything planned at the moment.

Addy's guarded look eased somewhat.. "Estimated timeframe?"

No idea. "Six to eight weeks. Most of that's travel to and from. Recovery time should be minimal." *Hopefully.*

"What's the offer?"

"Standard."

Addy gave a quick dubious laugh. "Standard for a run into the outer borders?"

"That's the offer," Sam proposed. Negotiations had never been her favorite aspect of business—all the back and forth was tiring—but she had always enjoyed the feeling when she'd given a term and held to it. The brief anticipation of whether it would be accepted. Knowing if she didn't like what they came back with, she'd just move on.

Only this time she was a little more stuck, so she hoped whatever the engineer was about to come back at her with wasn't too dear.

Fiddling with her tablet, but not looking at it, Addy was silent as she considered.

"Standard for six, one and a half for any time beyond that," she countered, with a note of finality. There was more interest now than concern lighting up her face, and Sam debated another round of give and take. But as far as counters went it was mild, and technically she was secretly endangering the engineer's life—

"Agreed," Sam said, holding out a hand. Addy's answering grip was strong and ended with a quick shake.

"When do we leave?"

Sam checked her wrist unit, tapping the band to bring the screen to life. It remained dark. *Right.* Squinting, she rocked back in her chair and counted in her head.

"My docking privileges expire tomorrow at seventeen hundred. I'm not interested in extending those privileges."

Addy turned back to her tablet, running her fingers across the screen again. "Then I better get started if you want the cooling unit looked at prior to launch." She pushed up from the table. "What bay are we docked in?"

"Twelve. Slot seventeen. Onboard code is 223-91." Sam dug into the front pocket of her jacket for her own tablet. Swiping to the correct screen, she held it out to the engineer, who pressed her print against it. "I'll have you authorized for entry and input."

The engineer nodded and tucked her tablet back into its holster. Then, taking them both in, she gave a surprisingly warm smile.

"Well, it's nice to be working with you?" Her voice and her eyebrows rose at the end of the statement. Sam motioned to herself with one finger.

"Sam." She jerked a thumb to the left. "Kate."

"And we already established that I'm Addy. Think that about covers it," the engineer affirmed. She stepped away from the table and then paused, looked back. "By the way, what happened to your face?"

"I got jumped in an alleyway."

Addy pursed her lips. "That's space for you." With a quick wave of one hand, she turned and strode away.

The moment she was out of earshot, Kate scooted over. "You didn't tell her anything," she accused. Sam frowned.

"That's not true. I told her lots of stuff. I gave her a goddamn rundown of my ship and—"

"I know we agreed not to say anything about Floodwater, but you made it sound like it's not going to be dangerous at all! Like it's just a normal job where we know exactly where we're going and what we're doing," Kate continued, as if Sam hadn't spoken at all.

"If all goes according to plan it will be just like a normal job."

"Oh, we have a *plan* now? Okay, great. That actually makes me feel better. Let's hear it." Kate sat back in the booth, her face open and attentive.

Sam rubbed a hand over her forehead. Why did it suddenly feel so warm? Must have been the chill of the compress.

"The plan is, we find whatever it is Floodwater wants and bring it to him."

Silence settled between them, brittle like the space frost that formed on the outer hull. Inclining further forward, Kate stretched her arms out and gently pressed her hands onto the top of the table, as if she were worried about cracking the surface.

"Do you have any idea where or even *what* it is?" she asked after a long, long moment, her words spoken as carefully as her movements had been. Sam found herself withdrawing from the table, feeling as if the area was on the cusp of exploding.

"I... might have an idea of *where* it is," she replied, inwardly wincing because it had sounded a lot surer in her head. "Floodwater was right; there's not that many places it could be."

"And one of those places happens to be in Secession Territory?"

Sam couldn't hide the flinch that time. She'd been hoping that bit of the conversation had slipped past Kate's notice.

"It's possible, yes." She wished she had something more solid, but she'd only been ruminating about it for an hour or so. Every time she went over it, there was a little tickle, a nagging tug that wanted her attention. Only she didn't have the attention to give it.

"What if we went to the authorities? Couldn't they do something?"

Sam laughed as she imagined *that* disaster. "Sure. Since they're pretty much all in Floodwater's pockets, they could kill us. Or just blast us off in pods into deep space. Personally, I'd like a quick death."

Kate dropped her head to the table, and her forehead *thunked* against the surface.

Right. Not everyone responds to potential demise with sarcasm. Scratching the back of her head, Sam tried to think of something reassuring. Something Jonah might have said.

"It'll be all right."

Kate rolled her head to the side, possibly to better show her disbelief.

Sam tried again. "Trust me."

"Sam, I don't even know you. How am I supposed to just trust you about something *like this*?"

Sam felt her chest constrict with the weight of responsibility she had never wanted to feel again: another person's life.

"Well, you know I had a friend that got me into a big mess," she attempted to joke.

But Kate's face as she lifted her head was solemn. "But what *happened* to him?"

The tablet in Sam's hand buzzed, giving her a start, and the screen lit up, drawing her gaze. The respite was brief when she realized the comm from a seemingly innocuous sender read, *As promised. MF.*

Shit. She'd somehow forgotten the nugget Floodwater had offered. Had tossed out like an unwanted toy. A recording of his meeting with Jonah. The tablet screen vibrated minutely, and it took a moment to realize it was because her hand was trembling. Involuntarily, her thumb moved to engage the file. She stopped; the last thing that she wanted to do was play out some of Jonah's last moments in a place as public as that one.

But the idea of walking all the way back to the ship with the transmission burning a hole in her pocket grated against her nerves. She stood up abruptly, scanning the area around them.

"Sam?" Kate asked, but Sam barely heard her. She caught sight of what she was looking for and shoved the chair back under the table.

"I need to use one of the privacy booths. Play a game or something," she instructed, waving an arm toward the space behind her.

Kate started to speak, but Sam was already walking away.

seven

"**P**lay a *game*?" Kate echoed, calling out in bewilderment to Sam's retreating figure. "Are you serious?"

If Sam heard, there was no indication. The captain was halfway across the room before Kate thought to follow her. By the time she got to her feet, a thickening crowd had folded around Sam. In the few minutes they had been conversing with Addy, the section had filled and the previously empty space suddenly held dozens of bodies, all hunched over tables or moving hands through holograms. A number of tables had queues forming up beside them.

"Hey, are you done with this one?"

The question came from a young man with a faded ball cap pushed back on his head, his flight suit spotted with grease. Two others stood behind him, another man and a woman locked in a heated discussion.

Kate glanced in the direction Sam had gone; there was no way to tell how long it would be before she came back. The last thing Kate felt like doing was muddling around in virtual reality. She waved a hand toward the table and stepped back.

"It's all yours," she invited. He flashed a wide grin as he slid past her into the booth and his two friends paused their argument long enough to give mirroring waves of thanks before joining him. Kate stood awkwardly to the side as she considered her next move.

If she left the section, Sam wouldn't know where to find her when she finally emerged from her secret retreat. That would probably irritate her.

Of course, if she'd taken two seconds to discuss it with Kate like a normal individual who didn't pathologically object to conversation, they could have designated a meeting place and Kate wouldn't be the one irritated.

"Fuck it," she muttered, spining on her heel and stalking toward the lift for the upper floors. The menagerie of games didn't interest her at all, but there was something in the building that did. Or more specifically, someone.

Once on the main level, she looked toward the private bar jutting out over the open floor. A handful of people milled about it, but none that resembled the tall, lithe figure of Link. She scanned the swelling crowd; in the flashing lights there was no telling anyone apart.

So much for that idea, she thought to herself, shifting out of the way of an enthusiastic dancer. She circled the edge of the section and found another bar set back into the wall so as not to take up any precious floor space. It, too, was crowded with more bodies than she was accustomed to being around, but she managed to maneuver her way through so she could rest her arms on the top. Mixing drinks with smooth, graceful movements was a short, dark-skinned woman whose mass of bright purple curls towered on her head. She steadily made her way down the counter, taking orders and filling glasses, hardly seeming to glance at the bottles she was using.

She was three customers away, and Kate was just starting to step back when Link emerged from another hidden door in the liquor shelf. They spotted Kate straight away and, after pausing to speak with the other bartender, took up a position beside her, taking the next order.

Kate waited.

"You and Sam depart company already?" they asked as they handed out two drinks to a lanky young man—this one in a long, fitted coat—standing next to her. From the way the man swayed as he accepted the glasses, she imagined they were not his first.

She shook her head. "Not quite. Sam had to... take a call," she settled on. As soon as she spoke them, she realized how ridiculous they sounded.

Sam was not the type of person who *took calls*.

Link, to their credit, made no comment. They were not particularly good at keeping amusement off their face, but maybe they weren't really trying to.

"Well, get you a drink while you wait then?"

Since she knew she couldn't very well stand at the bar and not order anything, she nodded.

"I'll take a Hot Jupiter."

They didn't seem to be good at hiding any emotions; surprise cascaded down their lean face like an ID scan even as their hands reached for the necessary bottles below the bar.

"Pretty potent," they noted as they took down a large glass from the rack above their head.

Kate watched them pull together the concoction, a mix of several clear spirits and then the final short pour of neon green liquid that began to smoke as soon as it splashed against the others. She was used to the mild shock and unspoken warnings that typically accompanied her drink of choice. It was a popular one for either those who wanted a one-drink ticket to utter inebriation-ville, or a tiny subsection of the population with an extremely specific genetic modification leftover from centuries-earlier experimentation.

She could tell Link was debating with themselves which group she fell into.

"I can handle it," she replied simply, feeling the glands in the back of her throat swell slightly.

They set the glass down in front of her, chin lifting. "Ah, a Purifier, huh?"

She met their eyes over the top of the glass. "That's offensive," she said, though it was hardly the worst thing she had ever been called. Bringing the drink to her lips, she took a hearty swallow. The taste was a punch, pungent and sharp; on a first try, most people did one of three things—coughed, choked, or teared up.

Kate appreciated the burn as it coated her throat and settled warmly in her stomach. Already she could feel the, for lack of a better word, *weight* of the alcohol and the way her body automatically adjusted. She wasn't interested in completely burning off the incoming buzz, but it was always comforting to know she could purge the toxins from her system.

Link laughed and held up their hands in a gesture of surrender. "I've got a few orders to fill. Don't disappear on me," they teased, with quick wink before directing their attention to the next customer.

Kate watched them make their way down the bar, quick hands and quick words, a quick grin always on their mouth. She sipped her drink because there wasn't any reason to rush. It didn't take them much time to make their way back to her.

"So," they said, folding their long arms across their narrow chest and tilting their head back, somehow giving the impression they were leaning against a wall.

"So," she repeated, setting her drink back down on the bar and resting her forearms behind it. "Has Sam always been so... chatty?"

"Oh, no. Used to be she'd hardly say a word."

Kate frowned. "God, I can't even imagine," she muttered, reaching for the glass again.

"Something in particular that you want her to chat about?"

There was a mildness to their tone that struck her as targeted, rather than easy going. And she couldn't quite tell if it was a warning or an invitation.

Well, she hadn't taken the safe route once in the last twenty-four hours, why start now?

To give herself a moment, she drank. The burn in her stomach was matched by a burn in her head, right between her eyes. She deliberated her way around it.

"Sam is on... unfriendly terms with Miles Floodwater," she began, choosing her words carefully.

She saw their gaze sweep the bar. Checking for customers. Or maybe eavesdroppers. Apparently, there were none to be seen because they remained at ease.

"Man like that doesn't have many friends," they volleyed back.

"They have a history." She made it a statement instead of a question. "But she's never done a job for him."

Their thin lips pursed, and they studied her with what might have been suspicion in their dark eyes. She wondered what it was they were debating and if they would tell her.

Link gave a casual lift of their shoulders, the suspicion shifting into consideration. "Best thing to do is ask."

"She told me to *trust* her."

Their arms fell to their sides, and they straightened, as if coming out of a slouch. Spotted an incoming customer.

"Can you?" they asked frankly.

Rolling her eyes, Kate pressed further forward on the bar, hoping to keep their conversation going for a few seconds longer. "How am I supposed to trust her when I don't know anything about her?" she pointed out. She caught the motion of a raised arm out of the corner of her vision.

"How'd you two get mixed up in the first place?" they asked, shifting toward the left, their gaze trailing.

She moved with them. "She saved my life."

They gave another grin, softer this time. "Tells you something, doesn't it?"

The door to the privacy room slid shut and locked automatically. It was basic as far as rooms went, modest sized, with nothing but a desk and data screen. That was fine. She had everything she needed on her tablet. The larger screen would be useful, at least, since she had left the glasses on the ship.

Without stopping to think, Sam moved to the desk and into the chair, bringing the computer online with a quick press of her palm. She didn't notice her hands were shaking as she interfaced her tablet with the screen unit. It took a few taps to bring up the file Floodwater had sent. Her finger hovered over the link, and she unconsciously braced herself before selecting it.

The video opened, crystal clear in quality. Another room, an office perhaps, dominated by a sleek console shaped like a U. Miles Floodwater sat behind it, elbows resting on the arms of a chair, gloved fingers tented in front of his face. Behind him, a large rectangular window bulged out into space. The hint of a bluish curve to a planet could be seen in the corner, along with some piece of structure that ran along the window edge. A satellite? A station? Sam didn't recognize the room; it clearly wasn't the one he maintained on planet nor was it the well-dressed space she had recently had the pleasure of visiting.

Could have been on a ship, she mused, trying to think back to the stops they had made on their last voyage. There had been a couple of stations for deliveries and supply pickups, and once just to get off ship for a few hours. She couldn't remember seeing anything to do with Floodwater at any of them, but there wouldn't have been anything to see unless he had wanted there to be. How had Jonah even known where to find him or how to get ahold of him?

Her train of thought halted as Jonah abruptly strode into the frame, wearing his brown canvas jacket with the zipper all the way up. Before she realized it, she had tapped the screen, freezing the image. She stared at his face, feeling a clutching pain in the base of her throat as if an object were stuck there, choking her. She closed her eyes and her breath shuddered in and out in uneven chops.

"I don't like it, Sam. Why don't we just split it even? Two in the shuttle, two on the ship? Hell, we could blow off both shuttles."

"Because it's a lot easier to mask one life signature than multiples. And I'm not leaving my goddamn ship. Besides, if it's a ransom they're looking for, one's cheaper than two."

"And what if they decide to just fire a couple of plasma rounds into the ship?"

"Then I guess I won't have to pay for those new heating coils."

"Dammit, Sam, that's not funny."

Sam opened her eyes. The memory was so vivid, so insistent, even six months removed. He had been angry in that last argument, but maybe not as much as he had been agitated. Concerned. Had there been something else she hadn't seen? There had been *so many* things to think about in that moment. He was supposed to be a constant, a variable she never had to worry about.

The look on his face in the frozen image before her was one she'd never seen him wear. Rage twisted his jovial features into someone nearly unrecognizable.

She let the video continue. Jonah fell forward, slamming his hands down onto the desk.

"What the hell do you think you're doing?" he demanded, his voice so sharp, so hard. So un-Jonah-like.

Floodwater did not so much as flinch at the showy display of temper. "Ah, Mr. Whent. So good of you to come."

Jonah hovered over the desk, his dark expression tightening further. "It's not like I had any kind of choice, is it?"

Floodwater's head tipped to one side, and his right hand lifted toward the ceiling before settling back into its former position. "That's not entirely true. Granted, the other option may not be ideal, but it is there."

"Tell me why I shouldn't just choke the life out of you right now?" Jonah growled, his fingers clenching as if he were already imagining them around the man's neck.

The quality of the video was so good that Sam could hear the sigh as it escaped Floodwater. "Don't make threats, Mr. Whent. Especially ones you know you can't follow through on." While Jonah continued to seethe, Floodwater spun in his chair and got to his feet. One hand tugged at the bottom of his suit coat and the other went to the top of his throat, lightly stroking the thin bit of roughened skin visible between his chin and the high collar of his shirt.

"Now, there's no reason we can't come to a mutually beneficial agreement in this situation," he added, looking out the wide window with the same assuredness he had with her.

Sam could see the little tremors in Jonah's body that told her he was holding back from launching himself across the desk.

"How much do you want?" Jonah spat out, pushing away and straightening up, his spine like a rod.

Floodwater clasped his hands behind him and continued to stare out the window. "I don't want any of your money, Jonah."

"Then what *do* you want?"

"I want you to undertake a quick, easy little job for me." Floodwater turned to glance over his shoulder, an almost-smile touching his lips. "That's all."

Jonah's jaw clenched. "Sam doesn't want to work for you."

Floodwater returned to the window. "That's why I'm not asking Sam," he countered smoothly.

Sam could see every single emotion as Jonah grappled with it; they played across his face. Anger. Guilt. Frustration. Desperation. Loathing. Resignation.

"If I do it, then Mac is clear? Completely clear?"

"One hundred percent."

She paused the video again; she already knew that Jonah had accepted. No need to hear the actual betrayal uttered aloud.

But the name he had spoken; that was important. Mac. Mac. It echoed through her brain as she brought up her tablet, flipping back to the communication that Floodwater had sent. The video had grabbed all her attention, but she saw now there were other attachments as well. She opened the one labeled *MW_contract_full*. Skimmed down.

"Dammit, Jonah. Why didn't you tell me?"

"Seriously?"

"Completely."

"Isn't that a little... unusual? For a ship captain?"

"There's not a whole lot about Sam that is usual."

Kate blew out a short breath and drank from a glass of water. "Yeah, I'm certainly finding that to be true."

Two Hot Jupiters and her head was buzzing a touch, a fact that had Link watching her with amazement. She'd contemplated a third—it had been a while since she'd put any kind of pressure on her system—but then figured water was the safer bet. She still didn't have any idea how long it would be until Sam found her or what kind of mood the captain would be in when she did. Considering how Sam had left, Kate guessed it would be some level of bothered, especially after having to search for her and then finding her pressing Link for information about her.

Though to be honest, Kate had learned more about *Link* in the past 20 minutes than she had about Sam. Link, who had lived on station for over 50 years, nearly their entire life, and who had three ex-wives, scores of ex-boyfriends, but only one true love.

She hadn't asked who or what that was, despite their repeated attempts to get her to do so.

Kate *had* asked why they only had ex-wives and no ex-husbands.

"In my experience, men make terrible husbands."

She had to chuckle at that one.

They also held majority ownership of the station and rented the lot from the satellite, apparently a common arrangement. Their favorite game was a card and dice combo called Unlucky—there were two tables in-house, but better action could be found in a station on the other side of the satellite or by invite only to one of the crew lounges. Twice a year (a designation they mentioned had little meaning) they traveled to the planet's surface, just to "touch base with real gravity."

What she had learned about *Sam* was that she'd been 21 when she first taken ownership of the kraken and she didn't really have much knowledge about spaceships in general. Apparently, a deliberate choice.

Kate wasn't sure how comfortable that made her feel in regard to traveling in one with her, but Link assured her Sam knew what she was doing; she simply wasn't much interested in the nuts and bolts. She usually left that to the one running the engine room.

The comment about the toaster made a lot more sense.

Had Jonah been the engineer? She frowned and took another drink of water, trying to decide if it would be out of line to ask Link about him.

"You done here?" Sam's voice broke in. When Kate turned to see her standing behind her, the captain's face was blank, devoid of the earlier turmoil.

"Are you—" *okay*? "—done?" she heard herself ask in response. Sam nodded, hands jammed into her jacket. Kate was surprised she still had it on and zippered up; it was hot enough inside the station that she'd slung her own onto the bar not long after she'd started speaking with Link.

"Yeah, we can head back to the ship."

Kate slid down from the stool, pausing to check her balance. The buzz from the alcohol was already fading, but she consciously burned the rest of it away. She took a final sip of water for good measure. Sam caught sight of the slender, nearly empty glass beside her water and lifted a brow.

"How many of those did you have?"

"Two," Kate answered, retrieving her jacket and folding it over her arm.

"She's a Purifier," Link supplied, grabbed both glasses and depositing them below the bar.

Rolling her eyes, Kate pointed a finger in their direction. "I told you, that's offensive," she stated. Those long hands went up in the air again.

"Right. So, what do I call you then?"

"Try Kate. It's my name."

They smiled a mile-wide grin. "All right then. Kate." They looked over to Sam. "I like this one," they added.

It was Sam's turn to roll her eyes. "You like them all, Link."

"True," they confirmed with a sober bob of their head. "And they like me back."

"Do me a favor and don't mention to Floodwater that I was here," Sam suggested, reaching over the bar. Link clasped her forearm, held it firm.

"We don't exactly have weekly check-ins. As long as I send him his money, I don't hear from him. And I *always* send the money."

The reassurance didn't seem to assuage her. "Doesn't matter. He probably already knows."

Sam was silent as they left, pushing through swarming crowds. Kate waited, assuming Sam didn't want to discuss anything within earshot of so many people. But the silence remained once they had spilled out on the street, which was virtually deserted in comparison.

It wasn't the other people keeping her quiet, Kate understood. It was just Sam. Only 24 hours in, and Kate thought maybe she knew the woman a little better than she had thought.

Well, Kate was tired of holding back questions.

"So?" she demanded.

Sam gave a start of surprise. "What?"

"What are we doing?"

"We're going to the ship."

"Don't give me that. What are we doing next? What's the *plan*?"

Sam rubbed a hand over her face; she looked exhausted, but Kate refused to feel guilty.

"I need to think," was Sam's reply.

Kate waved a hand toward the holo-station. "What were you doing for the last hour?"

"I sure as hell wasn't tossing back drinks at the bar."

Kate stopped in the middle of the street. It took Sam a few strides before she realized the other woman had stopped. She turned and looked back.

"May I remind you," Kate began, working to keep her voice calm, "that you walked off. You left me in the middle of that station less than two hours after we'd been kidnapped by some space gangster looking to strongarm *you* into doing him a favor. And yes," she snapped as Sam started to retort, "this was all after I asked—begged you really—to bring me up with you. I get that. I get that this is not your normal shtick. But we're stuck now, and this lone wolf bullshit isn't going to cut it. There are things that I need to know, and you need to figure out how to tell me, because if you think I'm going to sit backseat on this and wring my hands for the next however-the-fuck-long we're in this for, you've got another thing coming. So, you better figure it out quick. You want me to trust you? Then you need to trust me, too."

There was an implied *or else* in that final sentence that Kate wasn't at all certain she could follow up with, but it felt better to have it off her chest. Even if Sam did decide to leave her there on satellite.

The anger that had been growing on Sam's face during Kate's speech drained. She stalked away. Kate followed, careful to keep some distance between them, a bit concerned they were about to have another violent clash with a trash bin.

Instead, Sam set her hands on her hips and drew in a deep breath before twisting around.

"Okay."

"Okay?" Kate echoed.

Sam stretched her shoulders. "You have a point. I'm not good with… people."

"Yes, I noticed."

The look that Sam shot her was more irked than amused, but Kate could feel some of the conflict between them lessen.

"I'll explain… things. But I only want to do it once so let's get back to the ship first." Sam winced. "Besides, what I say is going to affect Addy as well."

"You're going to tell her about Floodwater?"

A shrug. "Yeah, probably should."

"Just answer me one thing first."

"I have answered you many things—"

"You said you'd never take a job from Floodwater," Kate continued, ignoring Sam's grumbled response. "So why were you going to sell him your ship?"

Sighing, Sam shoved her hands into the pockets of her jacket, her head tilting back in what Kate was beginning to think of as her standard pose.

"I guess it felt logical. He was the one who sold it to me in the first place."

"Really?"

"Yep. Gave me a deal, actually, one I couldn't turn down. I didn't find out until later that there were a few unspoken terms."

"Like what?"

"Like chasing down his shit for him, apparently. Let's go."

eight

When the ship had been docked in the abandoned service station, it had looked enormous, stretching out to fill the empty, ramshackle space. Docked in the satellite's utilitarian hangar and surrounded by other ships of vastly different shapes and sizes, it *still* looked enormous. It towered over the others like the undulating sea creature that was its classification's namesake.

Kate stared up at it as they approached.

"How did you ever fly this thing by yourself?" she asked before she could think of all the reasons not to.

The glance Sam gave the massive piece of flying machinery was a great deal less awe-inspired than Kate thought it deserved.

"There are some limited auto-functions, which helps. There was an emergency droid with co-piloting functions, but I shut him off. Program was buggy, I think. Really, the only tricky parts are take-off and landing," she explained. Her expression turned thoughtful. "Some inter-light maneuvers as well. Orbiting trajectories."

"So, in other words, everything?"

Sam shrugged.

They reached the base of the ship to find the cargo ramp already extended out. Tiny shivers of anxiety ran through Kate even as she reminded herself that Addy would be on board, running through the systems. That was all.

The stutter in Sam's stride told her the captain was having similar thoughts. Kate told herself to relax.

And then the largest gun she had ever seen walked down the ramp.

The weapon was in the hands of a strikingly large woman dressed in a dark jumpsuit with a distinctly military cut. Her face, hell her entire body probably, appeared to have been carved straight from polished onyx. Each of her steps looked like it would shake the whole satellite, but she made hardly a sound as she traversed the grated slope. At the bottom she stopped and stayed, holding the massive weapon as easily as if it were a teacup.

"You the captain then?" she asked, concerned apparently only with Sam. If the woman hadn't been holding a gun nearly the same size as her, Kate might have been offended by the assumption; there was no reason why she couldn't have been the captain. Except Floodwater had most likely given a description or rundown of them both. Kate simultaneously wanted and absolutely did *not* want to know how the Fisher King had described her to his henchwoman.

Sam, despite being shorter by at least six inches, managed to not look intimidated. Her head tipped in a way that appeared almost bored, as if giant gun-toting warrior queens were something she saw every day.

Maybe she did. It was only Kate's first day in space.

"That's right. My name is Sam."

The woman appeared unimpressed. "Captain will do."

Sam looked equally unimpressed. "You must belong to Floodwater. You got a name?" she asked. Though those were the only words that left her mouth, the air was thick with unspoken ones.

Kate saw the woman's hands tighten around her weapon and thought maybe Sam could stand to be a little *less* cool in that moment.

"Parker," was the clipped response. Her shoulders straightened, making her even taller than before. "And I work for Floodwater. He doesn't own me."

"Really?" Sam stepped forward, setting one foot on the bottom of the ramp. It put her mere inches away from one of Parker's bulging arms and the long barrel of her weapon. "Because that's what I thought. And I never even took a job from him."

With that, she stalked up the ramp, quickly disappearing into the cargo hold. So much for working on not being a lone wolf.

Parker's dark brown eyes shifted, practically boring holes into Kate. Up close the woman was so much *more* imposing; her long nose slightly crooked, as if broken at some point. Her jaw so heavy it looked like it could break any fist that struck it. The shadow-colored clothes did nothing to hide the thick muscles underneath, and the neck that emerged from the tight V of the suit was like the trunk of a tree. Her jet-black hair was pulled tight to her head and gathered into a dense braid that could have been another weapon if whipped fast enough.

Kate did her best to return the stare, because damn if she was going to pushed around by some hired—

The woman's eyes narrowed, and Kate felt her heart clutch. *Jesus, did she just say that out loud?*

"Who are you?" Parker asked, swinging her gun from one rippled forearm to the other in a move far too cavalier for Kate's liking. One of her hands could have easily spanned the entirety of Kate's head. Swallowing, Kate took a breath to seek out her voice from where it had scampered off to in the very far corner of her brain.

"Kate," she answered, proud the response did not squeak out as a question. She tried to think of something more to go with it but didn't really know the protocol for conversation with mercenaries. Were you allowed to chitchat with them? Were they just supposed to stand around looking broody and terrifying?

If so, *mission accomplished*.

Parker gave a short nod, then turned and stomped back into the ship. This time the ramp rattled with the force of her footfalls.

Stupid, Sam thought as she marched through the cargo hold toward the engine room. It was stupid to be annoyed by the appearance of Floodwater's goon. Hadn't she already known he was sticking one on her? Hadn't he made it abundantly clear during their *meeting* that she would not be out of his reach?

She'd been annoyed then, too. But it hadn't mattered as much because it had only been threats in a fancy office. Now it was like a piece of Floodwater was on her goddamn ship, and she worried it meant she'd never get him off again.

He doesn't own me. Ha. That was a level of wishful thinking Sam had never encountered before.

Of course, apparently, he'd already *been* on the ship, or at least his people, poking their fucking hands all over. Christ, she'd have to set fire to the entire thing to purify it.

"Heads up!"

As she stepped through the entrance to the engine room, Sam snapped her left hand up just in time to catch a small object before it could smack into her face. Across the room, Addy gave a sort of half wave, as if to signal "good catch" before turning back to a console screen.

Sam opened her hand and stared down at the blue rubber ball in her palm. A thin line ran the entire circumference of the sphere, the only mark that marred the surface. She recognized it instantly. Jonah used to bounce it whenever he was thinking. Addy's throw hadn't been the first time it had come flying at her head.

"Where—" her voice cracked, and she had to swallow before she could continue. "Where did you find this?" she asked, trying to think of the last time she had seen him with it. He had an irritating habit of leaving it all over the place. In her chair on the bridge. Tucked in the small alcoves above doorways. One time she found it in the freezer unit.

But all she could remember was the sight of his back as he jogged in the direction of the shuttle. It hadn't been in with his other things when she'd... she thought he'd had it with him. Maybe she just hadn't thought of it at all.

Addy didn't look away from the screen where a series of numbers were flashing by. "That's what was keeping the doors to the main bridge closed."

Sam frowned, her fingers curling involuntarily around the ball.

"This?" she asked dubiously, because that didn't seem like it could be right.

"Yep. Was jammed in one of the hydraulics. Looks like someone tried to pry the doors open which is what made me think to check."

Sam ground her teeth together. *Floodwater.*

"Couldn't open it enough to get inside. It's open now." There was no hint of a question in Parker's voice. The mercenary stood in the doorway, the massive gun still firmly in her grip. Sam wondered if she ever put it down or if she walked around with it like a fashion accessory.

"Open and operational," Addy confirmed.

Parker looked at Sam and the challenge was clear on her face. "Could be this mission's over before it starts."

Sam jerked a shoulder.

"You want to check, go right ahead," she invited, pushing down on her irritation until she could feel it bubbling in her stomach. Hell, maybe the damn thing Floodwater wanted was somewhere on the bridge and jamming the doors had been Jonah's stupid-ass way of hiding it, and this whole mess would fucking be over, and she'd only be out a couple hours' worth of work with a level six engineer.

And maybe she'd find a sack of money there, a unicorn, and the past year would turn out to be one of Triss's terrible practical jokes.

Parker held her gaze long enough to have Sam wondering if the woman was waiting for more than permission, before finally turning and walking in the direction of the bridge. As she left, Kate entered from the cargo hold and the sight of *her* had Sam cringing. *Shit,* she thought, belatedly recalling the conversation they had had less than thirty minutes before. Was she supposed to apologize now? She snuck a glimpse at Kate's face and didn't see anything that resembled the pissed-off expression she'd worn outside of the holo-station. That had to mean something, right? Damned if she knew. This was why she didn't like dealing with people.

That and all the talking.

But dealing with, and by extension, talking to, was what she had agreed to do, so she picked her way over a minor minefield of tools littering the floor. Addy automatically angled her body toward her but kept her eyes trained on the screen. Personally, Sam didn't have any problem with that—multi-tasking seemed like an efficient use of time—but then again, maybe a conversation about one's life potentially being put in danger was one you were supposed to have face to face.

"Can you pause that for a moment?" she requested.

"Not unless you want cooling pumps to misalign."

"What happens if the cooling pumps misalign?"

"Coolant can't get to the reactor."

"What happens if coolant can't get to the reactor?"

"The core will start to melt."

"Can't you just turn it off?"

"Yes. If you want us all to die horribly."

Sam raised her eyes to the ceiling, as if the patience she had never been gifted with could be found floating there. "How much time do you need? I have some important information you should be aware of."

Addy's fingers ran across the screen. "Just give me a couple of seconds to..." she made a few more strokes, and then revolved in the chair so she was facing Sam. The screen continued to blink, and Sam watched it warily.

"Why is it doing that?" she asked.

"That's the auto-run."

"Why didn't you just tell me you could put it on auto-run?" Sam demanded.

"That's not what you asked me," was Addy's response.

Momentarily, in place of the engineer, Sam saw Ollie, stiff-necked in his pristine medical tunic, his face long and serious. Addy's and Ollie's mannerisms, their whole beings, were completely different. But something in her tone reminded Sam of her very droll, very *literal*, former medic. He would have never lobbed a rubber ball in Sam's direction, but his voice—his entire person—had held the same dryness to it.

Shit. Not *now*.

She walked back toward the room's entrance, driven by the need to pace. "I may have been a little light with some of the details about this job," Sam began, trying to push past the memory before it could fully form.

"How light?" Addy countered. "Like you forgot to mention we need to make some undeclared stops?" Her face tightened with almost comical suspicion. "Is this actually one of those corporate-cover- up-insider-rendezvous?"

Sam had absolutely no idea what that was and no desire to know. She considered her approach and decided to go with her usual: blunt and direct.

"The item we're supposed to bring back belongs to Miles Floodwater." She paused and leaned out into the hallway, saw no sign of his goon. She didn't see any reason the muscle needed to be well-informed.

"He… coerced a member of my crew into locating and retrieving it for him. Before he could deliver it, we had engine difficulties near the Border. We were approached by an unidentified vessel; I evac-ed the three members of my crew in a shuttle which was then boarded by said approaching vessel."

She paused, drew in a thin breath, all she could manage, before forcing the rest out. "The members of that vessel jettisoned my crew before absconding with the shuttle."

She heard Kate give a quiet "Jesus" and deliberately kept eyes on Addy.

The engineer's face loosened with puzzlement. "That's unusual behavior for pirates," she mused. Sam bristled at the word "unusual." It had been a shock when it happened. Looking back now, she'd call it cruel. Monstrous.

"It is?" Kate's question was full of uncertainty as well, though Sam imagined it was of a completely different sort—confirmed by Kate's next words: "I mean, they are pirates. Isn't stealing and killing kind of their thing?"

"Stealing, sure. They'll strip a ship bare if it comes too close to their borders. But they're usually non-violent. They take the cargo and other supplies and leave the ship or crew intact. Don't want to draw the Core Corps in," Addy explained.

"There've been plenty of reports of pirate violence, especially near the border," Sam stated as calmly as she could manage, stomach twisting. She expected Addy to offer a rebuke; she was sure it was skepticism she saw skating across the engineer's features.

"So, what, you think the pirates have whatever it was that Floodwater wants?" Kate asked, her voice starting to tick upwards. "You want to go into Secession Space?"

Sam held up her hands. "It's likely but not definite."

"How likely?" was Addy's question.

One of Sam's hands twisted back and forth. "Fifty-fifty. We made one stop before... before. It's possible that my crew member left the parcel with someone he trusted, thinking we'd pick it up on our way back."

Addy's eyes grew thoughtful. "Did you have plans to stop again?"

Sam shook her head. "Not that I recall but it wouldn't have been hard for Jo—for this crew member to argue for it."

"How long ago did this happen?"

Sam shoved her hands into the pockets of her jacket and tried to even out her feelings as best she could. "Six months."

Six months that had somehow been longer and shorter than any other six-month stint she had ever experienced. Half a year that had sat in her mind as a distinctive blur, where each moment was excruciatingly detailed behind a foggy smear, like someone had run a hand over a painting before it had dried.

Steepling her fingers together, Addy tapped the tips of her indexes against her nose. "Okay, so just to recap: the job on offer is to track down a package belonging to one of the most dangerous men currently in existence. Said package is possibly in the hands of a friend but more likely in the possession of pirates beyond the bounds of civilized space. Is that correct?"

Sam squinted up at the ceiling again. "I think friend would be a generous term."

"That's great, Sam. There are an awful lot of *thinks* and *maybes* and *possiblys* floating around. One or two *certains* or *definitelys* would be appreciated," Kate stated, her hands going to her hips.

"Okay. How about, I'm *certain* that if we don't recover this package Floodwater wants, we'll *definitely* both be losing more than a couple of fingers," Sam snipped, holding up her right hand for emphasis. Kate frowned at the space where the missing digits should have been.

"Awesome. Thanks for that reminder."

"No problem."

"Ah, I need all of my fingers," Addy piped in, wiggling her own for show. "Kind of hard to engineer without a full set."

Sam folded her arms. "Floodwater isn't going to bother with you," she said. Paused. Then—"Probably."

"Reassuring!" the engineer noted with false cheer. Sam felt like throwing up her own hands but kept them pinched against her sides.

Fuck. "Look, I gave you the full details so you could decide if you were still interested. If you don't want to take the job after all, I'll pay you just to finish the on-satellite repairs. You can walk away, no harm, no risk of missing appendages."

With that, Sam clamped her jaw shut and shot Kate a look that she sincerely hoped conveyed, *there, I did what I said I was going to do*. Because she had, and if it cost them Addy's services, it meant she'd have to go back out and hire one of Link's mech heads, because she sure as hell wasn't flying into Secession Territory with just one of Floodwater's lackeys as crew.

There was always the outside chance she could trade the lackey to the pirates for the package—what the fuck would Floodwater care?—but it would mean she and Kate would have to fly the ship back alone. That was quite a distance to travel and hope nothing catastrophic happened. She'd managed it before by herself. Kate would probably have something to say about the ethics of—

"I've never dropped a job before. Not about to start now," Addy replied, cutting into Sam's ruminations.

Sam wondered if she looked as surprised as she felt. Then she wondered if there was more she was supposed to say, like *thanks-for-potentially-risking-your-life-for-me?* Probably not. The woman was getting full pay at a level six rate.

"So where is this friend-not-friend?" Kate probed. She appeared just as taken aback by Addy's affirmation of continued employment. Should Sam feel insulted by that? "On satellite?" she added when Sam didn't answer immediately.

As if it would be that easy. "No. He's on Dravanol Station."

"Dravanol?" Addy questioned. "Where's that?"

"It's a research station that orbits LFT4a, out in the Kaltar system." Parker's strong voice entered the room before the woman did. She took up space in the doorway. "That's a long way."

"It's on the way to the outer borders," Sam replied, feeling a tug of defensiveness. Parker's hands were empty, save for the ever-present gun. "No luck in the search?"

Parker's head gave a slow negative shake. "Bridge was clear."

"Is this tall drink of 70-round pulse rifle coming with us?" Addy inquired, studying Parker with considerable interest.

Parker's face was unreadable. "It's an MFG 545. Not a pulse rifle."

Addy tapped the bottom of her chin. "Oh. How embarrassing. I'd love an up-close explanation whenever you've got the time."

The potential pitfall opening up in front of her was so large that Sam decided the only way to avoid it was to ignore it outright. She moved her gaze to the center of the room and onto nothing. Absolutely fucking nothing.

"How much longer do you need before we can launch?" Sam wanted to know, directing the question to Addy without looking at her. There was the sound of a chair turning.

"At least five hours to complete the flush and recycling. The rest of the rounds I can run—hey a cat! Oh man, you didn't say there was a cat! Come here big guy," Addy cooed at the sight of Nata strolling in, pausing briefly to give a long backward stretch.

Ignoring her, Sam looked down at her wrist unit and tapped the blank screen out of habit. Cursed when it remained blank and pulled the tablet from her jacket pocket instead. "Five hours is approximately oh one hundred. We'll launch at oh seven hundred. Any objections?"

She said it more for form than anything else, but no one offered anything; she had half expected a token protest from Kate, but the young woman only nodded. Well, maybe they weren't in for a total disaster.

She turned to Parker. "Can you carry anything other than that gun?" she asked.

"Could carry four of your skinny asses," was the reply.

"Good. Because we need supplies."

nine

Space travel did not appear to be one of those things that improved the longer you did it. Kate blamed the myriad of advertisements on planet—flashing holo-boards, slickly edited commercials, even the rare, printed brochures—that always depicted a spacious cabin with curved furniture and a large window looking out over the endless expanse of stars or the whirling colors of a new planet on approach.

Those were usually portraying rooms on giant luxury space cruisers. She couldn't say she had ever seen an advertisement for living quarters on a *freight* class spaceship.

Standing in the middle of one, it reminded her a bit—okay, *more* than a bit—of her cramped cubicle back at the office. Boxy and mostly bare, with only a few pieces of furniture—a bunk, a small desk, a locker—all bolted securely to the walls. No window, not even a tiny round porthole. Just a place to sleep and store clothes along with a few other personal items. Not a full-time residence. Most of the vendors she had worked with in the past had on-planet quarters with families they could return home to. Kate wondered if whichever member of Sam's former crew who had used the room before her had had anyone to go back to.

Maybe it had been Jonah's cabin.

Maybe he and Sam had shared quarters. As soon as the thought entered her head, Kate shook it out. Whatever their relationship had been (she couldn't quite get a feel for it) she couldn't imagine Sam keeping a space with anyone, especially something as close and intimate as a sleeping cabin. Frankly, it was a miracle she let anyone on the ship at all. Or interacted with people in general. It was amazing she didn't just find some lost corner of the universe to hole herself—

A seed of frustration was sprouting, but before it could take root, Kate pushed it aside, shifting the direction of her thoughts.

Since Sam was the owner and captain of the ship, it meant she must have her own room, larger than the others and stamped with her... personality.

Just for fun, Kate tried to envision it. Bigger, sure. Fancier, maybe? Some touches of luxury for the vessel's owner? An actual bed instead of a simple platform that swung down. A dresser made of polished wood as opposed to beat up metal. A built-in bar stocked with gleaming bottles of booze? A golden, sparkling chandelier that dripped down from the ceiling?

She chuckled as the decadent images from advertisements merged with the sparse room in front of her. *Bet it's a no on the chandelier and bar.* She didn't know much about Sam's personal tastes, but she couldn't buy in to such a gaudy display. Then again, you never really knew what people were like in their private retreats.

And Kate wasn't quite sure what to think about the fact that she was wondering about Sam's. There was just something odd... curious... strange... well, something about the woman. A pull drawn by all those secrets she was clearly keeping. Oh, she had trickled out a few drops of information with half a promise for more, but there were much bigger pieces to the puzzle being carefully hidden away. Sam had intricately carved out the details as if cutting sections out of a book. She had given them just enough to understand the passage but not enough to know the whole story.

Anyone would be intrigued by that. Intrigued and annoyed. Possibly more annoyed than intrigued.

Okay, that was a lie.

Kate ran her hands into her hair and gave a quick tug to redirect her thoughts *again*.

According to the information Sam had offered, they had at least a week before they would reach the research station. There was no way she was going to just sit in her cabin and ponder the cryptic curmudgeon that was Captain Sam. Captain Sam who had, in their original agreement, said she would be one of the crew but who then, after delivering those scant details of their mission, had disappeared into the very fabric of the ship. And Kate was not going to search every single inch of it just to get a task to occupy the time. If Sam wanted to hide away, that was her own damn—

"Okay," Kate muttered out loud. That was getting her nowhere. She turned and walked to the door, pressing her hand against the palm plate to open it.

There were two other people on board the ship; one of them must have something for her to do.

Sam was not hiding. Not at all. She would have been insulted by even the insinuation. What she *was* doing was an extremely important and long overdue inspection of the backup gravity coils located in the upper crown of the ship. The small space happened to be all but inaccessible for more than one person and couldn't be reached without a separate access code that she had neglected to give Addy. It was unlikely the engineer would need them since the backup coils had been dead since she bought the damn ship and were no longer even wired into the systems.

There had been a moment, as she'd twisted up into the opening, when she had wondered if she would find the package that was the current impetus of her troubles nestled within.

But there had been nothing. Not even one of those stupid cross-eyed stickers that Jonah stuck to things he wanted her to replace. Hell, *he* might never even have been in there; she couldn't recall if they'd ever discussed the potential pitfalls of running without backup gravity. It was… strange to think there could be an inch of the ship that he hadn't set foot in.

Comforting too, in a way. At least she could be sure no ghosts would follow her there. Sam concentrated on breathing, on the stretch of her ribcage, the expansion of her lungs. The tightness in her chest remained.

She should have been down in the bridge, seated at the navigational console, looking over their course projections. That had been her intention, right up until the doors to the main bridge had whisked open finally after half a year.

Absently, she rubbed at an ache in her left knee. She wasn't sure what she'd been anticipating when the doors parted; annoyance at a layer of space dust or relief at not having to drag herself up a half-assed excuse for a ladder anymore. Maybe nostalgia at the sight of the wide display screens and consoles that had been the start and end of so many jobs.

Her eyes had gone immediately to the co-pilot's board and the shadowy specter of Triss sprawled out in the chair, one booted foot propped up on top and the other folded beneath her.

It had been a punch to the throat and had sent her scrambling back so the doors could slide shut again. She barely remembered stumbling down the hallway and climbing up into the crown.

Not that it mattered. The specter might not have followed her, but the memory had.

"This route is going to take us right up against the border, Triss."

"Actually, we're going to cross it. Twice. The other options are to either pass through a massive gamma burst that is working through this quadrant or take an out of the way route which will bypass the burst and give us a nice border cushion but will add about two weeks transit time."

"We don't have an extra two weeks."

"I know, Sam. Hence the dance with the border."

"Shit. What's the latest report on pirate activity?"

"Surprise! There are still pirates. But you know they usually haunt a few clicks in on their side. If we stay near the border, we shouldn't have a problem."

Shouldn't have. What an idiotic phrase. You either had a problem or you didn't.

Shouldn't have even taken the stupid job in the first place.

Sam rested her head against the hull. In her mind she could see the route displayed out on the screen; the breezy, unconcern expression on Triss' face.

Stupid. Stupid to have run the border.

Was she being stupid again? She ran a hand over the short hairs at the back of her head. Didn't have a choice this time.

Something brushed firmly against her right leg; she looked down to see the round head of Nata pushing up into the space. He craned his gaze up at her, twitched one ear, and made a *mhrrr* sound. Sam glared back.

"He's not coming back, you know."

Nata shook his head briefly then proceeded to rub along her side. In the tiny space, it was impossible to avoid.

"You know I hate when you do that," she complained though she couldn't bring herself to push him away or back down the access tunnel.

After a final rub, he curled up near her hip, his face smushed against her. Quiet purrs filled the air.

Sighing, she pulled out her tablet, bringing up the video that Floodwater had sent. There was no escaping the memories anyway. She stared down at Jonah's violent movements as they surged across the small screen. He was nearly unrecognizable beneath his expression of anger and hatred.

But anything was better than the last image she had of him, lifeless and still.

It was Addy that Kate came across first, which Kate was grateful for, because she doubted she wanted to consider the sort of tasks Parker might be willing to hand out. Surprisingly, Addy was not,as she had been ever since setting foot on the ship, hunkered down in the engine room. The precise woman was in the galley, seated at the sole square table tucked back against the wall. A cup of dark liquid sat by her elbow, apparently forgotten, and her head bent low over a small device.

Programming herself a mug of coffee, Kate took the cup and, as casually as she could manage, meandered over to join her. When she slipped into the opposite side of the booth, she could see it was Sam's wrist unit that Addy was tinkering with. The thin casing sat beside it and Addy was gently probing between circuits with a sliver of a tool.

Kate debated whether to speak; she didn't want to break the

engineer's concentration, but she wasn't sure if the other woman realized she was no longer alone.

"Help you with something?" Addy asked, without glancing up.

That answered *that* question. Kate took a sip of her coffee. "Any luck with that unit?"

With her face pinched in thought, Addy nodded slowly.

"A bit. I think I know what the problem is anyway."

"What?"

"It's a piece of shit. And about five years out of date."

Kate huffed. Addy glanced up, her brows arched and Kate held up one hand in response.

"Sorry, it's just... I'm not at all surprised," she explained.

"I take it you two have known each other for a while?" the engineer theorized.

Kate shook her head, though the morning before was starting to seem like *ages* ago. "About a day or so is all," she corrected. At Addy's disbelieving stare, she added, "It's kind of a long story?"

Addy's forehead wrinkled. "How could it be? It's only been a day or so," she pointed out.

"True."

"And anyway, we've got a week before we hit Dravanol. Spill it."

So, Kate walked back through the previous 24 hours, starting with her less than brilliant decision to visit Floodwater's on-planet station, being chased, Sam's timely arrival, convincing the less than enthusiastic captain to take her aboard (skipping the brief exchange in her apartment, no sense in giving out any wrong *ideas*). She considered leaving out the kidnapped by Floodwater part—but then again, it wasn't like the engineer didn't know who they were working for now.

"After that is when we, or I guess Sam, hired you," she finished. Looking back, she thought maybe it wasn't so long of a story at all. The experience had certainly *felt* longer. The telling of it though? Maybe 20 minutes tops.

Addy fiddled with the tool and a miniscule green light began to blink on the unit. "Ha!" she exclaimed triumphantly, setting the tool aside and reaching for the casing. Setting the inner electronics back into the housing, she snapped it shut with a quiet click.

Hard to tell if she had been listening at all.

"All fixed?" she guessed.

Addy gave a disgruntled snort. "God, no. But at least now I can interface it with the computer and get an OS onto it that's not completely obsolete." Checking the seams of the case, she flipped the unit over. Inquisitiveness stole over her face.

"What's this?" she hummed, running her fingers over the back plate.

"What?" Kate echoed, tipping forward unconsciously.

Addy swiveled the unit toward her.

"Looks like it was a gift."

Squinting, Kate could see text etched into the dark metal.

No excuses now for not getting our comms. -T.

Giving the unit a little pat, Addy placed it next to her tool and reached for the previously ignored cup. She took a long swig—if it was coffee, Kate could only imagine how cold it must have been. But Addy didn't seem bothered.

"So, what made you want to grab a ride on a spaceship?" she asked as she set the cup back down.

Clearly the engineer *had* been listening. Kate toyed with the mug's handle, and though she was no longer interested in the bitter liquid, she brought it to her lips just to give herself more time. She remembered the explanation she had given Sam, but that was only what had driven her to visit the Floods. She was starting to think something else had pushed her onto Sam's ship. And she wasn't sure she was ready to explore *that*.

"Were you really out on a ship for three years straight?" she asked instead.

Addy was silent; Kate thought maybe the engineer wasn't going to let her dodge her question so easily. Then Addy canted back, one hand stretching across the back of the booth.

"Sure, done it a couple of times. It's a pretty standard contract length for deep space work."

"But three years? I'm having a little trouble imaging a week inside this place."

"Well, the ships I was on were about 20 times the size of this one. Significantly more crew. Some colonists. On top of that, you spend almost half of the time in cryo-sleep."

"What about family? Or anyone… significant?"

Pushing a few stray strands of hair out of her face, Addy slipped her tool into a small leather case. She folded the case closed and tucked it into the pocket of her denim shirt. "Most of my family is scattered around the universe. If I get the yen for a visit, a three-year voyage is the least I'd need to sign up for. Last I heard, one of my brothers is somewhere in the Kenway Belt, and that's a good five years out on a freighter."

Five years. The number echoed in Kate's head.

"Haven't run into anyone significant, so that's never been a problem," the engineer added, with a bit of a smirk. She picked up her cup again and motioned with it, "But I've known a couple long distance spouses. Lots of comm drops. Hit the uplinks at every waystation. They don't usually do back-to-back runs though," she admitted.

"But you do?" Kate asked.

Addy nodded.

"Sure. I take a couple days, maybe a week at a station, but I like to keep moving. Plus, that way I don't have to keep a domicile. The rent they'll charge you nowadays is ridiculous. And for what? Half a box in an ant farm. No thanks. Could get something on planet, but are you aware that most interspace accidents happen on exit or reentry? Why risk it?"

Kate was pretty sure she *had* been aware of that, could remember reading something along those lines. She was thankful it hadn't occurred to her when she and Sam had made their trip up. Her mind jumped onto another point.

"So, where do you keep all your stuff then?"

"I don't have very much to begin with. Clothes. Some minor tools." Addy held up the leather case as if an example. "Most captains worth anything maintain their own sets specialized for their ships. Which is good, because if I had to keep a set for every ship I worked on, I'd need my own satellite."

Taking a last pull from her cup, Addy stood up from the table. She slipped Sam's unit into one of the cargo pouches of her pants.

"Well, I'm going to find that walking gun show and see if I can interest her in a nightcap."

Kate's surprise at the bluntness of the statement must have been clear on her face because Addy chuckled.

"Sorry, didn't mean to offend any sensibilities," she ribbed lightly.

"No, no. It's fine. I just... doesn't it bother you that she works for Miles Floodwater?"

Addy shrugged. "Don't we all kind of work for him at the moment?"

There was no arguing that. Kate sat back in the booth and chewed lightly on her lip. Addy gave another quick nod and ambled toward the crew quarters. She was nearly to the doorway when Kate remembered what had drawn her from her cabin in the first place.

"Wait, Addy?"

The engineer paused and turned back.

"Is there... if you want, I could... I mean, if... there's anything you need... help on, I mean, with? Like, fixing wise?" She cringed as the words came out of her mouth, thinking of all the sentences she could have combined, she'd somehow picked the worst.

But Addy didn't appear put off by them; she looked intrigued.

"You reworked those power lines?" she asked, after a moment of contemplation, sounding only *slightly* skeptical. Kate nodded, feeling only *slightly* offended.

Addy rubbed a hand under her chin and gave an answering bob of her head. "I've got a couple things that would go a little smoother with a second pair of hands. Tomorrow, oh eight hundred. Be in the engine room." She started to step through the doorway and then stopped, one hand pressed against the wall as she ducked back in.

"Better make it oh nine hundred."

Sam left the crown and headed down the corridor toward her quarters, hoping for, but not really expecting any reprieve from memory. She'd gone no more than a handful of steps before she spun in a complete one-eighty, realizing abruptly there was something very essential requiring her attention in the cargo bay. Immediately.

It had nothing to do with the fact she spotted Kate walking in from the opposite direction, clearly headed for her own room which, due to incompetent ship design, was directly across from Sam's.

Nothing at all to do with that.

She heard the steady patter of footsteps behind her and increased her pace, worried that Kate had spotted her and was following. But a quick glance over her shoulder showed an empty hallway. Seconds later there was the faint *thunk—thunk* of a door sliding open and then shut. Sam slowed and fought against the sharp, jittery feeling that had exploded in her chest.

Weird.

You did just spend the last eight hours hiding. Maybe if you hadn't, you wouldn't be feeling so guilty right now.

Sam had no idea what part of her brain was responsible for that garbage but a) she had *not* been hiding and b) she definitely didn't feel *guilty* about it. And c) she'd already informed Kate of everything the woman needed to know. Basically. Mostly.

It's not like knowing the entire story would lessen the chances of death or dismemberment. Anyway, Sam agreed to share information, not spill her guts. Not to mention the fact she had a spacecraft to operate and didn't have time for a barrage of questions. The last thing that she needed was—

She was so preoccupied with the one-sided argument even her brain didn't seem interested in having that she failed to notice the barrel of the blaster until she walked chest-first into the tip. Her forward motion ground to a halt as the metal dug into her breastbone for a second, before easing back. Sam stared down at the weapon and then met Parker's unwavering gaze.

"You shoot that in here and there will be more than just a hole in me," she pointed out mildly, even though all muscles from her lower back to her neck had tightened.

The tip of the gun pushed lightly against her chest again before Parker swung it up to rest against her shoulder.

"Don't worry. It's in standby mode. It can't fire."

"It's not the gun's decision-making skills that I'm concerned with."

The corner of Parker's mouth twitched but she offered no response. Sam looked to the left and the right to see if she could answer the question before she asked it. There was nothing but the open space of the cargo bay.

"What are you doing in here?"

Parker lifted one shoulder. "Standing."

Sam didn't allow her eyes to squint like they wanted to; like she had a feeling Parker wanted them to. Instead, she kept her gaze level. She didn't give a shit who the mercenary worked for; it was her goddamn ship.

Some of her thoughts must have shown, because Parker made an apologetic motion with her head before reaching up with her free hand to press a button on the side of her weapon.

There was a low whine and a flash of green as four points of light shot out in different directions. Green spheres no larger than a fist hung in the air at various distances from them. Before Sam could articulate anything, Parker whipped the gun down from her shoulder, took aim, and fired. Each time she pulled the trigger, a thin green beam blinked out, tagging the targets, and caused them to wink out.

The last orb disappeared, and Parker settled the gun back onto her shoulder.

"Just a little target practice," she stated with another shrug in her voice, as if she had not just displayed her prowess with a deadly weapon and didn't care in the least bit if Sam was awestruck.

Sam wasn't awestruck. She'd been in enough firefights to know the ability to hit stationary targets meant nothing. Nor was she unnerved because the Death card was already on the table, whether it be via mobster boss, pirates, or trigger-happy mercenary.

What she *was*, was amused and surprised by it. Surprised, because damn if she didn't appreciate the display of casual arrogance and disinclination to talk about it. Parker, she got the feeling, wouldn't ever need to know the why. Just what and when.

Simple.

And because she could appreciate that, Sam nodded as she looked around the space again. There wasn't any other use for it at the moment.

"Try not to blow a hole in the hull," she cautioned, turning back toward the exit.

"And Captain? Don't worry. I won't shoot you unless I have to."

"Comforting."

The ship's onboard clock read five after eight when Addy stepped into the engine room the next morning. Partly because despite a thorough walkthrough of the ship, she'd been unable to find Parker the night before (minus the mercenary's personal cabin, which wasn't a line to casually cross—especially not on Day One) but also because even though she had accepted Kate's offer of servitude, Addy was particular about other people mucking around in her engine room.

It didn't matter that the ship didn't actually belong to her. She was on board the ship now and all the machines within were her domain for the duration of the job.

Unexpectedly (she *was* rated Guild Level 6) Addy had been impressed by Kate's attempted repairs, in a not-many-people-know-how-to-separate-power-cables kind of way. The work itself had clearly been done with careful hands, though the lack of refined skill had also been evident, so she'd gone ahead and redone it anyway. But *theoretically* she could have left it as it had been, and there was a very good chance it *wouldn't* have led to catastrophic failure.

Whoever had overseen the engine prior to Kate's repair had been quite adept. That is, if one ignored the fact that he or she had tied the power cables together in the first place. Setting aside that single act of poor judgement, which, yes, *could* have led to complete reactor meltdown, the systems had been impeccably maintained, especially when compared to the…ruggedness of the rest of the ship. The engine had several downright brilliant modifications, if a bit unorthodox. Simple tweaks that supercharged an already powerful core. In fact, it didn't really make any sense that the mind that had conceived and implemented those upgrades would have made such a basic mistake as braiding together power lines. A desperate attempt maybe? Or someone else's—

"Thought you said oh nine hundred?"

Kate's voice interrupted her train of thought. Addy watched as Kate stepped into the room, rubbing her hands together as if to warm them. Drat. Hadn't had a chance to kiddie proof the area.

 Oh well. There wasn't much she couldn't fix in time if it came to it.

"Got an early start," was what she offered.

"No nightcap?" Kate guessed, with a ghost of a smirk.

Addy mimed locking her lips and tossing an invisible key. She appreciated the eye roll she received in response. Four weeks with the likelihood of more with someone uptight was never a pleasant experience. It was nice to see at least one of the others on board had a sense of humor.

"So. What can I help with?" Kate asked, pushing further into the room and casting an eye toward the main engine core taking up most of the space in the middle of the floor.

Definitely not that, Addy thought. Kate's other eyebrow lifted.

Oh, apparently said that out loud.

"Never a good idea to mess around with the engine core mid-flight if you can avoid it," she stated, which was true. "Besides, there's nothing to do there anyway." Also true. "Purrs like a kitten." A kitten heavily jacked up on…

She couldn't think of an appropriate metaphor.

"But," she continued, holding up one hand as she dug through a tangle of wires she had pulled out from under one of the floor grates, "how are you in terms of patience and perseverance?"

Kate looked at the mess of cords. "Moderate, I suppose. Why?"

she asked warily, as though she had already surmised the answer and was not pleased by it.

Addy nodded her chin down toward the wires. "Because I need to know where these all go. And it would be a good idea to check for fraying at the same time. Whoever oversaw this end of the boat was a genius but wouldn't win any awards for organization."

Lowering herself to the floor, Kate took hold of one section twisted in a seemingly endless mess.

"Isn't there a maintenance bot that could do this sort of thing?" she objected, running her fingers along one of the cords.

Because it wasn't a terrible idea, Addy reflected over the asset list she had been able to glean from Sam.

"Actually, there is a B-class service unit that would probably do the trick."

"Great," Kate said, extending her arms. "Where is it? Let's grab it."

"I think it's in the cargo hold. Though, now that I'm thinking about it, Sam did mention it was a little . . . wonky?"

"Wonky?"

"Yeah. I think her exact words were, 'I stopped using it because it got wonky.'" Addy's voice dropped at the end in a passable imitation of Sam's affect.

Kate returned to the cables. "Nevermind. I'd rather be bored to death than killed by some potentially homicidal robot."

Her lips pursed, Addy paused in the midst of grabbing for one of her tools. "I think we have vastly different definitions of the word wonky."

"I just think robot is one of the words you don't ever want paired with wonky. You know, kind of like you wouldn't want your surgeon to say, 'this laser scalpel sure is *wonky*.'"

"That's fair."

"Anyway, you can tell that the last engineer was organized?"

Addy could see Kate was already diving into the job she'd been given. Good sign. Enthusiasm was always a plus around technology that was necessary for survival.

"Sure," she began and then paused. She zeroed in on an odd flat cable amidst the usual round ones. Intrigued, she followed it, contemplating if it was another modification. There were benefits to a flat cable, but why replace one and not the others?

Captain could be a total cheapskate. Hadn't gotten around to it? Original cable could have just frayed and been replaced as needed.

"How can you tell?" Kate prodded, when the engineer failed to expand.

Addy stopped in the midst of sticking her head down into the open crawlspace. Her brow furrowed as she deliberated on the question and recalled where she had left off.

"Oh, right. Some of it's obvious, like nonstandard modifications. I mean, the captain could have hired the work out to a specialist, but then you run the risk of something going wrong and nobody being on board that could fix it. Other stuff is more a feeling, like the previous sequence for engine power-up. I have my own configuration that I like to use, but they had an interesting setup. Interesting to have the secondary fire first..." her voice petered out as she inched underneath the floor.

Kate hesitated in her sorting. If she was supposed to find the beginning to the other wires, it was likely she would have to climb down into the space as well. For now, she would wait until Addy was finished. No sense trying to cram two bodies where it looked like only half of one would fit.

She tried not to dwell in disappointment; she had been hoping for something a little more challenging, a little more exciting, a little more *demanding* of her focus and brainpower. A project that didn't remind her of the mind-numbing menial tasks she had done day in and day out at her old job. Because if she thought about her old job, she'd start thinking about what the hell she was *doing*, and that was likely to set off a chain reaction directly into a giant explosion of self-doubt.

Realistically she knew, as she continued to tease apart the cables, that any task higher up on the difficulty chain was out of her wheelhouse. Her father had been the rocket scientist. She was a project manager with an exceptional memory and an eclectic reading list—she could put together a process map with her eyes closed, but space engineering was not her special talent.

"Does it make you nervous at all?" she asked after a few moments of silence. The sound of shuffling and clanging drifted up through the grating. And then:

"Does what make me nervous?" came Addy's voice from what seemed like beneath Kate's feet.

"Going into Secession space?"

More clanging. A quiet, "Dammit." A not so quiet, "What the hell is—" Then finally a response that Kate knew was meant for her.

"Not really."

Kate set the mess of cables down. "Really?"

"Well, for one thing, we might not even end up in Secession space. Maybe Sam's not-friend has whatever it is we're looking for. And if they don't, we still might not have to deal with pirates because if they didn't strip the shuttle, which they probably did, they would have traded it. That thing could be halfway across the universe by now." A pause. "Though probably not. That'd be quite a distance to cover in the timeframe, even with modern spaceflight. Maybe a couple galaxies away but even that might—"

"Who would they have traded with?" Kate interrupted, because while she wasn't a rocket scientist, she could comprehend the size of the universe.

Big.

"Deep space crews. Any satellites that are off major routes. Transfer stations. Anyone, really."

"But... they're pirates."

"Yeah, and that usually means that they've got something on offer."

"But it's illegal." Kate was certain it was. Was pretty sure it was one of those things that had always been illegal. "The Core Conglomerates are constantly putting out bounties and increased activity warnings," she said. It was part of nearly every shipping contract she had ever signed off on.

"Yeah, and CC officers are probably the pirates' best customers. Not many of the independent stations like to trade with *gloms*. Most of the 'danger' of the Secession zone is rumor and exaggeration. I mean, sure, there are pirates that board vessels. It's a dangerous patch of space. People have been killed. But people get killed everywhere. Space is dangerous, period. A lot of pirates are just people trying to scrape by."

"You sound pretty familiar with them," Kate observed.

"I might have spent some time in the engine room of one of them."

Kate was about to demand a full account of that experience when a section of the floor to the left of her lifted and Addy emerged. She held a pocket-sized black case attached to the flat cable she had been following.

"What's that?" Kate asked, scrunching her nose.

Addy frowned and said the two words Kate thought should probably never be said while in an engine room. "Don't know." She lifted the object directly in front of her and studied it closely. "Looks like something fit in here, but whatever it was, it's not here now."

"It couldn't be anything important, right?" Kate motioned around the room with one hand. "I mean, the ship's still running?"

"You would think," Addy agreed in a voice that didn't sound like she actually agreed. She stared intently at the shell, as if she expected to find a full description written on the inside.

Kate wasn't sure what was making her more nervous—the idea that a piece (important or not) of the ship was potentially missing or the look on Addy's face as the engineer contemplated all the things it might have been. She was about to ask if it was something they should bring up to Sam when Addy tossed the box to the side as if it were no more than a piece of junk.

"I'll figure it out later. The engine core isn't going to maintain itself. Well, technically it will. Unless it becomes unstable. In which case we would all be supremely f—"

"I get the idea," Kate cut in. She picked up the bundle of cables again and sighed. "So, what are your thoughts on the Big Five merger?"

"Never gonna happen."

ten

Kate recalled once reading about a theory that it took ten thousand hours to master any given skill. She speculated on if that number had any correlation to how long or how many words it would take to get to know another person.

It had been a week, one hundred and sixty-eight hours, since they had left Icarus 3 and Kate was certain, based on her daily average thus far, that Sam had not spoken anywhere close to ten thousand words in the entire span of her life.

It wasn't even that Kate was desperate for conversation; Addy was more than willing to keep up a steady stream of speech as they worked, even as she manipulated various machines or settings. Outside the engine room, the engineer was just as talkative, granted mostly still about things pertaining to the engine room.

Even *Parker* was more verbose, usually pulled into maintenance work by Addy when the engineer needed another set of hands or extra reach. Her responses were generally mild—but not necessarily dissuasive—rebukes of Addy's brief but not-at-all-subtle flirtations. A few bits of genuine information were revealed in the galley where the three of them, four if you counted the cat, had taken to gathering for meals. Like the fact Parker was combat-rated in over *forty* different types of weapons. She'd rattled the stat off as if it wasn't anything big, but Kate was suitably impressed. And terrified.

Sam, however, seemed determined to keep their interactions under an unspoken word limit, and the more the captain deflected, the more Kate was resolute in finding a subject they could speak about at length. She knew she could poke or prod for intel, but what she wanted now was something... easy. Nice. *Normal.*

Since their present circumstances felt like a potentially fraught topic, she tried reaching back toward a hopefully less precarious commonality.

"Why shipping?"

The question slipped out of Kate's mouth before she could close her teeth over it. She made certain her eyes were pinned on the minute spot directly in front of her face and the insulation that she was replacing, so as not to give the impression she was at all interested in an answer. Nope. Not at all. Just a casual mixture of words, a totally random question, didn't matter in the least if anyone within earshot replied to it.

Out of the corner of her eye, she saw Sam pause whatever she was engaged with at the engine room's main console.

Kate continued to fiddle with the smear of *inso*-gel, even though she was finished and shouldn't have been touching it for three to five minutes.

There was a hint of confusion on Sam's face, which Kate couldn't be sure of since she absolutely was not looking at her except for maybe out of the very, very corner of her eye. Mostly the captain looked blurry. But possibly also confused.

"What?" Sam asked. Definitely confused.

Kate continued to stare at the wires in front of her. "I was just wondering, what made you pick shipping and transportation as a career." She looked over briefly in time to see the edge of Sam's lips lift and her eyebrows rise.

"I wanted my own ship. There weren't a lot of other options." Sam frowned, seemingly taken off guard by her own candor. She focused back on the comp screen.

Pleased and intrigued, Kate abandoned her pretend work.

"Why did you want a ship?"

Sam's mouth thinned. "I wanted to get off satellite."

"So why not go on planet?"

"Tried it. Didn't like it."

"You were on planet? When? For how long?" Unrealistically, Kate's mind flew backwards, wondering if their paths might have crossed earlier.

"Three days."

"Three days? That's it?"

"That's how long it took to buy and prep the ship."

"How—" Kate swallowed the question.

Sam glanced over. "How what?"

"How did you afford a ship? Especially one this big?"

"Old-fashioned way." Kate made a go on gesture and Sam continued. "I started signing on for transport jobs when I was sixteen, saved my chips. There wasn't anything else I wanted so I didn't have to worry about blowing my money."

"What about school? Aux training?"

Sam's lips twisted with distaste. "I did my required units and that was more than enough."

"Oh."

"What about you?"

"What about me?" Kate asked, startled by the returned interest.

"Why shipping and transport as a career?" Sam echoed, a faint smile on her lips.

"Oh. Well. I went to school for process management and—"

"Willingly?"

Kate chuckled at the skepticism. "Yeah. I actually like that sort of thing. Process and project management. Integration. The job I have is—was," she corrected herself, "kind of perfect for me."

At Sam's pointed look, Kate shrugged. "Yeah, I don't know. I just... I can't really explain it. It's not like I was completely miserable or anything. I liked my life. I liked what I was doing. And then one day everything felt like it... stopped. I felt stuck. Like everything was closing in."

"You felt caged in, so you decided the answer was to get into an actual confined space and go where you would have to remain in that space lest you die?" Sam summarized.

Kate huffed and shook her head, at the statement and at the dry, teasing tone it was delivered in.

"Honestly, I don't have any idea what I'm doing," she confessed in a false whisper.

Sam's smile stretched enough to display a faint dimple but before anything else could follow, Addy's voice cut in.

"Well, that is just the sort of thing you want to hear in the engine room of a vehicle in the middle of a cold inhospitable vacuum," the engineer wisecracked as her head appeared from one of the room's access tunnels. Her eyes narrowed when they landed on Sam.

"What are you doing? Did you touch anything?"

The hints of humor on Sam's face fled, replaced by traces of irritation and insult.

"I'm checking activity reports for the quadrant. Didn't I swear I wouldn't even attempt to replace one of the light bulbs?"

"No. I *told* you not to even attempt to replace a light bulb. To which, if I recall correctly, you scowled—yeah, like that—and stalked off."

Sam rubbed at her jaw as if to ease tightened muscles. "You know this is my ship, right? And I managed to keep it running for months without your expertise?"

Addy nodded in easy agreement. "Sure. I'm just asking if you want it to continue to be a ship or if you'd prefer it to be a paperweight."

"What will the activity reports tell you?" Kate slipped in, hoping to distract Sam with a practical question long enough to keep the discussion going. Sam hesitated, as if internally debating with herself, before she replied.

"Any recent pirate incursions in the area."

Addy's eyes widened. "We're still almost 20 jumps from the border," she pointed out. Judging from the timber of her voice, Kate assumed such activity would be unusual.

Sam keyed in commands with a few swipes. "I'm aware of that."

"Pirates don't usually run this far in," Addy continued.

"Not usually," Sam agreed, with no other reaction.

"But you think that they might?" Kate concluded, watching Sam's face closely. No hint of what she was thinking flickered across her expression. After a few more inputs, Sam turned from the comp.

"Doesn't hurt to check," was all she said before shifting to Addy. "We should be within communications range in about an hour."

Addy still looked quizzical. "Dravanol. That station set up for bay docking or extended?"

"Both. They'll assign us a spot after we've communicated with Receiving."

"Aye, aye." Addy noted lightly as she returned to the panel.

"I'll be on the bridge. I'll send the access codes down once they've been transmitted." Sam's gaze came back to Kate and, briefly, it looked as if there were more she wanted to say. Then she gave a shake of her head and ducked out of the room.

"You really going to haul your ass up into that crawl space instead of using the bridge like a real captain?"

Parker's voice was low, smooth, and devoid of judgement despite the words, but the muscles in Sam's neck and shoulders still locked. One hand rested against the groove in the wall while the other hung in mid-stretch, reaching for the next rung. She debated in her head simply ignoring the comment and pushing up into the auxiliary bridge anyway. Could even close the emergency hatch in case Parker tried to follow, though honestly, she wasn't sure the mercenary wouldn't be able to tear the hatch off its track. Still, she considered the idea, if only to spare herself yet another fucking conversation.

The past week had been full of them between maintenance updates from Addy—which were fine—and questions, *always questions*—which were less fine—from Kate, who one would think had never even *heard* of space before. All right, maybe this job wasn't a typical, normal, run-of-the-mill job, and perhaps there were things about that ship that she wouldn't necessarily know, and you can't know if you don't ask, but fuck, Sam felt as if she had spoken more in the past week than she had in the other thirty-five-plus years of her life. Didn't anyone appreciate the *silence* of space?

She'd assumed Parker did, judging by her succinct speech patterns, but there she was, commenting on something that required no comments.

It was Sam's goddamn ship. She would captain it from wherever the fuck she wanted.

She turned, intent on saying just that—Floodwater's goon or not—but she got a look at Parker's face and stopped. The normally stone-faced woman had what looked a hell of a lot like anxiety pinching her otherwise smooth skin. Sam's right eye twitched involuntarily.

Yeah. Another conversation for sure.

"Something you need, Parker?" she waded in, barely withholding the sigh.

Parker's hands flexed at her side before disappearing behind her back. Her shoulders straightened. Sam might've been amused by the formal stance if she hadn't been so annoyed.

"Just wanted to know how long we were planning on being station-side."

That sure as shit wasn't all she wanted to know. "Hopefully not long," Sam replied, curiosity slowly overtaking irritation. Something had the big woman rattled. "Couple hours maybe."

The mercenary's shoulders straightened further. "I'll need some of my own time."

That raised suspicions in Sam, who couldn't imagine what sort of personal business a mercenary would have on a research station. But asking would require extending the conversation, which she was not in the mood to do, nor, based on the tightness of Parker's features, did she think the other woman would welcome. The small tells reminded her of all the times Jonah had known when things were bothering her.

The idea had Sam pulling back and squashing even the faint interest. "So long as you're back on board when we leave, doesn't really matter to me." Even as she said it, it occurred to her that Secession space or not, there might be an opportunity to rid themselves of Floodwater's oversight.

As if she could read Sam's thoughts, Parker hmphed. "That won't be a problem," she stated, giving one final hard glare before turning and walking away. The doors to the bridge slid open as she passed. Sam stared through the doorway to where the front view panel looked out into space. She raised her gaze to the opening of the auxiliary bridge. Then back to the main bridge. A wave of fatigue hit so strongly that she rested her forehead against the access ladder.

"Shit."

Six months in space was hardly any time at all. The average length of a transport job from the inner ring to the outer reach. On planet, the changes that took place in six months might be substantial, rendering sections unfamiliar or unrecognizable. But in space, change was slow, and somehow, despite great advances in technology, things always seemed to look just as you left them.

At least, that was how Sam felt. Looking out the viewscreen, the sight of Dravanol station was exactly the same as it had been on that previous visit. A long, spear-shaped structure, it orbited like a massive needle above a planet of swirling blue and green clouds. She couldn't remember the planet's designation, but someone— Jonah maybe—had likened it to a great crashing ocean they had once seen.

Before she could think more on it, she clicked open the comm link.

"This is ship registration number MCV-09890-1B, direct out of Icarus 3, requesting docking privileges station-side and a conference with a member of station crew."

Silence. *On break maybe,* she thought to herself with a roll of her eyes as she sat back in the flight chair to wait for comm station one to get back with their fucking coffee.

Triss must have handled the communication last time. She usually did. *Saving lowly admins from your sparkling personality, Sam.*

Sam kept her eyes on the console. The bridge had been void of ghosts when she finally managed to drag herself inside following Parker's offhanded comment, but she wasn't willing to risk looking to see if an idle thought could summon them back. She couldn't help thinking how empty the room felt, in a way it never had in the past. There had been plenty of hours spent by herself on the bridge over the years. But she hadn't been alone.

How was it she was only realizing it now?

"How long does it usually take for them to answer?"

She flinched, her heart thudding painfully against the front of her rib cage at the sound of a voice from beyond the grave. After a second, she realized her mistake, caught the difference a moment before she glanced over to see Kate leaning in the doorway, hesitation written across her face.

The difference: Triss had never asked questions, had never hesitated.

Rather than the exasperation she expected to feel, Sam found herself grateful for the company. She would answer a hundred questions if it kept the past in the past.

"Depends on how long it takes them to notice our signal," she replied. Rubbing at her right temple, her eyes roamed toward the navigator's chair directly in front of her.

It was empty. If Kate noticed the falter in her response, she kept it to herself.

"Ah, Addy asked me to check the PA comm? Specifically to the engine room," Kate stated instead, still hovering just outside the room.

Sam motioned with one hand. "Sure. It's uh… right there. That panel."

Kate stepped in, drifting in the direction that Sam had pointed. She paused over the console, squinting down at the flat screen and controls.

"This panel? With the ninety thousand buttons?"

Sam felt a smile threaten. The corner of her mouth twitched. "Lower right. It's got PA right above it."

Leaning down so that her nose was inches from the board, Kate peered closely, the fingers of one hand lightly brushing over the controls, as if she were trying to read with her fingertips.

Shaking her head, Sam stretched over and pressed her right index finger directly underneath a large green switch. Looking up, she was taken aback by how close the movement had put them.

Their eyes met; she watched Kate's flutter down, then back up, and the quick movement jerked Sam out of her temporary stupor.

"That one. Just… just click it and uh… the uh… screen will ask," she fumbled out.

Kate eased back, appearing a little out of sorts as well. "Will ask?" she prompted.

Sam stared at her. "What?"

"What will the screen ask?" Kate reiterated.

"Oh. Uh, it'll ask what rooms you want to connect to."

"Right. Okay." Kate set her finger over the switch and clicked it up. The screen directly below it blinked on and she bit her lip as she scanned the readout. Her finger swiped across the screen.

"Addy? Can you hear me?"

Silence.

"Addy?"

There was a click, followed by a *"Ye—"*, immediately trailed by a violent crashing sound.

Then silence again.

Sam and Kate exchanged looks and Sam pushed up in the chair. "Addy? Everything okay down there?" she asked with concern.

Another click and Addy's voice came in over the channel. *"Yeah, sorry. Kate, did you by chance leave a container of SR4 fasteners out?"*

Kate pursed her lips before answering. "Yeah. I thought you might need them."

"Okay. Great. New engine room rule: don't leave open containers of fasteners out where someone can trip over them."

"Sorry about that. But at least the PA works?"

"What? You sound terrible. I can barely understand you. Some kind of feedback. Maybe one of the wires is frayed."

"Oh. Well, you sound fine on this end."

"Really? Huh. Could be something on this end. I'll check the speaker unit itself. Might be that—"

While Addy rattled on, Sam shifted, and with her focus on Kate, clicked the comm switch off. Addy's voice cut out. Kate gave her a questioning look.

"I'm sure she'll figure it out."

Nodding, Kate offered a dim smile and motioned over her shoulder. "Well. I should get back there and see if she wants any help. There were a lot of fasteners. And um… we'll be docking soon, right?"

Sam glanced at the comm board. "Hopefully."

"Right. So, I'll… see you in a bit then. Hopefully." With that, Kate pulled away from the console and stepped outside the bridge doors. Sam felt a quiet tug she couldn't identify, but it was more than the desire not to be alone.

"Kate," she called, and as soon as the sound entered the world, she realized it was the first time she had said the other woman's name outside of introductions. Four letters had never felt so strange rolling off her tongue.

Kate paused and turned. Waited.

As Sam opened her mouth, no idea of what she wanted to say, a new voice clipped over the comm line.

"Ship MCV-09890-1B, this is Dravanol station. What is the name of the individual you are seeking and the purpose of your conference?"

Almost apologetically, Kate gave a quick wave and disappeared down the corridor. Sam swiveled in the chair back to the console, even as she felt drawn in the opposite direction.

"Dr. Mac Whent. And the purpose is personal."

"And who is seeking the audience?"

"Tell him it's Sam. Tell him Sam needs to speak to him about his brother."

"Wait, wait, wait. Just wait a minute. What do you mean, stay here?"

The words echoed through the voluminous space of the cargo bay, and Kate was pleased with how calm they sounded even as they reverberated.

"I mean remain within the area denoted by the exterior walls of the ship."

"Sam."

"I literally don't have another way to describe it."

Kate crossed her arms. "I don't want you to describe it. I want a reason for the request," she gritted out, barely resisting grinding down on her teeth.

Sam didn't look away from the small viewscreen she was occupied with. "It wasn't a request."

Sliding her hands down to her hips, Kate stared at the side of Sam's head and imagined it to be as thick as the ship's hull. "What was it then?" she challenged, her voice dropping.

Finally, Sam slowly turned her head, eyebrows up. "An order. And *crew*," there was a strong emphasis on the word, "follows orders, remember?"

"Even if they're really dumb orders?"

"Especially if they're dumb orders." Without turning back, she jabbed forcefully at the screen and then zipped up the front of her jacket, as if both actions were punctuation. She stomped over to the controls for the cargo ramp.

"I'm going to murder you."

Sam took immediate note of that. "What?"

Kate had her fist pressed to the center of her forehead. "I meant, metaphorically," she asserted.

"No, you didn't," Addy chided as she stepped into the bay, her arms full of an assortment of parts and wires. She sauntered toward the large bay doors and, upon reaching them, let the burden cascade to the ground in a cacophony.

"Hey, easy," Sam snapped, making a sharp gesture at the noise and mess.

Addy lifted her hands. "Whoops," she apologized, without a hint of sincerity.

Dropping her fist, Kate reached for patience, hoping there was still some left in the well after a week. "Look, why do we have to stay on board while you go out there?"

"She didn't say anything about us," Parker stated. Her sturdy boots clomped over the floor grating as she strode into the space. Suddenly the room felt reduced, with the ceiling significantly closer to her than the others. In her hands she carried a heavy-looking crate, while her gun was slung over her shoulder. She paused, halfway to Addy, and asked, "Where do you want this?"

"There is fine," the engineer replied.

It hit the floor with a jingling crash.

"Hey!" Sam shouted again, both arms spread out.

Parker gave her a blank look. "Whoops."

Twisting to look over her shoulder, Kate looked sullenly at the mercenary. "What do you mean?"

"Technically, she just said for you to stay on board," Addy clarified when Parker gave no further response.

Kate turned back to Sam, the muscles in her face pinching in frustration. "But you *meant* all of us. Right?"

Sam didn't reply, fiddled instead with the access controls for the ramp.

"Sam," Kate prodded, her voice heating.

With a long exhale, Sam rotated her shoulders and let her head drop back.

"Addy's the engineer. She'll have to leave the ship to check the hull and coordinate with dock personnel."

"And Parker?"

"Parker has an enormous gun."

"Sam—"

Sam brought her head back up and gestured, palms up. "Come on, Kate. This is a research station, not an entertainment satellite. It's boring. It's full of science nerds who won't talk to you about anything. They won't let you go anywhere. They'll probably want you to sign some bullshit NDA documents. I'm just going to meet with my contact, hash out a few things, and then we'll be on our merry way."

"What are they studying?" Addy piped up, cutting into the

tension. She lifted two wrenches into the air, hefting them in both hands, as if checking their weights.

"What?" Sam barked.

Addy set the wrench in her right hand down and tapped the other against her shoulder. "You said it's a research station, right? So, what are they researching?"

"How should I know?"

"You've been here before, right?" Addy swirled the tool in a lazily circle. "How else would you know it's full of nerds who won't tell you anything? Plus, it's not on any of the major transport routes. I'd never even heard of it till you mentioned it."

A myriad of expressions flittered over Sam's face, and her gaze tracked the entire footprint of the bay before finally landing on Parker. Kate wasn't sure how to describe the silent exchange that passed between the captain and the mercenary, but she was glad she wasn't in the center of it.

"They're studying the effects of temporal catatonia," Sam answered after several long, heavy seconds.

"The effects..." The realization hit Kate and her jaw dropped open. "So that means there's—"

Sam nodded. "It's also a containment facility. This is where the poor bastards get sent. So will you please just stay on board?"

"It's a containment facility, Sam. I'm sure they have everyone safely secured."

"Yeah, because that's how every zombie film starts."

"Zombie—you have the strangest hang-ups. I'm coming with you."

"I dunno, Kate," Addy interrupted, her usual cheer dampened. Her forehead wrinkled with worry. "Have you ever seen anyone who's been afflicted? It's... not good."

"I bet it isn't. But I'm not a helpless idiot or a child, and I'm not letting Sam go anywhere without someone she can trust." Kate's eyes paused briefly on Parker, and she dropped her chin in a dip of concession. "No offense."

Parker rested her arms comfortably on her gun. "None taken."

Sam rubbed her hands over her face, drawing them slowly down over her chin. "Ironically, this is probably the least dangerous place on our itinerary. It's not like we have to worry about Benny popping up and clobbering me out here. It's just a bunch of science geeks."

"Well, you didn't expect Benny to pop up and clobber you back there on Icarus 3, did you?"

Sam jammed her hands into the pockets of her jacket. Her mouth opened and then closed almost immediately. After a moment, her shoulders fell.

"The guy that I'm meeting with… we have… kind of a… complicated history."

"Were you married?" Kate asked.

Sam started and shook her head vigorously. "What? No."

"Ex-lovers?" Addy guessed.

"No, absolutely not—"

"Bad roommate? One of you break the lease?" Parker added, in an oddly sympathetic tone. Addy made a face and shook her head.

"I hate when that happens. Once this guy I was seeing tried to—"

"Fuck, no. Like I said before, we're not exactly… friends," Sam expounded, reluctantly.

"Shocking," Kate muttered. At Sam's glare, Kate threw her hands up into the air. "Isn't that a good reason *not* to meet with him alone?"

"Worried he's going to murder me in the middle of a research station?"

"I would!"

Addy leaned against a crate behind her, the wrench dangling casually in her hand. "This is great," she said offhandedly to Parker. "The last job I was on was really missing this kind of dynamic."

Parker cast her gaze downwards at the other woman. "You mean your other crew didn't shout themselves hoarse at each other over stupid shit?"

Addy shook her head. "Nope. They were all teamwork and compliments. It was weird. And so boring." She paused and then added, "Were you planning on following Sam around the station?"

"No. I have my own business here."

"Ooo. Mysterious. I like that."

"Hush."

After a solid ten seconds of attempting to stare Kate down, Sam capitulated.

"Okay, fine. You want to come with me, fine. Just let me do all the talking, okay?"

Kate nodded and did her best to keep the gloat off her face. "Of course. I'm just backup," she promised.

Sam mumbled, "Shit." And then something that kind of sounded to Addy's ears like, *alone my ass*.

"I heard that," Kate stated.

"Great," was Sam's reply as she hit the release mechanism for the cargo ramp. As it lowered with a rumble, she added over the noise,

"Anyone not on board by the time I'm ready to leave is getting left behind. Got it?" she bit out before looking forward again, hands clenching by her sides, almost rhythmically. Kate turned her head and mouthed *that won't happen*.

Sam stalked down the ramp even before it finished its descent, Kate close on her heels.

Sam was a dozen or so steps out of the ship when a door set in the nearest wall of the docking bay slid open and five figures strode through; four more than she had been expecting. Those additional persons were dressed in black jumpsuits, similar to Parker's, but with "SECURITY" emblazoned across the front. Weighty tactical belts and sleek hand blasters hung around each of their waists. Nerd police.

It was the figure out front that drew most of Sam's awareness. Even from a distance of six months and 30 feet, she recognized him. Though she had never given it much thought before, Sam was beyond grateful that Mac Whent looked nothing like his brother Jonah.

Everything about him was different, from Mac's close-cropped blonde hair and blue eyes to his tall, lean, and somewhat crooked frame, currently wrapped up in a long white lab coat. Even the shoes, boots in a highly polished black and peeking out from dark slacks, were a far cry from the brightly colored canvas footwear Jonah had been fond of.

"You know, I can't actually think of one good reason why I should listen to a thing you have to say."

She couldn't keep from recoiling; she'd forgotten. Even without the infectious humor in the tone, the low baritone that flowed from Mac's lips was uncannily similar to Jonah's. As she schooled her face back into more neutral lines, she knew from the narrowing of his eyes that he'd already seen.

"You're already here so might as well?" she offered, not put off by the cold greeting. She'd sort of been expecting worse, so all things considered, a decent start.

Beside her, Kate adjusted and she couldn't tell if the other woman was stiffening in some level of outrage or was simply uncomfortable with the tension. A second later Kate muttered, practically into her ear:

"You weren't kidding about the 'not fond of' bit."

Across the way, Mac began to speak, and Sam only had a moment to wonder if he had somehow managed to hear Kate before a piercing alarm blared out. It echoed through the cavernous space and sent all of them down into a crouch in a vain attempt to escape the harsh siren.

"What the hell is—" Sam half-shouted at the same time one of the security officers pressed a hand up against his ear and called out:

"Unidentified ship has breached the security barrier!"

A robotic voice pitched over the shrill of the alarm, "Security breach. Security breach. Unauthorized ship approaching station."

"It's in the docking tunnel, sir!" the same officer exclaimed.

With both hands over his ears, Mac shook his head. "How in the hell did it—"

Before he could finish, a narrow white ship burst into the docking bay at a shocking speed, its nose wavering like it was out of control. Smoke trailed from one wing, billowing dark gray and smelling of sulfur. Without thinking, Sam grabbed hold of Kate's arm, yanking her down the remainder of the ramp and into a sprint behind Mac and the security officers. They all, in turn, bolted toward the bay's far end where a series of dividers rose from the floor.

There was the tumultuous scream of metal against metal as Sam vaulted over one of barriers, dragging Kate along with her. She pressed her back against the divider and felt the rush of force blow overhead. Mac slid behind another barrier a few feet away and their gazes met. After a deliberate hesitation for potential debris, they lifted their heads up together.

The ship had crashed into the bay, ground across the floor, and come to a halt a good fifty, but-not-quite-far-away-enough-for-Sam's-comfort, feet from the kraken. The alarm continued to blare while smoke plumed, filling the overhead space like cloud cover. Otherwise, the ship was still.

Sam and Mac eyed each other.

"Friends of yours?" they asked at the same time.

A door in the side of the shuttle slammed open and a dozen figures poured forth with a flurry of laser streams blasting out ahead of them. The beams cut wildly through the cargo bay, streaks of red light bombarding the walls, the floors and, much to Sam's indignation, the hull of the kraken.

"Sonofabitch!" she snarled at the sight of sparks showering off her ship. Enraged, she had nearly gotten to her feet before her brain booted into action and reminded her that she, unlike the ship, was *highly* susceptible to laser fire.

She dropped back behind the barrier and saw across the way that Mac had done the same. Twisting to her right showed Kate was hunkered down not far away with one of the security members beside her.

When Sam rolled back to Mac, he was speaking rapidly to the guard closest to him and being passed a hand blaster. The other two guards were already returning fire, popping up to let loose streams before taking cover again.

"Who the hell are those guys?" she hollered. Mac looked to her before rising to fire his own shots.

"I was hoping you could tell me. They came in on the same access code as you," he returned, once he had ducked again.

Sam scowled. "They must have hacked our communications. They didn't show up on my proximity scan."

"Ours either." Lift, fire.

One of the guards stood and caught a blast directly in the chest. He crumpled to the floor, close enough for his companion to drag him back behind the barrier. Cursing, Mac raised his blaster, fired without looking, and crawled over to where the man lay motionless. He tugged the weapon out of his hand and shoved back over against the divider. Firing again, he tossed the unit to Sam, who caught it in both hands.

Her scowl deepened. "I hate these things."

"If you don't mind, spare me the nonviolent lecture at the moment."

"I've never claimed to be *nonviolent*," she retorted, curling her fingers around the grip of the gun. She peeked out the side of the barrier.

Their return fire had halted the incursion of the intruders, now spread out behind the scant cover the cargo bay offered; a handful of crates and one particularly large maintenance vehicle. Four bodies lay motionless that she could see, evening up their odds.

She heard a *grunt* followed by a *thump* and revised the thought when another one of the guards dropped. He pushed back to his knees though, his right arm hanging limp at his side, and transferred the blaster to his left.

Not seeing any other choice, Sam fired off three quick blasts of her own, not at all surprised when none of them hit the mark.

"Not one fucking word," she growled darkly in Mac's direction despite the fact he'd said nothing, concerned with his own targets.

Out of the corner of her eye, she noticed the guard closest to Kate hand her a weapon.

"What? No, don't give that to—do you have any idea how to use one of those?" Sam protested, hunching down as a laser streamed over her head.

The guard rose up and fired twice; one of the intruders spun out from behind his cover, collapsing to the floor.

"Point at hostiles, squeeze trigger," he instructed, crouching.

Kate's hand tightened on the blaster as she looked over at Sam. "Seems easy enough?" she ventured, shifting so her left shoulder rested against the barrier in a clear attempt to mimic the stances of those around her.

"Oh yeah? Killed someone before have you?" Sam pressed, firing again. Again, none of her shots landed.

"Can't I just use the stun setting?"

A laser stream blasted between the barriers, catching the corner closest to Sam's face. The metal melted and curled in on itself, burning bright orange and smoking.

"It's a laser. It doesn't *have* a stun setting!"

"What the hell is she doing?" Mac wondered, his voice tight.

For a split second, Sam thought he was speaking about Kate, even though she was looking directly at the other woman and could see the hesitation clear across her face. Then her head swiveled, and she had the exact same question ring through her brain when she saw who he actually meant.

Parker stormed down the open ramp of the kraken with her massive gun pressed up to her shoulder. A ferocious volley of beams burst from the weapon, each one slamming home. Her broad frame wove between the enemy blasts as she strafed the floor, firing unrelentingly.

Until there were no more streams cutting through the air and no more movement.

Mac stood and Sam followed suit. She held a hand out to indicate Kate should remain down and, *for once*, Kate did not protest.

"She one of yours?" Mac asked, nodding his head toward Parker. Sam rubbed at the base of her throat and felt her eye twitch.

"Yep. Or. Sort of."

"Sort of?"

"Kind of a complicated story actually."

"Anything to do with what you're doing here?"

"Yep. Got somewhere private we can talk?"

"And if I don't?"

"Then we can talk right here. But I don't think you're going to like what I have to say."

Mac shook his head. "You never bring me any good news." He frowned and shook his head again. "We have to wait until more security arrives. Then we can talk."

No sooner had the words left his mouth than the door to the bay whisked open and a full dozen guards raced in. Sam raised an eyebrow.

"That's a lot of security for a research station."

"Lucky us, we're well funded. Come on, we'll go to my—"

A loud crash came from the downed ship, and they whipped around in unison. Pushing out of the wreckage was a sole intruder, a blaster in his hand. Sam lunged toward Mac, tackling him just as the laser whined. She felt a shock of pain in her knee and, as they hit the ground, she saw Parker pivot at the base of ship's ramp and fire off a single shot, striking the intruder directly in the chest.

Kate lurched out of her frozen state as Parker lifted Sam onto the med-bay bed with hardly any effort at all. Mac waited, medical tools already in hand.There was a tear in the knee of Sam's right pant leg, burned around the edges where the blast had hit. Sam grimaced as she struggled up into a sitting position, and her fist slammed against the cushion as Kate reached her side. Mac pulled back the singed fabric.

"Going to have cut these," he stated.

Sam's response was a grunt through clenched teeth.

Taking that as agreement, Mac traded what was already in his hand for a pair of heavy-looking shears. Kate tried not to imagine what else they might be used for besides cutting cloth. She felt a shot of queasiness run through her as he began to slice through the material.

"They're just fabric shears," he explained, as if he were reading her mind. When she glanced at him, he gave a tight smile. "It's not uncommon to have to cut clothing away from an injury," he added with surprising gentleness.

"Right. Makes sense," she replied, leaving off the part that it was the *injury* she didn't really want to see.

"Can we maybe have the medical fashion lesson later?" Sam asked, teeth gritted. If she had more to say, it was cut off as a spasm wracked through her body. Mac snipped through the last piece of cloth and pulled it out of the way. Kate braced herself for some vicious mixture of blood, bone, and burn.

Her brain shuddered to a complete stop from what she saw instead: twisted metal framing and sparking wires. The laser had burned through alloy and circuits, leaving a smoldering hole through a metal plate that bore some resemblance to a kneecap.

An electrical spark snapped and zapped as another spasm coursed through Sam.

"Feedback loop?" Mac guessed, studying Sam's face.

She nodded, eyes clamping shut briefly as she sipped in air.

"I'll need to cut the inputs. The blast destroyed the override," he said. Sam's head bobbed again, and Mac started to turn toward a tray of additional tools nearby. He paused; fingers outstretched.

"I can't give you anything for the pain. Not yet. Not until they've fully discharged," he warned.

Beads of sweat gathered on Sam's forehead as the rest of her face contorted. "I know," she managed to get out, hissing through her teeth.

Kate remained stock still next to her, stuck in a mixture of shock, uncertainty, and concern. She didn't want to leave, not until she knew Sam would be okay, but she wasn't sure being there was doing any good, especially if she was in the way. And Sam couldn't be keen on the idea that someone else was viewing her in such a vulnerable state, that is, if she was thinking about anything beyond the obvious amount of pain she was in. Probably should go take Parker and find something else—

"I'm going to need you to help brace her," Mac instructed.

Or—or she could do that?

"What?" she and Sam voiced at the same time.

Mac returned with a slim tool in hand: something that looked like it would be more at home in Addy's leather case. He set his free hand below Sam's knee and motioned with the tool.

"She's going to jump as I sever the inputs. I need you to hold her still, or else I could end up doing more damage."

More damage?, Kate thought with a note of incredulity, even as she surveyed the med-bay, because surely there was someone else that could—

Nope. No one. Even Parker had somehow disappeared.

With a quick exhale, Kate carefully placed her hands on Sam's thigh, pressing down firmly. The muscle seemed to jump beneath her palms. At least, it felt like muscle.

"So—what—you're some kind of droid or something?" she joked, shooting for levity. She winced when her voice came out more panicked-hysteria. Her eyes narrowed in on the neutral space between Sam's face and her leg; that familiar, well-worn jacket still zippered.

"Ha. It's just a… shit… robotic leg."

"Old war injury?"

"Some… something like that."

Irrationally provoked by the latest in a seemingly never-ending series of evasive answers, Kate glowered. "You *really* don't like people knowing anything about you," she snapped.

Sam grimaced but Kate figured it was most likely from the pain.

"Ready? I'm severing the first link," Mac cautioned.

Kate automatically bore down with more of her weight on Sam and saw the moment the pain coursed through her. Sam's mouth contorted, but instead of a scream, or a yell, or even a stream of curses, the only thing that escaped was a ragged gasp. Kate felt her own throat close.

"How many more?" she heard herself ask.

"Three," was Mac's response. "Hold on."

Sam's eyes nearly rolled back into her head, and the only sound she made was a thin intake of air through her nose.

"Two more."

Sam dropped her head slightly. Kate looked into her eyes, glassy with shocked delirium, and thought, Shit.

Then she leaned forward and pressed their mouths together. She felt Sam's body tremble beneath her and hoped this wouldn't go down in history as one of her worst ideas ever.

"Last one," she thought she heard Mac say, but it was hard to hear over the buzzing in her head.

Sam shuddered, differently than before, and as Kate pulled back, she heard the other woman inhale sharply. When their eyes met again, Kate could see pain, confusion, and something she was certain was not anger swirling in Sam's pale irises.

It took two swallows before Sam could speak, and even then, her voice was weak.

"What... was that for?" There was a hitch in her voice that had nothing to do with pain.

Kate eased back, lifting her hands from Sam's thigh. She suddenly needed space. Lots of it. But she found she couldn't quite make herself step away.

"To take your mind off the pain," she breathed out. *Walk to the door. Now.*

She stood there, eyes locked on Sam.

Sam stared back.

Kate was barely cognizant of Mac moving nearby until he pressed a long cylindrical object to Sam's neck. Her body twitched, and a moment later her eyes clouded over, drifting shut. Mac maneuvered her without trouble into a supine position.

"She'll be out for a couple of hours at least," he said. His face was blank, but Kate heard the implied dismissal. She took another step back.

"Right," she said. "I'll just..."

She stole one more glance at Sam—unconscious, face unnaturally relaxed—and then hurried out of the lab.

eleven

*I*t *just always figured*, Addy thought as she made her way down one of Dravanol's numerous and nearly identical corridors. You stock half a dozen XR443 intake cup-links and the damn pirate lasers skip right past them. All 26. Not a scratch on any. Instead, they somehow zero in on the much tinier, much harder to see SS526 stabilizers, of which you have exactly none to spare. Actually, Addy wasn't even sure of the last time she had worked with an SS526 so she wasn't exactly shocked to find there weren't any replacements on board.

Luckily, you could swap out the SS526 for the newer TK300 model, which was more efficient and reliable. But, of course, there weren't any of those on board either.

She was banking that, judging by the level of tech packed into the station—*someone sure as hell had deep pockets*—there might just be a spare or two (or four hopefully) on site. Asking around had netted her the name of the head of maintenance, a stickler for in-person communications named "Ed." All she had to do was find him, but Ed apparently liked to move around. She'd already checked his office and the security center and been told he was out "making the rounds."

Well, if she didn't run into him in the next ten minutes, she was making her way to the supply depot and stealing the stupid things if she had to. She had been in more than a few deep space stations, and while they all had a creepy sort of emptiness to them that came from too few people in too large a place, Dravanol was the first station she'd stepped foot onto housing a population that was, according to medical research, violently, bat-shit crazy.

As she turned down a new corridor, idly pondering if anyone ever got lost and what their chances of survival were if they did, Addy froze in mid-step. The clunky maintenance-like hallway abruptly gave way to smooth white walls and almost painfully bright lights, heralding the section of the station she had actively been trying to avoid—the patient wing. Along both sides of the hall were thick doors, each with small glass panels set at head height so passing doctors or researchers could peer inside.

Frowning, Addy glanced back over her shoulder the way she had come. Shouldn't there have been a door or a security desk or checkpoint? How secure was the facility if anyone could just accidentally wander into the ward of dangerously disturbed individuals?

Maybe rerouting that maintenance elevator hadn't been her best idea. But honestly, who didn't triple lock their maintenance elevators?

Addy whipped around as one of the doors on the hall swung open, but it was only a man in a lab coat and a woman that could have doubled for Parker, just without her enormous gun.

She tilted her head and looked closer.

No, it *was* Parker.

The door shut with barely a click, but the deep *thunk* of the lock as it engaged echoed down the hall. In a voice that Addy could only catch the tone of, the doctor or researcher spoke rapidly, hands gesturing to the room and then seemingly to the station itself. Parker didn't appear to be paying him any mind. She peered through the window, riveted by whatever or whomever was inside. Judging by the expression twisting the muscles of her face, Addy had the feeling it wasn't the *good* kind of riveted.

Finally, the man in the lab coat stopped talking. He reached out a hand, possibly to pat Parker's shoulder and then stopped, clearly thinking better of it. Withdrawing his arm, he turned and walked away, his footsteps soundless against the polished floor.

Creepy, Addy thought. She began to make her own retreat, because it seemed like the sort of... thing people, specifically pulse rifle toting mercenaries, didn't want you stumbling upon. And she had a feeling Parker was as deadly without the gun as she was with it.

Parker's head turned immediately, her dark eyes pinning Addy in place.

Whoops.

"I'm just… going… uh, back to the… um… ship?" Addy tried.

Parker's face was carefully blank, smoothed out in a manner it hadn't been moments before. If she hadn't been concerned about the potential volatility of the following moments, Addy would have thought the transformation quite a feat.

"Do you really think that's going to work?" the mercenary challenged, her voice simultaneously sharp and blunt.

"It could work," Addy proposed cautiously. "I'm actually pretty adept at forgetting things. Well, unless they have to do with basic physical and mechanical principles. That's all pretty much burned into—"

She stopped talking when Parker's eyebrows nearly reached her hairline. They traded stares and exchanged silences until Addy was about to move on—she did still need to find the maintenance chief—when Parker gave a quick jerk of her head. Her eyes shut briefly, and when they reopened, resigned irritation swam within. "Look, there's no sense in pretending you didn't see. Pretending doesn't mean it didn't happen," she stated.

True but— "I said forgetting," Addy pointed out. "I'd never pretend."

"Get over here."

Since it didn't seem like she had a choice, and maybe she was a little bit nosy, Addy closed the distance between them until she, too, stood in front of the door. Parker angled her big frame so Addy had a full view through the window. Not sure what she should be expecting, Addy peeked in.

It was a room, simple in form and function. She noted a sleep bunk, a desk, and a chair. And on the bunk, back against the wall, legs hanging but not swinging, was a young man, not more than 20 or so. His eyes were closed, his hands folded in his lap. He might have been sleeping, though the position hardly looked comfortable.

His absolute stillness was loosely unsettling—everything about him suggested life, except for the lack of movement. The few cases of temporal catatonia that she had ever seen had been from a distance and marked by frantic, uncontrolled outbursts of motion. Addy continued to watch, but she wasn't sure what she was supposed to be seeing.

"That's my brother," Parker finally explained. Addy looked closer, wondering if the new information would adjust her perception. She thought maybe she could see... his face sort of... if she squinted the resemblance was—

Eh, she had never been good at that sort of thing. If Parker said it was her brother, then he was her brother. No further clarification needed.

"Last time I saw him, I was fifteen. And he looked exactly the same," Parker added, almost absently.

Okay, some clarification was suddenly needed.

"What? Really?" Addy balked, because sure, Parker wasn't old by any stretch of the imagination—not that she was going to try and guess, because that certainly was another skill she did not possess. But it was nearly impossible to believe the boy in that room was older.

Unless—

Addy began to recall the other perplexing symptom of temporal catatonia.

"How *long* has he been here?" she asked. A weight came into Parker's gaze, as if Addy's response had not quite been what she had been expecting.

"Nearly fifteen years. Went out on a mining job—preliminary search. Was out two years when he caught—developed—the tempers. Didn't know he'd been brought here until almost a year after. This is the first time I've been here."

Parker's voice changed—it wavered but didn't break. "He's still just a *boy*. How is that possible?"

Probably a rhetorical question, Addy thought, considering the quiet manner in which Parker spoke the words. Like a whisper, if Parker had been capable of whispering. But maybe there was something she was supposed to add to keep the silence from descending upon them again. Most of the information she had on what everyone called "the tempers" came from secondhand accounts; people who had known people who had come back from deep space dramatically altered. Or was it more accurate to say unaltered? Frozen in time. She didn't have any medical knowledge—she wasn't a doctor, she was an engineer, which reminded her that she was supposed to be looking for a TK300, except maybe it was more important that she—

Doctor. There had been a doctor. Or a researcher. A dude in a white coat.

"Maybe the doctor could explain—" she started.

Parker waved the thought away before she could finish it. "Not really. Apparently, as far as they can tell, there is no explanation. They have a massive facility like this running for who knows how long, and they don't have a damn clue why or how it causes people to stop aging and lose their damn minds at the same time."

At the end of her speech, Parker swung her fist at the door, but at the last moment pulled up short, resting her palm against the glass instead.

Addy wasn't sure what the right thing to say was, but she knew a change in scenery would be beneficial. Nothing could be accomplished just standing outside a door. Motion was the key to *distraction*.

"You need something to take your mind off of this," she decided, because it was evident that thinking about this was not doing Parker any favors. "You know what would help?"

"Sex?" came Parker's unexpected reply.

"That..." Addy paused, her brows pulling together, "...was what I was going to suggest, yes."

"Yeah, I had a feeling. You're not exactly subtle."

Her frown deepening, Addy mentally flipped back through the past week, trying to pick out any moment where she might have been too forward.

She came up with nothing. "We've barely had three full conversations since being onboard. Two of those involved me asking you to turn the landing jack two quarter turns." She paused. "And that wasn't an innuendo."

Parker nodded. "True. But you don't just talk with your mouth."

It took Addy a moment to parse that, and once she did, it occurred to her that while gazing wistfully at someone might be okay in a novel from three centuries past, in practice it probably came off a little weird. She had to remember shorter jobs came with different.... social parameters.

"Right. Sorry about that. Didn't mean to make you uncomfortable." That was certainly true.

For the first time since Parker had noticed her, she turned from the window. Her lips were curved marginally, less than a grin, but definitely a smile.

"Didn't say it made me uncomfortable."

Addy went back over the conversation. That was also true. She perked up a bit.

"So that means—" she began, hopefully.

"What I need are a couple of drinks. We can talk about the rest another time," Parker countered, in a *this-is-your-final-offer* tone. Addy nodded.

Sounded like a reasonable deal.

She'd find the maintenance guy later.

"I've got the better part of a bottle of scotch back on board," she suggested.

Parker shook her head slowly. "I've got something much better than that," she promised. She shifted her body as if she meant to start moving but then paused, giving one final glance through the window.

"You speak to him at all?" Addy asked, as they began walking.

"No. Doctor said there isn't any indication that he's aware of external stimuli."

"Yeah, that sounds like something a doctor would say."

Parker chuckled. Her shoulders jumped in the most casual gesture Addy had ever seen her make.

"Wouldn't really matter anyway. I doubt he'd even recognize me now."

"Is it because you left your gun on the ship? I mean, I hardly recognized you without it."

Parker's lips pressed together in a manner that suggested she was either not amused or trying very hard not to be. Addy was confident it was the latter.

The lines of Parker's face drew together, and her shoulders tensed.

"He didn't have a sister when he left."

The words were so palpable in the air that Addy could almost see them as they leapt forth from Parker's mouth. She looked beyond them to Parker's face, to the tightness around her eyes and the upward tilt of her chin. To the way the mercenary stared straight forward as if the only thing she was concerned with was continuing to move from one place to another.

"Didn't he? He just didn't know it. But don't worry Parker, anyone would be pleased to see you," Addy replied, looking ahead once more.

Silence drifted between them. Then a quiet "hmph".

"I bet you think you're pretty slick," Parker hummed, with a touch of heat.

Addy relaxed her eyes as the bright light of the patient wing fell back and the dimness of the maintenance tunnel took its place. Her mouth lifted.

"Oh, I'm all right."

Kate hesitated outside of the med-lab. On one hand, she was dying to see that Sam was recovering well firsthand; the short comm message that had come through to the ship had been irritatingly short. On the other hand, the comm message had read, *Am fine. Ensure ship ready for departure.* It was no doubt Sam's way of saying "Don't bother checking up on me." And maybe Kate wouldn't feel the need to check up on her if her message hadn't included more words about her stupid *spacecraft* than it did about her own welfare.

The thought frustrated her into walking forward so that the lab doors slid open a second before she strode through.

Mac looked up from where he was hunched over Sam's cybernetic leg. Completely detached from her body, it appeared more like a piece of machinery than a limb.

In the measured pace of everyday, Mac seemed more distant than he had during the post-assault medical drama, and she wouldn't go so far as to call his cool blue gaze welcoming.

"Hello. Kate, was it," he greeted, without a hint of question coloring his tone.

She paused a step inside the doors, the aggravation that had driven her into motion flagging in the face of his reserved demeanor. It wasn't *his* fault Sam was incapable of appropriate levels of communication.

"Yes, that's me. Um, and you're Mac? A friend of Sam's?"

Friend wasn't the term Sam had used, but Kate couldn't think of a polite term for *someone-who-isn't-fond-of-another-person*.

One of his eyebrows lifted. "I wouldn't call us friends. And it's Dr. Whent, actually."

There was a bite to his second sentence that hadn't been present in the first. Neither the stark white lab coat, close cropped haircut, nor the steady expression changed the fact that he was very young, probably still in his twenties.

Before she could give any response, his face shifted into a wince, followed by a self-deprecating smile.

"Sorry, that was unnecessary. I just wasn't expecting..." One of his hands waved in a vague circle. "...this." His smile widened, and any lingering animosity seemed to disappear with the transformation of his features. "I take it you're here about Sam?"

Kate nodded, a bit thrown by the change in his manner. She cast a glance around the lab, but all the visible beds were empty.

"Where is she?" She tried to keep the panic that leapt up into her throat out of her voice, tried for a normal, acceptable level of distress. "Did... something happen? Is she okay?"

Mac's gaze was questioning. A totally, *reasonable* level of worry for a... shipmate.

He shook his head and held up one hand. "Don't worry, nothing happened. There were a few follow-up tests and scans necessary, and those required the main facility's equipment. Sam is fine. Did you receive the comm?"

There was an odd note in his voice. A subtle rebuke or a gentle concern? She sighed. It didn't matter anyway. She didn't know what she had been expecting.

Nothing. Shouldn't have been *expecting* anything. Just charged emotions due to adrenaline and chaotic events. Nothing that warranted more than seven words in a brief message.

"Yeah. I saw it. I just... Well. Doesn't matter. I'll—we'll—I'll be on the ship if... there's anything..." her voice faded as she realized she wasn't even sure what she was trying to convey. She waited another moment, without knowing what she was waiting *for*, before turning tail the way she had come.

Kate exited the lab with considerably less gusto than she had entered with, and the doors whisked shut behind her. Mac studied them, eyes scrunched at the corners, as if wagering with himself the likelihood they would immediately spring open again. Was she standing just outside the range of the motion sensor, silently arguing with herself?

The doors remained closed.

Shrugging, he bent his head once more over the robotic limb, peering through a magnifying lens at tiny circuitry. Several minutes slipped by before he said to the seemingly empty room:

"You can't avoid her forever, you know. Your ship isn't that big. Neither is this station, for that matter."

No one answered him, yet he continued to work, making minute adjustments to the multifaceted equipment in front of him. Then there was a click followed by three quiet beeps, and a large panel in the med-lab wall slid open. A seat slowly lowered down and out with Sam carefully perched on it, hands curled around the sides to keep her balance. Across the lower half of her face was a breathing apparatus, which she promptly removed the moment the seat came to a stop. Underneath it, her mouth was curled up with displeasure.

"I'm not avoiding anyone. You're the one that said I needed these stupid scans," she rebuked, pulling sensors from various spots on her body.

"I did. I could have told her you were nearly done. But you didn't want anyone to—"

"How much longer is that going to take?" she interrupted, nodding toward his worktable and her disconnected leg. He raised his head, directing at her the same unseen regard he had given the doors moments before.

"Another few hours," he replied, with a complete lack of the urgency Sam would prefer, considering it was her leg on the table. Sam could feel frustration, always at a simmer those days, begin to boil up but he continued before she could complain, "It wouldn't take so long if the calibrations weren't so far off. When was the last time you had a fitting?"

The clipped, clinical question had the effect of knocking her indignation askew as her brain scrambled to recall the mundane information. She rubbed an arm and tried to remember a time when things had been settled enough for *routine*.

"Sam?" he prodded. Her eyes dropped from where they had been idly inspecting the ceiling to his; she wasn't sure if it was the beginnings of impatience or sympathy that she saw in them. Didn't know which she would *prefer*. "How long?" he repeated.

"Not sure. A while."

A quiet settled between them, like a blanket over unspeakable things. She watched the precise movements of his hands as they torqued and twisted his tools with an abundant level of force.

"If you don't have it adjusted at regular intervals, the misalignment will cause other issues. You know that. It was probably causing you to limp, right?" he asked, his voice sharp with accusation. She bristled as the jab hit its mark, even as she told herself she didn't give a damn about his opinion.

"If I agree I'm terrible at maintenance, will it spare me the lecture?"

One of his tools crashed onto the table and his hands came to rest on the surface. He glared at her and while she wanted to take comfort in the fact that she clearly wasn't the only one out of sorts, mostly it made her feel tired.

"I don't even know why I'm helping you. I don't have to do this, you know. I don't owe you anything."

Sam was wildly aware of that and could admit, to herself, it was part of the reason for her seesawing mood. Casting her gaze over the assortment of blinking and beeping machines housed in the relatively small-scale medbay, she tried to reorient to a topic that might placate him for the moment.

"I'm guessing you're helping me because you don't get a lot of opportunities to play bioengineer in your current role as space station doctor."

There was a pause. He gave a exhaled firmly before picking up his tool again. "That's true." Pausing, he flexed the fingers of his right hand before reaching down to pull back one of the panels on her leg. "So, are you going to tell me what brought you all the way out here?""

Rather than respond immediately, she continued to watch him work. Was there any hint in it as to how to approach him? Should she simply lay out everything she knew? Simple. Clean. Unemotional. No bullshit. She liked that idea. There was no sense in pretending there was any sort of relationship between them; Jonah had been their only connection and Jonah was gone.

The only trouble was, she wasn't entirely convinced she could remain aloof when part of the reason she was stuck running a job for an unhinged space mobster was sitting in front of her twiddling around in her detached limb.

"There are a couple of things that I've learned," she finally replied, making a concentrated effort to keep her voice low and even. With her gaze fixed on him, she noted the deliberate relaxation of his shoulders and jaw.

"I learned about your contract with Floodwater," she began, eyes steady.

His hand tightened around the instrument it held.

"I learned Jonah took a job from him to try and get you out of it."

Mac set the tool aside once more.

"I learned he found whatever it was that Floodwater wanted. And," she stopped, waited for his full attention before continuing, "this I haven't learned yet, but I have this *feeling* maybe he told you all about it when we stopped here that last time."

He folded his arms, defiant. "If you've learned all that already, what do you need from me?"

She wanted to snap at him. Grab him by the scruff and give him a good shake. Maybe aim a short, stiff-armed punch to his nose, wipe the expression off his face, the one she couldn't parse. Jonah had never looked at her like that.

But she didn't do any of those things. Because there was one thing she *hadn't* learned, and it was the only thing she was desperate to know.

"Why didn't he tell me, Mac? Why didn't he tell me he'd taken that job?" she asked, because if anyone in the universe might know, it would be him.

The muscles in his face contracted, then went slack with something that looked akin to exhaustion. He ran a hand over his clipped hair in an impatient gesture. "Fuck, Sam. He knew how you felt about Floodwater. No fishing for the Fisher King?"

"And he didn't think I'd make an exception? Like this wouldn't have been more important than some stupid rule?"

Mac shrugged. "Would you have?" he challenged.

Sam pushed against the bench with her hands; if she could have, she would have been up and pacing. The added immobility to her already restricted situation was one more fuel cell in the engine of her vexation.

"I don't know. I want to say yes. But I don't know. I'll never know. Because he didn't ask. He didn't tell me." She could feel her anger burning in her cheeks. "How in the hell did you get mixed up with Floodwater anyway? Why does he have a contract with you?"

He shook his head and grabbed a dry wipe from off the table, rubbed it over his hands as if they were coated in some invisible residue.

"None of your business," he retorted.

Her eyebrows lifted. "Guess again," she shot back.

Mac crumpled up the wipe and tossed it down. "What do you care? Jonah's dead. Job's over. Has nothing to do with you."

Her eyes were like steel. "Guess again," she repeated, quieter. She saw the second comprehension dawned on him; his eyes darted away.

"Shit," was all he said.

"Yeah. Shit. You think I'm hauling around one of his mercs for fun?"

His eyes jumped back. "That big one is his?" She nodded. "I thought you'd just gotten skittish," he admitted.

She thought about cuffing the back of his head for that but figured there was a better way to get recompense.

"I want to know how this whole thing got started. And don't even think about leaving anything out," she warned.

He left some things out.

There wasn't time to or any purpose in going through it all, he argued. What did it matter how Floodwater had gotten his contract? There was no changing the fact, no changing the past.

Sam could have pushed; she thought about it. She had no doubt that Jonah had. Jonah had probably heard the whole damn story.

But they had been brothers. Jonah had been her friend, the one person she trusted more than anyone else but that didn't— couldn't—compete with familial ties. As close as she had been to Jonah, she wasn't foolish enough to think for a second that the closeness transferred at all to Mac. She might have spent the better part of nearly 40 years alone, but that didn't mean she didn't understand the concept of family.

You weren't alone. You had them—Jonah, then Triss and Ollie.

That was different.

She let him gloss over his dealings with Floodwater, let him skip ahead to that last visit, that final conversation.

"Jonah sent me a comm ahead of time, before you got here, telling me that he knew about it. That he was going to fix it." Mac gripped the edge of the table with both hands, his knuckles white. "I told him I didn't need him to fix anything. I didn't know he'd already taken the job. He didn't tell me he'd met with Floodwater until after he got here."

"Did he tell you what Floodwater hired him to do?" Sam asked.

Mac lifted his shoulders. "Pick up some package. Something dumb like that. I was surprised. I thought it would have been something… I don't know… bigger."

"Bigger?"

"Yeah, you know. Like pull some heist or kidnap a Corp VIP."

The idea of Jonah secretly planning some high-stakes activity along the lines of either of those thoughts was so impossible that Sam bounced right past it.

"Did he say what was in the package?"

"No. He just said he'd gotten it and once he got it back to Floodwater, my contract would be voided." His mouth tensed, as if he had tasted something unpleasant. Sam caught it and pressed.

"What? What else did he say?"

"I asked him what made him think Floodwater would keep his end of the deal." Mac's face tightened at the memory, trying to recall the conversation from half a year past. "He said he had insurance. And if he could find the right people, he'd make sure Floodwater was finished."

It was Sam's turn to be perplexed. "What did he mean by that?"

Another shrug. "I thought it was just Jonah being Jonah. Tough, big brother Jonah. Talking big like he always did." He gave a short cough of exasperation; one that sounded painfully similar to the one Sam had given countless times before.

She pushed away the thought. "Did he show you the package?"

Mac shook his head. "No. He said it was on the ship."

"Did he say where?"

His forehead wrinkled. "No. I assume he meant in his quarters."

Sam dragged her fingers against her chin. "It's not on the ship. Not anymore. Not anywhere… I looked," she fumbled slightly, averting her gaze. The fact that it had been Floodwater's creeps that had searched her ship still rubbed wrong.

Mac looked confused. "Okay. So then why did you come all the way out here? Did you think he gave it to me? You could have just sent a comm, saved yourself a trip." He tapped a finger against the cybernetic limb. "And a leg," he jabbed.

She let the weak jest slide past. "I think he might have hidden it on the emergency shuttle."

The information didn't seem to sink in. "The shuttle," he echoed dully, as if he were trying to follow her logic but was failing.

"It's the only place we haven't looked. The only place he had access to before the attack," she pointed out.

"Okay. But you said the pirates took the shuttle."

"They did," Sam confirmed.

"Okay, well it's been six months so even if they haven't scrapped it, they've definitely burned out the locator and any other beacons," Mac reasoned.

"Yeah, probably."

"So, what? Are you planning on flying around the Secession Sector until you run into some pirates and then just hope *they* know where it is?"

"It sounds stupid when you put it like that."

"It is stupid!" he agreed heatedly.

"I know that!" she roared back. "But what other option is there?" She stared at him, willing him to answer, wanting *someone* to tell her the next step that would pull her out of this fucking *black hole* she was being dragged into.

Spinning away from her, Mac paced to the other side of the room. He taken only a few steps back when he stopped.

"Did Jonah touch the shuttle?"

"He was *on* it, wasn't he? Kinda hard not to touch it."

Mac cut a hand through the air in a frustrated wave. "No, I mean did he do any upgrades to it? Any software enhancements?"

Sam blew out a breath. "Christ, probably. The shuttle came with the ship; it's been fifteen years. I don't think there was a part he didn't do something to." *Except for the gravity coils*, her mind added unnecessarily.

Something approaching a smile crossed Mac's face. It was sharper than Jonah's, with none of the charm or easy amusement.

"Then he probably buried his signature somewhere in the code. You could track that. Well," he amended, the grin shifting into a grimace. "Not *you*, but someone competent could."

She lifted an eyebrow. "Someone like you?"

His face went dismissive. "You have an engineer. She could dig it out."

"But you already know it, don't you? I bet you've seen his code. You could do it faster."

Sam paused and searched for what to say. What would or could convince him. She wasn't good at that part. Jonah had been the talker. She shouldn't have ignored him so much when he was schmoozing.

"I need your help, Mac. Maybe if I can track this thing down, I can finish what he started," she tried. Closure, right? Those grief guides always talked about closure.

Not that she'd read any of them all the way through.

She could almost see the indifference slide down over Mac like a wall, neatly separating them.

"It won't bring him back, will it?"

Another pause and Sam shook her head. Let out a long breath through her nose. "No. It won't." She plowed ahead. What was there to lose now? Couldn't afford pride, or to pretend the situation was anything less than dire.

"But it's not about him. Or you. Or me. Not anymore. My… friend? Kate? She's on his list now."

Mac continued to stare at the table, the subtle tilt of his head the only sign he was listening.

"If we don't do something, next time it'll be someone else. Maybe someone you care about. His list is never empty."

He remained silent, and Sam had nothing more she could think of to say. No other reason to offer up, no incentive that might convince him. She couldn't even think of an insult or threat that might goad him into action.

To top it all off, she couldn't storm out in frustration, because half of her mobility was on the fucking table.

She opened her mouth to try again; there had to be something that she could—

Exhaling loudly, Mac threw his head back and glared upwards. The gesture was so much like one she was always making that Sam nearly choked on the unknown words building in her throat. She swallowed them back.

"This won't be quick," he warned. Nodding, she motioned to the table.

"Well, fix my damn leg first."

Alcohol on a spaceship had the same perks and pitfalls as it did on planet or station, with a few notable exceptions. For starters, one had to keep a careful eye on the supply, a feat oddly more difficult than keeping track of foodstuffs or medical necessities. Maybe it had something to do with the regularity at which one drink became two drinks, became five drinks, and then who emptied the damn bottle and put it back in the pantry unit? On planet, one can run to the store. On satellite or station, there's the routine supply delivery. On a ship in between transfers, there's only the hope the next waystation has extra they're willing to trade. Sudden dryness could be a shock to the system.

And poker night was never the same.

In the opposite vein, if one got too drunk and ended up missing a ship's departure time, it could be a very, very, very long time before another ship came along. It was worse for those who liquor had a disruptive hold on—being left on an outer colony or deep satellite could easily be a five-year sentence without an actual corporate ruling.

Addy had seen both happen—there was always one fresh-faced recruit or long-timer who couldn't bear to stare into the wide expanse of space without a heavy dose of liquid spirits.

She didn't think that was going to be a problem with Parker, who had been nursing a tumbler of unknown amber liquid for nearly an hour. The mercenary had poured it from an unlabeled bottle. Addy was on her second glass and hadn't yet been able to identify the taste. She had enough experience to know if she couldn't figure it out by that point, a third tumbler would *not* help, despite repeated assurances from her brain.

Parker drank in slow, thoughtful sips, and it did not appear as if she were trying hard to keep her mind off her brother and his condition. Addy assumed that was what she was thinking of, since the furrowed line between her brows remained firmly in place. Even the presence of Nata, fluffy and stretched adorably in front of the mercenary did nothing to loosen it, though Parker was stroking her long thick fingers through his fur to loud appreciative purrs.

Addy paused after taking her own small swallow. A thought pushed its way through the other increasingly fuzzy thoughts until it reached the front of her mind.

Maybe *she* was supposed to be providing a distraction?

Was it time to bring up sex again?

Should maybe wait a little longer, she decided. Just to be sure. Light conversation would be good. Something easy and non-confrontational, a little fun banter. She considered the possibilities briefly before settling on:

"So... why'd you start working for Floodwater anyway?"

Nailed it.

The look Parker gave in response was laced with suspicion, as if she assumed a hidden reason behind the question. Had she called Addy on it, the engineer wouldn't have had an answer beyond general interest. She knew who Floodwater was, of course. Knew his reputation and by extension, the reputation of the people who "worked" for him. And she did wonder how closely Parker herself skewed toward that reputation. So far, the mercenary had the "ruthlessly efficient" and "highly dangerous" aspects down cold. She figured the "complete badass" bit was simply part of Parker's natural charm.

Parker continued to glower, but Addy waited. She was getting used to the cautious silences. Finally, Parker leaned back in the booth, her shoulders settling minutely as she took another of her sips. Nata's head lifted up at the absence of pets to shoot her an accusing stare, though she showed no notice.

"I was part of the Corporate Corps for a while. Negotiation mostly. Didn't like the way they handled things, though."

Negotiation. Not a skill Addy would have thought to attribute to her. "What kind of things?" she cut in. Corporate reach didn't fully extend into the wilds of deep space, so she had to admit she was a bit out of touch with the current state of the universe. Politics could be so *boring*, but at least it was out of the realm of the tempers and its effect on families.

"Disputes. Sure, with big ones between the Major Companies, they would respond quick enough, but the smaller guys? The independents? More likely they wouldn't even raise a finger."

Addy could recall hearing similar talk in the crew halls between shifts. The little guys were always getting the short end of the stick.

"And Floodwater? He gets... involved?" she asked, carefully, because you could technically call extortion, assault, and the host of other things the Fisher King was said to engage in as being "involved."

Challenege flashed in Parker's eyes, but Addy didn't get the feeling it was directed at her.

"Yeah, he does. Look, it's not all busting kneecaps and hush money. He helps a lot of people that don't exactly have any other options."

"And how much does he charge them for that?"

Parker shrugged but her gaze skittered away. "Pay him or go under. At least there's a choice," she points out.

Addy thought there might be a specific term for that kind of "choice", but it evaded her.

It was probably fine to bring up sex again, anyway.

She was about to do so when Kate stepped into the galley. Taking in the bottle at the center of the table and the glasses split between them, her gaze tracked first to Addy, then to Parker, and then back to Addy.

"Is this a private party?" she asked with a levity sounding only partially forced. On the surface, it felt like it was directed at them both, but Addy caught the quick glance shot her way.

One didn't have to be a genius at math to know that three bodies lowered the probability of sex except in certain circumstances, none of which Addy was currently interested in. Plus, there was the whole *taking-the-mind-off-of-upsetting-events* shtick she assumed was still supposed to be happening.

She resisted scratching her forehead. It was exponentially easier on a three-year job, where the only potential pitfall in sexual partner selection was getting involved with someone who might get themselves stranded. Instead of answering, she took a drink and let Parker field the question.

Parker's response was to lift the bottle in Kate's direction. After a moment's hesitation, Kate retrieved a metal cup from one of the cabinet units and held it out over the table. Parker gave a generous pour and when she finished, Kate brought the cup to her nose and sniffed.

"What is it?" she asked, and it occurred to Addy that asking had not been an option she had contemplated enough.

"Something a friend of mine rigs up special."

Kate looked down into the cup. She took a taste and her eyes widened as she swallowed.

"Some friend," she managed.

Parker smiled, a full grin, crooked at the corners, that did absolutely nothing to lessen the ferocity in her face.

"Yeah, it's strong as hell. Couple glasses of it'll get most people giddy," she agreed. Addy found herself frowning into her own glass.

"Why'dya give me two?" she asked. To her surprise, Parker turned to her and winked.

"Wanted to see what you looked like giddy."

Winked. Addy sat up straighter. *That* was a good sign.

Kate chuckled and drained the rest of her cup in one go. She set it down on the table and tipped her head as if ruminating on something profound. After a few seconds, she shifted her head back and forth.

"It's good, but wasted on me," she declared cryptically. Confusion stole over Parker's features, but Addy watched the subtle ripple along the underside of Kate's jaw.

"You've got the acetaldehyde mutation," she guessed out loud.

Acknowledgement washed over Kate's face while Parker's puzzlement only grew.

"What?" the mercenary asked.

"She's a Purif—"

"Don't call me that," Kate warned. Addy held up a hand and readjusted her thinking. Her thoughts sloshed in her head.

"She has a gene—well, a couple of genes that allow her body to metabolize certain substances faster than average," she explained. At least, she thought that was what she explained. Her tongue honestly felt a bit numb.

"What?" Parker repeated.

Addy made another adjustment to her thoughts. Slosh.

"She doesn't get drunk. Can't really."

"Oh." Parker nodded and squinted. "That's rough," she added.

Kate shrugged. "Well, really strong alcohols can sometimes give me a little buzz if I want them to. And on the upside, I don't really have to worry about accidentally ingesting poison," she reasoned.

"Is that... a big concern where you're from?" Parker asked. It sounded to Addy like maybe the contents of her single tumbler were starting to catch up with her. Addy felt comfortable enough to reach over and give her arm a light pat to show solidarity. Only her depth perception was a little off, so she ended up smacking the tabletop next to the mercenary's hand. It was enough to irritate Nata, who rolled up and off the table in a quick motion. He exited the room with his tail fluffed.

"No, but it was a problem back in the last century especially among rising executives. There was a lot of experimentation with genes..." Addy lost her train of thought for a second. "... anyway, it was a big mess, they shut down a bunch of programs that got a *little* too out of hand but by then they'd already had some success with human trials..." she faded again and glanced between Kate and Parker, trying to gauge their interest in the topic.

Both women were watching her with nearly identical perplexed expressions on their faces, quite a feat considering the vast differences in their bone structures.

"What?" Addy demanded.

"Well, it sounded like you just mumbled something about hairless dogs and twin intakes," Kate replied. She exchanged a look with Parker. "I was just waiting to see where you were gonna go with that."

Addy looked back down at the drink in her hand. Pointing at it, she looked at Parker. "What is *in* this?" she hiccupped. And then drank some more.

Parker laughed, her head dipping back to lean against the booth seat. "I don't ask questions. I just enjoy it."

Sound advice.

"We ought to offer the captain a shot or two. Might help with her disposition," Parker continued with another chuckle.

If Addy hadn't raised her eyes then, she would have missed it. But she caught the twitch in Kate's cheek at the mention of Sam.

"How is the captain doing, anyway?" she asked, out of curiosity and also—no, pretty much all curiosity.

Another twitch. "According to Mac, fine."

"What'd Sam say?"

Kate arms folded around herself. "Nothing. She wasn't there. They were running some tests on her somewhere else."

Addy could feel the tension in the room rising, which was the opposite direction she wanted it to go. Only one thing to do.

"Well. Who wants to open the engine core and watch the particles interact?"

To her astonishment, neither Kate nor Parker gave any response. Parker took another taste from her glass, while Kate glared at the other side of the room. Addy frowned and wiggled her jaw slightly; had she spewed nonsense again? Usually an offer to open the engine core got more of a reaction.

"Who do you think they were?" Kate asked abruptly.

Addy shot a glance over at Parker to see if… yep, just as mystified.

"What?" Addy asked.

"Who?" Parker added.

Kate shifted her gaze back to them; already Addy could see the haze of intoxication was gone. "The ones on the ship that attacked the station?"

Addy felt her mouth pull downward further than it already was. "Whoever they were, they owe me four SS526s and the six hours it's gonna take to replace them."

Clearly vexed, Kate slouched in the booth. "At the end of that firefight, it didn't look like any of them would be up to giving anything to anyone," she stated with a sour note. She nodded her head toward Parker. "What do you think?"

Parker flicked a hand dismissively. "It's a medical and research facility with no security stations nearby. There are all sorts of folks who would find that an appealing target. But that's station security's problem, not mine," she replied, disinterested.

"What if it's not?" Kate protested.

Lifting an eyebrow, Parker asked, "What do you mean?"

"The ship came in on our heels. Maybe it was tracking us. Maybe we were the target."

Parker shook her head with slow confidence. "Only an idiot would target this ship," she scoffed.

Unease slithered down the back of Addy's neck, and she sat forward to try and dislodge it. Instead, it perched like a snake coiled around a tree branch waiting to drop on unsuspecting prey. She wasn't going to ask, but she knew Kate would.

And sure enough… "What's that mean?"

Addy wasn't sure if it was courage or naivety powering the question; it was anyone's guess how long either would last.

Draining the rest of the liquor, Parker set her glass down on the table with a quiet click. "It means that no one in the galaxy is going to attack a ship that belongs to Floodwater."

"This ship doesn't belong to Floodwater," Kate argued.

"It sure as hell does. Until you put that package in his hands, as far as the universe is concerned, this whole boat is his property. And if Sam is lucky, she'll get it back in the end."

"What if she's not lucky?"

"You better *hope* she is."

twelve

"**I** told you this was going to take a while."

Sam eased back from where she had been leaning over Mac's shoulder and scowled. He remained as he had been for most of the past two days: slouched in front of a screen, the contents of which made Sam a little dizzy to look at.

Not that it stopped her from staring. Neither did the fact she had no idea what she was looking for. She hoped it would be something obvious, like a pop-up message that read "Target acquired." Presently, it bore a strong resemblance to the maintenance sequence she sometimes had to run the ship's main computer through.

That only took eight hours, max. Not 48 and counting.

"It's a massive distance from here to the border and beyond. First the signal has to travel that far. Then it has to search any databases it hooks onto. Then the signal has to return."

"You already told me this," Sam pointed out.

"Yes, and it doesn't appear to have sunken in, because you've been practically perched on my shoulder for the whole time we've been running the search."

She caught herself tilting forward again and straightened. Cupping her elbows, she deliberately walked over to the room's long window. The swirling red and orange clouds of the planet below captivated her for a few beats before her head swiveled back toward the screen.

"That's not true. You locked the room down twice for sleep breaks."

Mac turned in his chair, hands linked in front of his chest. "Did you sleep at all?"

"Some," she replied. An hour. Maybe two. Mostly she'd just restlessly rolled around on one of the lab bunks. She heard a sigh escape him and when she looked, he was watching her with a mixture of exasperation and frustration.

"Sam. What are you really going to do if, and I do mean a huge *if*, you find this thing?" he asked bluntly.

She turned her back to him and pressed her hands down onto the sill of the window. Despite the iciness of space inches away, the surface was warm beneath her skin.

"Suppose Jonah did find some grand evidence against Floodwater. Suppose it still exists and you manage to get your hands on it. What then? Who the fuck are you going to *give* it to?" he pressed, his voice full of all the same doubt and incredulousness she felt but had been trying not to dwell on.

She had been asking herself that question for the past two days; in between searching through navigational charts, recent incident reports, shipping routes, and memories she dredged for any hint in conversations, facial expressions, or even goddamn body language that would have clued her into Jonah's plan. And further back, where she'd managed to tuck it away for the moment because she didn't have time to spend trying to dissect it, was what was happening with Kate and—

Sam stopped before the thought could escape the tiny box she had crammed it into. She shifted again, setting her back against the sill. In two days, she hadn't exactly come up with a solution, but there were at least a couple options.

One of them might not even get them all killed.

"Could turn it over to one of the Big Five. They'd love to get him into their courts. Probably jump at the chance to dismantle his business. Or absorb it," she proposed.

His hands tented together and the first two fingers pressed against his lips. "Would they, though? How do you know he doesn't have ties to any of them? The guy's been around forever; don't you think if they wanted him gone, they would have managed it already?"

The thought had occurred to her. But— "Well, the UNE isn't an option. It barely has a presence out here and almost no authority. Even if I could somehow get him to Earth, I don't know that there's anything they could do. They ceded jurisdiction in deep space matters to the Cores," she reasoned. She had never been to Earth, but all the stories gave the same general account—bit of a backwater, really.

"Unless he's violating one of the Fundamentals," Mac pointed out. Sam raised her hands to her forehead and rubbed at the dull ache pulsing at the center.

"He's probably violating several of the Fundamentals. And if Jonah had proof of that and didn't tell me, I'm going to be doubly pissed at him."

"Are you?"

"What?"

"Are you pissed at him?"

She started to give the kneejerk answer—*of course* she was pissed he left her with this shit to clean up—but the weight in his tone made her pause. The brief repose gave the feelings enough time to slip in before she could block them.

"No. Not at him. I mean, maybe I was for a little while when I first found out. When it felt like a total betrayal. But now... Now I'm just pissed at myself."

"Why?"

Another question she had been asking herself; another reason she'd been racking her memories. And the two answers she had come up with were both like a blow to the solar plexus.

"Because either he had a reason not to tell me, something I did to make him think he couldn't trust me, that I couldn't handle it. Or he *did* try to tell me, and I just didn't hear it."

The words hung in the air between them. Sam could nearly see them in the shifting light cast from the screen. She wondered if she should try and pull them back. If they'd done more damage than good.

Sam was by no means fluent in Mac's expressions after two days of close proximity, but she knew it wasn't anger he was looking at her with. And when he spoke, his voice was almost gentle.

"Maybe he didn't want to get you involved. Maybe he was trying to keep you safe."

She had thought about that too. The reality was— "When Floodwater is involved, no one is safe." Jonah had been smart enough to know that.

"Jonah wasn't always that smart," he replied, as if he were reading her mind.

It was true. For someone with a genius-level IQ, Jonah's unwritten rule of action had been "Act first, consider later." The fact might have made her laugh if not for the nagging feeling she *had* that she had missed some communication from him. Things had always been easy between them. Maybe she let them get too easy. Maybe if she had put more effort into reaching out before, it wouldn't feel so impossible now.

Maybe she wasn't as good at being alone as she had always believed.

Mac stood up and crossed to the other side of the room. He brought another screen to life with a few quick taps, this one above a small dispensary slot in the wall. After a few beeps, a cup appeared in the slot, followed by a hiss. When he turned back to Sam, he held the mug out to her. She shook her head, and he sipped from it instead.

"What about the Peacekeepers?" he offered. And like that, the conversation was set aside.

She shook her head, grateful for the change in subject. "Too unpredictable."

"They're UNE sanctioned," Mac noted.

"That's because the UNE has no sway over them whatsoever. Easier to say it's a sanctioned group than admit you can't do anything about them."

"They are supposedly neutral; you wouldn't have to worry about Floodwater having his hooks in them."

"Supposedly. Look at their record. They're more like hired hitmen than bounty hunters."

"Are you worried about the personal safety of Miles

Floodwater?" he asked, with no small measure of doubt.

"I sure as hell don't want to send a hit squad after him. That's not justice. That's revenge."

Mac spread his arms out wide. "Aren't they the same thing?"

Sam met his gaze and held it. His eyes were the same shape as his brother's; had she ever realized that before? But there was a coolness to them that didn't remind her of Jonah at all—perhaps a relic of loss, or servitude, or maybe just the vacuum of deep space.

Whatever it was, it reminded her people were not always what they seemed. Even the ones you thought you knew best.

"Not to me," she replied finally, shifting her hands to her forehead again. The dull ache had grown into a full-blown headache wrapping all the way around her skull. Mac took a long drink from his cup before setting it back down into the slot it had come from. A couple touches to the screen had it retracting into the wall, out of sight.

"Look, Sam. Why don't you go lie down for a bit? I'll send a comm the minute anything hits."

She dug her finger and thumb into the bridge of her nose to try and relieve some of the pressure. Even though every single part of her body was all but begging for rest, sleep was the last thing she wanted. There was no comfort in sleep. Just memories and no way to escape them. At least while she was awake, she had a chance of fighting them away.

"I'm fine," she insisted.

"You're not fine. I can see your headache from here. You had cybernetic links severed and reattached less than *seventy-two* hours ago. Your body needs rest. It makes absolutely no sense for you to stand here, staring at a screen. It could take weeks to get anything. That's if it even works at all."

Ping.

Both of their heads swung toward the screen. Sam searched for the hoped-for pop-up window but there was only the same cascade of endless code.

"What was that?" she demanded.

Mac had already retaken his seat and had his nose almost

pressed to the screen, his nimble fingers cruising over the bottom of the display.

"Huh," was his reply.

"Huh?" Sam repeated, with no small measure of impatience.

He nodded. "Yeah. There was a match. Off a relay comm about… four sectors from here. A bounce signal."

"Meaning?"

"Meaning it's not from the source, so hold your excitement. The signal probably originated much further out. In order to link with a factory update, it needed to boost off this relay."

"Can it be traced back to the original source?" she asked, peering over his shoulder, the pain in her head steady but nearly forgotten.

"Well yeah, but—"

"Send those coordinates to the ship," she ordered, already jogging out the door.

It didn't occur to Sam, until she entered the docking bay and saw her ship sitting in the middle of the room like a waiting puppy, that she hadn't been on board in nearly a week. She stopped and stared, not sure if she could remember the last time she'd spent—

That wasn't true. She remembered; she just didn't want to.

Shoving the thought aside, she stormed forward, her stride long and mostly even, save for a barely noticeable hitch. Her right leg felt strong and sturdy—thanks, she knew, to Mac's careful repairs. The hitch, though—that was just muscle memory.

As she approached, she could see the cargo loading ramp lowered. Nearby, one of the two repair lifts loomed. Addy stood atop it, arms disappearing into a panel below the nose of the ship.

Parker was there as well, the tall mercenary leaning casually against the side of the lift. Pulling her arms back, Addy flexed her fingers and then bent over the railing. She pointed with one hand and pulled her goggles down around her neck with the other. Her mouth moved and Parker stooped down, picked a cylindrical object off the ground, and passed it up to her. Sam couldn't be 100% sure because of the distance, but she thought she saw the engineer wink as she took it.

Wink.

Parker's response was a roll of her eyes and something suspiciously like a grin.

A grin.

Shit.

Before she could even consider what the fuck she was supposed to think about that development, Addy caught sight of her. The engineer set down the object she was holding and raised a hand in greeting.

"Hey, Captain. Looking much improved!"

Sam's shoulders hunched at the comment, but she nodded briskly and tried to shrug off the unease. She let her eyes roam over the ship's hull, taking in the scorch marks from the laser blasts and the numerous signs of repair.

"How soon can we take off?" she asked. The engineer pursed her lips and let them fall open with a light *pop*.

"Just finishing up the last install now. I'll need to run a QC, and if everything checks out, then I'd say two, maybe three hours at the most."

Parker shifted beside the lift, raising one arm and resting it against the bottom railing; the metal frame squeaked with the redistribution of weight.

"We going somewhere?" she asked, an unusual pitch to her voice that Sam was not inclined to decipher. In her peripheral vision, she thought she saw Addy's face twist up with concern.

She ignored them, heading up the ramp instead. Leave a crew on their own for a few days...

"Yeah. We're leaving as soon as the ship is ready," she replied, boots stomping against the grating as she struggled to ignore the sudden, strange inclination she felt to soften her footsteps. As if she was trying to sneak onto her own damn ship.

She was halfway up the gangway when Kate appeared at the top. The other woman's head was lowered, and she held a small assortment of containers in her hands.

"Addy, did you need bonding compound or fluxum tape? And I couldn't find anything labeled chlorofrax so I grabbed everything in your…"

Kate raised her head and her sentence trailed away as soon as she saw Sam, who was rooted in place, as if her legs were super magnets stuck to the ramp.

Stupid to get involved, her mind whispered. Sam felt her mouth drop open, despite the fact she had no idea what she was about to say and no desire to say *anything*.

"Sam! Goddammit, Sam, wait! I'm coming with you." Mac's voice rang out and Sam's mouth snapped shut. She twisted around and took in the sight of Mac hustling across the docking bay, as if he expected the ship to take off at any moment. A soft bag was slung over one of his shoulders, not fully closed, with a bit of fabric and part of a canteen sticking out. He might have looked nothing like his brother, but for a split second, it was Jonah who Sam saw scrambling toward her.

"Goddammit Sam, wait! Don't even think about closing that door!"

"We're two minutes past our dock time. Do you know what this is going to cost me?"

"Nothing, because I was the one signing us out!"

"Oh, that's right. Must've slipped my mind."

"Don't you think that joke's getting a little old? Ha, ha. Leave without me. I mean, you do it at every port. It can't possibly still be funny to you."

"The funny part is that you keep agreeing to sign us out."

Sam blinked and it was Mac's scowling face directly in front of her. She ran a hand through her hair, barely resisting grabbing hold of it and tugging.

"What the hell do you think you're doing?" she demanded. Mac adjusted the strap of his bag from where it had fallen down his shoulder.

"I'm coming with you," he repeated. From the look on his face, she could tell he certainly *thought* that was true.

She bit back the response that immediately jumped into her mouth; clamped her teeth to further hold it in. Down the gangway,

Addy and Parker were watching the encounter with entirely too much interest and amusement.

Sam jerked her head toward the ship and stalked inside, not waiting to see if he would follow. She marched through the cargo bay, past the engine room, down the main corridor, turned sharply before the crew quarters, and stopped in front of one of the only sections of the ship that currently still required a passkey. With a steady hand, she punched in the short sequence and was stepping in almost before the door slid open.

She wasn't sure what had driven her to choose the med-bay as the battleground for the impending argument—maybe the proximity of first aid supplies or the fact it was the room farthest from the cargo bay and potential eavesdroppers—but she was grateful she was too irritated to have any kind of flashbacks of Ollie inhabiting the space, except she was still *thinking* about him and, fuck, she wasn't sure how much more crowded her brain could get.

With more anger than was probably warranted, she whipped around as Mac strode through the door.

"You are not going anywhere," she shot off immediately, one hand cutting through the air. "You are staying right here on this fucking station until I finish this job, and then you can do whatever the fuck you want."

Mac's eyes narrowed. "You need me to trace the signals. Wasn't that the whole point of coming here?" he argued, his voice rising.

Sam shook her head. "Now that we have a starting point, I can trace the signals. You know that. And even if for some reason I can't, Addy'll be able to," she retorted.

"If I share the coordinates," he warned, fists clenched at his sides.

She didn't even bother responding to the implied threat, merely stared at him flatly until he deflated.

"What if the signal is corrupt and you lose it? We're talking lightyears of space here; it's a possibility. An engineer isn't going to know how to pick it back up again. But I will. You know that. That's why you asked me in the first place," he countered, shifting tactics.

Sam ignored the part of her brain that felt it might be prudent to at least consider his logic.

"You're not coming," she said again, reaching for a serenity she had never before managed, but damn if she didn't want it now. Anything that would keep her from bending. From swaying instead of holding firm. She *owed* Jonah.

Mac turned away, giving a nearby crate a swift kick that he probably would have liked to have delivered to her instead. That was fine. He could be as pissed as he wanted. She had made a lot of mistakes in her life; this would not be one of them.

He glared at the sterile white cabinets bolted to the far wall, the line of his shoulders rigid. She considered, briefly, how long to let him stand there; she could always have Parker escort him off if for some reason he—

"Is this because of Jonah? Did you guys make some dumb pact about me?"

Sam started at the question, confused. The first part she could understand easily enough, but the second—

"What?" she asked.

Mac waved his hands through the air as if trying to motion to everything around him at the same time. "You know, like 'Promise me you'll never take my baby brother into danger' or some stupid shit?" He lowered his voice as he spoke, as if trying to mimic Jonah's cadence.

Sam stared at him, the idea and the impression running together in her mind until she couldn't help it—she chuckled. She tried to imagine Jonah speaking those very words or anything even remotely similar and a full-blown laugh escaped her. Something about the term *baby brother*... she laughed again, and some of the tension balling up inside her chest released.

"No, nothing like that," she replied with a shake of her head, her lips still curving. It occurred to her that, if she and Jonah had their positions reversed, Jonah would have offered his brother a spot on the ship before they were even fully docked.

Of course, if their positions had been reversed, they never

would have been in the position in the first place, because *she* didn't make shady deals with space mobsters.

Focus.

"Then what's the problem? You know you could use my help. The help, to remind you, you came all the way here for," he insisted.

Sam tried to hold onto the irritation she had been feeling moments ago, but the unexpected laughter seemed to have washed it out of reach.

"I already got your brother killed, Mac. I don't want to add you to my conscience," she confessed, laying her metaphorical cards out on the table. A royal flush, as far as she was concerned.

"You didn't get him killed."

Sam shook her head. "I put him on that ship."

"And did you force him out of the airlock?"

The visual that came to mind was sharp and stark. "No."

"Then his death isn't on you. I wanted it to be," Mac admitted, quietly. "I wanted it to be your fault because there was no one else to lay it on except some faceless pirates a million lightyears away. But it's not your fault. Jonah made his own choices."

Sam shook her head again, not willing to accept that. "On a ship, the captain makes the choices. Crew follows orders. Jonah was my best friend. But he was still my crew."

"It would piss him off to hear you say that."

"It always did."

Mac was silent. Determination crept across his face until it covered it. "Let me help you. Let me help you, for him. For Jonah."

Folding her arms, she pressed back.

"You've got a contract here, remember? Don't think Floodwater would look too kindly on you abandoning your place."

He shrugged. "Isn't this job supposed to nullify my contract? How much could he really care if he's so willing to release me? And fuck him," he spat suddenly, his eyes alight. "Who do I have left for him to threaten me with?"

Yourself, Sam thought, but the word didn't make it past her lips. Because it didn't matter; even if Mac stayed on station, performed his job perfectly, and never said another thing about his employer, Floodwater could still decide to "nullify" his contract in a completely different manner. Would she still feel responsible then? She watched her perfectly dealt hand fold.

Part of her continued to refuse. There were already too many people on the ship she felt beholden to. She had never wanted to put herself in the position of captaining another crew, of being responsible for multiple lives. It was starting to feel like some horrible sense of déjà vu.

What ultimately decided it was the look on his face. Strong, unwavering, just a little ticked off and so completely sure he was right. She couldn't help seeing Jonah when she looked at him now. And she'd never been able to say no to Jonah.

Well. Except for once. And look how that had turned out.

"You've got two hours to get whatever you need together," she ordered, before starting toward the door, wondering if the mistake had been then or now.

Something akin to a smirk passed over Mac's face. He turned to let her pass. "I've already got everything in my bag," he declared, motioning to the soft rucksack he'd dropped. Sam gave it a cursory glance and shook her head.

"Doubt it," she replied, as the door slid open again. Waiting just behind it was Nata, sitting with his tail idly flicking back and forth. He started to push forward against Sam's legs and then paused, his tail curling up almost in question as his eyes darted to Mac.

Mac looked at the cat in shock. "You kept Nata."

Sam fixed her eyes straight ahead. "He sheds everywhere," she replied, slipping past Nata into the hall. She paused but did not look back. "Make sure to bring your med tote. You just signed on as ship's doctor. Hope you like the space," she added, motioning to the room a second before the door slid shut.

On her way to the main bridge, Sam nearly collided with Addy as the engineer burst in from the engine room, a small black box in one hand and a data tablet in the other. Since she already had an up-to-date report on the ship's status, Sam didn't see a reason to chat but stopped when Addy held up a hand in a bid for her attention. She bit back her impatience when the engineer didn't immediately look up from the tablet.

"Something wrong with the repairs?" she asked, after another moment had passed without any words being offered.

Addy's forehead wrinkled but she said nothing. Her thumb swiped over the tablet repeatedly until something must have appeared to her liking because her brow cleared, and she glanced up.

"Nope, repairs are finished. Running the checks now. This is something else," she replied, and held up the black box.

Sam raised an eyebrow. "What is it?"

Addy appeared uncharacteristically perplexed. "Dunno."

Frowning, and annoyed to find herself curious, Sam looked closer. "Looks like some kind of casing," she hazarded, hearing the impatience in her own voice.

"Sure, but to what?"

Digging at the tense muscles of her neck, Sam lifted her other hand toward the nearest wall. "There are a million things on board that could have a housing like that. Where did you find it?"

"In the engine room. Attached to the core with a CVC cable."

Sam dropped her hand, her scowl deepening. "And that's… not good?" she settled on because things with acronyms usually weren't great.

Addy brought the box closer to her own face, rotating it slowly. "Could be nothing. The guy that mucked around in your engine before me—"

"Jonah," Sam supplied automatically.

"—yeah, sure. He made a lot of modifications to the original specs. It might have been something he was planning but didn't get around to actually installing."

"It's possible," Sam agreed, but there was a nagging little tug in the back of her brain that she couldn't quite close in on. It wasn't like Jonah to leave unfinished projects, at least as far as the engine went. He'd bug her until she bought whatever parts he needed.

"Anyway, just wanted to let you know," Addy finished before shuffling back toward the engine room.

She was nearly at the end of the corridor before Sam called her name.

"What would you attach to the core with a C-whatever cable?"

Addy considered it, head tilting back, as if the answer were written on the ceiling.

"Could maybe rig a thermal boost. Wouldn't do much on a core this size, but every little bit counts to some people. It'd be a smart place for a syphon setup."

"What would that do?"

"Divert a small amount of power, enough to run an ancillary unit. Something you'd want kept under the radar. The power drain isn't usually enough to show on any systems check."

Sam bit the inside of her cheek and mulled over the information. "Anything else?"

Addy scratched the side of her temple. "Not off the top of my head."

"Do me a favor? Think about it some more."

The engineer gave a quick little salute and started to retreat again.

"Oh, and Addy?"

The engineer paused.

"You and Parker…" Sam began and then shook her head. "You know what? Never mind."

Addy grinned. "Is the doctor going to be joining us?"

Sam nodded. "Any problems with that?"

Shaking her head, Addy turned the corner, her voice trailing behind her. "Just good to know who you're flying with."

thirteen

Time was definitely a problem in space, Kate reflected.

There was the pace of things, of waiting and its effect on the human psyche. More specifically on *her* psyche. Kate felt like she was mostly getting used to that part—it wasn't so different from waiting on planet. The only variable was the artificial gravity, which did not improve the sensation at all.

It was the absence of daylight, or more specifically day *and* night, that was the bigger problem for her. The lighting throughout the ship was set to mimic sunlight, and the lights in her cabin automatically dimmed when the clock blinked past twenty hundred hours, but neither of those things seemed able to convince her brain to fall into any sort of remotely normal sleep pattern.

Which was why, at what would have been around three in the morning back on planet, she was in the galley, tucked into the booth with a cup of tea that was slowly getting cold.

Sleeplessness was not something she was accustomed to; at home it was a rare night that she did not sleep straight through until morning. Nor was it an experience she was enjoying. During the "day" she felt foggy and off balance, but for some reason, once "night" rolled around, her mind was filled with random, infuriating thoughts about random, infuriating people.

Well, not precisely *random*. But *definitely* infuriating.

It was a problem. She was half-worried she was going to accidentally fall into the core if she didn't get a decent amount of rest soon.

That is, she *would* be worried, if Addy ever let her *near* the core.

What she needed was a distraction. Addy already had one, if the completely unsubtle looks passing between her and Parker were any indication. Of course, that kind of distraction probably wouldn't help, considering the current subject of those infuriating thoughts.

Maybe it would help if she could figure out what she was supposed to *do*. Apologize? Pretend it hadn't happened? Apologize *and* pretend it hadn't happened? The only clue she had been given by the other party was extreme avoidance, which seemed to at least lean toward the *pretend-it-never-happened* option.

Irritated with herself, Kate swiped a finger over the wall screen beside the booth and called up a random entry in the ship's onboard library. A bit of boring reading: the tried-and-true method for dozing off, right? She skimmed over the entry heading the computer had chosen for her.

Insomnia.

She resisted letting out a thin scream of frustration. She also restrained herself from smashing her fist against the screen, because despite appearances to the contrary, she was certain the computer was not trying to mess with her. Instead, she calmly swiped again, shuffling to the next entry.

Sleep Deprivation.

Suppressing another groan, Kate swiped the screen closed. Rising up, she snatched her mug off the table and shuffled to the sanitation area. She rinsed the cup with cleaning agent and set it in the drying unit. Behind her, she heard the quiet thud of boots passing over the small rise of the entryway. She peered over her shoulder, wondering if it was Addy's or Parker's turn to fetch some necessity. It wouldn't be the first time she'd run into one of them on an early morning galley raid. Each time she'd grinned at Addy's near-incoherent sleepy mumbling or Parker's silent *don't-say-a-word* expression. Now, she just wanted to slip back to her room and pretend she knew what sleep was and how to do it.

But it was Sam she saw crossing the threshold: her head down, the tufts of her nearly-white hair matted, moving with a stiffer, straighter parody of her normal scuffle. Stopping in front of the rack of mugs, Sam took one down—her usual, chipped, pale blue—and sorted through the cabinet as if on autopilot. It wasn't until she shifted to the water dispenser that her head lifted, and their eyes met.

The only sound in the room was the whisper of hot water streaming against ceramic.

Kate felt like every single word she had ever learned was running through her head, yet try as she might, she couldn't force any of them together into a sentence. *Where was she supposed to start? Where have you been? Why are you avoiding me? Are you okay? What's going on? Where are we going now? What's the plan? Are you angry with me?*

The water cut off with a quiet gurgle. Sam picked up the mug, dropped her gaze, and ducked back out of the galley without a word.

Kate blinked.

"Are you kidding me?" she asked the empty space.

Admittedly, probably hadn't been the best way to handle that. Sam could recognize her behavior as avoidant, unhelpful, and borderline childish. Maybe.

She also knew that if time suddenly rewound and she was forced to replay the events, they would unfold the same way. Early morning conversation was not something she indulged in, even when the other person didn't unnerve her.

There. She admitted it. It was bad enough before, what with the talking, and conversation, and general presence. And then, with one little action, Kate had managed to nudge her just enough off balance into an orbital rotation she had not been prepared for, and she was not enjoying the sensation at all.

Because, okay, she had been getting used to it—to other people again. Acquaintances. Crew. People interested in knowing her and who she—maybe, possibly—was interested in knowing back. But there was a huge gulf between interested and *interested*, and how exactly was she supposed to act now?

Were they supposed to talk about it? She knew she didn't *want* to talk about it, but maybe they were supposed to. Maybe that was a rule. She wanted to ignore it, but what if that made things worse?

Ideally, they could pretend it didn't happen.

If they did talk about it, what was she supposed to say? Was *she* the one that was supposed to say something or was Kate? After all, it wasn't as if *she* had started it.

Most of the time, she was 100 percent sure she wanted to go with the ignore, pretend, amnesia options, because there were at least a dozen much more important things that needed to occupy brain space but then she'd go ahead and remember—and it would— just—

Shit.

She wasn't ready; she couldn't possibly be ready. Not if it was this hard to simply reach out. To connect on that level, to lose that? Again? She'd never survive it. She'd never been more alone than riding back to Icarus 3, the bodies of her crew—her friends—in cryo-storage.

Sam stumbled as she came to the door of her quarters. Hot water sloshed over the rim of her cup. Hissing, she switched hands and shook out the offended appendage before keying in the code to her door.

She was tired; so, so, so tired. Her body felt like it was on fire. Mac's adjustments to her leg might have evened out her stride, but the rest of her was responding like every single step was a four-foot drop onto uneven rocks.

It would take three days to reach the coordinates Mac had uncovered. She could use the time to catch up on sleep, indulge in that respite he had been bickering at her about taking. And then, *perhaps*, she would be in a better position to deal with her reaction to Kate. Obviously, some kind of... talking would be necessary. Not an apology or anything. Just. A discussion. A *short* one. Something that would... settle things.

She'd do a search of the archives. There was probably a script somewhere she could modify.

Nodding to herself, she took one step into her room and then pulled up short, nearly spilling more tea, when another body slipped in front of her.

Kate strode to the middle of the space, *her* space, and stopped, arms folded across her chest, her back to Sam.

Sam hesitated in the doorway, free hand still hovering over the keypad, and contemplated if she should let the door close or if it was better open. If she kept it open, then anyone passing by might hear whatever it was the other woman had come to say. And Sam had a feeling the things Kate had come to say, might be said in a louder than average tone.

But if she let it close… what would that mean? Should she—?

This was not how crews were supposed to work.

"I was expecting something nicer," Kate announced, and the sound of her voice pulled Sam forward into the room. The door slid shut behind her. She considered if she should be insulted by the statement or unnerved by the fact Kate had been thinking about her living quarters.

Both, she decided.

"A captain is only as good as her crew," she offered. Kate turned around halfway and raised an eyebrow.

"Really?" The single word managed to be both a question and a contradiction.

Sam shuffled slightly and resisted hunching her shoulders like she wanted to. "That and I… don't really care for decorations."

Kate gave a short, sharp huff. "I think that's the first thing you've ever told me about yourself," she mused.

Sam felt her shoulders touch her ears. "Look, it's late… or ah… early, I guess. We should probably—"

"Why did you agree to take me along with you?"

Sam snapped her mouth shut so quickly she nearly bit her tongue. An entire three-volume set of responses flashed through her head, but she wasn't stupid enough to speak any of them out loud. She went with what she felt was the obvious answer. "You asked me to."

"I did. Now I'm asking why you said *yes*."

Sam started to jam her hands into the pockets of her jacket and realized her jacket was currently tossed across her bunk. She settled on flexing her fingers by her side; the movement didn't give her the same sense of comfort. She thought back to the conversation on planet, when it had been a choice between casting off the last tie to a former life or going back up into the memories she had been trying to escape.

And there had been Kate, with such a simple request that had been anything but. Sam felt every single one of the millions of miles of space between then and now.

"You wanted something different. I... sympathized," she allowed, because it *was* true. They had been in the same boat, just at opposite ends; Kate pushing forward and her, pulling back.

"And that was enough?"

Kate was studying her, the inconceivability of it written clearly across her face.

"That was enough to get you to scrap your plans and take a complete stranger onto your ship? Sympathy?"

Jerking her shoulders, Sam glanced away and took a sip of her tea. She felt like she was trying to walk along a very, *very* narrow path and the stabilizers in her leg were misfiring.

"You fixed the engine. I owed you." Also true.

"You could have just paid me. You didn't even offer."

Sam was abruptly stunned to realize she *hadn't* offered. Hadn't even *thought* about offering. Shit. She set her mug down on the desk near her bunk and was momentarily distracted by the little blue rubber ball Jonah used to toss so casually. Absently, she touched her fingers to the smooth surface before folding her arms in. She tried to clamp down on the irritation she felt toward her past self.

"What is it that you want from me?" she asked, with a bit more heat than she intended.

Kate took a step forward and Sam felt herself instinctively lean away, even though Kate made no other motion toward her.

"That's the thing, isn't it? You already gave me what I thought I wanted. A ride into space, a job that's grown more dangerous with every second. I'm not bored now, am I? Nothing's been routine about this. And yet..." she went quiet. Her left arm rose as if she were going to reach out. Instead, she folded her elbow back and, making a fist with her hand, tapped it lightly against her own forehead.

"I don't know. I guess you're not the only one who isn't good with people," she said, with a humorless chuckle. Sam wasn't sure if a response was wanted, or what she would even say if one was *required*, so she remained silent. Safer that way.

"Anyway," Kate began, looking up, her lips lifted but not quite smiling, "I guess I realized that maybe I got a little caught up, you know, with the—with you rescuing me and then, uh, being, *kidnapped*—"

Sam watched, a little mesmerized by the way Kate's hands began fluttering through the air, like she was trying to sculpt out the various events that had transpired.

Almost like she was nervous.

"And then there was that ship that attacked, and your leg was blown off—"

Lifting a finger in objection, Sam interjected, "Hold on, my leg was not *blown off.*"

Kate paused and fumbled, as if she hadn't expected the interruption. Frowning slightly, she ran a hand through her hair. "Okay, fine. I mean, there's was a gaping hole in your knee but—"

"It wasn't *gaping.*"

All of Kate's movements stopped, her hands lifted near shoulder height, fingers spread upwards. She curled them into her palms before dropping her arms to her sides.

"You were in a lot of pain," she said quietly.

Sam nodded because *that* had certainly been true. She simply wasn't sure what it had to do with whatever Kate was getting at.

Kate continued, "So. I... wanted to apologize. And... I mean... there's no..."

Sam lifted an eyebrow.

"...*expectations*... or, you know. Anything. Like that. We can just forget. It."

Sam stared.

Letting out a soft laugh that might have also been a puff of frustration, Kate pressed her hands to the sides of her face and met Sam's gaze directly.

"Look. Can we just be… okay?"

"Be okay?" Sam echoed, lost.

A faint smile worked its way across Kate's face, a hint of either amusement or vexation, Sam couldn't tell.

"Yeah. Can we be okay?" Kate repeated.

"Okay," Sam agreed, because it sounded like a better deal than what had been going on. Even if she still wasn't sure she knew *what* that was. Kate's smile widened a fraction and she nodded.

"Okay," she said. She started to say more, but then seemed to swallow it, and murmured "goodnight" instead. With that, Kate stepped around her.

A flood of relief coursed through Sam, unexpected in its intensity. The knowledge that things didn't have to change, that they could go back to being *normal*, released a palpable weight from off her chest.

But underneath, there was something uncurling. Something reaching out. And Sam knew she just had to wait five seconds for Kate to pass through the doorway. Just five seconds and she would be alone again without the distracting tug of company. Just five—

"I needed a reason to go back up." The words slipped out before she could stop them.

Shit.

Like a cabin fire, more words rushed free.

"After… after it happened… I saw them everywhere. In the corridors. The galley. The engine room." The words came faster, almost quicker than her mind could process. "Whenever I closed my eyes. And then, one day I didn't. I didn't see them. That was worse. Like I had forgotten them. I couldn't take it, so I sent a comm to Floodwater. Didn't think anything about how quickly he agreed, but I guess I know why, now. Then I was in that station, waiting, waiting, and I didn't want to sell to him or to anyone else, but I kept thinking about their faces. And how it was my fault."

"Why? Why was it your fault?"

Sam opened her eyes; she hadn't realized she had closed them. "Because I ordered them onto the shuttle. I made us split up. I figured the pirates would go for the ship. We had a fairly full cargo; it would have shown up on their scanners. And the ship was disabled. Easy target. But they went for the shuttle. Killed everyone on board. Blew them out the airlock."

Her voice broke on the last syllable; her eyes stung but remained dry. She tried to swallow down the lump that had formed in her throat, but it stubbornly remained, pressing like a hand against the front of her neck. Kate stepped closer, and this time, Sam held perfectly still.

"Gonna tell me it wasn't my fault?" Sam asked roughly.

Kate was quiet. So was her reply. "You were the captain. Crew follows orders."

Sam looked down into her mug. The surface of the dark tea rippled ever so slightly from the hum of the ship. She felt the faint vibrations come up through the soles of her boots, buzz along the circuitry in her leg, and tickle the hairs on her arms. It made it easier to ignore the churning in her gut.

"You remember what you said on Icarus, about the Trident Research Station?" At Kate's nod, Sam continued, "That commander, Jack Hero, evacuated the other eight members on board. With one decision, he saved his entire crew. All eight."

She paused, transfixed by the minute tremors in the liquid. Her voice sounded far away in her own ears, as if she were listening from the other side of a wall. She wasn't sure if Kate was still there, but suddenly it felt imperative to say the words, even if no one else was around to hear them.

"I couldn't even save one. Not even my best friend."

There was the whisper of movement and a faint pressure on her shoulder.

"You saved my life," Kate said, her voice low.

Sam turned her head, saw the fingers resting lightly against the curve of her arm, and followed them until she met Kate's steady gaze.

"Did I?" she questioned. "Or are you just not dead yet?"

It hung in the air, an impossible question. She watched Kate struggle for a reply, but what response could there be?

Sam cleared her throat.

"You should get some sleep," she said, more gently than she imagined herself capable of.

Kate looked reluctant, as if she wanted to argue.

"Okay. I—" she cut herself off, then nodded. "Okay."

Sam watched her move to the door, her steps unsure, like someone walking over uneven ground. When she reached the exit, she paused and looked back over her shoulder.

"You can't take responsibility for other people's actions, you know. I'm here because I wanted to be here."

"But I agreed to let you on the ship," Sam countered.

Kate was not deterred. "I convinced you to let me," she insisted, her tone allowing for no further argument.

Sam tipped her head in acknowledgement.

The small movement lifted the corner of Kate's lips. "How about you own the things that you do, and I'll own the things I do, and we won't feel guilty over each other's choices?" she bargained.

It seemed a logical enough request, though Sam doubted the future success of its implementation. She bobbed her head anyway. "Agreed."

Something like relief came over Kate's face. "Goodnight, Sam."

"Goodnight. Kate."

The door to Sam's room slid open soundlessly and Kate stepped into the corridor. Before she could go any further, she felt a hand drop down onto her shoulder. Surprised, she gave no resistance to the pull that spun her back around.

She had half a heartbeat to think what, and then Sam's mouth was on hers rougher and more insistent than the brief lip lock she had initiated in the med-bay. The scrape of teeth over her bottom lip was followed by a soothing brush of tongue. Her breath punched out of her and was replaced with a warm, quiet exhale.

The kiss ended just as abruptly as it started. Kate opened her eyes in time to catch sight of Sam with her rarely seen crooked grin.

Then the door slid shut in her face.

Kate stared at it, her heart racing, and her blood pumping loudly in her ears. An airy laugh escaped her.

"Touché," she murmured.

It almost felt like she was back inside the vintage arcade pod, only instead of a horde of alien ships surrounding hers, there was only one. One single cruiser drawing closer while her boat sat dead in the still waters of deep space. And apparently there wasn't a damn thing she could do about it.

That meant all the crates carefully stocked in her cargo bay were going to go missing, which meant she was going to have one very unhappy client and one very big loss on her books.

That meant putting off replacing the axom wiring, which Jonah said wasn't a problem, but then Jonah had also said he could have the ship back online in an hour or so. Three at the most.

That was six hours ago.

Now they had a pirate cruiser approaching their coordinates, and unless it was full of revelers at an intergalactic costume party, that meant her ship was about to be raided. She didn't keep weapons on board, because no cargo was worth getting lasered over—and that meant there was no avoiding the inevitable.

Well, she could always try reason, diplomacy, or just straight charm, but none of those were her strong suit.

First things first, though.

"Jonah, what's the status of the engines?"

He shook his head, tossing his ever-present rubber ball between his hands. "Still a no-go. I've got the problem isolated, but it's going to take more time to bring everything back online."

"Isn't that what you said four hours ago?" Triss asked from the nav seat, where she was propped against one of the arm rests.

Jonah ran a hand through his unruly hair. "Yeah, I fixed the original problem. There are a few new issues now."

"How sure are you that you've it figured out now? What's to say that after you fix this problem, the same thing won't happen?" was Ollie's question. He was seated at the

comm station, straight-backed with his shoulders not touching the chair at all.

Sam held up a hand to cut off any response. "It doesn't matter at this point. Triss, you're sure the cruiser is homing in on us?"

Triss nodded, crossing one ankle over the other. "Unless there's something not showing up on our scanners, we're the only thing in this section of the border."

"Maybe they're planning on offering assistance?" Jonah proposed.

Triss shot him a look. "We didn't send out a distress beacon."

"How much time before they reach visual distance?" Sam asked, ignoring the exchange.

Frowning, Triss tipped her head back and forth. "About 40 minutes."

"Okay. That gives you enough time to prep one of the emergency shuttles."

"You're going to abandon the ship?" Jonah protested.

Sam shook her head. "No. You three are. I'll remain on board. Because it's my ship, and if there's any chance of negotiating, then I will be the one to do it," she stated, before Jonah could object.

He did it anyway. "No way. If you're staying, then I'm staying. We should just split up, two in the shuttle, two on the ship."

"Chances are high that they're just looking to score some easy cargo, but if that's not the case, then I want you all somewhere safe. The sooner the shuttle releases, the better chances we have of you being undetected, so I don't want any arguments."

Jonah held out his hands toward Triss and Ollie, in a bid for support. "You guys are fine with this? Not a single argument from either one of you?"

Ollie folded his hands on his lap; the rest of him was motionless. "Captain has given the orders. The plan seems sound enough to me. And I would certainly rather not be on board when the pirates are," he supplied.

"But you'll let her be here? Alone? Against god only knows how many raiders?"

Triss pushed up from her seat. "C'mon Jonah. We all know what's going to happen. The pirates'll board, they'll demand the cargo, Sam'll hand it over, and they'll leave. Last thing they want to do is bring the Corps down into this space. Some cargo gets lost, no big deal. People start dying? Traders won't want to make this run anymore, and that'll be a problem."

Jonah gave a half-hearted laugh. "You really believe that?"

Sam held up a hand before Triss could answer. "There's no more discussion. You're going. Triss and Ollie, I want you to prep the shuttle. Jonah, I want you in the engine room on the odd chance you can pull a miracle and get us moving before they get in range. But once we're down to ten minutes to visual, you get your ass to the shuttle. No arguments."

Triss and Ollie both hustled from the bridge while, unsurprisingly, Jonah remained behind.

"Something you didn't understand, Jonah?"

He frowned and stared hard at her, fidgeting with the ball in his hand. After a moment, he reached up and set it into the nook above the bridge door—Sam noted the location for when he inevitably asked where the damn thing was.

When he spoke, there was confusion in his voice. "You don't have to do this alone, Sam. Let one of us stay. Someone ought to have your back."

Sam waved that off. "You heard Triss. Hell, Jonah, it's not like this is the first time we've ever been boarded. Why are you so squeamish?"

His frown deepened. "It feels different. And you didn't ship us all off those other times, so why now?" he argued.

"We weren't this far out the other times."

"Yeah, so what if something goes wrong?"

She couldn't understand his insistence, and the next words she said came up with hardly a thought. "If for some reason things go that bad, then I'm the only one who doesn't have a family. No one to deliver bad news to."

His confusion instantly morphed into anger; the transformation in his face was startling. "What about us?" he demanded. "It'd be pretty fucking bad news for us to lose you!"

The force of it pushed her back, both physically and emotionally.

"Jonah, I—"

He held up his hands; they were shaking. "I'll be in the engine room," he snapped, breaking off the conversation and leaving a jagged edge behind.

She was left staring at his back as he stormed away.

fourteen

Sam wasn't sure what she had been expecting. She knew what she had been *hoping* for—that they would find the shuttle simply floating in space at the coordinates Mac had uncovered—even though it might have been unrealistic.

Pleasantly surprised would have been a nice change of pace.

Instead of the shuttle, there was a relay satellite, a twisting hunk of metal in an otherwise empty section of space. She brought the ship as close as possible to the small beacon, and that was when Mac chose to make an announcement.

"What do you mean I have to bring it on board?" Sam questioned.

"I need to physically access the main memory," he explained, as if the reason for the request should have been obvious.

Sam did not think it was. "And you need to do that *on* the ship?" she pressed.

"Well, I can't exactly do it in the middle of space. Unless you have an EVAC suited rated 500dsi?"

She did not. And so, using one of the ship's robotic arms, she dragged the cumbersome object into the cargo bay.

Well, Addy *finessed* it inside because, as the engineer quipped, she'd made a few modifications Sam wasn't familiar with, and everything would "probably go smoother if she handled it." Sam agreed, because it was quicker, easier, and involved significantly less talking. It did leave her wondering what the hell her ship was going to be like once the job was finally over.

"Think of it as an adventure," Addy suggested.

"I want to think of it as a *ship*. My ship," was Sam's reply.

They gathered in the cargo hold, where the satellite took up half of the floor area and reached nearly to the ceiling, some 20 feet overhead. Sam frowned, craning up. It hadn't looked so big floating out in the darkness.

"Try not to break it," she implored, as Mac began unscrewing a side panel. Nata stalked nearby, sniffing here and there, his fur occasionally rippling as if there were something about it he found offensive. "And for fucksake don't let the cat get into it."

Mac paused, the whirring of the tool in his hand falling silent.

"Don't worry. It's not like they'd ever know it was us anyway." He reached to run his hand along Nata's back, but the cat slipped away before he could make contact. "And I doubt there's much damage this little guy could do," he added, before returning to his task.

"See, you say that now, and then I get a bill in two years because there's some kind of corporate alarm system that alerts headquarters whenever one of their stations gets busted up."

Mac glanced over at her. "You're very paranoid, aren't you?"

A healthy amount of caution did not equal paranoia in her book. What kind of stupid question was that? "Why do you need to take it apart anyway? Tell me again why you can't just scan it?"

He set down the power driver and pulled the panel off, tossing it to the side where it clattered loudly against the bay floor. Sam held out a hand toward it, glaring pointedly. He shrugged.

"Sorry. And I could scan it, if I wanted it to auto-delete all the files that are currently stored on it."

"Why is it that every single thing auto-deletes when you scan it?" Sam demanded.

Addy popped her head up from where she was examining the underside of the satellite. "That's because most developers of this kind of software, or specifically the major corporations they work for, are paranoid as shit."

"Oh. Well, it's good to know I'm not alone in my apparent paranoia then."

"So why is he taking this thing apart?" Kate asked, perched on the edge of a packing crate.

"He's not actually taking it apart," Addy corrected, standing up and sounding disappointed. "I mean, I don't think he is. Right? You're not taking the whole thing apart?"

"Wasn't planning on it," came Mac's muffled reply from within the structure. Addy turned back to Kate.

"He just needs to get the memory core out. Do we need to put this thing back?" she asked, tilting her head toward Sam.

"Yes."

"I really don't think it has any kind of alarm system on it. I mean, I can check, but it's pretty obsolete. We'd really be doing this sector a favor by taking it. They'd have to replace it with something newer."

Sam stared at her, trying to ascertain if she was joking.

No. Not joking.

"What would you do with an obsolete communications satellite?" she voiced and then immediately wished she hadn't.

Addy's eyes lit up. "Well, for starters I would—"

"What does he need the memory core for?" Kate interrupted and Sam shot her a grateful look. Until she realized abruptly that she had unwittingly wandered over to stand a few feet from where Kate was seated. Flustered, Sam shuffled closer to the satellite and tried to look like she was interested in it.

Big ugly hunk of metal panels and weird antennae. Like every other relay unit she had ever seen.

"Once I connect the memory core to the computer, I'll be able to see when and where the cloned signal came from," Mac explained, pulling another, smaller piece of paneling from the satellite.

"And then... " Kate cued.

"And then we'll hopefully have the coordinates of the shuttle. Or possibly another relay station."

"So basically, we could be jumping around the universe chasing signals forever?" Kate suggested dryly.

"I think you've been hanging around Sam too much."

Sam felt her shoulders bunch and glared at the dull gray of the satellite's hull. "There's been no hanging," she muttered, just loud enough to be heard. Something suspiciously akin to a snort of laughter sounded from where Parker reclined against the railing of the stairway to the bay's catwalk. The mercenary didn't even try to hide the smirk on her face.

That seemed a little rude in Sam's opinion.

"Don't you have any questions about this whole... thing?" Sam asked, waving one hand wildly at the satellite.

Parker shook her head. "Nope. I just shoot things. It's much less complicated."

"I feel like that should be *more* complicated," Sam pointed out.

"Not when you know who the bad guys are."

"So, what happens when you don't?"

"That's not a problem I've ever run across."

"You sure about that?"

Parker didn't so much as blink. "I am."

"What exactly is the plan for if we do find the shuttle?" Kate cut in before Sam could respond. The look she was given this time was considerably less grateful. "I mean, to play pessimist for the moment, what happens if whatever Floodwater wants isn't on the shuttle?"

The only noises that followed were the muffled clinks of Mac's tools, dulled from inside the hull of the satellite. Sam thought about his recounting of Jonah's message, about the insistence there was something that could damage Floodwater permanently. While she had never been particularly motivated to take action against the scumbag, had in fact been content to simply avoid employment with the man, she thought it safe to say her attitude had changed. She was more than willing to push further now, to risk a bit more, to deliver a blow he couldn't shake off.

Maybe for Jonah.

Maybe also because she could still feel a phantom ache where Benny had clobbered her.

Maybe for the marks she still remembered on Kate's throat.

She wasn't ready to push that choice and risk on anyone else though.

"Maybe you could tell him you couldn't recover it? I mean, if you can't find it, you can't find it, right? What's the worst he would do?" Addy reasoned as she came around the side of the relay to peer in over Mac's shoulder.

"Torture and kill you," Mac and Parker said at the same time.

She straightened, skeptical. "Really?"

"Yes," they replied in unison.

Addy frowned. "That seems excessive," she mumbled, mostly to herself.

"Floodwater's not really concerned with excess," Sam stated. "And if anyone else has a better idea of what we should be doing right now, this is, shockingly, the time to say it."

The clanking of Mac's tools ceased as Addy turned to Parker. Her subsequent question rang out across the room like a hammer strike against metal sheeting. "Did the captain just make a joke?"

Three heads turned so that six eyes were looking straight at Sam, all widened slightly.

It was *unnerving*.

"What does that mean? I make jokes. I can be funny," Sam snapped with indignation.

"Sure, absolutely," Addy agreed. Too easily.

"But are you actually asking for our input?" Kate ventured.

Sam glared at the ceiling. "Yes," she gritted out.

After a beat, Kate replied, "You picked this course. We trust your judgement."

Sam saw all three women nod. Her chest burned and tightened; she tried not to think about the last time there had been three sets of eyes on her.

Mac backed out of the satellite and triumphantly held up a small rectangular drive, seemingly oblivious to the heaviness in the room.

"Got it!" he announced, bringing it close to his face. He squinted and then frowned. "Wait, no. This is the backup. Hold on one second!"

He stretched back inside the machine and came out a moment later with another drive, slightly larger than the first.

"Here's the main memory."

"Can you access it using the ship's computer from here?" Sam asked, cutting through the tension. Mac was already stepping toward the console near the bay's back wall. He pulled down the key plate and dragged a crate over in front of it to straddle.

"Should be able to. Addy, can you grab me an AXA cable? I'll need to hook the—"

Sam reached over his shoulder and pulled open a small panel on the right side of the screen. A thin tray extended; several different types of connectors attached.

"You should be able to hook in here," she explained with only half the impatience she felt.

Without a word, Mac set the memory drive into the tray, pressing until the correct pins aligned and sank in.

Sam hovered beside him, trying to hold in the question that was ready to leap off the tip of her tongue. She already knew what the answer was going to be.

"How long is it going to take for you to find anything?" Kate beat her to it.

Sam's mouth shut. She hadn't noticed the others draw in close. Mac's shoulders rippled and she waited for the snippy reply. To her astonishment, his response was evenly measured.

"It depends on the level of security. There are at least a couple petabytes of information on here. Running a simple search is going to take some time. If there's encryption, it could be a lot longer."

"So, what do we do in the meantime?" Kate groused.

Before Sam could point out that there were approximately one thousand things they could be taking care of on a spaceship at any given moment, Addy brightened and held up a finger.

"I know what we can do! We can—"

"Addy, there is nobody in this room that wants to do what you are about to suggest," Parker interrupted flatly.

Addy's brow furrowed. "—Play Intergalactic Risk?" she finished, confused. Sam wasn't sure if the look that came onto Parker's face was because she hadn't expected the engineer's answer or because she didn't believe it for a moment.

A chuckle drew all of their gazes. Kate had one hand pressed lightly to her mouth. She shook her head and smiled at Addy.

"I haven't played since college. The star I was orbiting went supernova and wiped out all my colonies. It was heartbreaking."

"That's a tough break," Addy sympathized.

Sam resisted pressing her hands to her forehead. "I have an idea," she said instead, holding her arms out. "Why don't we get back to our stations? Mac, send me—" Pause. "—send out a comm when you find something? I'll be on the bridge."

As she headed toward the exit, she heard Kate ask, "Do we *have* stations? Was that another joke?"

Technically, there were lots of things she could—and probably *should have* been attending to or at least monitoring—but Addy was curious. (She was curious about a lot of things really, maybe more than she should have been, but at the moment, she had a very specific area of interest.) She lingered off to the side of Mac, rummaging idly through an open crate of random parts—*oh, it looks like they did have spare SS526 stabilizers after all, weird*— until both Parker and Kate had wandered away, ostensibly to find their own distractions. The moment they were both gone, she shifted to stand directly behind Mac.

"Was there something you needed?" he asked, after a few moments of her silent staring.

"You're a doctor," she began with.

"I have medical training. I'm not technically a doctor," he corrected.

Her eyebrows rose. "What are you *technically*, then?"

"A biomedical engineer. With a specialization in cybertronic health."

"So, that deals with the creation and maintenance of cybernetic limbs, right?"

"Among other things, but largely that, yes."

"Hmm." She moved closer, examining the screen. "And hacking, that's just a side hobby?"

Mac rotated away from the screen, smiling as he looked up at her. The smile, she noted, did not reach all the way up to his eyes. Too weighed down with condescension. "I don't think running a search query on a hard drive can really be considered 'hacking,' do you?" he replied, with the drawl of false modesty.

Addy shrugged and grinned as well, letting her own insincerity show through. "No, definitely not. But circumventing the security protocols that would exist on a hard drive belonging to the Telsen-Nozirev Corporation would."

His smile dimmed but remained on his face. He mirrored her shrug. "It's not all that different from getting the human body to link with an artificial limb."

"Well, guess it's a lucky thing for us. Though, I suppose it's the reason Sam went to you in the first place."

"Why do I get the feeling you could've managed on your own?" Mac inquired, scratching behind his ear. "You sound like you know quite a bit about relay systems."

She held up her hands in a mock gesture of surrender. "I wouldn't say that. Besides, I'm sure Sam feels more comfortable having someone she really trusts handling it." She lingered on the word *trust*.

His head lifted back slightly. "Are you saying she can't trust you?"

"Hired crew, old friend..." Addy made a motion like a weighing scale. "Anyway, there are a couple things I need to check on. I'll let you get back to it." She took the few steps back to the open crate she had been pretending to sort through and started to reach inside.

"Hey," she said, as if an idea had just occurred to her. Peeking up, she saw Mac was still watching her. "Seems kind of weird to have a biomedical engineer on a psychiatric research station, doesn't it?"

The smile slipped away entirely. "I always felt useful," he said simply.

Pursing her lips, she nodded and pulled up a few objects: a spool of cable, a packet of clips, and the small rectangular plastic box she had taken from the engine room. She held the box up in front of her face, rotating it back and forth.

"Any ideas?" she asked, pushing it toward him. He perked forward unconsciously, distracted from his task. She watched him consider his answer and knew the next words out of his mouth were not the first ones he thought of.

"Looks like the housing for a power displacer. Or a disruptor maybe."

Her gaze sharpened on the box. "A disruptor?" she echoed. He nodded.

"Sure. There's the tunnel for the input and the room for the dampener," he explained, pointing with one finger, despite being well out of reach. Addy shifted back to him and wondered if she imagined the slyness in his eyes.

"Huh," she mused.

Though the engineer was uncharacteristically subtle about it, Kate could tell Addy was loitering near Mac and waiting for her and Parker to disperse. Partially because she wanted to know why and partially because she couldn't think of anything else to do, since Addy still wouldn't let her in the engine room by herself, Kate ambled back to the satellite to wait. It wasn't hard to feign interest in the object—she had never seen one outside of a televised launch in grade school. She found Parker taking up the exact same space she had been occupying earlier; the mercenary openly watched Addy and Mac's interactions.

After an internal debate between pretending to examine a hunk of space metal and joining Parker's blatant observations, Kate abandoned the satellite and wandered over.

"So..." she offered as an opening statement.

Parker said nothing.

"What do you think they're talking about?"

"I have no idea. And even if I could hear, I still don't think I would have any idea."

Kate nodded. She thought there might have been an undercurrent of frustration in the statement. "Right. You just shoot things."

A noncommittal sound that still managed to sound like a warning was the response.

Kate shifted topics. "So, you and Addy? How's that going?"

Parker's eyes swept over, one eyebrow rising ever so slightly.

Kate nodded again. "You're right. None of my business. Are you at all concerned about dealing with more pirates?"

"Just part of the job."

"Uh huh. Listen, you don't happen to have any more of that booze, do you? This would probably be less painful with alcohol."

Parker looked momentarily confused, and then a smirk broke over her face. "Sorry. Not much of a chatterer."

"Totally understandable. We could talk instead," Kate suggested. Parker's smile flattened a bit, turning dubious.

"About what?"

"Well—"

"Don't ask her about her gun. She won't let you hold it," Addy announced, coming up behind her.

"I won't let *you* hold it," Parker clarified, some of the stress in her posture relaxing. Addy frowned and jerked a thumb toward Kate.

"But you'd let her hold it?" she asked, sounding insulted. Kate wasn't sure how to feel about that. Parker rubbed her chin and gave Kate a quick once over.

"It's pretty heavy," was what she said.

"What's *that* supposed to mean?" Kate asked, feeling insulted.

Parker motioned with her head back toward Mac. "What was that little meeting about?" she redirected.

Addy was studying something in her hand. "Hmm?" She glanced up and seemed to realize the question directed at her.

"I was just curious."

Parker and Kate exchanged glances.

"About what?" Kate asked, when Addy did not elaborate further.

The engineer tapped a finger against the end of her nose. "There's something not quite right, but I can't put my finger on it."

Kate stole a glance in Mac's direction and lowered her voice. "Something not right with Mac?"

"He does seem a little... off."

"No offense, but you're a little off, too," Parker stated.

"Yeah, but in a charming, sort of endearing way, right?"

Neither of the other women responded.

"No? Not charming? Or endearing? Huh. That's weird."

Parker nodded. "Yeah, weird would be the word I'd use."

Kate rolled her eyes. "Can we focus just a little bit? What do you mean by *off*?"

"I don't know," Addy replied with more than a hint of vexation. "Something about him being on that station bugs me. A medical research satellite seems like a strange place for a biomechanical engineer with superior subspace tracking skills."

Parker looked unconvinced. "Captain said it was a station full of nerds. Seems like the perfect place for him."

Addy appeared to be mulling something over, her jaw shifting back and forth minutely. She made a *tsking* sound with her tongue. "Yeah, but it's the type of nerd. It's like if we found you on a Peacekeeper outpost. You wouldn't fit."

"I'm offended," Parker replied, face perfectly even.

Addy raised the object in her hand, holding it out in front of her.

Squinting at it, Kate asked, "Isn't that the casing you found in the crawlspace of the engine room?"

Addy nodded, her face thoughtful. "I assumed it was some modification Jonah made or was going to make. But maybe it was something that wasn't supposed to be there. Something somebody removed before someone else could find it."

"For what reason?"

"Sabotage," Parker supplied. She lifted both her brows when Addy met her gaze. "That's what you mean, isn't it?"

"But Mac wasn't on the ship last time," Kate pointed out as Addy nodded again.

"It would've had to have been someone else," Addy agreed.

"One of the crew," Parker insisted. "They would have had the best opportunity."

Addy rotated the piece in her hands but wasn't looking at it any longer. "What do we know about them? Anything?"

The mild feeling of discomfort that had started to rise in Kate's chest grew exponentially. She couldn't quite understand its source, but it made her want to fidget.

"Sam doesn't really talk about them, other than Jonah. The engineer," she admitted.

"Hmmm," was Addy's only response. She and Parker exchanged a look that had the feeling in Kate's chest tightening.

"We have to tell Sam," Kate declared, but something in Addy's expression gave her pause. "What?"

"What if it *was* Sam?"

Kate blinked. "That's crazy. Why would Sam sabotage her own ship?"

"People can get pretty crazy when they've been in space too long."

"So, what, you're saying Sam contracted the tempers and murdered her crew?"

Addy held up her hands in a defensive gesture. "I'm saying we need to think about this carefully. This was supposed to be an easy pickup job. I think we can all agree it's a lot more complicated than that."

There was a sudden scraping sound; they all turned in time to see Mac leap to his feet. He spun, saw them staring at him, and pointed to the screen with a fierce smile.

"Found what we were looking for."

The main bridge looked different from the last time that she had been on it, Kate thought, settling back against one of the flight chairs. That had been before they had docked at Dravanol, way back when Addy had sent her on a minor errand. As Mac fiddled with the controls to a holographic display—to project his findings, she assumed—Kate tried to pinpoint what it was that had changed.

The dust coating many of the screens and instruments had been wiped clean, so that the previously dulled surfaces glossed under the overhead lights. All the panels were active, not just the ones Sam had been navigating from. With all the blinking and humming from the consoles, it looked like the command center she had always imagined when thinking of spacecraft.

Even with all five of them present, there was more than enough room to spread out. Parker posted herself near the doorway; Kate pondered if the mercenary's habit of always setting up near an exit was a protective one or a desire for easy escape. Addy hovered near the largest bank of screens; every few seconds she turned to view the readouts, as if she were waiting for results of sorts. Mac was closest to the engineer.

Sam sat in the first flight chair and would have looked mildly bored if it weren't for her stare practically burning a hole in the back of Mac's head.

Oddly, Kate found she kind of missed the smaller blueprint of the auxiliary bridge.

"Give me one second to program a quick readout," Mac explained, despite the fact no one had asked for an explanation. Maybe he felt Sam's impatience. Kate certainly could, and it wasn't even directed at her.

A star map suddenly projected up into the center of the room. Mac keyed in a few more commands, and the map shrunk to fit the air between them.

"Okay, this is our current location." He stepped close to the holograph and circled a section. As his finger passed through the area, a white dot appeared as a marker. Taking two long steps to the right, he added, "And this is where the signal is coming from." He drew a second circle. On the map it appeared as if hardly any distance separated the two, but Kate knew she was looking at lightyears of space. She chanced a glance at Sam and saw the other woman's expression of impatience had shifted to concern. A quick look around the room showed similar reactions. It felt as if she was missing something obvious. Obvious and important.

"So. What's the problem?" she asked because it was evident there was one. Mac lifted one finger to point at a red dotted line cutting through a section of space, not far from where they were. She hadn't noticed it.

"Well, this is the border. And this..." he motioned to the second circle again.

"...is deep inside the border," Kate finished for him as it dawned on her. "And that is bad," she added. It probably went without saying.

"It certainly doesn't make our task any easier," he agreed.

"What's out there?" Sam asked abruptly, pushing up from the chair. "Is it charted?"

Mac nodded and input several commands into the projector. The map zoomed into the second circle, expanding into a small system with two planets and a dim star. Both planets had at least half a dozen or so moons in orbit.

"Can you get a lock on the coordinates? Exactly where in the system the signal came from?"

He shook his head. "No, we're too far away. If we get closer, I'll be able to pick up the signal itself and trace it back to the source. But we're going to have to get a lot closer."

Sam rubbed a hand over the spot just below her left collarbone and said nothing.

Kate shuffled closer, but the view did not change. The visuals of the star and planets had no more details than their circular shapes. There was no corresponding tiny image of a shuttle anywhere to be seen.

"Why would the shuttle be there?" she puzzled out loud, scrunching up her eyes as if that might bring new understanding or clarity. Mostly, it just made her forehead hurt.

"Might have dumped it," Mac suggested, sprawling over one of the other flight chairs. "Or it could have crashed."

Addy stepped up, staring at the map with a thoughtful intensity.

She scratched along her jaw and jutted her chin toward the two planets.

"There could be a trading den, maybe on one of the moons." Her hand paused at her throat. "Can you bring up any known planetary information?"

A few seconds later a handful of text and numbers appeared beside each orb. She hummed and nodded slowly. "Gas giants," she confirmed, though there was concern in her voice. Her hand began to move again, shifting down to squeeze the skin of her throat lightly.

"What is it?" Kate asked.

"The orbits look like they're degrading. Eventually, the two planets are going to collide. That's going to make quite a scene."

Kate eyed the holograph warily. "Not while we're there, right?"

Addy shrugged. "Space is unpredictable."

"That's great. Thanks. I'm really happy to have that to think about now."

Across the room, Sam took her seat again. "It doesn't matter so much why the shuttle is there," she mused, shifting back and rolling her head so she could still see the map. "The real question is how we are going to get there without... interference."

"It's a lot of space. There aren't that many pirates to begin with. Could take our chances and go in fast. Might get lucky," Mac suggested.

Sam shook her head. "I don't get lucky," she replied, flexing the two fingers of her right hand as if they were evidence of that statement.

"We don't have any cargo or anything. Would they even be interested in us?" Kate asked.

"If we were running close to the border, probably not. This is deep into Secession space. They're going to want to know why we're there. That's if they're feeling generous," Sam noted, sourly.

"If they're not feeling generous?" Kate pressed, despite knowing the answer.

"Then they'll most likely bombard the ship."

"Why don't you have any guns on this ship?" Parker cut in abruptly. "I checked; there's not even any disrupters."

"Because it's a transport ship, not a military cruiser. And I hate guns," Sam replied without looking in her direction.

"Seems like that puts you in a tough spot right about now."

"If you have guns, they have to shoot. If you don't, then they don't."

"Doesn't mean that they won't," Parker pointed out.

"Maybe. But it gives them the option not to."

"What if *we* were pirates?" Kate asked and found herself in the uncomfortable situation of having all eyes on her. "You said they were traders. Do they ever attack each other?" she posed to Addy. She remembered the engineer's description of the pirates what seemed like ages ago. Traders. Scavengers. *Non-violent.*

Both Sam and Mac followed her gaze. Addy fidgeted, obviously uneasy with the question.

"I mean, there are always outliers—" she started, and Kate waved impatiently.

"Yeah, of course, but in general?" she pressed.

"In general, no. They're like... their own corporation," Addy answered, after searching for the right term.

Mac appeared skeptical. "What are we supposed to do, then? Paint the Jolly Roger on the side of the ship?"

"The what?" Kate asked.

"We're not painting anything on the ship," Sam denied, firmly.

Mac held up his hands and Kate continued, "They must have some way of identifying other pirates, right? Some kind of communication or code that gets sent out?"

"Like a sign and countersign?" Parker proposed.

Kate could see the engineer was following the direction she was headed and was struggling with it.

"You said you had worked in the engine room of a pirate ship before," Kate reminded her, feeling a slight pang at having to pry. She chose her next words carefully. "Is there anything you know that could help us?"

She was sure Addy would shake her head and say no. Or remain silent. Judging by the parade of expressions that crossed her face, she must have been considering it. Maybe weighing loyalties she hadn't expected to have.

Addy's eyes swung over to Sam and the expression in them was unexpectedly, fiercely cold.

"This is still about a retrieval job, right? Not a revenge mission? Not payback?" she interrogated, her voice as chilled as her gaze.

Sam looked startled before her face closed off. "We go in and out. All I'm concerned about is getting out from under Floodwater," she replied, her own tone flat.

"What about after?" Addy pushed, sounding unconvinced.

"I captain a ship with no guns. Do I seem like the revenge type?"

They exchanged a long stare, neither blinking, until finally Addy gave a short nod.

"There's a particular sequence they add to their ships' identification signal. Yes, I know it. And yes, I'll add it to this ship's. On one condition." She paused and held up a finger. "I enter it and no one else reads it."

"Agreed," Sam replied, without a second of hesitation. Addy's gaze slid over to Parker, who frowned.

"What are you looking at me for?" she asked. Addy bit her bottom lip and gave a short sigh.

"Because I don't know what you're required to report back to your boss and I don't want Floodwater's hired soldiers cleaning up Secession space."

"Hired soldiers like me?" Parker asked, a hint of reproach in her voice. Maybe hurt.

"I'm guessing you're not the only one who likes to shoot *bad guys*."

"I'm here to make sure Floodwater's property is retrieved and returned to him. Everything else is noise."

Addy nodded again, seemingly satisfied with the answer. "Then let's be pirates."

fifteen

The transformation from freelance freight transporter to space pirates took less time than Kate would have guessed, based on television and movie streams. A few numbers and five minutes (most of which were spent by Addy insisting the others turn their backs to the input console before she would make the change) and suddenly the ship and everyone in it were something and someone else. Like a mag train shifting tracks, almost imperceptible, save for an uncomfortable tug in the pit of her stomach. On the train it was the adjustment in speed and direction, but she suspected the feeling now was due to the sudden increase in probability. As in, they *probably* were going to end up dead. Despite Addy's earlier insistence that most pirates were nothing more than traders of ill-gotten gains, Kate couldn't help but think they would not take kindly to the deception were it uncovered, hypocritical as that might sound.

Well. It wasn't like the level of danger before had been "moderate." It was like going from "on fire" to "more on fire."

At first, it was almost too easy to forget the transformation had even taken place. Space was massive. Endless. Empty. In the entire time they had been traveling, Kate had been aware of other spacecraft twice; both times when she had been on the aux bridge with Sam. Once on approach to Icarus 3, when ships had been floating serenely in and out of the bays, and then again at Dravanol Station, when one had come crashing into the hangar.

Otherwise, being down in the engine room or even roaming the winding corridor of the kraken, it was impossible to tell what was beyond the thick, curving walls. Just endless empty void.

Sometimes, she almost forgot the *purpose* of their excursion. Caught up in one of the monotonous fixes Addy seemed to find solely for her or sitting in the quiet of the galley when no one else but Nata was around, it felt like nothing more than a routine job. Or what she imagined a routine job would be. Nothing to hint at coercion or an unveiled threat of death.

And then Addy would need Parker's help with something, or Mac would appear to rummage for a late "night" snack, and the sight of the mercenary's blaster and the doctor's family ties were blatant indicators of why they were out there.

Three days after they passed over the invisible border into Secession space came another stark reminder.

A ship. Much too far away to see through the view screens, barely a blip on the long-range sensors. But a blip nonetheless, which meant they were close enough to receive the doctored identification sequence if they bothered to scan for it, according to Addy.

"What's the likelihood that they'll scan for it? Or that they're even pirates?" Kate asked, her chest constricting, despite the evenness of Sam's comm announcement regarding the unidentified ship. It didn't sound like it was time to panic, but she wasn't sure she could trust Sam to accurately portray when panicking would be appropriate.

Addy, who had read off the distance to the other ship from her tablet before tucking it back into a pocket, shrugged, and turned back to the display she was working on. It was some kind of simulation, but the engineer didn't seem inclined to explain it to Kate, based on how often she had waved away her offers of help.

"Well, there aren't a lot of reasons to be in Secession space, so they're probably pirates. And if I was a pirate and I was in my territory when some other ship came by, I'd definitely scan it."

The pressure in Kate's chest increased. "If they figure out we're not pirates, how fast could they get to us?"

Addy gave another lift of her shoulders. "Who knows? Depends on their ship and the type of engine they're running with. Then again, a kraken's not really built for speed, so there aren't a lot of ships we *could* outrun if it came to that."

"You're very calm about all this."

"We're separated from a vacuum by a couple of feet of metal and circuitry. There are a thousand things that could go wrong at any second that would lead to our immediate deaths. Pirates figuring out we're not pirates doesn't even crack the top ten."

Kate stared. "And that's supposed to make me feel better?"

Pausing, Addy glanced away from the screen, her eyebrows lifted. "Oh, am I supposed to be making you feel better?"

"I'd appreciate it, yeah."

"Appreciate what?"

Kate jolted at Parker's voice. The mercenary stood in the far doorway of the engine room, leaning against the wall with one elbow, her long gun slung over the opposite shoulder. Did Parker even notice that she carried the weapon everywhere or was it automatic at that point? Leave room, take gun.

"Kate's concerned the pirates are going to see through our ruse and come murder us," Addy explained, which was not exactly what Kate had been thinking, but it certainly was *now*.

Parker's shoulders rounded, two small mountains rising briefly. "Nothing we can really do about it. They either will or they won't."

Kate felt her stomach pitch downwards. "Oh my god," she murmured quietly, worried she was about to be sick.

Addy tilted her head back toward the screen. "Does that help?" Kate got the distinct impression the other woman found her apprehension amusing.

Pinching the bridge of her nose, Kate shook her head and tried not to imagine death via pirate invasion. "No, not really."

"Does what help?"

In the other doorway, Sam stood with her arms folded across her chest, a nearly mirror image of Parker across the room. The captain and the mercenary appeared to notice each other at the same time. Both frowned and dropped their arms to the side almost simultaneously. Kate opened her mouth, but Addy was quicker.

"Kate's worried the pirates are going to kill us all."

"Please stop saying that," Kate groaned. After a couple of seconds of silence, she snuck a look at Sam. To her relief, there was none of the easy acceptance and faint amusement that colored Addy and Parker's expressions.

Catching Kate's eye, Sam shook her head. "They wouldn't kill us," she stated.

The twisting in Kate's stomach eased at the unexpected reassurance in Sam's tone. "No?"

Sam shook her head again. "No, not at first. First, they'd probably try and figure out if we were worth something to someone. And if we weren't, they probably still wouldn't kill us. Just leave us on some remote planet or moon, maybe with enough rations to last until some survey team picked up our distress call or we ate each other."

While Kate's jaw dropped open, Sam turned to Addy. "I picked up an odd discharge pattern from engine one when I ran the proximity scan. Can you check the venting system? I'd rather not explode before the pirates get their chance to kill us."

"You're not funny."

Silently, Sam moved to the comp screen on the wall opposite where Addy was working. After a few inputs, a quadrant map blipped onto the screen, all the squares empty. Sam jerked a thumb toward the screen.

"They're already out of range. Probably didn't even notice us."

Kate's heart felt like it was pounding up in her throat. She glared at Sam. "You know, for someone whose entire crew got taken out by pirates, you're pretty flippant about them," she snapped back. And as soon as the words passed her lips, she regretted them. Her stomach roiled again, for a different reason.

Sam's jaw tightened and she swiped the map clear. She looked to Addy, who seemed fully engaged by the screen in front of her.

"The venting system?" Sam repeated, the question weighted in a way it hadn't been only a moment before.

If Addy perceived the sudden tension in the room, she didn't show it. "Everything looks normal. I'll take a closer look in a little bit, but I'm not seeing any spikes. Could have just been an off-cycle flush."

"Keep an eye on it?"

"Of course. That's what you pay me for." The engineer let her hands fall away from the screen. "Hey, if you die and I live, I still get paid right?"

"Addy." Parker's voice had a sharp note of disapproval that was reflected in the contraction of her normally smooth countenance.

Addy wore an expression of open curiosity. "What? It's a legitimate concern," she insisted.

Kate watched as Sam wet her lips and one cheek twitched.

"I'll make an amendment to the contract," was all Sam said. Her tone was even, devoid of any debris that might have been knocked loose by two careless statements.

Addy nodded, clearly satisfied. "Great. Now get out of my engine room before you break something," she ordered, returning to her work.

With a shake of her head, Sam started to turn into the corridor and then paused. With one foot out of the room, she looked back, easily matching Kate's stare. Kate expected to be blasted by anger, annoyance, or some mixture of the two, but that wasn't what she saw at all. Instead of irritation or some cousin to it, Sam's face was full of remorse.

Sam started to speak, and Kate had the weirdest feeling she was the one about to get an apology.

"Try and relax, okay? I won't let anything happen to you."

Kate blinked and Sam was gone, her boots clinking in the hallway.

"Shit," she muttered. *Tactful. Extremely tactful, Kate.*

"Nice, bringing up the boss's trauma. Real smooth," Addy noted, cheerfully.

"Addy." This time the engineer's name was a pained groan from Parker.

Without looking over to see if she was watching, Kate extended her middle finger in Addy's direction.

"When you're done with that, can you finish checking the tension levels? Unless you want the hull to shred and for us to be sucked into space."

When they had first come up with the ruse, Kate had assumed the most nerve-racking moment would be the first time they came across another ship. She had imagined intermixed feelings of dread, terror, and nerves battling for dominance while they all waited, gnashing their teeth, to see if their disguise would pass muster.

It turned out she had an excellent imagination, even if she was the only one who had been psychologically biting her knuckles. No one else had shown any signs of unease, but despite the flippant behavior Sam, Parker, and Addy had displayed, Kate figured they each must have been feeling at least a little anxious.

Of course, she had also imagined feelings of relief and triumph when it became obvious the pirates had fallen for their very simple trick and the rest of the trip would pass in relative peace and calm.

That did not turn out to be the case.

Kate's dread, terror, and nerves seemed to multiply every hour until she was sure that she would choke on them. The other ship had been too far away for them to know if it had even picked up the identification sequence, and she became convinced that not only had it read the code and seen through their disguise, but it was also now trailing just out of range of the scanners with an entire army of pirate ships, waiting to descend on them.

Two days later, wretchedly tired but unable to sleep because the confines of her cabin only made her thoughts that much more claustrophobic, Kate pressed her forehead to the table in the galley and tried to breathe in slowly enough to keep from having a panic attack, but fast enough to keep from blacking out. Nata had stretched himself across her lap; his weight was comforting, and she ran one hand back and forth across his fur.

"You're not going to throw up, are you?" Parker asked from across the table.

She exhaled sharply at the frankness in Parker's question but didn't bother to lift her head. With all the pressure that was squeezing her, she wasn't sure she could, even if she tried.

"I hope not," she muttered, eyes tightly closed.

"Yeah, me too. I got one of those sympathetic stomachs, so if you blow, I blow."

"Sympathetic isn't a word that I would associate with you, Parker."

"Why? 'Cuz I'm mean-looking and carry a big gun?"

"Yes," was Kate's muffled reply.

Parker chuckled. "That's fair. Still worried about those pirates?"

"Do you know what I did before this? I was a project manager. The only things I fought were schedules. And sometimes Alan in IT, but only because I know he was the one stealing receivers from the storeroom."

"Weren't you the one that told Miles Floodwater to go fuck himself?"

"Not in so many words. And I don't think I'd fully grasped the situation at that point." She'd been out of her mind, Kate thought. That was the only possible explanation for *that* behavior.

"Is that what you're doing now? Coming to grips with it?"

"Looks like it." Kate paused and rolled her head to the side so she could peer questioningly at the mercenary. "How did you know I said that?"

"You might have an admirer or two among Floodwater's guys now."

"Great. I'm always looking for new and exciting friendships."

"Don't know that friendship is what they'd be looking for."

Kate pressed her forehead back onto the table. "Hard pass then."

A quiet *click* broke the silence that followed. Lifting her chin, Kate could see the dulled metal of a mug a few inches from her face. The scent of vanilla drifted into her nose and her stomach clenched, balking at the idea of anything entering it. Not that she thought she'd be able to get it down her throat.

"Drink it. It'll help you sleep."

Kate wasn't sure at which point Sam and Parker had traded

places, or if Parker was even still in the room, but she supposed the vanilla should have been a strong hint. She rolled her head back and forth slightly.

"I'm never sleeping again."

"Well, eventually you're gonna pass out, and I'd rather you didn't do that while doing something important."

Something nearby hummed as Sam finished her admonishment, and Kate raised her head, buoyed by her need to know. Sam looked down at her tablet briefly before tucking it away. Her pale gray eyes were steady.

"There's another ship, isn't there?" Kate guessed.

Sam didn't answer, just reached out and pushed the mug a bit closer.

Ignoring it, Kate blinked her eyes shut briefly. "Tell me something. Anything."

"Like what?"

"Anything. Tell me… how did you meet Jonah?"

Kate blamed it on the overwhelming combination of pirates and impending doom on her brain; she had been studiously avoiding questions about him, not wanting to upset the balance they had finally achieved. With five little words, it felt like she had flipped off the gravity coils and reversed the polarity in the room. She figured the conversation would be abruptly over in three, two, one—

"I met Jonah when we were twelve."

The statement hung in the air, suspended by Sam's slightly shaky voice. "At the holo-station?" she prompted quietly when the waiting became unbearable.

"Yeah. I was skipping class, in one of the old gaming cabinets that most people didn't bother with. I didn't realize he was watching until I reached the end of a level and he cheered. *Cheered*. He wanted to try it. I told him how to play and what all the controls were, but I don't think he listened because he died immediately. I thought he was annoying." Sam's voice stuttered, as if she hadn't meant for the last sentence to escape, and she fell silent again.

"If twelve-year-old you was anything like you are now, I imagine you thought everyone was annoying," Kate pointed out, reaching for levity like a balm against a burn.

"I've always been discerning."

"You're a fucking curmudgeon."

A real laugh rattled out of Sam. "Yeah, well. He was annoying. Cheerful. All the time. And he always had this grin on his face, like everything was funny. He didn't look on the bright side. He *was* the bright side. And he talked. Talked, talked, *talked*. Sometimes, I'd leave the room and he'd still be talking. He'd talk to anyone, too. Total strangers. He *enjoyed* it." Sam said the word *enjoyed* as if she couldn't possibly imagine anything *worse*. It had Kate wondering if her disinterest in conversation was natural or a learned defensive strategy.

Sam gave a little jerk of her head and sipped from her own mug. "So, I made him do all the docking check-ins and outs."

"Why did you start working together?" Kate managed to prop an elbow up on the table and rested her head in her palm. Nata chirped in her lap as he was jostled but remained in place. Sam glanced down meaningfully at the cup in front of her, and Kate reached for it, curling her fingers around the warm surface.

"I wanted my own ship, got one. Jonah didn't know what he wanted, didn't really care what he was doing. He liked working on engines. Was good at it. He offered to work for me."

Kate paused in the middle of bringing her cup to her mouth. "He offered? To work for you? You didn't just ask him?"

Sam shrugged, took another drink.

"So, what, you were just going to take this ship out by yourself?" The memory of Sam half inside one of the engine bays, cursing her way through a repair manual flashed into Kate's mind as she took an unconscious swallow of tea. The warm liquid and the slight incredulity helped further relax the muscles of her stomach.

Sam looked out into the empty galley, distant.

"I don't know what I was going to do. I hadn't thought that far ahead."

That far ahead of what? Kate wanted to ask. Sam was quiet and contemplative. Was she looking back, trying to see if there was some way, some *thing* she could have done to save him? Before Kate could voice the thought, there was the faint rumble of vibration. Reaching back into her pocket, Sam tilted the tablet up to read the display. Their eyes met.

"Out of range. Looks like we get to live another day." Sam rose to her feet. Kate remained where she was, feeling calmer than before, but saddened. She thought about Addy's speculation that some part of Sam's crew, maybe Sam herself, had sold them out to killers. Seeing the feelings that passed over Sam's face as she spoke, muted or restrained as they had been, Kate found it hard to even consider. She knew grief, was still close enough to her own to touch it. It might not burden her the way it obviously did Sam, but the weight was still there, right above her heart.

One of Sam's fingers tapped lightly on the table next to the mug that Kate had set down.

"Finish that. Then get some rest. Take the cat. But be warned; he snores."

As she left the room, Kate looked down and stroked a hand over Nata's head, smiling as the cat butted up against her in response. "Is that true?" she asked, rubbing lightly at his ears.

An expression of pure, blissful innocence was his response.

A thought occurred to her. "How does Sam know if you snore?"

If anything, Kate was surprised it hadn't happened sooner. A non-guild rated (or trained for that matter) engineer mucking around the engine room of a complex spacecraft with marginal supervision (if that) was practically begging for an accident to happen.

One minute she had been reaching between two conduits, aiming for a failing fuse, and in the next second she heard Addy curse. Her focus drifted and so did her fingers.

Kate's left hand rocketed out of the panel, propelled by an arcing electrical current. A cry escaped as she instantly cradled her hand to her chest, bringing her other hand to fold over it protectively. The searing sting and the heat coming off her skin had the right hand hovering uselessly.

"Med-bay. Right now. Go." Addy's voice was firm and insistent, cutting through the insistent shouts of *pain, pain, pain* blaring in Kate's mind. She felt a gentle push on her lower back, and as she scrambled toward the door, she looked over her shoulder to see the engineer hadn't paused her work.

However, she did make a shooing motion when Kate hesitated in the doorway. "Go!"

As far as accidents went, it could have been a lot worse. All her fingers were still attached to her hand, even if they were blackened and blistered. When she was fourteen, she'd fallen backwards and cracked her head against some stairs. The concussion alone, never mind the skin patch to seal the wound, seemed far worse than being a little singed.

The pain, though. Maybe the distance of time had pushed away the memory of pain, but the sharpness crawling through her far exceeded the dull throbbing she vaguely remembered. It burned from the tips of her fingers and spread up her arm and into the rest of her body in waves, as if the electricity were still coursing through her.

Mac was rummaging in a cabinet when she entered, holding her hand outstretched before her like she was worried about it exploding.

He took one look at it, closed the cabinet door, and yanked open the drawer below it.

"Sit down," he ordered, jutting his chin toward the med-chair as he snatched up a silver foil package. He cracked it against the counter then shook it quickly, coming to stand beside her as she hopped onto the gray padded seat.

"Keep your fingers spread," he instructed, ripping a strip off the top of the packet and squeezing it in his hand.

The neon blue ointment slowly coating her marred skin immediately helped cool the flames; at the same time, even the soft pressure of the gel made the hurt flare. She didn't try to hide her grimace.

"So, what happened?" Mac took a firm hold around her wrist as she flinched back. He paused for a second before returning to the task—*ha*—at hand.

It was starting to look like she'd dunked her hand in a vat of cake frosting.

Before she could answer, the med-bay doors swished open and Sam stormed inside. Judging from the tightness of her features, the captain was not just happening by.

"What the hell happened?" For half a moment, Kate almost thought the other woman was going to reach out and grab for her arm, coated as it was. But Sam's arms folded across her chest in a familiar movement.

Kate questioned how she had even known about the injury. As far as she was aware, Sam had been holed up on the bridge. Again. Then she scolded herself. Addy. Probably relayed it to her over a comm.

"I caught a little jolt from one of the access cables. Not a big deal." Kate tried for casual, an effect which was somewhat ruined by her sharp gasp when Mac pressed a bit too firmly.

He gave a sympathetic smile. "Sorry. Almost done with that part though. Keep your hand raised and try not to move your fingers. She's still got all of them," he added helpfully to Sam as he spun away from the table and reached for the drawers behind him.

Sam did not appear appeased. "Oh, in that case." She shot him a glare that bounced off his back. "What were you even doing messing around with the access cables?"

Kate tried to remember to keep her hand still. Ever since Mac had said not to move her fingers, she'd been struck by the overwhelming desire to make a fist.

"Just doing what Addy asked me to. Something she's working on."

Sam's expletive had her raising her eyebrows at both its vehemence and creativity.

"I'm not sure that's physically possible," she murmured, watching as Sam paced over to the comm on the wall and jabbed it with one finger.

"Addy? What do you think you're doing?" Sam all but snarled into the speaker.

"Do you mean in general or right now, specifically?"

"I mean, why is Kate sitting in the med-bay with electrical burns from the access cables?"

"Oh. Well, I can't say with 100% certainty since I didn't see it, but I assume it's because she made contact with the cables while the power was on."

Sam's mouth opened and then closed but no sound emerged. She pressed her forehead against the wall above the comm. The next words out of her were clipped and controlled.

"Addy. What were you having Kate *do* with the access cables?"

"I'm trying to figure out what—oh. Hold on a second."

The comm connection dropped and Sam banged her head lightly against the wall a few times before straightening.

Mac tugged on a drawer. It held fast and the tools on the counter above rattled. "Is everything on this ship broken?" he complained.

Sam reached past him, pressing first in and then jiggling the handle. The drawer popped open a quarter of the way. A second, sharper pull had it sliding out all the way.

"What, you don't have stuck drawers on your fancy research station?"

Ignoring Sam, Mac rooted through the drawer before pulling out a two-pronged tool with a length of cord wrapped around it. He shook the tool over the counter until the cord fell free and then turned back to Kate.

"Do you even know what access cables are for?" he asked over his shoulder at Sam.

"I know you're not supposed to touch them," Sam shot back.

Mac lifted the tool and placed it over Kate's hand, one prong on either side of her palm. The blue ointment had solidified so that her fingers were completely immobilized.

"And how do you know that?" A smirk formed on his lips. When Sam remained silent, he chuckled and explained to Kate, "She touched one. Jonah said it practically blew her across the room."

"It wasn't across the room," Sam muttered.

Kate glanced over and saw that Sam was glaring up at the ceiling, a hint of red staining the base of her throat.

"I barely brushed one and my arm nearly flew off," Kate acknowledged.

"You're going to feel a little heat, possibly some tingling. But it shouldn't hurt," Mac advised, just before he pressed a switch on the device over her hand.

"What is that?"

At first, Kate thought Sam was talking about the apparatus Mac was using but then saw she was motioning toward the cord on the counter.

"Hmmm? Oh, it's called a stethoscope. Doctors used to use them to listen to a patient's heartbeat. Pretty outdated nowadays. By about 500 years," Mac answered, without looking up. "I assume it was Ollie's?"

Kate could feel mild warmth seeping in, as if she had placed her hand into a bowl of heated water.

"Yeah. He liked weird old junk," Sam recollected, still staring down at the scope.

"That how you got him on this ship?" Mac pressed a button on the side of the tool and the buzzing stopped, along with the heat. He set the instrument down, took Kate's blue hand in both of his, and lowered it onto the table as well.

"He was a passenger. Was traveling out to a mining station to take a physician's post. When we got there though, the mine had closed and the post was gone." The words seemed to tumble from Sam's mouth, as if she were not aware she was speaking to them. Kate held her breath, partially so as not to derail her and partially in anticipation of whatever Mac was about to do to her hand.

At least, she assumed her hand was still in there.

She thought she was starting to see a pattern in Sam's actions, and it ran contrary to the impression she appeared determined to uphold. Was it a result of the pirate attack or simply another facet of the captain's personality? Would it ever be possible to separate pre- and post-attack Sam?

Did it matter?

"So, I offered him a place on the ship. Figured it would be handy to have someone with medical skills on board."

Thwack!

Both Kate and Sam jumped at the crack that rang out, interrupting the moment of reflection. Mac set aside the long, flat bit of metal he had brought down squarely against the top of Kate's hand. He took hold of the top of the blue casing and tugged upwards. It came away easily, like a piece of a shell, revealing Kate's unblemished hand. She lifted it free from the rest of the blue fragments and flipped it over, wiggling her fingers as she did so. Stiffness faded with each movement, but the pain, and the burns that had caused it, were gone.

"Good as new," Mac declared, brushing the scattered bits of cast into a vent in the table.

"I'll say," Kate agreed.

"Try not to brush up against any more major power sources, okay?" Sam suggested, looking significantly calmer than she had earlier.

"Pretty sure I got what we needed, so we shouldn't have to open those again."

They all turned to the doorway. Kate wondered how long Addy had been standing there; she hadn't heard the doors open.

Sam's mouth thinned. Rather than speak, she jabbed a finger in the direction of the hall and pushed her way past the engineer, clearly expecting Addy to follow. Addy gave a little wave before backing up and letting the doors slide shut in front of her.

Kate stayed where she was, certain Sam wouldn't appreciate her following. She looked from her healed appendage over to Mac, who was busy cleaning up the space. She watched, once everything else had been put away, as he placed the stethoscope carefully into one of the drawers.

"You mentioned him before. Ollie," she clarified when he glanced up at her. "Did you ever meet him?"

"Once, when they stopped at the station. Just before…" he cleared his throat. "Well, before the incident. But Jonah talked about him—everyone really, on the ship—enough that I felt like I'd met him a thousand times."

"What did Jonah say about him?"

He shrugged and turned in the chair. "Usual sort of things. Conversations they had that I might have been interested in. Jonah was pretty far off most of the time, but there were a couple of things we probably agreed on."

"Like what?" she pressed and knew it was too much when his eyebrows drew together. His hands folded atop the table.

"Why are you asking?"

Biting her bottom lip, Kate wasn't sure she knew the answer to the question. She recalled Addy's earlier suspicions and wasn't sure she would want to answer it even if she *did* know. So, she settled for a shrug of her own.

"Curious, I guess." She pushed up from her seat and wiggled her hand at him. "Thanks for your help."

"No problem."

She paused at the door, out of range of the motion sensor and turned back. He sat watching her retreat and a quizzical look came over his face when he saw her hesitation.

"How long was he on the ship?" she asked.

He frowned in deliberation. "Not sure. A couple of years, I think. Certainly less than Jonah or Triss. Why?"

"Just wondering how well Sam knew him."

"Well, they say you can really never know someone. Not entirely."

Sam continued walking once she passed through the med-bay doors, confident Addy would be trailing. After a few steps, she could hear the heavy clunk of the engineer's boots behind her. They progressed beyond the engine room and the crew quarters, moving through the looping hallway until Sam felt like they had put enough distance behind them. Then she turned and folded her arms.

"Now. What exactly is it you're trying to do? Besides endanger the other members of my crew," she asked bluntly. *My crew* slipped so easily from her lips that she almost missed the fact she had spoken it. She couldn't quite gauge how she felt about it in the moment, save for it wasn't the all-encompassing guilt she had once imagined.

Addy didn't so much as flinch at the sharp tone. "I went through the computer logs to see if I could figure out what happened to the ship on your previous pirate encounter."

"Why?" Sam asked, hearing the stiff defensiveness in her own voice.

In contrast to the tension Sam could feel crawling up her spine, Addy appeared perfectly at ease. She slipped her hands into her pockets and rocked back onto her heels.

"You told me to," she replied. At Sam's blank look, she added, "'*Do me a favor? Think about it some more?*'" lowering her voice in an obvious imitation of Sam's own.

Sam frowned and tried to trace the words back to their origin. When had she—

Right. She pressed a hand to her forehead. "You think what you found in the engine room is related to the attack?" she clarified.

"Maybe. Maybe not. Either way I'd like to make sure whatever happened then, doesn't happen now."

Sam resisted the sudden urge to rub at the base of her throat. "How might they be related?"

"I have a couple of theories."

"Such as?"

"I need to run a few more tests before I could really say."

Dropping her hands to her sides, Sam straightened to her full height. She had a good four inches on the engineer, but Addy's easy expression never shifted. Sam shook her head and dropped back, feeling unsettled for reasons she could probably name if she wanted to look.

She didn't.

"Try and be a little more careful with your testing then, okay? I'm not interested in losing any more crew members."

sixteen

At first, the ship was nothing but a speck surrounded by billions of other specks glittering in the endless blackness. She wouldn't know it was there if not for the sensor map on the console screen in front of her and the tiny blinking image approaching at a steady pace.

The shuttle had disappeared from the screen, much to her relief. It wasn't the first time she would be boarded by pirates, but even knowing what to expect, it was still comforting that her crew would be out of the possibility of danger.

Now it was simply a matter of waiting for the other ship to close the gap. She squinted at the numbers on the screen and noticed a pair of Ollie's thin wire-framed glasses resting atop the console. Slipping them on made the numbers far clearer and reminded her she'd need to have her eyes tweaked next time they were on a station. Maybe argue with Ollie, again, about why he should have his done.

Twenty-six minutes to interception. Probably already slowing down to capture speed. She hoped whatever the hell it was they were planning on using for seizing was not the same claw-like contraption the previous pirates had employed. That delightful machine had necessitated hull repairs in four different places. Like it wasn't expensive enough to lose an entire shipment of—

Twenty minutes. Might be better if she met her soon-to-be guests in the cargo bay. She had run into reasonable ones before. It was possible she could convince them not to take the entire shipment. Losing half a ton of product would be significantly better than losing all of it. She could work out an acceptable loss clause in the contract. After all, she had warned that the accelerated schedule combined with the projected route could lead to trouble. Obviously, she should listen to herself more often.

Fifteen minutes. Of course, it would just be her luck to

end up meeting the one pirate captain that liked to take fingers as trophies. And she didn't really have any fingers to spare at that point.

Eight minutes. She narrowed her eyes at the screen again. Then blinked and leaned closer. Were they increasing speed? Why? They couldn't have been so stupid as to think ramming the ships together would be a good idea? Fuck, she'd throw the damn cargo into space herself if they wanted it that bad. They could fish for it out of their own airlocks.

Three minutes. They weren't on course to ram the ship. They were going to shoot past it. But why? Why give up that close to the prize?

Sam felt her stomach drop and shook her head. No. That wouldn't make any sense. Something must have spooked them. She stared down at the screen, expecting to see the massive image of a Corporate Corps transport crawling up behind her ship.

But there was nothing.

With her pulse skittering, she grabbed a comm piece and jammed it into one ear just as she caught sight of the pirate cruiser flying past. She punched in the shuttle's communication line.

"Jonah? Can you respond?"

There was the empty sound of silence.

"Jonah? Respond?"

Silence.

"Jonah? Triss? Ollie? Are you receiving?"

Silence.

And then— "Sam? We're receiving. What's going on? Pirates wrap up already?" A strained mixture of forced levity and the disapproval she knew Jonah still had for her decision came over the line. She was starting to worry he had been right.

"Jonah, the ship went past me. I think… I think it's headed for the shuttle."

"The shuttle?" She could hear his frown. And something else. "Why would it—wait a second. Ollie, punch up the viewer and—"

His voice abruptly cut off and silence flooded back in.

"Jonah? Jonah, can you hear me?"

Silence.

She turned back to the console, checked the communication line.

Closed.

Her throat closing, she re-entered the number, tried to raise the shuttle again.

"Jonah? Can you respond? Triss? Ollie? Anyone? Are you there?"

Silence.

One moment her mind was terrifyingly blank, as if every single thought had frozen in place, and in the next, a thousand different potential actions were running through her brain, each one shouting at her to pick it. It took another moment to break free from her paralysis. She scrambled out of the flight seat and burst out of the bridge—

Sam jerked awake, her hands digging into the arms of the flight seat. She stared down at the console in front of her, and for a second, she saw the flashing indicators of the shuttle and the incoming pirate cruiser.

Then she blinked rapidly, her eyelids weighted with fatigue, and the display showed only the system scan she had been in the process of setting up. Atop the dash Nata lay stretched out, watching her with his round green eyes, his tail curling down just above the screen. Sam stared back and recalled finding him tucked away in Jonah's room, no doubt as a safety precaution. Probably the last thing Jonah had done before he had gone to the shuttle. When she had popped open the door to his crate, the cat had simply peered from the depths of it, making no move to wander out.

As if he had already known.

She released her grip on the seat and brought both hands to her face, rubbing the heel of her palms against her eyes and then dragging her fingers down her cheeks and over her chin until they slipped off. Her sighs were loud and deep in the quiet of the aux bridge.

A glance at the onboard clock in the upper right of the screen told her she hadn't fallen asleep for long, less than half an hour.

Shouldn't have been sleeping at all. It wasn't even halfway through a ship's day.

Then again, she hadn't been sleeping during the ship's night.

Not more than a few hours, anyway. Not since they'd crossed the border and the dreams had started up again.

She almost laughed to herself. Again? They'd never stopped. But the proximity to the border made them so much more vivid. Like she was back in that exact moment when she realized what would happen and how she could do nothing to stop it.

There were differences. Not the panic or the terror or the helplessness. Those remained the same. But underneath those emotions she could recollect so easily, were tiny rivulets of doubt and distrust and suspicion, running through like drips of water off the outside of a condenser unit. She could hear the echo of Jonah's laughter and over it, Addy's cautious warning.

Sam wiped a hand down her face once more, as if she could push away the remnants of the dream, and sat up in the seat. Nata continued to watch her, gaze unblinking. Unsettled by the memory, she felt a flash of hot anger shoot through her and swiped a hand towards him.

"Go on, get out of here," she muttered as he easily avoided her, jumping down to the floor and shooting through the exit. She turned back to the console: her half-finished inputs were on screen. Before she could start on them again, the tap of footsteps drifted up through the floor hatch. She paused, waiting to see if they would continue past. Instead, they were replaced by the quiet rustle of fabric, as if someone were shuffling in place.

After nearly a month on the ship and, by extension, nearly a month in space, Kate thought she was about as used to life without sunlight as she was going to get. It was awful, exhausting, and completely disorienting, but she had adjusted, in a functional sense. With enough time, she thought she might, possibly, in a *hey-anything-can-happen* sort of way, come to appreciate, if not actually enjoy it, like Addy seemed to.

It would only necessitate the complete loss of her mind and will.

Certainly, it would take more time than Kate was planning to stay on the ship. As thrilling as being forced into a fetch quest by a homicidal space mobster, blasted at by possible pirates, and hurtling deep into forbidden territory in search of actual pirates was, Kate found she kind of missed the comparably dull atmosphere of her office. On one hand, no one ever fired a laser at her from behind the water cooler, and on the other hand, *no one ever fired a laser at her from behind the water cooler.*

Whatever ennui she had been feeling that had driven her to leave everything she had known had now been addressed and sorted, thank you very much.

There was also the pervasive feeling of dread as it pertained to being discovered by pirates, but she felt like she'd made improvements. The last two flybys of other ships had only inspired a mild sense of agitation in her, despite being less than an hour apart.

She didn't consider it paranoid to wonder if they might have been the same ship, circling.

Still, she thought as she walked along the corridor toward the auxiliary bridge where she was certain she would find Sam holed up, she never got the opportunity to put her hands on a boson engine core in the office. Technically, she didn't get to put her hands on one on the ship either, since Addy was all about "safety protocols." ("Look, you wouldn't open the hood of a car while you were driving it, right? Same principle." "I don't have a car. I take the mag train." "Oh, in that case." "Really?" "No.")

And it was no longer the need for something new, something *different*, that was drawing her forward. She had thought she had been looking for *something*, but maybe it had actually been someone—

Oh boy. Stop that thought right there.

She didn't *need* someone, or to attach herself to someone. But sure, she could understand it now. She had been lonely. Detached. Missing her father long before he had passed. She had withdrawn to prepare for the inevitability, and once it had come, it turned out nothing could prepare her. She had simply been alone, surrounded by unfamiliar things that brought no comfort.

That's what she had been fleeing. And what she had been looking for was a connection. Any connection. The way back.

Kate reached the bottom of the ladder as Nata came bouncing through, gracefully landing a few feet from her. He craned his short neck up at her and curled his tail behind him. The expression on his face seemed to say, *you don't want to go up there.*

"That bad?" she mouthed to him and couldn't fathom what kind of response she was expecting to get in return.

He gave a quiet chirp and stalked off, his tail twitching with what *felt* like indignity.

Suddenly skeptical about her next steps, Kate was careful to keep her body out of sight of the opening in the ceiling. Leaning, she stretched her neck up and over until she thought she could see the dark khaki of Sam's pant leg. As an extra confirmation, there was a quiet cough and the leg pulled back, hidden from view. Sam was up there. All Kate had to do was decide if she really wanted to climb up and open the can of worms she had rattling around in her brain.

She thought about the theory Addy had proposed, one they hadn't discussed again since first genesis, not during one second of the testing and simulations of the original attack that Addy had been running through in an attempt to ascertain what had happened.

The idea that one of the crew, or even Sam herself, had sabotaged the ship.

Kate knew Sam felt responsible. Maybe there wasn't any reason to share Addy's suspicions with her. Maybe the idea that one of her crew had set them up was one of those things she should keep to herself and never speculate further on. Really, what help could it be? Suspecting, or even flat out knowing, what had happened wouldn't change the events themselves. Her crew would still be dead. They'd still be in their current predicament.

And if it *had* been Sam? Then tipping her hand could be a really, really stupid mistake. Surrounded by nothing but empty space, it would be the last mistake she ever made.

But Kate kept thinking about the look on Sam's face as she recounted her guilt. If there was anything that might shift that weight, it had to be worth it. She wasn't sure if Sam was aware of it or not, but that weight was slowly and surely crushing her.

Or she was a tremendous actor.

Possibly the paranoia talking.

Plus, and Kate was honest enough to admit it, there was still that little—okay, possibly more than little—tug that kept pulling her in Sam's direction, despite the various warning signs, like the (however unlikely) murderer scenario and Sam's own *apparent* disinterest.

Apparent might have been the wrong word, considering there had been kissing, and Sam also appeared (was that egotistical to assume?) to be feeling a tug of her own. Yet Kate got the impression Sam didn't *want* to be interested, and how different was that from *actually* being uninterested?

They are two entirely different things, her mind helpfully supplied.

Were they? Or did she just *want* them to be different things?

Completely different.

Yeah but—

"Are you going to stand down there much longer? I can hear you breathing. It's creepy."

Kate jumped as Sam's voice interrupted her internal debate. Sam's face peered down through the ceiling hatch, eyebrows raised, as if trying to comprehend what reason Kate could have for lurking in the hallway beneath her.

Her brain momentarily leapt back to the first time she had been on the ship and had been trying to follow Sam's simple invitation, *you can come up to the bridge when you're done.*

A month felt like a lifetime.

"Kate?"

She felt a little buzz in the back of her head. "Uh... is it okay if I—" she pointed up at the opening. The expression on Sam's face shifted to wary, and Kate wondered if all the thoughts running through her mind were somehow visible. After a moment of silence, Sam nodded and shifted back out of sight.

With considerably less difficultly than the first time—hey, maybe she was getting the hang of space travel after all—Kate pulled herself up, remembering at the last minute how small the room was. After a quick calculation of available space, she perched on one of the arms of the only other flight chair, twisting her body so she could be facing Sam. The movement put their legs in close proximity, and Kate tried to lean backward without making it obvious she was doing so or drawing attention to their nearness.

The physical and mental gymnastics were exhausting, and she had yet to start talking.

"So, what's up?" Sam asked when Kate didn't immediately speak.

Kate stared, feeling completely blank. For all that she had been thinking about Addy's theory and Sam's guilt and the odd peculiarities of the story she knew, she had not at all considered exactly how to tell someone you thought one or more of their friends might have set them up. How were you supposed to do it in extremely tight quarters, which were very, very distracting? Did Sam notice the lack of space and was ignoring it, or had she not picked up on it but was about to if Kate kept just staring at her. Say *something* for crying out—

"Why don't you ever use the main bridge?" she blurted out, before the question had fully formed in her mind.

Could have been worse, she decided.

Sam looked confused, but not necessarily bothered, which Kate felt was a major improvement from the early days of their working together, when every one of her questions had caused Sam's face to shift between irritated and *more* irritated. Real progress.

"Habit, I guess."

Kate pushed her hair back behind her ears and avoided tugging on the collar of her shirt. "It's like a shoebox up here. Don't you get claustrophobic or anything? There's all that empty space below," she rambled, mentally wincing as she tried to find the right foothold for the conversation she really wanted to have but was failing miserably at it.

Sam gave a faint grin. "If you're claustrophobic, you probably shouldn't be in space."

Kate rolled her eyes. "You know what I mean."

One of Sam's shoulders lifted. "I'm more comfortable up here. It's quiet. Harder for someone to barge in on you unexpectedly. Triss always—"

Sam stopped, jaw tightening, all traces of humor chased away.

Kate waited, watching. She could almost see the debate playing out in Sam's head. She'd already told stories about the others, about Jonah and Ollie. Why hold back now?

Unless there was something special about—

Kate diverted her gaze to one of the small comp screens, not wanting her own thoughts on display.

After a few seconds, Sam sighed and rubbed at the base of her neck. "Triss always preferred the first chair, right in the center of the bridge. Practically slept in it," she finished, clearing her throat at the end before falling quiet again.

Shifting her eyes to a closer screen, Kate waded in carefully, oh so casually. "Mac, uh, mentioned her a few times. She was your pilot?"

Still worrying the skin along her collarbone, Sam nodded, her gaze distant. "Yeah. She did all the course navigation for jobs. Which was good because I always hated that mess. Figuring out the best route, which depots to hit, which corporate stations to avoid. How far we could push before we'd need to stop for inspection or supplies. She was good at that. Liked it."

"Was she another passenger that you picked up?"

"No." The hesitation in Sam's voice was gone. "We were in this station bar in one of the outer sectors. Jonah and me. Had finished a job and were killing time before our dock time expired. And Jonah was babbling on and on about something. Maybe ideas he had for the ship, maybe jobs he thought we should take. I wasn't really listening. The place was mostly empty, and his voice rattled around the space like a tomb. This woman appeared at our table. Like she'd materialized out of thin air. And she said something along the lines of, 'If you don't shut the hell up for five fucking minutes, I'm going to shove my fist so far down your throat I'll be able to tell what you had for lunch.'"

Kate felt her face twist at the image. "That's a visual."

"He laughed. And said if she waited just a bit longer, I'd probably do it for her. She looked at me and said she'd be happy to lend her expertise to the occasion. I asked if she was looking for a ship, since I was apparently about to be down a crewmember due to violent and sudden stomach removal."

"And she said yes."

"Yep. Wanted to see the ship first. Didn't believe it was a kraken until she saw it. She said it had always been a dream of hers to fly one. I said great, because I fucking hate it."

"Really? You hate flying your own ship."

Sam gave another sigh. "No, not really. It's just... with navigation, there's a lot of numbers and math. The computer does all the hard number crunching, of course, but when you're plotting the job run, you're still surrounded by it. All the checks and re-checks and corrections to keep track of. That's the part I don't like. But she did. It was weird."

There was such unaccustomed affection in her tone that Kate could feel the nagging little question form in the back of her mind and slowly push its way forward. She wouldn't ask though. Absolutely not.

"Were you and she...?" She couldn't finish the thought when faced with Sam's puzzled look. Definitely shouldn't have asked.

"Were we what?"

Feeling herself start to flounder, Kate racked her brain for a way to extricate herself. "Do you, uh... think any of the others knew about Jonah? About him working for Floodwater, I mean?" she redirected instead.

One of Sam's eyebrows lifted at the shift in conversation, and Kate was sure she was going to be called on it. But Sam shook her head, and there was no mistaking the frustration that worked onto her face.

"I don't know. I didn't think he would keep something like that from me. I didn't think he was *capable* of it. He usually couldn't keep a secret to save his life," Sam huffed. "One time he does manage, and it still didn't save him." She shook her head again, as if pulling herself back from some memory.

"If any of the others knew about it, I didn't pick up on it. But you know what I really don't get?" Sam pushed ahead without waiting for a reply, "*When*? When did he do the job? Because Floodwater told me Jonah found whatever it is we're looking for, and Mac pretty much confirmed it, even if he doesn't know what the hell it is either.

After we left Icarus 3, we didn't take any detours. Didn't make any stops at any stations except for Dravanol. We were on a tight schedule—couldn't afford any delays."

Sam's voice was laced with frustration, like she was rehashing an old argument.

"What was the job you were running?"

"Just a cargo run. Not even a full capacity one, but the client was very insistent."

"Why?"

"Because clients are always very insistent. Plus, the planet we were picking up from was under quarantine. Guess maybe that was making him nervous."

"Quarantine? For what?"

"Don't remember. Not even sure if they said. But they put a limit on the amount of cargo that could be lifted offsite each week. That's why the payload was small. I offered to stick around for a week to double up, but he said it was more important to get any amount out as fast as possible."

Kate frowned. "That seems kind of odd, doesn't it?"

"It's not the oddest thing I've ever been hired to do," Sam replied, and Kate really, *really* wanted to ask, but it seemed bound to derail the current conversation. She made a mental note to bring it up again another time.

"Where were you taking it? The shipment?"

"All the fuckway to the other side of the galaxy. Which is part of the reason we were anywhere near the border. Wouldn't have crossed over, except Triss detected a gamma cloud right smack in the middle of our main flight path. Had to make an adjustment. One way took us over the border. The other route would have blown our schedule by two weeks."

Sam dragged a hand through her short hair; soft spikes tufted up in the wake. "Should have just blown it," she finished, anger and guilt dripping from the words.

Kate wasn't so sure Sam would have been permitted to make that choice. Because she had a sinking suspicion something else would have happened to divert the ship onto another path. There was something else she was curious about, though.

"What did you do after? The attack," Kate clarified when Sam glanced up.

"There wasn't anything I could do at first. The ship was still dead. Jonah had almost finished the repairs but…" she trailed off and held her hands up. "It took me hours to cobble it together enough to the get the engines back online, and I'm probably really lucky I didn't blow myself up or something."

She paused and swallowed. "I went to the shuttle's last coordinates. I… found them. Brought them inside. Bagged them."

Her voice went distant, as if coming from far away. "I've been alone my whole life. I mean, my father died before I was born. I barely remember my mother. No siblings. If I have aunts or uncles or second cousins, they've never made themselves known. I figured I was used to it. That I didn't need anyone. Just a ship and a crew.

"It wasn't until they were gone that I realized… they were my family. How dumb is that? Surrounded by three people every hour of every day and still thinking you're alone?

"Flying back, with them… stowed… I've never felt more alone. I think it broke something in me." Sam seemed to speak the last words to herself, as if she had forgotten Kate was there. "I can't feel that way ever again."

Her voice changed again, hardening.

"And then I finished the job. Dropped the cargo off at the drop site. Was only a day late. Client didn't even make a fuss."

Kate flinched at Sam's flat, clipped tone. Her mind spooled up images to accompany Sam's words, and she couldn't help but wonder if Sam's face then matched the blank expression she currently wore.

Sam's eyes shifted to meet hers and Kate was startled by the fury suddenly reflected in them.

"So. Which one of my family do you think played the traitor?"

Sam watched surprise and confusion battle their way across Kate's features and figured there were a couple of possible reasons for that.

1. Her tone might have been a bit harsh.

2. The word "family" might have been a bit out of character.

Possibly a combination of both, Sam thought, as Kate opened her mouth to speak.

"You already suspected."

It was nearly an accusation; Sam felt herself bristle. She pushed back at it, trying to remember hers was not the only life on the line. The ship was no longer full of only memories.

"Addy said she found something. In the engine room. Something that shouldn't have been there. She wasn't sure what it was; thought it might have been one of Jonah's upgrades that hadn't been finished."

Kate nodded slowly but said nothing in return.

"She's been running simulations, using data from the logs and your help?" Sam continued, holding up her left hand and wiggling her fingers. That drew a faint smirk to Kate's lips, and Sam saw her fingers twitch at her side, as if reliving the feeling of current running through them.

"So, I'm assuming, since you've come all the way up here, she has a new theory on our mysterious black box that you've decided to share with me." Sam saw Kate's eyes dart briefly away before returning. "Even though she would rather you didn't."

Kate remained silent for another moment before she steadied herself and said, "She thinks it might have been a kind of modified power disrupter. Something that could have overloaded the engines."

It came out quickly and carefully, as if she had rehearsed the lines.

"She thinks someone sabotaged the ship," Sam construed, and Kate nodded again. Sam watched her gaze flitter around the small room, touching every panel and instrument, every screen and button, until it seemed to hover just over Sam's right shoulder. She wasn't sure what could be causing Kate to feel so nervous—beyond, of course, trying to inform Sam one of her friends had potentially double crossed her—but considering they were on a job forced on them by a space mobster, personal betrayal seemed par for the course.

Then she caught a flash of guilt, and a light bulb went off in her head.

"She thinks I did it," she reasoned aloud, and knew she was spot on when she saw Kate flinch.

"That's one theory," Kate replied cautiously. Sam slouched back in her chair, though it felt like every single muscle in her body was tensed.

"You agree?"

Kate shook her head. "No. I have a different one."

"Oh?"

"Did you ever wonder why the pirates went for the shuttle instead of the ship? I mean—" Looking annoyed at herself, Kate pressed her lips together and took a deep breath. "Of course, you wondered. What I meant was, what if wasn't about what they wanted, but *who*?"

Sam frowned, not sure she understood. "How could they have known who was on the shuttle?"

"What if Jonah wasn't the only one working for Floodwater?"

"What do you mean?"

"Look. What if someone sabotaged the ship to ensure you would be stuck in that spot, waiting for the pirates to arrive? You sent the others off the ship. Whoever set up the disruptor could have contacted the pirates to let them know. And that's why they bypassed the ship and went for the shuttle."

"But they killed everyone on board the shuttle," Sam pointed out. "Jonah, Triss, *and* Ollie. What does that do to your theory?"

Kate held her hands palms up. "Maybe Floodwater decided he didn't need whoever it was anymore. Maybe he thought he had gotten everything he wanted. Or maybe the pirates fucked up. Maybe that's not what was supposed to happen."

Sam considered, half listening to the storm of thoughts raging inside of her and half wishing she could tilt her head sideways and have them all drain out. She pressed the tips of her fingers against her forehead, wondering if she was imagining the bulge in her skull from the pressure.

"So, the competing theories are either I set up my own crew or one of my crew set me up. Since you don't think it was me, have you hazarded a guess as to which one it might have been that drove the knife in?" She couldn't keep the bitterness out of her voice, even though it wasn't really directed at Kate. Or, at least, not solely.

She supposed the situation warranted it.

Kate fidgeted, her arms shifting from leaning against the console behind her, to crossed in front of her chest, to down by her sides. Her mouth opened and closed a few times as she made several aborted attempts at a response, before she finally exhaled,

"I don't know, Sam. They were your crew. You knew them best."

Sam was shocked by the laugh that escaped her; it burst out, as if her body were expelling the very idea.

Obviously not, she thought. What else was there to say?

But as she sat there, those four words cutting through the din in her mind, she realized she did have something to say. *You knew them best.* Without looking at Kate, the words slipped from her mouth.

"You asked me if I wondered?" She stared at the view screen ahead, currently displaying empty space. "I've wondered every single second for the past half a year.

"At first, I wondered why the hell I ordered them off the ship.

"Then, I wondered why I had taken that particular job.

"Why had I taken us over the border?

"Why hadn't I bought Jonah those damn uplinks he was always complaining about?

"Why hadn't I sent out a distress beacon?

"Why hadn't I done something?"

Kate's eyes were filled with something that Sam didn't recognize, wasn't sure she wanted to recognize.

"And yeah. A couple of times I wondered why we went dead once we crossed the border when we hadn't had a single issue the rest of the trip.

"And why it took Jonah so long to patch things up.

"Why he argued with me when I told them to get on the shuttle.

"Why Triss and Ollie didn't."

Sam shook her head, whether in denial or to try and clear her thoughts, she couldn't say. Now that she had said everything she had been swallowing for the last seven months, the final truths came up easily.

"I don't know if I don't see it or if I just don't want to."

She jumped slightly at a touch on her shoulder. When she looked over, she saw Kate drawing her hand back. A thoughtful expression tightened her features.

"I've never been alone," Kate began, clearing her throat. "Growing up, no matter what I was going through, my father was there. Even when I went away to school, he was just a comm call away.

"And then he got sick. I was in the same room with him, but he wasn't there. Then, one day, the room was empty. It's hard to think about. It's hard to remember. Even good memories. Sometimes, it feels like there's a hollow space in the center of my brain.

"Suddenly, everything about my life felt unbearable. Everything was a reminder of this thing I couldn't think about.

"Being on this ship, caught up in this complete insanity—" Kate paused. "I don't think about it. About—" her voice broke, "—about how much I miss him."

She coughed quietly, blinking back tears. And though she wanted to, Sam couldn't bring herself to look away.

Appearing similarly affected, Kate replied, "I know you miss them. But isolating yourself isn't going to keep you from being alone."

Sam could feel herself shaking her head, an unconscious movement. "It's not being alone that scares me so much. It's... it's having people I... care about. And losing them again."

"You know, I think I was wrong about you."

Sam looked up at her. "What? What do you mean?"

Kate nodded. "Yeah, you see, I thought you were this cranky, badass grump who never wanted to get close to people because she thought they were a waste of time and space."

Sam narrowed her eyes because there was something about Kate's tone—

"But it turns out you're actually kind of a sap."

She sniggered and it felt like something hard and heavy had broken off in her chest; the next breath she took in came easier than the last. And yet—

"I don't want to think that any of them could have... or might have... done something like that," she murmured.

Kate reached out again, setting one hand lightly on Sam's knee.

"I know. And hey, I could be wrong."

Sam could feel the corner of her lips turn up.

"You could, huh?" she asked, not even bothering to hide her disbelief. Kate nodded, returning the smile.

"On rare occasions, it's been known to happen."

"Right. Like when you decided it was a good idea to go into the station of a suspected criminal head, looking to bargain for a ride on a ship?"

"So! What are you doing up here anyway?"

Sam's smile widened, but she didn't comment on the new direction. "I'm setting up a system scan for comparison against the ship's current map information." That's what she was *supposed* to be doing. She hunched forward over the screen, squinting slightly, and absently reached her left hand up to the collar of her shirt. Her fingers closed over air.

"Why?"

Something tapped against her shoulder. Glancing over, she saw Kate holding out the pair of glasses her hand had been searching for.

"Thanks," she said, slipping them on. "This part of the system wasn't fully chartered before the border was established and what was mapped was done a long, *long* time ago. By running a scan and comparing it to the database, we should be able to pluck out any interesting anomalies near the coordinates that Mac picked up from the last relay."

Comprehension relaxed the muscles of Kate's face. "Anomalies like a pirate base?" she suggested, maneuvering around the small space until she could peer over Sam's shoulder. Sam started to point out she hadn't run the scan yet so there wasn't anything to see but then… she didn't.

"Yep," was what she said instead, flexing her fingers over the inputs and mostly ignoring the reduction in space between their persons. It wasn't as if she had given any further consideration or contemplation of their previous two… physical exchanges.

Kisses, Sam. They were kisses. Please never use the phrase 'physical exchanges' again, she berated herself. They had mostly settled the first instance, what with Kate's apology, and then Sam had gone and completely lost her mind by instigating the second round, which they hadn't discussed or acknowledged in any way, which was *just fine* in Sam's opinion. Except for how sometimes she found herself sharing things she didn't intend to, or drifting closer when she didn't realize she was moving, or watching Kate's mouth whenever she was talking—

Wait, what? "What?" she asked as her brain caught up to the fact Kate had been speaking and she hadn't heard a word of it. In her defense, she wasn't the only one that seemed to be having a problem.

"Uh… I said, how long is that going to take?" Kate stuttered, her own gaze jumping away for a second before being pulled back the next.

Beep.

 Sam lifted a finger. "Not that long," she replied, shooting for casual and feeling like she got at least within ten feet of it. It likely would have been more convincing if she hadn't had to wet her lips before speaking.

Sam glanced down at the readout on the screen. She frowned, her forehead wrinkling as she peered closer. After swiping a finger across the screen, her frown deepened.

"What is it?" Kate asked, drifting toward her again, and this time Sam barely noticed, too intent on deciphering the information the system was presenting.

"This is the map that's in the database." Sam's finger dragged over the screen again and the view shifted. "And this is the map that was just returned with the scan. Notice anything different?"

Kate chewed thoughtfully on her bottom lip. "No. Looks like a small system. Two planets. Both gas giants. Half a dozen moons for… oh. Not six moons."

"Exactly." Sam swiveled away from the console to the screens to her right.

"Could we be in the wrong spot? The wrong system?"

Sam's shoulders gave a short bounce. "Highly unlikely."

Kate managed to wait almost a full minute before she gave in. "So, what are you doing now?"

"I'm running a GX scan."

After a moment, Kate opened her mouth—

"It will tell me the radiation levels of the system. Which will tell me if there were any major body collisions in the recent past," Sam explained.

"Doesn't the fact that there are four moons instead of six kind of already tell you that?"

"Some scientific evidence would be nice."

"So, while you're doing that, maybe we could also talk about why it would matter if there were only four moons instead of six? I mean, we don't really care about the moons, do we?"

"It depends on when the collision occurred."

"Why?"

"Because when any bodies in space collide—stars, planets, black holes—it sends out a massive amount of radiation."

"Okay."

"And radiation is bad for living things."

"Yes, I'm aware."

"So, if there was, say, a pirate base in the system?"

"It might have been wiped out in the blast. Did anything come up in the first scan?"

Sam slid back to the main console. "It's hard to tell. If there is large-scale radiation it could be interfering with the scan." She brought the system map back up on screen. "There are a couple of objects around this planet here that weren't there before, but they could be debris from the collision that got pulled into orbit."

Kate fell silent and Sam shifted from one screen to another. After what felt like forever, but might have been as short as five minutes, Sam sat back again and stared at nothing.

"Okay then," she said, suddenly.

"Okay what?" Kate asked.

"We're just going to have to go to the exact coordinates and see what we see."

"Just show up?" Kate stated. "And what, hope there isn't a giant armada of space pirates waiting for us?"

"What's the worst that could happen?" Sam threw out, already drawn into course calculations.

"I literally just said it. Why are you like this?" Kate inhaled sharply.

"Like what?"

"It was a rhetorical question. You really want to go in blind?"

"Isn't that what we've been doing this whole time? Why stop now? I could send a probe, but if there is a *pirate armada*," Sam wiggled her index fingers, "and they spot it, it's gonna look real suspicious."

"Yeah, maybe, but—"

"Besides, we've got the ID code. Nothing suspicious about a ship coming back to base. And—" Sam hesitated, unsure if it was fair to mention the next bit out loud. She already knew Kate had been struggling with the more dangerous aspects of their current situation. What she had been about to say wasn't likely to help.

"Go on," Kate prodded gently, after a moment.

Well. Honesty, right? "I don't know what else to do. This is our one lead."

Kate was silent. Her hands fidgeted in the twisting way they did whenever the woman was nervous. And still, she nodded.

"I trust you."

seventeen

It took three days, measured by the onboard clock, to reach the coordinates of the planetary system. Three days uninterrupted by ship sightings, crew accidents, or revelations of any kind.

The back of Sam's neck itched, as if some microscopic organisms were burrowing through the short hairs there. She couldn't quite figure if the anxiety was due to memory or anticipation—either way, there was the sense of standing in front of an airlock, peering out into the void of space, and hoping the steel door wasn't about to blow away.

As they drew closer to their destination, no armada on the radar, the sight that did greet them was enough to take her mind off the feeling.

It was too large to be a satellite. It looked nothing like a space station. Sam had never seen anything like it. She didn't know how to describe it.

She didn't even know how to *begin* to describe it.

"What the hell *is* that?" Kate breathed, staring at the monstrosity that floated outside the ship's view screen.

"It's got to be a station," Mac insisted from behind the navigation console. Instead of observing out the front viewer, he brought up the image on the computer screen.

"*That's* a station?" Kate's voice was unbelieving.

Mac tapped on the display, zooming in further on the picture. "That's a ship, coming out of what I assume is a docking bay. And here—" he pointed to another section of the structure "—those are gravity wells for artificial gravity. It's definitely a station. I've never seen one like this before. This…" he frowned. Sam had an idea of what he had been about to say.

"It looks like a scrap heap," she said, flatly. "There is no way some pirates stuck this thing together out of stripped vessels or whatever other weird thing you're thinking."

"Could have been an orbital mining base," Addy suggested, leaning over the nav console. She waved Mac's hands aside and swiped at the screen with her own fingers. After a second of looking at it upside down, she placed her index fingers in opposite corners and rotated the image. She nodded.

"Yeah, that could definitely have been a heavy core platform. It looks like they built up on it, added structural support underneath and along the sides. It's not pretty, but it looks functional."

"Why would there be a mining base out here?" Sam asked, her mind flipping back to the star chart for the system.

Addy pursed her lips. "To… mine?" she hazarded.

"Let me rephrase that: Why would someone set up a mining base in an unstable system?"

"Maybe they didn't know it was unstable?" Addy offered.

"Then they hired some pretty shitty system surveyors. But who the hell cares why it's here." Sam turned toward Mac and jutted her chin at the screen. "You're sure the signal is coming from there?"

Mac nodded. "Yes. Now that we're close enough, I can get a fixed signal from the shuttle. It's definitely on board that… thing."

"Okay." Her attention shifted to Addy. "Any special pirate docking procedures we should know about?"

Addy held up her hands. "I've never docked at a secret pirate base before. This is a new and joyous experience I am sharing with all of you."

Great. "Well. I guess there's only one thing left to do."

Sam hoped it didn't get them all killed.

It turned out that docking procedures in a secret pirate space station were exceptionally basic. Non-existent, really. No communications. No flashing displays or locked gates. Sam simply piloted the ship into the bay and set it down in a nearly empty hangar. If it weren't for a small scattering of shuttles and cruisers, she would have thought the base abandoned. The prickle at the nape of her neck flared as she looked out the front viewscreen and saw no signs of life.

"So where is everyone?"

"Out pirating?" Mac suggested, quietly.

Sam frowned over at him. "Why are you whispering?"

"I don't know."

"Hmmm." Sam pushed up from the pilot's seat and walked out of the bridge, Mac right behind her. By the time she reached the cargo bay, Addy and Kate had secured the final landing stages and were preparing the exit ramp. Parker loomed close by with her massive weapon cradled in both hands. They all turned expectantly to Sam as she crossed the threshold; it struck her that, despite her reservations, she had somehow ended up with a new crew.

With a little luck, things would turn out better for this one than it had for the last.

A lot of luck, she amended, as she considered what they were about to do.

"Okay. Mac, you've got the tracker?"

He held up a small tablet and nodded. "Right here."

"Good. Here's the plan. Mac and I will go out, find the shuttle, search it, grab the package for Floodwater, come back, and we'll all get the fuck out of here," she outlined, holding her hands out. "Any objections?"

"Is that a real question or—" Kate started. Beside her, Parker shifted her stance, slinging her gun into the cradle of one elbow.

"If you think I'm sitting on this ship while you go out to get that package, you've got another thing coming." The mercenary's face may as well have been carved from granite.

Sam tipped her head slightly in acknowledgement. "Well, you are kind of... conspicuous. Maybe we don't take the big gun, huh? New plan. Parker, Mac, and I will go out. You two will stay here with the ship. If something goes wrong, you can—"

"We can what? Blast on out of here? And what if something goes wrong *here*? On the ship? While you're out there?" Kate interrupted.

Sam rubbed a hand over her forehead. "Try not to let anything go wrong with the ship."

"Like what?"

Addy began listing items, ticking them off her fingers. "Well, I'm guessing we'll want to keep the core heated so we can take off immediately. But if it gets too hot without proper exhausting, we could blow it, which would lead to a massive—"

Kate held up a hand to cut the engineer off. "You are not helping. Why don't we all just go out together?" she pressed.

"You want to just leave the ship unsecured in a pirate dock?" Sam questioned, arms folded, determined to win this argument. "Because I would like to make sure the ship is still here when we go to leave."

"Can't you just *lock* it?"

"Yeah, that worked real well on Icarus 3, when Floodwater's goons traipsed all over it, didn't it?" Sam tilted her head toward Parker. "No offense."

"None taken. Your locks are garbage."

"You'll be fine. Just don't open the doors to anyone you don't know," Sam suggested.

Kate rolled her eyes. "The doors open from the outside."

Sam shrugged. "Only if the pressure seal is off."

"You know, the sooner we get out there and find the damn shuttle, the sooner we can get gone from this place," Parker pointed out, her annoyance obvious.

Fighting down impatience, Sam took hold of Kate's arm and tugged until there were more than a few feet of distance between them and the others. And then, since she could see the others looking on with interest, she turned her back to them for at least the illusion of privacy.

"Look. This ship is the most important thing in my life. I need... I am *asking* you to watch it for me," she stated, as quietly as she could manage, because what she wanted to say was *there is no fucking way I am letting you off this ship.*

She had a feeling that sentiment would not go over well.

Kate glared back and Sam could see the arguments brewing in the depths of her eyes. She braced herself for a stirring defense of her position and was astonished when the other woman let the fight drain out of her.

"You are so… frustrating," Kate replied with a quick shake of her head. Before Sam could comment on that, Kate reached out, grabbed hold of her jacket lapels, and dragged her close. She held one finger up in front of Sam's face. "I will look after your ship. But I swear, if you die, I will fucking kill you."

Sam lifted her eyebrows at the words but reconsidered her response in light of the tone they were delivered in. "Okay."

Giving a short nod, Kate pressed a brief but hard kiss to Sam's mouth before releasing her grip. Sam stumbled slightly and had to regain her balance before she turned back to the others, eyes narrowing preemptively. But Mac appeared absorbed in the screen of the tracker, and Addy had moved to the room's console, her hands already tapping commands into the screen. Only Parker stood exactly as before, weapon readied, face blank. Sam had the urge to lift her fingers to her lips and instead smoothed them down the front of her jacket.

"Okay. Anything else? Or can we—"

At Addy's raised hand, Sam sighed. "Yes, Addy?"

"Real quick. What if the parcel is *not* on the shuttle? Did we ever decide?"

A pressure began to swell in Sam's lower chest, between her stomach and her heart. She heard herself speak, but it sounded like she was underwater.

"You mean, what if I dragged you thousands of lightyears through space to a dangerous pirate base for nothing?"

Addy rocked back on her heels slightly. "Kind of? But mostly, I was wondering if we had a Plan B."

Sam recognized that a Plan B would have been smart. She *wanted* to have a Plan B. However, every time she had considered the possibility of Plan A failing, she had been paralyzed by a complete and utter lack of other options. And if she thought about *that* for too long, paralysis started to seep into everything.

"Plan B is we get off this station and reassess our options." Kate's voice was firm and confident; when Sam turned to her, the look on her face was the same. The statement seemed to satisfy Addy, who gave a quick two-fingered salute.

"All right. Drop the ramp. Once we're clear, lift it back up and lock it down," Sam ordered.

The grind of the ramp descending swallowed the last of her words, but she saw Addy bob her head and figured she had gotten the gist.

Or maybe it was less of a nod and more of a startled jerk because as Sam descended the walkway, Mac, and Parker thudding along beside her, she found half a dozen figures waiting for them in the once-empty bay. Each one armed, with their weapons pointing directly at them.

"Shit," she muttered even as her brain added a long drawn out *fuuuuuccckk*. She felt Parker tense, saw the rise of the mercenary's shoulders out of the corner of her eye, and could almost hear the heavy whine of seven lasers firing at once. Her hand shot out before she could think to stop it, latching onto Parker's bicep.

It was like taking hold of a piece of the hull—hard and inflexible.

She had no sense as to what Mac was doing, but he wasn't a shining beacon of violence, and luck willing, had none of Jonah's propensity for spontaneity.

Then again, luck had been handing out some real shit bags throughout the entire endeavor.

One of the figures stepped forward from the others: a man with a full black beard and skin just a few shades darker than her own. His irises were an odd, pale purple, as if a cosmetic dye job had faded over time. The idea of fearsome space pirates going for dye jobs bounced around her head and, combined with the stress of the situation, nearly had Sam letting out a wild whoop of laughter.

She managed to keep it to a small, strangled noise.

"You have a choice, Sam, for you and your crew," the man said, his voice steady and nonthreatening, despite the muzzles pointed at them. Sam narrowed her eyes at his familiarity with her name. "I hope you make the right one."

Under her fingers, Parker's arm flexed as if it were seconds from wrenching from her frankly symbolic hold. She wanted to close her eyes but wasn't sure which view would be worse: the one in her mind or the one about to unfold before her.

"Captain?" Parker growled, clearly seeking permission to unleash.

Get to the shuttle, Jonah.

"Easy, Parker," she heard herself say as she lifted her hands in surrender, hoping like hell she wasn't making another mistake. "Easy."

eighteen

Addy recognized most people might describe her as laid back. Actually, there were probably a lot of *other* words people might use—weird echoed through her mind in Parker's flat drawl—but she was confident laid back were two of them.

Take, for instance, her current situation—being marched like a line of convicts with her crew, surrounded by armed pirates, through what basically amounted to a homebrewed space station. Parker's broad back was in front of her while Kate was at the end of the line.

She assumed Kate was still behind her.

As nonchalantly as she could manage, she twisted her head to peek over her shoulder and—

"Eyes front," came the barked command.

Addy obliged, but she had gotten enough of a look to confirm Kate's presence. That had to bode well, right? She wondered if their decision to surrender immediately had factored into the so far peaceful handling or if she had just been *that* right about the demeanor and nature of your average space pirate.

Not that she had ever doubted her ability to accurately judge character.

Since Kate was silent, Addy imagined the other woman was of a similar mind.

Or freaking out.

"So. What do you guys call this place, anyway?" She looked to the guard marching alongside her. The woman didn't quite match Parker in mass or height, but she did boast an intimating scar that ran vertically through one of her oddly purple eyes. No answer was forthcoming.

"What kind of ore did you mine on it?" Addy continued, undeterred. The guard seemed to jolt in surprise, though the movement was quickly suppressed.

"Yeah, I noticed the platform on our approach. It's real impressive what you've managed to do with it. Turning a heavy core frame into a habitable station with, I'm guessing, foraged parts is—"

"Be quiet." One of the guards snapped out the order from up front, where Addy could just see Sam walking with head bowed.

Addy held out her hands and shut up.

As if annoyed by the easy capitulation, the guard, a young woman with a harsh demeanor, spun back around.

They had traveled from the wide-open bay of the hangar to a segmented corridor with anemic lighting. The guard at the front halted at a set of doors and punched at the buttons of a keypad beside them. They slid open soundlessly.

Addy was impressed; WD-40 had to be a bitch to get out there.

The woman pointed at Addy and jerked her head toward the room.

"Separate the others. We'll take her in here."

That doesn't sound good, Addy thought as she felt a firm push at her back. She stepped forward into the room; it was dark, and the glow from the hall did little to illuminate anything within. Luckily, she didn't have to go far. After a few feet, a hand gripped her shoulder and jostled her down into a seat.

"How long have you been working for Miles Floodwater?"

Addy squinted up at the bright light abruptly pointed at her. It was impossible to see who asked the question, which she assumed was the *purpose* of the bright light, but she recognized the irritated tone of the guard that had snapped at her. Was she having a bad day? Or was that just her normal cadence, in which case, *rough* for anyone working with her on a daily basis.

Were the others were being questioned as well? Probably.

"I don't work for Floodwater," she replied, blinking away from the light. There wasn't much else in view. The room was small, a few feet wider than the table she was seated at. She couldn't tell how much further back the room went as it plunged into darkness deepened by the light. "I work for Sam. Six-week contract with a standard added-time bonus."

There was a dismissive sound, followed by murmuring she couldn't make out.

So, there was more than one person back there. She wasn't sure how useful the information was, but she tucked it away for now.

"Well, then how long have you been working for... 'Sam'?"

Addy could practically hear the quotes in the speaker's voice and debated the possible reasons for them.

Did they think 'Sam' was a euphemism for Floodwater?

Did they think Sam's name wasn't Sam?

She tapped both index fingers lightly against the smooth surface of the table. Time in space was always so *tricky* to keep track of, no matter how many jobs she did.

"Little over four weeks," she answered when she'd finished her mental calculation.

"And where did you first come into contact with her?"

"With who?"

There was a pause, followed by a sharp, *"Sam."*

"Oh. A holo-station on Icarus 3. I had just finished a two-year stint on a mining vessel in the Haldron system, which I do not recommend. That system is woefully underdeveloped in terms of supply and transit stations. The ship I was on was a real piece of shit, too. But you can't really expect a class two vessel to—"

"When did she bring you to Floodwater?" A second voice interrupted, closer than the other. Addy thought she saw the blurred edges of a figure hovering on the border of the shadows.

If the first voice had sounded irritated, then the new voice was *pissed*.

Addy folded her hands together on top of the table and shook her head. "I've never met the guy. I went straight from the holo-station to the ship. Which was lightyears ahead of my last job. A little misaligned, needed some light maintenance, but otherwise in good shape, considering—"

A dull thump was followed immediately by a tremor through the table. The second voice issued what sounded like a reprimand, and maybe a name, but it hissed out too quickly for Addy to catch.

Another pause and Addy thought she could hear air being sucked aggressively in through someone's nostrils.

"Why did Floodwater hire you?" the first voice asked, as if through gritted teeth.

Leaning back in the chair, Addy crossed her arms and shook her head again. "I told you. He didn't. I signed a contract with Sam; the paperwork is on file on the ship. I'm just here to make sure the engines don't melt. Which is more or less impossible considering all the safeguards but—"

"I hardly think a guild level six engineer would be necessary just to keep the *engines from melting*," the first voice stated, scornfully.

Addy smiled faintly. "The kraken has a very complex core design. Which reminds me; I'd love to see the power setup you have for this station. Any chance we can wrap this up and go take a look?"

There was silence.

And then the quiet swish of doors opening and closing.

"Guess not."

"How long have you been working for Miles Floodwater?"

Parker stared blankly ahead. The only sound she made was the quiet shift of one arm folding over the other. Slow and methodic, the movement was somehow threatening; maybe it was the flat expression on her face or the controlled rage simmering in her dark eyes, both of which stared into the bright light without blinking.

There was a pause, and the voice cleared its throat.

"We know you're part of his organization. Why did he send you here?"

Parker remained silent.

"What was your mission? To eliminate? To retrieve?"

One breath in. One breath out.

"Are you in contact with him? Are there others coming?"

In. Out.

"If you're expecting a rescue, you can forget it. You and your friends are nothing to a man like Floodwater."

The shadows behind the light receded slightly and the fuzzy outline of two figures came into shape. Against the back of her biceps, Parker's fingers flexed.

"You don't owe him any sort of loyalty."

The corner of Parker's lips curled up; it annoyed her, but she couldn't help it. Sometimes they were all just a little too predictable.

She did wonder where her gun was though.

"How long have you been working for Miles Floodwater?"

Kate raised a hand up to block the light shining in her face and scowled at the disembodied voice that floated in from the dark side of the room.

"Who are you? What do you want from me?" she demanded, swallowing down the nerves bubbling in her throat. At least this time there wasn't a muscled lackey with a hand around her throat.

Yet.

"How long have you been working for Miles Floodwater?"

Pressing her palms down against the table, Kate shook her head. "I am a United citizen. I have rights. You can't hold me against my will."

"You're not in United territory, Ms. Anvers. And I wouldn't expect a UNE lawyer to make the trip out here."

The hairs on the back of Kate's neck stood. "How do you know my name?"

"I don't think you're in any position to ask questions, Ms. Anvers. After all, you're the one that broke into our station."

Kate settled back in her chair, willing herself to stay calm. What would Sam say? Nothing helpful, most likely. Addy?

"It's not like your doors were locked," she replied, trying for flippant. The shake in her voice probably gave her away.

"Ms. Anvers, this will go a lot easier if you just answer our questions. We already know that you met with Miles Floodwater on Icarus 3, approximately five weeks ago."

How?! she wanted to snap, but it seemed unlikely she'd get an answer. Instead, she huffed and rolled her eyes at the thought of the words "meeting" and "Floodwater" in the same sentence.

"If you call kidnapping and threatening to kill someone 'meeting with them,' then yeah, we had a grand old get together. Where are the others? What have you done with them?" A cold thought raced through her brain and down her spine. "If you've hurt them in any way—"

"You'll what, exactly?"

"Keira." A second voice chastised. There was shuffling, the sound of someone moving further back in the room.

"Your friends are safe. We have no intention of harming them."

"And I'm supposed to trust you? After what you did to Sam's crew?" Kate asked, glaring into the shadows. "I can't even see you. Why would I believe anything that you say?"

The bright light shut off, casting the entire room into darkness. Then, slowly, the room brightened as the main overhead lights came on. Kate blinked away the spots in her vision.

Across the table from her sat a woman with dark hair pulled back from her face. Her hands were folded in front of her, and she watched Kate with purple eyes narrowed in consideration. She didn't look angry, more thoughtful, as if one of Kate's questions had managed to sway her in some way.

Behind her stood another woman, one who did not appear calm or thoughtful. Her face was drawn tight while her lips pressed together in an obvious attempt to keep from speaking. Kate had a feeling she was "Keira."

The woman at the table drew forward. "Tell us—" she hesitated. "Explain to me your... encounter with Floodwater," she rephrased, an underlying sense of urgency in her tone. "Please. It's important."

Kate shifted in her chair, trying to gauge the woman, wondering if it was a setup or trap. Wasn't that how they did that sort of thing in films? One nice guy, one asshole, and they go back and forth until the person being questioned cracked? If she trusted now, what kind of price would she be paying later?

Still, it wasn't like she had a lot of options.

"His goon smashed Sam unconscious, grabbed me, and dragged us both into some office where Floodwater was waiting. He told us we'd either do a job for him or die. Well," Kate held up one hand with a mocking little wave, "actually, he just started talking about cutting off fingers. I inferred the whole 'death' part. I guess whoever told you about the meeting left that part out."

The woman sat back and brought her fingers up under her chin. Behind her, Keira stepped forward.

"They still—" she began, but the seated woman cut her off with a motion.

"We may have gotten this wrong. Bring Marcus to me. I need to speak with their captain."

"But—"

"Now. And release the others while you're at it."

Keira looked appalled at the command. "Even the merc—"

"All of them."

Choking down what looked like a painful amount of words, Keira spun around and stormed out of the room, taking with her the feeling of potential immediate harm, for which Kate was grateful.

Until the woman at the table looked up, her expression sharp and intense. Kate realized the possibility for harm was still there.

"But first. Tell me about Sam's former crew."

Sam contrasted her current situation with the last time she had been in a chair, in an unfamiliar room, and held against her will for reasons unknown. It helped that her face didn't throb with the echoing force of a Benny secret handshake. On the downside, with Floodwater, she'd had the advantage of being aware of his temperament.

She'd only seen the aftermath of what the pirates were capable of. As far as she knew, Addy, Mac, Parker, Kate—they could all be drifting out in the cold of space at that very moment. A swirling mix of anger, guilt, and fear was crawling up from her stomach and threatening to choke her.

The door slid open. A woman, tall with black hair drawn tight against her head, entered carrying a slim tablet. Another figure appeared in the doorway momentarily, but the woman held up her free hand in a clear "stay back" gesture. She stepped in and the door swished shut.

Sam did not know how long she had been in that room. Half an hour? More than an hour? Several hours? However long it had been, there had been one thought she had kept at the forefront of her brain, in front of the thoughts of attempted escape or deception or negotiation.

As the woman approached the table, Sam spoke that thought out loud as calmly as she could manage.

"I'll tell you whatever you want to know. Do whatever you say. Just let my crew go unharmed."

The words caused a momentary hitch in the woman's stride, a brief stutter before she reached the table. She laid the portable screen down on the table, folded her hands over it, and met Sam's gaze.

"Did you kill Jonah Whent?" she asked.

Sam stared, caught between repeating her plea as many times as necessary and by the woman's eyes, which were the same unnatural purple as the man from the hangar. It took a moment for the sentence to interrupt the dueling thoughts, cleaving to the center of her brain like a sharp knife.

"What?" The sound of Jonah's name coming from the woman's mouth was so unexpected, Sam was certain she had misheard. A second later the full comprehension of the words hit, and she pushed back in the chair. "*What?*"

"Were you in any way responsible for the death of Jonah Whent?" the woman reiterated and there was something calculating in her countenance, ready to add up every syllable spoken into an ultimate judgment.

Sam had started to shake her head but froze as the question changed. *You get your ass to the shuttle. No arguments,* she heard herself say. She closed her eyes and watched his back recede.

"I was his captain. I was responsible for him."

When she looked again, the woman's face had softened.

"Did you *knowingly* contribute to the events of his death, Sam?"

The question sat atop the other two, teetering out of place. It was gentle where the others had not been, and though she understood all the parts, Sam was confounded by the whole.

"How do you know who I am?" she asked, stepping to the side of it.

A brief smile crossed the woman's lips. "You're not as anonymous as you might think. Your refusal to work with Miles Floodwater, for instance, is quite well known. So well known, in fact, that we considered if it was a ruse. When Jonah contacted one of our agents, we weren't sure how much to trust him. Or you."

Sam tried to sink further into confusion to escape the sharp sting the information brought. More secrets. There had been more secrets. "Jonah contacted you."

"He did. And it was decided that what he was offering was worth the risk. We arranged a meeting, not far from our borders, along your intended flight path."

A low hum droned in Sam's ears. Almost against her will, she could see the pieces fitting together. "He was going to give you whatever was in Floodwater's parcel."

The woman nodded and slid the tablet across the table. "Our ship was delayed, and by the time we reached the coordinates, you were gone. It was on our return trip that we discovered this."

The screen of the tablet blinked on, and Sam's gaze lowered to it involuntarily.

Displayed was the interior of a room; it took Sam a second to recognize her shuttle. The screen shook slightly, and the view began to pan, a time lapse running in the corner. An unintelligible murmur of voices played.

Her entire focus was on the bodies splayed out around the small space; the unnaturalness of their positions made it obvious they were dead. The camera steadied and then lowered to one of the corpses, zooming in on the face. Sam felt her heart clench in her chest.

Surprise and relief flooded into her when she saw the face was not one she recognized.

"What is this?" It came out quieter than Sam expected. Quieter than she would have liked. She cleared her throat. "What the hell is this?"

With anger she thought she should feel, she shoved the tablet away from her. The woman's hand dropped down over it and slid it to the side.

"We found your shuttle drifting approximately two marks beyond the border. We assumed it was a distressed vessel and boarded with the intention to assist. As you saw, assistance was... no longer possible."

Sam frowned at the description, wishing she hadn't pushed the tablet out of reach. Still, the images were clear enough in her mind.

"Who were they?" she wanted to know.

"According to some items that we found on their persons, they belonged to an outlier group that occasionally raids along the border. We've had dealings with them before. Deeper investigation, however, proved them to be men in the employ of Miles Floodwater."

Lifting a hand to her face, Sam tried to let the information upload into her brain, past the other swirling thoughts that scattered each time she brushed against one. Jonah had been in contact with pirates. Had planned a meet. Pirates hadn't killed Jonah. Hadn't killed Triss or Ollie. That's what the woman in front of her was saying. What the evidence, if it was real, seemed to be saying.

Sam had no reason to believe her, but then, she couldn't think of a reason the woman would be lying.

And she sure as shit didn't have any trouble believing Floodwater had more of a hand in how things had gone down. Had he set Jonah up? Why? Had he known what Jonah had been planning? How? Did it prove there had been a traitor?

Why the hell hadn't he *told* her any of this?

Her hand lifted to her temple and rubbed the skin above her brow. She barely noticed the woman had risen to her feet, had maneuvered around the table so she sat against it, well within Sam's reach.

"Did you kill Jonah, Sam," she asked again, though this time it was barely a question.

Sam shook her head. "No. He was my friend. I would have died for him."

"Do you know where the parcel is?"

Sam lifted her head at the urgency in her voice. "Where is my crew?" she asked instead.

The woman's jaw rippled. "They're safe, Sam. I promise."

If ever there was an appropriate time for an eye roll, Sam felt like it was then. "Why should I trust you? Why should I trust *any* of this?"

"They are—"

Before the woman could finish, the door to the room slid open and Kate rushed in, frantically searching the space. When her gaze landed on Sam, she lurched forward so violently that Sam braced herself, not sure if she was anticipating an attack or an embrace.

Neither occurred. After two steps Kate drew herself up short, as if she had hit an invisible wall. It might have been comical if not for the strain evident on her face. Her eyes flicked over to the woman before shifting back to Sam's.

"Are you okay?" Her voice was heavy with relief.

Sam nodded and considered Kate's frantic demeanor and the potential causes. "Are you okay?" she echoed, searching for any visible signs of physical discomfort or distress. There were no bruises, no marks that suggested harm had been done. When Kate mirrored her nod, she felt her own rush of relief warm the icy ball where her stomach usually was. "Where are the—"

As she spoke, Addy stepped through the doorway, followed by Mac and finally Parker, without her weapon. Sam speculated momentarily at the condition of the unlucky pirate who had been tasked with taking it off her.

When Addy caught sight of Sam, her face brightened. "Hey, you're alive! That's great."

"Addy." At the low warning in Parker's voice, Addy turned.

"What? Is that not great? We should celebrate the little things."

Pressing her fingertips to her eyes, Sam shook her head—she was paying level six rates for this and had no one to blame but herself. Plus, the flood of serotonin was making her a little giddy.

"Are you all okay?" she wanted to know, dropping her hands back to the table.

Addy's head bobbed and she sat on the corner of the table. "Yeah, sure. No sweat. Well, Parker sweated a little, but only because they took her gun."

"And they better be giving it back," Parker stated flatly, crossing her arms as she stood against the wall, just behind where Kate had halted.

Mac pressed his palms down on the table.

"We're fine. You?"

"Yeah." She turned back to the woman, who had remained silent through the exchanges. Sam wasn't sure if she was impressed or annoyed by her patience, but it did help to see a crinkle of irritation on the woman's brow. "Before I tell you anything, I want to know who you are."

The woman straightened, opening her body up to the rest of the room.

"My name is Iris."

When she offered nothing more, Sam stretched forward, impatient. "Why are you so interested in Miles Floodwater and his parcel?"

"Does it really matter?"

Shit. Sam decided that, fuck it, she couldn't pull off the taciturn badass who could convince her opponent to give up details with nothing more than a hard glance. She'd just have to settle for grumpy old fuck who got the answers she needed.

"Whatever it was Jonah found, that he promised you, it's not on my ship. I figured the only *other* place it could be is on the shuttle."

"And this is the only reason that you came here? Nothing else?" Iris prodded, the same intensity from before evident in her tone. Sam wondered if it was worry or anger fueling it and was baffled to think Floodwater could have some reach or presence even all the way out there, beyond the borders of so-called civilized space.

She nodded. "Yeah, that's it."

A ghost of a smile appeared on Iris's lips. "And why should I trust you?"

Shit, Sam thought, annoyed at hearing her own words echoed back at her. Well, they'd come that far. She held up her right hand in front of her face, making sure to look through the space where her middle and ring finger should have been.

"I don't exactly have any reason to be loyal to Floodwater. In fact—" she cut herself off abruptly, her gaze shooting over to Mac. She wasn't sure that they had come quite *that* far.

Iris bent closer. "In fact?" she questioned.

Mac looked back at her, but his face was inscrutable in a way that Jonah's had never been. Or maybe it was just the fact that every time she looked at *him*, she expected to see Jonah, and it made it impossible to read him.

"Jonah thought there was something in the package that might, I don't know, bring down Floodwater. Or at least cause him a lot of trouble if anyone found out about it." She huffed out a laugh as her brain caught up with her mouth. "And you know what it is. He would have told you. Or maybe you already knew." Sam shook her head and laughed again. What did it matter?

"It's on the shuttle. It *has* to be," she concluded. She couldn't tell if Iris was convinced. She didn't know if she had convinced herself. But Iris nodded.

"We will help you search for it."

Iris led them herself through the station to a much smaller hangar— "For ships we decommission or decide to strip for parts," she explained as they walked, escorted by two other pirates, their weapons holstered.

Sam was barely listening, her stomach knotted with anticipation while her mind tripped over itself. They were so close—she wanted it to be over, while another part of her whispered that it might never be. An even quieter voice lamented the idea of returning to her solo state.

And then the shuttle was directly in front of them. It was a generic emergency vehicle, one of a million or more made. But she knew.

Without a word, she scrambled until she was ducking low to slip inside the open airlock. Inside it was dark and she hesitated, trying to remember the space. There hadn't been much use for the craft; it had been one of those things that had to be kept on board, like a med-kit. Something you didn't expect and hoped never to have to use.

The layout was simple. Room for the crew. A cockpit. Some storage in the form of tall lockers and bins.

She crept in, pressing a hand against the ceiling to balance herself. The ship was tilted somewhat, and the angle played with her sense of direction. Her fingers rang along thick cables leading— she was fairly certain—toward the nose.

Triss would have been in the navigation chair, and the tiny cockpit held a maximum of two. Had Jonah been in there with her? He had responded to the comm, but he could have done that from either of the two secondary consoles located in the main chamber.

She bumped her shin and, bending low, saw that one of the bunks was pulled down from the wall. Had someone stretched out in an attempt to relax? Probably Ollie, trying to quiet his nerves. Sam could envision him with folded legs, breathing slowly and deeply. She shuddered and shook her head to clear the image.

There was debris scattered all over the floor: panels, spare parts, random equipment. Some of the lockers hung open, the bins emptied. As if they had been ransacked or thoroughly searched. She bit her lip as she picked her way over the mess. Ever since she first realized Jonah might have stashed something in the shuttle, she had considered all the places he could have hidden a thing too important to leave out of his sight. If he hadn't wanted her to know about the job, then he probably hadn't told the others either.

Sam paused, because what if he had? What if she was the only one who hadn't known?

Didn't matter, she thought abruptly. Didn't matter right now. All that mattered was where he had put it.

She passed the lockers, intending to leave them untouched. Too simple. Jonah liked to make hiding spots out of less obvious things. She stopped, reconsidered. He would have been in a hurry and under pressure. And maybe she didn't know him as well as she thought.

She pulled open the doors, one after the other. Empty.

The space narrowed as she drew closer to the cockpit and she stopped, gaze catching on an empty terminal docking station. She pushed a finger into each of the two connector flaps, searching the small spaces. Nothing.

The gap behind the airlock sign? Empty.

The dip above the entry to the cockpit? Clear.

The cockpit itself was even smaller than the aux bridge on the kraken. To the right, the pilot's chair was still tilted nearly 30 degrees, as had been Triss' habit. On the left, the second chair was turned so its tall back was facing the other. Sam climbed into it, her hands resting against the console. Everything on the pilot's side was mirrored on the left, backup controls in case they were needed. The only difference was the addition of the higher mapping, scanning, and comm functions. But nothing Jonah would have been able to open and sneak something inside. Not unless—

Her eyes landed on a speaker box that jutted out slightly from the bulkhead.

Almost without conscious thought, she fumbled through her pockets. After a bit of searching, she came up with a screwdriver she didn't remember stashing in her jacket. She watched, as if it were someone else's hands, as she methodically twisted the slender tool. Four screws dropped onto the dash, one quiet *ping* after the other. With the index fingers of both hands, she tugged the box forward. It pulled away easily, revealing a crevice the size of two fists jammed full of wires, a circuit board, and nothing else.

"Sam?"

Kate's voice came from the doorway, pulling her back to the present. Sam twisted in the seat to see the other woman leaning into the cockpit, a look of caution on her face.

It took Sam two tries to get the word out. "Yeah?"

Kate appeared to hesitate and then asked, "Can I help in here?"

Blowing out a long breath, Sam nodded.

"Yeah, sure."

They searched.

For hours.

Over every inch of the small, compact space. Through drawers and lockers. In every instrumental panel. Behind the casing of every string of lights. They dug into every single pocket of air that could be easily reached and many more that could not.

With each crevice she dug into, each panel she tore free, Sam's awareness shrunk to a laser-like beam, concentrated solely on the next centimeters in front of her.

There was no room for any thoughts—not for the distance they had traveled, the revelations about what had happened to her crew, her family. No space for Floodwater or pirates, for past mistakes or future disappointments. She dug through metal, fabric, wires; pushed past feelings and memories, for the one thing that would make it all stop.

There was nothing.

Sam sat, staring at the open recycling unit she had finished dismantling. She saw nothing, because there was nothing to see. It wasn't until a hand touched her shoulder that she realized she was staring simply because she could think of nowhere else to look.

"Sam?" Kate's voice was quiet, gentle. It might have been comforting if Sam could feel anything beyond a creeping numbness.

"Sam?"

Somehow, though she felt completely disconnected from herself, Sam turned her head. Looked at Kate, recognized the concern in her expression. And behind the concern, fear.

"It's not here," Sam breathed out.

nineteen

This isn't right, Kate thought. *This isn't how it was supposed to go.*

It felt as if the gravity had been turned off, as if everything and everyone were seconds from drifting off, nothing to tether them to safety. Kate stood in the middle of a pirate hangar half a galaxy away from home where the expected taste of triumph had soured.

She couldn't imagine how Sam felt. Sam, who hadn't said a word since that single hopeless exhale. Her anger, frustration, and disappointment were evident through the entirety of her body when she emerged from the shuttle empty-handed. There had been no comments; not a flippant remark from Addy or pointed question from Mac. Even Iris, so unreadable during interrogation, appeared unsettled.

Sam's expression was perfectly blank as she scrutinized the shuttle. Kate was certain she knew Sam well enough to know the captain was thinking about something, though she had no clue what. She hoped it was something productive, like what their next steps were, and not something stupid, like guilt.

Frowning, because knowing Sam it probably was guilt, Kate opened her mouth to point out just how stupid that was, when she realized Iris was already speaking.

"—arrange to have it moved to the main hangar." Iris paused, clearly waiting for Sam to respond. When Sam gave no indication that she had heard or was even listening, Iris turned to Kate, eyebrows lifted.

Am I the decision maker now? "Uh, sure. That sounds good?" Kate looked to Addy for support. The engineer nodded, massaging the crown of her head, near where her hair was tied up.

"Parker and I can go back and prep the ship for reattachment. If the shuttle's not too damaged, it won't take long."

Kate glanced at Sam for a response, but Sam had returned to the ship, seemingly fixated on a spot near the main airlock.

Iris was also watching Sam, a frown twisting her lips. She started to move in Sam's direction but stopped when the door to the hangar swooshed open.

A bearded man stepped through; Kate recognized him as the one who had originally captured them. He went immediately to Iris without sparing any of them a glance and murmured quietly into her ear.

There was a hint of irritation in Iris's face before it was quickly smoothed away. "Right. Marcus, escort these two back to the main bay and have Phillips and Carse tow the shuttle there as well."

A deep furrow appeared in Marcus's forehead. He nodded stiffly.

"And the others?" he questioned, his voice devoid of the doubt so clear in his raised brows.

Before Iris could respond, Mac stepped forward, one finger lifted as if to say, *actually*.

"Do you have any doctors on station?" he asked.

Iris nodded. "Yes, two. Are you injured?"

He shook his head. "No, I just... I'm a doctor. Sort of. I'd be interested in discussing with them their practice of deep space medicine on a colony this size." He shrugged and smiled faintly. "And maybe I could help if it was needed?"

After a moment of consideration, Iris nodded again, though with a measure of reluctance. Or, at least, it appeared so to Kate. "Marcus can take you to our medical facility."

"Okay. I mean, you could also just point me in the right direction? I'm sure he has more important things to be doing," he offered, turning up the wattage in his smile slightly.

Is he flirting with her? Kate thought, with no small sense of incredulity.

Iris responded to his smile with an arched one of her own. "Marcus will show you," she repeated firmly, lifting one hand dismissively toward the door. If he had any other suggestions, Mac refrained from verbalizing them and instead stepped through the doorway, Iris close behind. Marcus, Addy, and Parker followed and suddenly the room that had felt a little crowded was uncomfortably empty.

Which was ridiculous, considering the entire thing had started with her and Sam alone in a small room together and oh, yeah, that had been uncomfortable too, what with the whole being saved from certain death by a total stranger who had seemed, frankly, a little annoyed at having done-a-save. But while the Sam Kate remembered from that first meeting had been standoffish—awkward in a way that had implied a long time away from people—she'd still been considerate and present. Kate recalled the tea and offer of dry clothing, the gentle insistence on taking her someplace safe.

In contrast, the Sam standing in the room with her now was as distant as the planet Kate called home. She had withdrawn completely into herself, consumed entirely by whatever was going on in her head. Disappointment had to be part of it: fear and uncertainty as well. Kate felt those emotions keenly herself. She couldn't help but think maybe Sam's discontent went deeper than the letdown of not finding what she had been looking for. Finding the package would probably be like finding a part of Jonah; not finding it must have felt, in some small way, like losing him again.

Kate knew Sam wouldn't much appreciate the observation, so she kept it to herself.

"Well… I guess it's nice to be off the ship for a bit? And not in mortal danger? Though, I guess we still *could* be, but I sort of got the impression everything was… fine. You know. Friendly." She managed to rein in her rambling with some effort and chanced a look in Sam's direction.

Sam had one hand pressed against the hull of the shuttle, her eyes drawn to some specific point Kate couldn't see.

Stepping closer, she tried again. "Iris seems… helpful. I mean, she was kind of intimidating when she was questioning me, but once I told her we weren't working with Floodwater because we *wanted* to, she dialed that down."

Nothing.

Frowning, Kate crossed her own arms as she ruminated on the pirate leader's queries. "Actually, she seemed really interested in knowing what Floodwater was up to. Like she was expecting him to send someone out here for something. Maybe we should talk to her about it. Maybe she can help us?"

Just a few feet away and still having received no response, Kate blew out a sharp breath. "Sam? Are you listening? Sam?" She reached out and pushed gently against the other woman's forearm. The force was enough to knock it from the hull, revealing a burned patch of metal that might have once been a control panel.

Sam's head shot up. "What?" she snapped.

"Did you hear anything I just said?"

"About what?"

"About talking to Iris?" At Sam's continued look of incomprehension, Kate felt her eyes strain upwards. "About why she's so interested in Floodwater? Maybe she can help us somehow."

Kate had never seen incredulousness so perfectly inhabit someone's face as it settled into every single one of Sam's features.

"What kind of help do you think a bunch of space pirates on the far edge of the galaxy are going to be able to give us against one of the most powerful men in the universe?"

The dismissiveness in Sam's tone made Kate's shoulders curl upwards.

"I have no idea; that's why I suggested asking them. It sure as hell sounds like they have some animosity toward him. That might help us. You know, the whole the enemy of my enemy?"

Sam shook her head. "There are more important things we need to be thinking about."

"Like what?"

"Like figuring out someplace safe to take you."

Kate jolted in astonishment, both at the words and the vehemence with which they were spoken.

"What?" she heard herself ask, though her lips felt numb.

Sam straightened; her face animated now with an intensity Kate found unnerving. Her eyes were like storm clouds, and Kate could almost feel lightning building in them.

"Floodwater is not a patient man. If he hasn't sent someone after us already, he will soon. And he's not going to accept 'I couldn't find it.' So, we get you someplace you can disappear, and I'll go back, maybe figure out somewhere else to look. If he catches up to me, he won't care that you're not there. It's me he'll want." She said the last part quietly, almost under her breath, as if it were the least important part of the entire speech.

Running a hand through her hair, Kate tugged lightly at the roots. The sharp little pain proved that no, she wasn't dreaming. She was actually hearing this. Her heart began to knock in her chest, ringing loudly in her ears, as if it could block out the sounds coming from Sam's throat.

"So what? You're going to… to… *sacrifice* yourself?"

Sam shrugged, but the movement was too jerky to be casual. "He might be satisfied with the other fingers."

Kate glared. "Is that supposed to be *funny*?"

"No." Sam took a deep breath and a step forward. One of her hands hovered in the air before dropping to her side. "Look. Floodwater… he'd hurt you because it would hurt me. If he has me, he'll just hurt me. He won't bother looking for you." She smiled, without any humor. "He's not a *patient* man."

Kate searched every inch of Sam's face and saw the resolve etched there. She was sure this was what Sam had been ruminating so thoroughly on once they realized the parcel had not been on the shuttle. This was the argument she had been constructing, the decision she had been coming to while staring blankly into space.

"And I'm supposed to be okay with that?" she asked, softly.

The resolve didn't weaken, but a touch of remorse seemed to filter through Sam's mask. Her shoulders softened. "I guess you don't really have a choice."

Silence dropped between them, heavy and stifling. Kate felt it press against her like a hand physically pushing her backwards.

After a moment, Sam pressed her forehead against the hull of the ship. "I need to think," she muttered.

Kate cleared her throat, trying to get the words out before she choked on them. "You do that," she snapped, spinning and stalking out of the room.

She was not prepared to find Iris waiting in the hall. Kate pulled up short at the sight of the pirate leader leaning rather casually against the wall only a few feet down from the door.

"We should speak," the other woman declared calmly.

Looking back over her shoulder as the door whisked shut behind her, Kate shook her head. "I don't think Sam's interested in or willing to talk just now," she pointed out.

Iris straightened, clasping her hands in front of her, fingers twisting slightly. "But you are," she pressed.

Kate was about to deny it, to point out that it wasn't her place or her ship. But it was her life, wasn't it? And you couldn't start making a plan without first gathering the facts.

So, she nodded. "I'll listen," is what she offered.

"That's all I ask."

Addy had to hand it to the guy; somehow, he managed to *almost* look unintimidated by Parker's silent glower. Even more impressive, he offered the line, "Your weapon is safely secured," without so much as a flinch, despite the way Parker's eyes narrowed down to pinpoints resembling raging plasma fire.

"It'll be secure when it's in my hands," she stated flatly, flexing her fingers as if she were gripping the stock of the blaster. Or Marcus's neck.

"It will be in your hands when you leave this station. Not a moment before," he countered, matching her tone.

"I thought we weren't prisoners?"

"You're not. But you're also not one of us. And I don't trust you."

Parker shifted her stance and Addy tried to decide if that was the moment to jump in. Before things got too dicey.

"That makes two of us," Parker agreed in a low growl.

Addy held her breath. Maybe the moment had already passed.

Marcus tipped his chin up slightly. "So long as we understand each other."

Addy got the feeling several other things were exchanged through the lengthy stare that followed, but the threat of physical blows appeared to have passed. She was glad the daggers Marcus had been shooting at Parker were gone by the time he looked in her direction. Not that the strange purple orbs were particularly friendly, but at any rate she didn't feel compelled to check for knife holes.

"Remain within the bay at all times."

"Sounds pretty prisoner-y to me," Parker remarked dryly, as he moved to leave.

"It's a large station." He made a faintly mocking flourish with his hand. "Wouldn't want you to get lost."

He strode off, and if he'd had a cape or cowl, Addy imagined he would have flipped it over his shoulder.

She would have. Maybe she was just projecting.

Addy regarded Parker, who continued to glare at his retreating figure as if she could cause him to spontaneously burst into flames through sheer will alone.

Sighing, Addy shifted the bag on her shoulder and waited.

"I don't like him," Parker voiced after a solid minute. Or what felt like it.

"Well," Addy began, starting across the bay toward the ship, "the good news is that once we leave here, there's like a one in one hundred billion chance you'll ever cross paths with him again."

"Yeah, that's what I'm afraid of."

Addy chuckled at her companion's annoyance and, as she had a few times already, thought it was strange she and Sam were constantly at odds when they appeared to share the same disgruntled impatience with other people. Probably a case of being too much alike.

"Why are you so worried about your gun anyway?" Addy asked as they entered the docking bay. "Don't tell me you're one of those people that feel naked without it?"

Parker huffed but didn't reply. Addy continued.

"I mean, it's not like you even need it. You could probably kill someone just by scowling at them."

When Addy glanced up to see how that had been received, she found Parker eyeing her with not even thinly veiled skepticism.

"Obviously, that's not true or Captain Stick-In-His-Ass wouldn't be walking around upright. And no," Parker added, while Addy snickered again, "it's not about the gun. It's about it being *my* gun. I don't like it when people take things that belong to me."

That sounded reasonable enough to Addy. She started to say so when it became apparent Parker wasn't finished.

"The place where I grew up? If you didn't keep an eye on your things, someone took them. And even if you did watch, they *still* took them." Parker's hands curled into fists at her sides. Addy watched her arms swing as she walked and couldn't envision anyone trying to take something from that grip.

She felt the subtle press of being watched and glanced around; they seemed to be the only ones in the bay, but she figured there were cameras somewhere. But unlike most docks, which usually wanted you to *know* you were being watched, these were hidden amongst the rough infrastructure.

Addy was *very* curious about how the station had come into being.

She turned her attention back to Parker before she could get sidetracked.

"Where did you grow up?" she asked, figuring the question was simple enough. But Parker slowed and a wariness crawled across her face.

Revolving so that she was walking backwards, Addy reduced her speed to match but kept moving. Some distance, it looked like, was called for.

"What? I'm good enough to drink with and good enough to sleep with but trading home planet stories is a no go?" She said it jokingly, but there was an underlayment of hurt. Because she was fine with casual. She had been operating on casual, but there was casual and then there was *professional*, which was a little further removed than she thought they were being.

Parker rolled her shoulders. On closer inspection, Addy thought she saw a hint of embarrassment in the other woman's stiffness. Figuring it for a sensitive subject, Addy began to suggest they go directly to the ship to get the shuttle into place before Sam had a chance to view the extent of the repairs necessary. Nothing *difficult*, of course, but everything always went better without the boss underfoot.

"Ekan V," Parker answered before Addy had a chance to open her mouth. At Addy's lifted brows, Parker explained, "That's where I grew up. Some folks call it—"

"The backwater moon." Addy nodded, coming to a stop in front of the still lowered ramp. "I've been there. Couple times. Never had anything stolen, but I travel pretty light."

Parker's expression seemed to relax. "So?"

"So?" Addy echoed and Parker made a small impatient gesture with her hand.

"So, where did you grow up?"

"Oh. Just about everywhere in the galaxy actually." At Parker's puzzled expression, Addy grinned. "I was born two years into a five-year contract, and my mother is not the type to quit a job. I think we were on a station in the Nanda quadrant for a year or so and then it was tag along. Don't think I've spent more than three months on a terran surface."

"Guess that explains it."

"Explains what?"

Parker rolled her eyes and her lips pulled back faintly. "Why you're so damn weird. Too much artificial gravity."

Addy shook her head, not the least bit offended. "I think it's more genetics than gravity. Though to be honest, I'm the most normal one in my family. All my brothers and sisters are way weirder than I am."

Parker's mouth didn't move, but her face was practically shouting her doubt. The next words she spoke, however, were not the jab Addy had been expecting.

"How many do you have?"

"How many brothers and sisters?" Addy clarified. At Parker's nod, she replied, "Twelve."

"*Twelve*?"

"Yep. Four sets of triplets and then me. Lucky thirteen."

"Your poor mother."

"She's a saint. We don't often all get together. Too far apart. Last time I saw them all I think I was fourteen? Fifteen? Can't quite remember what the occasional was. She tapped a finger to her nose and did some more mental math. "Out of everyone, I probably see my brothers Bendigo and Ballarat the most. Their routes are always passing through Icarus. Ballina—that's our sister who's the third in their triplet—works with them, too, but she never joins us for drinks. Kind of a bitch really."

One of Parker's eyebrows lifted nearly to her hairline. "Your brothers' names are Bendigo and Ballarat? And you got a sister name Ballina?" Parker recited the monikers as if she were memorizing facts for a test and was not at all certain she believed the information she'd been given was correct.

Addy nodded, pleased to finally be sharing something substantial. "Yep. They're the babies before me. The oldest are my brothers Darwin, Perth, and Hobart. Then three sisters, Melbourne, Cairns, and Canberra. Then two more girls, Sydney and Geelong, and another brother Warwick."

When Parker offered a long blank stare in return, Addy added a polite, "What's your brother's name, by the way?"

"Ronny."

After waiting a beat to see if anything else was forthcoming, Addy shrugged. Apparently not everyone used centuries old navigational charts to name their kids. Nobody was perfect. "You ever go back? To Ekan?" she clarified when Parker remained silent.

"Floodwater's not big on vacation time."

"What about after?" Addy asked, curious. She vaguely recalled a conversation with Sam along the same lines and figured a half-baked notion was working its way around her brain. No doubt it would spring forth at some completely random time, so she didn't dwell on it too much.

She enjoyed how her mind worked.

"After what?"

"You know, after Floodwater. You're not planning on working for him forever, right?"

Parker didn't immediately reply. When Addy looked, the mercenary's face was drawn tight. It made Addy replay the question over in her head, just to double check the words she had spoken, in case she had accidentally slipped something wildly offensive in.

No, seemed pretty norm—

"You never stop working for a man like Floodwater."

As she trailed Iris, Kate speculated on where the pirate was taking her for their talk. Back to the interrogation rooms? Or would it be more like Floodwater's office, a reflection of her power and status on the station?

Because it was obvious she *did* wield power. If her actions and the way Marcus deferred to her hinted at it, the journey through the winding halls of the station cemented it. They passed by a number of individuals, all of whom started to approach but were waved off.

Could just be popular, part of her mused, but Kate dismissed it. She knew exactly what it looked like when someone wanted something from you because you were the only one who could give it.

When Iris finally led her through a door as plain as all the others they had passed through, the room Kate stepped into had the feel of both a laboratory and a conference space. It was large but packed with an assortment of items. Some stacked on metal shelves pressed against the walls. Others strewn across long tables. All it needed was either an e-board and hologram suite or a massive tank with an unknown creation growing in it.

Thankfully, she saw neither.

"What—" Kate made a circle motion with one finger, "—is this?"

Smiling faintly, Iris backed against one of the tables and gave a little half shrug. "Part storage. Part junk room." She glanced around, her gaze lingering in a few spots, as if remembering something specific in each. "Part historical archive. It may help to answer some of your questions."

Kate picked up a random object from the nearest table—a twisting cylinder that looked more like a sculpture than anything practical—and held it up, one eyebrow raised.

"I think I have more now?"

Iris dropped her hands to the table, resting on them. "Let's see if I can answer some of them. You want to know how we knew who you were? That's simple enough. You are, all of you, listed in some capacity in various databases and systems. Once you became of interest to us, it was just a matter of searching out the information."

"Okay, but who accessed those records? I can't imagine you have a link to on-planet records from all the way out here. And how did we *become* interesting? Just by meeting with Floodwater?" Kate queried, with no small amount of exasperation.

Iris shook her head. "No, not just because. We couldn't possibly monitor everyone that meets with Floodwater. Think of us like a corporation. We have agents and advisors that live beyond the border. One of them intercepted details of the job Floodwater offered you, and that was what put you on our radar."

"You know what's in the package he wants Sam to recover," Kate guessed. Sam had said as much and because she had been trying to pull pieces together to see how they fit. What else could it be?

Iris nodded. "Yes, we do."

Kate flung her hands out. "So, what's in it?"

A small struggle played out across Iris's face. Her bottom lip folded in between her teeth. Kate waited, feeling jittery with anticipation for the revelation to come, but after another moment's pause, Iris's response was underwhelming.

"Files."

Kate waited another beat in case something a bit more profound was on its way. "Files," she repeated when Iris offered nothing more. "*Important* files?"

"In a manner of speaking."

"In a manner—no, you know what?" Kate waved her hands through the air in front of her. "Forget it. This is stupid. Sam was right." She muttered the last part to herself as she marched back toward the door. The knot that had been slowly tightening in her stomach since her argument with Sam twisted further as she tried to think about what to do now. Playing a cryptic guessing game was not on her list of priorities.

"Wait, wait."

Stopped in front of the door by Iris's voice, Kate inhaled sharply before looking back. Iris had lifted both hands, palms out, as if trying to calm a wild creature. Not far off. Kate felt a little like a wild creature.

"I'm sorry. It's… difficult to know exactly where to start."

Frustrated, Kate replied, "Then just start anywhere."

Dropping her hands, Iris shifted around the edge of the table and gazed down at the items scattered across it. Reaching out, she touched what seemed to be a small-scale model of the station.

"This is not a normal station," Iris began, slowly. Kate rolled her eyes.

"Yeah, I figured that out and I've only seen one other one."

Iris smiled before continuing. "It was originally chartered as a mining colony, the first in this section of the galaxy, over 200 years ago. Before the establishment of the border."

"You not about to tell me that you're over 200 years old, are you?"

"No. My grandparents were members of the original team of colonists. They saw an opportunity, a good one, and took it. But, as you might have guessed, mining was not the true purpose of the colony. That was just a cover. The real purpose was—"

"Genetic experiments," Kate interrupted. Looking surprised, Iris nodded, and Kate gave a shrug. "Well, what else could it have been?" she pointed out. "The distance to any other trade port would hardly make it worth it for drug synthetization, and 200 years ago was right around the time of—"

"The Genetic Accord. Yes. Experimentation with the human

genome was outlawed so they moved beyond the UNE's reach under the guise of business."

"Who's 'they'?"

"We're not certain. Many of the records were corrupted or lost when a large asteroid struck the moon the colony was originally built on. The colonists were forced to evacuate to what was, at the time, the mining platform. There were no long-range spacecrafts, a failsafe against escape, so there was no way to return to civilization. Every so often, though, another ship would come within range of the crafts they did have."

"And that's how they became pirates," Kate assumed, earning another nod.

"Yes. Unfortunately, our predecessors were a bit more desperate than we currently are, which accounts for the violent reputation we have. Contrary to what is often believed, we make every effort not to take lives."

"What about the pirates that attacked Dravanol Station? They sure as hell seemed intent on taking us out."

Confusion passed over Iris's face.

"We committed no attack on Dravanol Station. A station of that size and that distance; there's no benefit for us."

Kate couldn't see any reason not to believe her, so she tucked it away for now.

"Okay, forget Dravanol. I'm guessing those files have something to do with the experiments?" Kate asked, trying to shift the conversation back on track.

"Yes. We only recently discovered them in part of the original archive the colonists were able to preserve. They were downloaded and wiped from our system by one of our own, who then took the files and offered them, we believe, to Floodwater."

"Who 'hired' Jonah to pick them up, and when that failed, strong-armed Sam into finishing the job." As far as space conspiracies went, Kate figured it was easy enough to keep straight. "Okay, so then what? If we find these files, you want us to deliver them to you instead of him?"

"There are two benefits to handing the files over to us. The first is that nothing pertaining to those experiments belongs in the hands of a man like Miles Floodwater."

"Yeah, sure. That seems obvious. I can't really think of anything that belongs in that man's hands. But there is the small, not-insignificant fact that he threatened to kill us if we didn't bring him that package. And, no offense, how exactly are you suggesting we keep *that* from happening? We join your happy colony way out here on the edge of space?"

Iris appeared amused. Okay, maybe that was a *little* flippant.

"That is where the second benefit comes in. We have been in communication with someone very keen to see Floodwater's organization unraveled. The evidence in those files would go a long way in helping with that."

Something didn't quite add up. "Why? If these experiments happened 200 years ago, how could Floodwater be involved?"

"Ask yourself Kate, why would someone of Floodwater's disposition seek out illegal documented genetic experiments?"

Because he's an evil bag of human garbage felt like too simplistic an answer. "I don't know, for tips and tricks?" Kate gritted her teeth together as it hit her. "Because he's running his own experiments."

Iris nodded. "Even his desire for such information would be enough to warrant an investigation into some of his holdings, despite previous... reluctance. And if the files were found in his possession?"

Kate narrowed her eyes. "You just said that the files shouldn't be in his hands. Now you want us to give them to him? The files we *don't* actually have?"

"If they were recovered, they could be used to lay a trap. One even Floodwater would not be able to extricate himself from. And the threat against you would be removed."

"You want us to be bait," Kate hypothesized, because she could see the way it all made sense. A tidy little workflow where the critical path could either lead to locking up a monster or being destroyed by one.

Since the latter was already on the table, it wasn't the worst idea. Though Kate wasn't one hundred percent sure she agreed that arresting Floodwater would negate the threat against them. "I don't suppose you would mind sharing a little more information about this someone you've been talking with?"

For the first time, Iris hesitated. "Not at this time. Not unless you agreed."

"Great. So, bait or run." Kate shook her head and stared hard at nothing. If she looked long enough, maybe the answers would drop out of thin air. Bait or run. Was this another deal that would put them further upside down? How much could they trust Iris? She seemed forthright, but there was no way to know for sure. No certainty.

It wasn't as if certainty had been abundant before.

A small part of her was wondering what she was even doing there. Talking with Iris, negotiating with the leader of a community—that should have been someone else's job. Someone else should have been figuring out how to keep them alive, what they should do next, someone else who was off god knew where, doing god knew what—

Okay, so it was more than a small part of her. Was this how Sam felt? Or was there some wellspring of captain's confidence she tapped into?

Regardless, she was the one who was there.

"I'll talk to the others about it."

As the doors to the docking bay swooshed closed behind her and Kate started toward the kraken, she tried to put her thoughts into the same ordered lines as her steps. It would have been easy, if not for the fact that all her thoughts were flying off in wildly different directions. Should she trust everything Iris had told her? What reason would the woman have to lie? Should she tell Sam? Even if everything Iris had said was true, what did it really *mean*? They still didn't know where the files were. What if they couldn't find the parcel?

Prior to this excursion, she'd never been off-planet before; now she was just supposed to pick someplace in the galaxy, preferably one that wasn't within Floodwater's reach—*ha!* —and, what, settle down there for the rest of her life? Was she supposed to change her name? Her face? How much did facial reconstruction go for in the backwaters of the galaxy? Fuck, what if her facial reconstruction went horribly wrong and she ended up as some unrecognizable—

"Kate? Kate? You... okay?"

It took Kate a moment to comprehend that someone was speaking to her and another to recognize it was Mac. He was up against one of the landing struts, tablet in hand. She caught the strange look he gave her and realized she had been running her hands lightly over her face. Dropping them to her side, she shook her head and then nodded, trying to reorient herself.

"No. I mean, yes. Yes, I'm fine. Just... thinking."

She waited, expecting the next words out of his mouth to be "about what?" But the question didn't come. Instead, his head turned, and he peered behind them, as if trying to retrace her steps.

"Sam with you?" he asked.

For one wild moment, she was certain he knew exactly where she had been and who she had been speaking to. The idea zipped through her like a bolt of lightning, startling her with its ferocity. Just as quickly, she pushed back against the paranoia, dismissing the notion—how the hell could he have known and why would it even matter? She felt like she was seeing Floodwater everywhere now, and it occurred to her that she might be about to spend the rest of her life looking over her shoulder for him. The thought had her exhaling slowly, as if she could force some of the sudden weight out through her lungs.

She decided to keep her visit with Iris to herself. At least until she had a chance to speak with Sam about it.

"No. She wanted some time by herself, I think."

Mac nodded and made a *tsking* sound with his tongue. "She in a mood?"

After a beat, Kate replied, "I think she's a little disappointed."

"It's a long way to come for nothing. But it was kind of a long shot to begin with. I'm amazed we even found this place. The Corps have been searching for the pirates' home base for decades."

She frowned at the note of satisfaction in his voice. "Planning on cashing in a reward?" she asked, her tone clipped.

His brow furrowed. "What? No, of course not. But tracking down a ship across a galaxy? That's pretty incredible."

"Yeah, well, it's too bad Floodwater's parcel doesn't have a tracker on it. Would have saved us all a lot of trouble."

"I guess using FedUPS Express Shipping isn't very space mobster-y."

"I don't know, have you seen their rates lately?"

He chuckled. "Actually, I haven't. Their service zone doesn't include Dravanol. Parcels only come in and go out every six to eight months with the supply drops."

"Are you going to go back?"

Mac's eyebrows lifted. "To Dravanol?"

She nodded.

"Yeah, most likely. I mean, that's where my work is, so it's not like I have a lot of other options."

"Not interested in tooling around the galaxy on a spaceship?"

"You mean with Sam? Ha. Even if she did offer, and I can't imagine she would, the chances one of us would murder the other after three weeks would be pretty high."

Kate bit her bottom lip, annoyed. She was sick of talking about Sam, tired of wondering and worrying about what Sam was thinking or feeling.

"See any interesting things on your tour?" she asked, casting around for anything to change the subject.

Mac looked at her blankly, as if he didn't have the faintest idea what she was talking about. Before she could begin to elaborate, he nodded enthusiastically.

"Their med-lab, right! Well, considering what they probably had to start with and the lack of routine scheduled upgrades, what they have is pretty functional."

He frowned and rubbed the back of his neck. "They didn't want me looking too closely at anything, but even from four or five arm's lengths, I could see there were a couple of higher-end machines I wouldn't have expected to find outside of a major Corp research facility."

Kate considered what Iris laid out for her and pondered if the files Floodwater wanted so badly said anything about *which* Corporation had been running the experiments. Even two centuries later, that kind of information could be incredibly damning. Maybe Floodwater had more than one reason for wanting it.

Beside her, Mac continued to ramble, apparently taking no note of her wandering awareness. "I suppose they could have lifted it from one of their raids, maybe from a research vessel, but why bother? I can't imagine what they would use an infusion table for, for example."

Kate tilted her head. "What's an infusion table for?" She considered whether she should explain the pirates' dark origins. It wasn't as if Iris had sworn her to secrecy.

"It's used in intravenous fluid transfers where—"

Wincing, Kate held up a hand. "You know what? I don't want to know." She hesitated. Might as well wait until they were all together again. That way she wouldn't have to explain anything twice. It had nothing to do with any weird or completely off-base feeling that she'd somehow be betraying Sam by not telling her first.

"Come on," she said, shaking her head slightly. "Let's get inside."

twenty

Empty. Empty. Empty. Emptyemptyempty.

The word chattered through her mind over and over, until Sam wasn't sure if they were talking about the shuttle or her own brain. What she had been looking for was supposed to have been in the shuttle, and since it wasn't, she didn't have any clue as to what she was supposed to do next.

Couldn't go back to Icarus 3. That much was blatantly obvious. Like she'd told Kate, Floodwater wasn't the type to accept any reason for ending a job. And it's not like she had volunteered for the job in the first place.

Couldn't just fuck off to space. He'd find them. Had to be smart, had to have a plan, a place to go to. People to trust. That was where being an antisocial misanthrope was really coming back to bite her in the ass. Jonah had been the one with the contacts, and with him having been mixed up with Floodwater, she wasn't sure she could trust any of the names in his onboard codex.

She could, maybe, use her own name. Her father's name. That could maybe open a few doors, some offers of assistance. The idea of using something she'd thrown away years ago came with a peculiar feeling of discomfort, as if some important piece within her core wasn't balanced correctly. Like it was wobbling in its frame and a sharp tilt in any direction would send it crashing to the ground.

But, as she drew back from the idea, her mind helpfully supplied her with the image of the red marks ringing Kate's throat back on Icarus 3.

Blood-filled eyes. Frozen, blistered skin.

Could she really afford to turn her nose up at any potential safe""" havens? Lives were in her hands. Again. Couldn't fuck it up this time.

Sam sat on her bunk, legs dangling just above the floor, the fingers of her right hand curled around the metal frame. Her left hand squeezed the blue ball that Addy had tossed at her weeks earlier. Her nails dug into the hard surface, but it barely registered. Beneath the bunk, Nata idly watched the slight swing of her legs with interest from the middle of a plaid, round bed.

What to do next?

Try and figure out someone, somewhere to run to?

Or stick with the job?

Maybe Floodwater had more patience than she thought. Maybe it was too soon to panic. She could go back over the original timeline, the flight path, the logs. Maybe they had stopped somewhere else she wasn't remembering. Would Jonah have been so desperate he would have altered the ship's course while she and the others were sleeping?

She thought of the black box Addy had shown her and squeezed tighter. Or maybe he'd had help in covering his tracks? Triss had been the one to set the nav courses. She could have shifted them easily without anyone noticing. Or Ollie, with his medical knowledge, could have sedated them, given Jonah any window he needed.

Suddenly, her empty head wasn't empty anymore. It was overflowing with *ifs* and *maybes* and fuck, nothing actually helpful at all.

Her arm whipped downward, sending the ball shooting toward the floor. It hit with a solid *thunk* and raced back up toward her face. She snatched it from the air, felt the smack of hard rubber against her skin. The noise in her head paused.

She did it again. *Thunk. Smack.*

Could check the nav logs and the medical supply record.

Her hand moved. *Thunk. Smack.*

Either Triss or Ollie could have overridden protocols and covered their tracks, but Mac might be able to pull some shadow from the system.

Thunk. Smack.

Not much to go on, but a start at least. And while Mac was combing through the computers, she could look over old jobs, see if there was anyone she could reach out—

Thunk. Click.

Sam blinked and looked at her left hand. It was empty. She leaned over the side of the bunk, scanning the floor. It took a moment to find the ball, mostly because it no longer resembled a ball. It had cracked into two almost perfect halves. Nata had pushed up from his bed and was nosing curiously at them.

Nestled in the center was a thin shape no bigger than half the length of her thumb.

Sam hopped off the bunk and knelt beside it, plucking the item out of the makeshift rubber casing, and bringing it close. Just an ordinary micro memory drive.

"That sonofabitch," she murmured with a nostalgic mixture of fondness and exasperation. She glanced down at Nata who playfully swatted at the broken pieces. Straightening, she hurried over to the console at the foot of her bunk. Her hand paused inches away from sliding the drive into the docking port. If she opened any of the files on the drive on a ship's console, it would be accessible by anyone on the ship. She couldn't say why the thought raised a flag, but it was there all the same.

She glanced around her space for a spare tablet, but for once, there wasn't one within range. After a moment of consideration, she pushed up her sleeve and stared down at the wrist unit Addy had returned to her, "good as new," supposedly. And supposedly, it could access and display a vast array of file types, audio, video, and holographic included. Then again, Sam was uniquely familiar with what a piece of shit it was.

Screw it. Sam uncovered the input port and fiddled with the drive until it snapped in. She had barely touched the command prompt when the audio file began.

Sam. If you're listening to this, I know you're probably pissed. Hopefully, you're pissed because I've explained everything to you and not because something happened, and you've discovered this after the fact. But, I guess if I had told you, then there wouldn't be any reason for you to be listening to this.

And if you're not Sam, well then fuck you for listening to other people's messages.

Jesus, Jonah.

Anyway, I picked up Floodwater's wonder package. Here it is. Unimaginable horrors packed onto a micro-drive. What this is, a man like Floodwater can't get his hands on. It's insane, Sam. Experiments. Human experiments. I sent a couple files to Mac because it's all medical mumbo jumbo to me and I didn't want to drag anyone else onboard into this. He says it's bad, like beyond illegal bad. This could shut Floodwater down permanently; maybe wipe out his whole operation. Just got to get it to the UNE and someone I can trust. Someone not in his pocket. I have a few ideas.

There came the dampened sound of knocking and then another voice, faint as if through a wall or a door. *Dammit Jonah, move it!* Jonah chuckled.

Hopefully, I'll be able to share them with you shortly.

The audio cut out and a visual file displayed in its place, projecting out in front of Sam's face. She stared through it, not seeing anything, still hearing the light-hearted twang that came over the speaker, sounding fearless even knowing what he had possession of. Had he had any clue that the "pirates" approaching were Floodwater's men? Is that why he left behind the files? Why the hell hadn't he trusted her *sooner*? She tried to think of what she would have done if she had known, if the facts had all been in her possession. But trying to reach back through time and space was impossible.

Sam frowned at the nearly hieroglyphical medical jargon on the document displayed in front of her. Tapping her wrist unit had the pages shifting, some with diagrams and charts, others with numbers she didn't even try to decipher. She shook her head slightly—she'd take it to Mac. Jonah had said his brother had already seen it, so he'd be able to break it down for—

Time froze. And the next audio loop she heard played directly inside her mind.

"He said he had insurance. And if he could find the right people, he'd make sure Floodwater was finished."

"What did he mean by that?"

"I thought it was just Jonah being Jonah."

"Suppose Jonah did find some grand evidence against Floodwater. Suppose it still exists and you manage to get your hands on it. What then?"

Shit.

Shit.

Shit, shit, *shit*.

Mac hadn't said *anything* about knowing about the files. Had made it seem like Jonah hadn't spilled anything about them.

Dravanol was the only place they had stopped before the attack. The only place where someone else might have been able to slip on board and install a piece of equipment designed to incapacitate the ship. No one would have questioned seeing Mac on board.

Sam pressed her hands down against the desk, feeling as if her legs had been swiped out from underneath her. Mac. She remembered his face, the way it had crumpled on screen when she had told him about Jonah. Then the absolute fury that followed. Just an act? Or hadn't he known what Floodwater's men would do once they boarded the ship? Had it been one more of Floodwater's twists?

Time to fucking find out.

Her balance was shored up by the anger swelling through her. Sam stalked forward, slapping a hand onto the control panel for the door and not bothering to lock it behind her. It took two seconds of contemplation to decide where he might be, bouncing briefly between the bridge and med-bay before settling on the med-bay. She hoped he was there, because if he so much as attempted to lie to her again, he was certainly going to need medical intervention.

Fuck, who was she kidding? He was going to need it anyway.

As she stormed along the corridor, she couldn't help but hear echoes in her head:

"Then his death isn't on you. I wanted it to be. I wanted it to be your fault because there was no one else to lay it on except some faceless pirate a million lightyears away. But it's not your fault. Jonah made his own choices."

No, his death isn't on me. It's on you.

The doors to the med-bay whooshed open and there he stood, his back to her, inspecting the contents of one of the small cabinets, tablet in one hand. She remembered seeing Ollie doing the same thing countless times. The memory made the anger inside her flare.

"You bastard," she snarled. Mac's head lifted, though he didn't turn completely around.

"Sam? Something you need?"

The calm collected voice only served to enrage her further.

"I know it was you. Do you even *have* a contract with Floodwater? Or is that a lie, too?"

He turned, and for less than a second, she saw the answer in his face. It was a quick, barely noticeable flicker of twisted glee that fell immediately into puzzled confusion.

But she saw it.

"What are you talking about? You saw my contract," he pointed out. Sam shook her head.

"Yeah, I saw it. But I didn't think to run it. And I bet Jonah didn't either, just saw your name and panicked."

Mac raised his eyebrows. "Where is this coming from, Sam? I mean, what happened that—"

"I found the files, Mac."

That look again. Hidden just as quickly. "Jonah's files?" he asked, and she knew she wasn't imagining the hint of excitement in his voice.

"Yeah. The ones he said he shared with you. The ones you said detailed Floodwater's experiments."

The calculation in his eyes was more apparent as he watched her silently.

"Why'd you do it, Mac? Floodwater could have had anyone go after those files. Why Jonah? Why your brother?"

He sighed and his gaze fell to the floor. One hand slid idly over the screen of his tablet. And then he lifted his eyes and smiled. One finger tapped the screen, and white-hot pain lanced up her leg, forcing the breath from her lungs. She lurched forward and grabbed the side of a med-chair to keep upright.

"I'd love to explain the whole thing to you, Sam," he began, turning back toward the cabinet and sliding out a drawer. He rummaged through it before retrieving a med-injector. With slow and easy movements, he adjusted a dial on the tool and pivoted around to face her.

She watched him approach, but the pain made it impossible to move.

"But I think it's worse if you just never know," he finished, before pressing the injector against the side of her neck. She felt the pinch of the needle. A cold chill flushed into her.

"And don't worry. I'll take care of the cat."

And then nothing.

Something wasn't right.

That was the feeling in Kate's gut as she sat in the galley with her companions. Parker and Addy sat across the table, while Mac had his back pressed against the short counter. It left one conspicuously open space, not that Sam was likely to have sat there if she had been there.

But the captain wasn't there.

At the very least, Kate had expected an inspection or an acknowledgement once they had finished mounting the shuttle. A *can we go now* or *good*.

There had only been a short comm text, instructing them to disembark as soon as the ship was ready.

Maybe that *had* been the acknowledgement. Considering where Sam's head seemed to be, maybe it was all she could offer at the moment.

No one else appeared particularly concerned by Sam's absence. Addy had simply fired up the engines once her repairs were finished and navigated the ship away from the base.

And that felt off as well. When had Sam left the navigation of the ship to anyone other than herself?

Something wasn't *right*.

Or maybe it was that too many things weren't right, Kate thought. Weren't they at the part in the story where the group pulled together their master plan to thwart the villain? Instead, they were seated at the proverbial kitchen table, trying to figure out what metaphorical stone to look under next. A task that would have been more fruitful if their leader had deigned to join them. She couldn't help thinking it was a discussion they could be having back at the pirate base. Why had Sam been in such a hurry to leave? So reluctant to trust anyone?

You don't exactly trust Iris either, she reminded herself.

"Shouldn't one of us go get Sam?" Kate asked, for what felt like the millionth time, interrupting Addy's description of job opportunities on the far edges. She set her hip against the table. "I mean, shouldn't we at least consider some next step that *doesn't* involve us running from Floodwater for the rest of our lives?"

"Who said anything about running? For all we know, Floodwater's parcel *could* be on the outer rim," Addy pointed out. "I'm just trying to be thorough."

"How about being helpful?" Kate suggested waspishly. Addy peered over at her, and Kate felt her neck flush. "Sorry." She turned to Mac, hoping for an ally.

"But seriously, you agree with me, Mac? Sam's the only one of us that could have any idea of a next place to look." She left off the part about Sam's emphatic decision they hide her somewhere a psychotic space mobster wouldn't look. Sam could make *that* announcement to the others herself.

If she ever bothered to come out of her cabin. Like an adult.

Mac rubbed a hand over his jaw. His expression looked both sympathetic and apologetic. "Well, I do, except I wouldn't suggest disturbing her just now. She was having pain earlier, so I gave her a sedative to help her sleep. Won't be awake for a least a couple of hours."

"Oh." That was new. The idea that someone had spoken to Sam should have been comforting, but the contents of the conversation were worrying. Kate's mind flew back over the last time she'd seen Sam, as if she could ferret out any signs of discomfort in the memory. "But she's okay?" She tamped down on the urge to go see for herself.

He nodded, smiling faintly. "Oh yes. It's not uncommon to have residual pain after reattachment, especially if you're not careful with your usage."

"Oh." That made sense. "Careful" wasn't a favored word in Sam's vocabulary. Kate found herself watching Mac's face for longer than intended, because even though the words made sense, something about his concern, or rather lack of it, seemed peculiar. "Should... should you check on her?"

His smile widened, and he lifted the tablet from off the counter. "There's a biometric monitor in her leg. If there are any issues, it will send an alert. Don't worry. She just needs some rest."

Kate nodded, vaguely reassured. Yet the odd nagging sense remained. Before she could think of how to vocalize it, Mac was reaching into the cabinet and pulling down a set of glasses. From a side pocket in his pants, he removed a tall flask and set about pouring a bit of dark liquid into each cup.

"We've got time to plan what our next move should be. For now, maybe we just celebrate the fact our previous move wasn't our last one," he said, handing out the glasses.

"What?" Addy asked as she accepted the drink.

"He means we should be happy those pirates didn't kill us," Parker responded bluntly, taking the drink and motioning with it.

"Not pirates," Kate corrected as Mac set a glass down in front of her. "Scavengers."

Parker rolled her eyes. "They can call themselves whatever they want; it doesn't change the fact they steal shit from other people."

"Yeah, but to survive," Addy pointed out.

"Maybe that was true 30 years ago when they were just trying to hang on. But now? Now they just like it. Now they've been getting away with it for so long that they feel entitled."

Mac lifted his glass toward the women. "Here's to getting out alive."

Kate thought it was a little early to be celebrating, but both Addy and Parker were raising their hands, so to do otherwise seemed petty. She brought her glass to her lips and took a long drink. The burn of the alcohol hit the back of her throat, but then a darker, unexpected flavor stung her taste buds. She rolled her tongue around her mouth, feeling a distinctive burr as she brushed over her teeth, a numbness creeping over the muscle.

Her eyes shot up just in time to see both Addy and Parker set their own empty glasses back on the table. She opened her mouth in warning, but it was too late; a glassy distance had already come into their gazes.

She looked to Mac and found him observing her, his expression no longer controlled. He waited, expectantly, and she had only seconds to decide if she should strike out. The deadness on her tongue spread, even as her cells fought against it. She closed her eyes and her respiration slowed while the rest of her fought to burn through whatever toxin was pushing against her system.

She could hear him moving and felt the sudden press of his fingers against her pulse. A moment later, he forced one eye open, flashing a light into it.

It didn't take much for Kate to remain limp—the substance was unfamiliar and *potent*. She could feel her body straining to remove it. Her limbs felt heavy and unresponsive.

Seeming satisfied, Mac let her eye close. Her consciousness slipped.

When she resurfaced, he was speaking.

"Yes, I've got them incapacitated. Are you sure you want all of them? Seems more trouble than its worth."

Even to Kate's scattered mind, it was obvious he was speaking to someone. Over a comm? She couldn't hear the response. Only his voice again after a short while.

"Yes, I'll keep them in cryostasis for the return. That way I won't have to worry about maintaining their sedation."

Another pause.

"Barring any issues, they'll remained dosed until well after we've arrived, I assure you."

Kate struggled to maintain awareness. He was alone now. If she could...

Exhaustion crept over her, dragging her down. There was the heat of her system working to purge the toxin, but a chill was crawling up through her chest. Her consciousness slid away—

—it returned as she felt hands underneath her arms, dragging her. She could hear the stutter of her heels against a grated floor. The corridor? The weight of the poison was heavy, a steady pulse in her body. Blackness descended again, a muffling curtain.

She jostled awake as her body rolled. Pillowed fabric pressed against her cheek; she cracked one eye enough to see a gray bed. The med-bay.

Her body was shifted onto her back. The first tingles of sensation prickled her fingertips. An apparatus was strapped over her face—the next breath she took was frigidly cold.

Have to move... now, she thought sluggishly. Before—

There was the faintest pressure at her neck, near her collarbone. She could have imagined it.

Darkness.

—

—

Cold.

Burning pain.

Awake.

Pins and needles. Everywhere.

Light. Color. Movement. Voices.

Kate came to, her awareness forced through a tunnel into the space behind her eyes. Her mind was clear and her body vibrating with excess energy. She had to fight to remain still, to take stock as quickly as she could.

She was alive.

The toxin was gone.

There were voices again but muddled. Not close.

She peeked. Saw no one. Tiny shimmering flecks floated across her vision. Kate blinked, but they remained.

Okay, the toxin was not *entirely* purged.

Looking around, she was still on the ship, still in the med-bay. Whatever had been on her face had been removed, and there were no straps or IVs holding her down. Experimentally, she tried moving her arms and legs—felt a surge of relief when both sets responded without issue.

She was okay. For now. But what about the others?

Further inspection of the room located Addy, stretched out on one of the other three beds. Her eyes were closed, and the laxness of her features indicated she was still unconscious.

Before Kate could whisper her name, the door to the room swished open.

"—move them to Holding."

"No restraints?"

"They're heavily sedated. Won't give us any trouble."

Strong hands gripped under her shoulders while another pair encircled her ankles. She was lifted easily and felt the sway of movement.

Her heart began to pound. Holding did not sound like a place she wanted to be. Every part of her screamed escape, but she knew she would only have one shot at it. If she messed it up, there'd be shackles or, probably, death. Had to take advantage of their ignorance while they had their guards down.

So, she waited, mentally traveling the map of the ship. From the med-bay to the main corridor, through the kitchen, to the cargo bay, down the ramp.

She felt her legs dip first, followed by the rest of her, felt the move back to balanced. The hands beneath her shoulders shifted, changing their grip.

Two things happened at once.

There was a sudden yowl and a blur of gray just as Kate twisted, throwing her body into a free fall toward the ground. Catching herself on her hands, she kicked out with her feet before the first carrier had finished an exclamation of surprise. There was a symphony of growls and hisses as her heels connected solidly with a body—she heard an "oomph," and shouts of pain, followed by a crashing sound. She was completely free of any hold and shot up into a crouch.

Kate took in the wide open, seemingly empty space of a hangar—familiar—and bolted toward the first door she saw.

twenty-one

Addy was dead.

She was 95% sure. There was darkness. And silence. And a god-awful feeling permeating every single part of her.

Well, if she were dead, she probably wouldn't be feeling anything, right? Wasn't that the only thing death had going for it?

With no small amount of skepticism, Addy tried opening her eyes. Her lids felt far heavier than she remembered. Or maybe they were stuck together, like after a long cryo-sleep when the dryness was almost unbearable before the soothing ointment was applied.

She had nearly given up on it when finally, they cracked open. Light, brighter than she could stand, seared in. Immediately, she squeezed her eyelids shut again.

As far as reconnaissance went, that had been awful. She was either dead and in a nebulous afterlife that included pain and clinical lighting, or she was not dead and in a place not at all concerned about the electric bill.

Forgoing sight for the moment, Addy took another approach. She attempted to shift her body, assuming it was the part feeling a bit like… someone was pressing on every single pain point in her nervous system. No *body* meant she was probably dead. If she had pain, she had a body, which meant she was most likely just *near* dead. Small, but important distinction.

Again, everything seemed slower and muddier than it should have, as if the message for movement was strolling idly along the neural pathways from her mind rather than zipping with its usual pep. Eventually she felt her arm move, her fingers sliding across a smooth, unyielding surface. At the same time, a solid plane of discomfort registered underneath her shoulders, back, and legs.

Lying down then. On something that shouldn't be lain down on. She briefly considered trying to sit up, but that seemed like a lot of effort for potentially little gain, especially if she was near dead.

"You're not dead."

The voice, familiar, came out of nowhere, a slight static hum to it. After the all-encompassing quiet, it was like a shout to her ears, and she might have rolled away from it, if only that wouldn't entail moving.

"I'm becoming aware of that, thank you," she endeavored to say, but wasn't sure how much got past the dryness in her throat.

"You're not even close to dead," the voice continued, as if it had been privy to her previous line of thought.

Addy could feel responsiveness seeping back in. She flexed her fingers, felt the stretch in her arms. Her legs lifted and her toes wiggled.

She thought it was probably time to try opening her eyes again. Addy raised a hand to her forehead first before cautiously blinking. Her vision was blurry, and the light still stung, but she rubbed with her fingertips until the world took a shape she could comprehend.

Oh.

She was in a cell. The shape and space left no ambiguity. It looked exactly like the holding rooms she had observed on countless stations and satellites, possibly once or twice from this very perspective. Three of the walls were dark metal, while the fourth, straight out in front of her, was a clear force field that taunted freedom. On the other side, standing tall and *not* caged, was Parker, once more devoid of her trusty firearm. In fact, she didn't appear to have a single weapon on her person. Addy thought she was actually getting used to seeing the woman disarmed.

Weapons or no weapons, Parker was still on the other side of a cell door, which could only mean one thing.

"Must be nice to have friends in high places," Addy drawled, scratching at her cheek idly. The muscles and skin felt abnormally formless underneath her still waking fingers. Parker flinched behind the haze of the field, a minute movement Addy hadn't thought her capable of.

"Floodwater's no friend of mine."

Addy shrugged and then regretted it when the motion made her head swim. "No? You're still on the other side of the door."

"That doesn't mean I'm not in a bad spot."

Addy gave a snort and wished she hadn't. Even the quick puff of air had her vision rippling unpleasantly.

"Why? Because they took your guns? That's rough. Wonder what they're going to do to me?"

Parker didn't respond, and Addy risked turning her head, to see if the mercenary was still there.

She was.

"Parker. What are they going to do with me?"

Parker shook her head, and the helplessness in the action was as unsettling as the flinch had been. "I don't know."

Addy sighed and turned her gaze to the floor. The overhead lights reflected in the glossy surface, resembling a pool of still water. She tried to remember the last time she'd seen standing water. It randomly occurred to her that she hadn't even had a chance to try the beach on Icarus 3. "Yes, you do. So much for my bonus pay."

Idly, she wondered if last requests were still a thing.

"Addy, I—"

"Where's Sam? And Kate? They in a couple of these cells, too?"

"No."

Addy turned her head again. Parker was pacing back and forth in front of the field, arms folded tightly as if trying to restrain herself. The sight of her in constant motion, the complete antithesis to her normal stillness, was strangely fascinating. She tried to categorize Parker's gait. Forceful? Guilty? Frustrated?

It certainly beat thinking about death.

"They took Sam somewhere. I don't know where. Probably to see Floodwater."

"He's here?" Addy paused and then added, "Where are we?" She had her ideas, but it'd be nice to have them confirmed.

"Dravanol. The facility belongs to him."

"Ah." Confirmed. "That's convenient, I guess."

Parker froze in place and faced the cell. "I didn't know."

"You don't know a lot of things, apparently," Addy mused. This time she ignored the wince. "Where's Kate?"

"She's gone."

Addy rolled over onto her side and pushed up, cringing as the world spun briefly. It was nothing compared to the clench in her stomach. "What do you mean, *gone*?"

"Mac put us all under in order to transport us here. But whatever it was, I guess it didn't fully take on her? When we got here and they took us off the ship, she bolted. They've got half the personnel on the station looking for her and some of the floors locked down."

"How many personnel are on station?"

"Addy—" Parker began in warning. Before she could finish, the door behind her slid open and another mercenary strode in. A hand blaster sat comfortably in a holster at his waist, and a smaller stunner was strapped to his upper thigh. He stopped at the sight of Parker and one hand dropped to rest on the blaster.

"Parker. Don't think you're supposed to be in here."

Parker lifted her shoulders but said nothing.

"Do I need to call in backup?"

"That depends on what you're doing here," she said.

His hand curled around the handle of the blaster. "Checking on our guest."

Addy chuckled humorlessly. "I guess we're about to find out what's going to happen to me," she stated, trying to ignore the sinking in her chest. Pointless, wasn't it? If she was gonna go, she'd rather go in a good mood.

"Be quiet in there."

"Any point in my mentioning that I'm just the hired help?"

"Quiet," he reiterated sharply. He made a small motion with his head. "Step away from the cell, Parker."

Parker remained still. "She's telling the truth. She's just some engineer hired to run the ship."

"Uh, not just some engineer. A guild level six, thank you."

"Be quiet," both the man and Parker snapped at the same time. Addy pushed herself up into a fully seated position with a pained grunt. She expected another call for silence, but they were absorbed in one another.

"You don't have to do this," Parker stated, calmly. Even through the barrier, Addy could see the tension in her large frame. Evidently the man could as well—he pulled the blaster from its holster and curled his finger around the trigger but left it hanging at his side.

"Step away from the cell."

They exchanged long stares. Wordlessly exchanging threats? Seeking out weaknesses? Whatever was going through Parker's head, absolutely nothing showed on her face. Then, abruptly, Parker lifted her hands and stepped back, her movements slow and obvious. The guard watched, stationary, until she had moved out of Addy's sight, seemingly far enough away to satisfy him. He approached the cell and gave Parker one final, almost apologetic look as he hit the control panel to lower the force field.

"Don't worry. I'm guessing it won't be long before Floodwater sends down word to take care of you, too," he offered, before turning his head toward Addy and lifting the blaster to head height.

"It's nothing personal," he added. Addy nodded in understanding as she kept her eyes on his.

"Of course."

"Any last words?"

"Just that—oh!" Her eyes widened as she looked over his shoulder.

Parker was moving, hardly aware she had made the decision to, a split second before she heard a grunt followed by the whistle of the blaster firing. She recognized the heavy thump of a body hitting the floor, and as she rounded into the cell, she saw Addy standing over the motionless form of the guard, blaster in hand, a bemused expression on her face.

"Huh. Can't believe he fell for that," Addy murmured, with no small amount of relief.

Parker looked down at the guard, surprised as well. "What did you do to him?"

"Oh." Addy held up her free hand, motioning with the blaster at her wrist. A thin wire ran from a simple looking band down to the body on the floor. "Taser band." She gave a quick twist of her hand and the wire snapped free, disappearing into the band. "He's probably going to have a nasty headache when he wakes up. Friend of yours?"

"Hell no. Come on. Let's get out of here," Parker insisted, waving with one hand. Addy stepped over the guard and the movement put them side by side. Pivoting, Addy jammed the blaster underneath Parker's chin.

"Give me one reason why I shouldn't just shoot you."

Parker's hand was a blur as it reached up and snatched the gun from Addy's grip. The engineer exhaled.

"Well, fuck."

"Come on."

Addy held firm. "Why should I trust you? You could be taking me straight to Floodwater."

"I told you already, I don't know where he is. And who else are you going to trust?" Parker pointed out.

"At this point? *Literally* anyone else."

Parker motioned into the cell. "How about him?"

"Bad example."

"Addy."

"Parker."

Parker exhaled, feeling as if her skin was too tight. "Look. My brother is on this station, remember? If they're doing something shady here, then it might involve him. Believe me, I want Floodwater shut down."

Addy hummed, then shook her head. "Under protest," she announced.

"Noted. Can we get the fuck out of here now before someone else shows up to kill you?"

Addy knelt and unclipped the stun-rod from the guard's holster. "They already sent someone to kill me. Are they that redundant that they would try and kill me twice?"

Parker plucked the stunner from her hand and pocketed it into her own holster. "Maybe they'd be coming for me."

"Hey, don't I get a weapon?" Addy protested, arms wide.

"No. Follow me and act normal."

"Right. Because I was just going to go running down the hall screaming 'free at last,'" Addy mumbled, sounding insulted.

The corridor was empty; Parker waited to see flashing lights and scores of troops running by in combat armor, laden with weapons, but it looked the same as it had the last time they visited. Borderline deserted.

"Where are we going?"

"Cargo bay," Parker replied, already trying to map the route they would need to take. It would require some seriously good breaks to make it without running into any more of Floodwater's men. Her limited freedom had at least netted her the information of where on the station they currently were.

 Addy's brows pulled together.

"Why the cargo bay?"

"We'll grab a ship and get the hell out of here. Hopefully before anyone notices."

Addy stopped midstride. "Woah, no way. We have to find Kate and Sam."

"Didn't you hear me? They already took Sam. And if they took her to Floodwater, she's probably already dead. Or wishing she were."

"You said Kate escaped."

"I said she *ran off*. Most of the damn station is looking for her."

"So, you're just going to leave?"

"Addy, if we want to live, we need to get out of here." It was so obvious to Parker. They were woefully underpowered. Now was not the time to—

"And what about your brother? You going to leave him behind too?"

"We come back. With more firepower. With help." Parker struggled with the argument. Words were not what she typically used to convince people. That wasn't her job.

"From *where*?"

"I know some people."

"You *know* some people? Really? Are they also of the 'work for Floodwater' variety? Because I dunno how much help they're gonna be. I hope you plan on being a lot more convincing than you were with Captain Here-To-Kill-You-Now."

"I still have contacts in the Corps. We can notify the Peacekeepers. And fuck, maybe get word to those damn pirates. But we're not going to be able to help anyone if we die here."

Addy shook her head and took a step backward. "I'm not going anywhere without Sam and Kate. You do what you want."

Parker stared at her. "You know I could knock you unconscious and just drag your ass out of here, right?"

"Don't think that would look very normal."

Squeezed uncomfortably behind a mass of pipes that were more than a little warm to the touch, Kate tried once again to take stock of her situation.

Out of immediate danger. She didn't know precisely how long she had been hunched in the can't-believe-she-fit-there space, but she had watched at least three small groups of uniformed individuals run by. None had so much as glanced in her direction, nor had any returned, so she felt as safe as possible, all things considered.

The problem was, what to do next?

She knew they were back on Dravanol. She might have recognized the hangar bay if there had been anything on her mind other than the exit she had bolted to, but the large, bold lettering on the walls of the corridor that spelled DRAVANOL RESEARCH STATION was also helpful. Unfortunately, the only part of the station she knew was the route to the med-bay and, since she wasn't familiar with her current surroundings, she assumed she had most likely sprinted past the turn for it. Not that she necessarily wanted to be anywhere Mac might be, considering what had occurred the last time they were in a room together.

What she did want was to know where Sam, Addy, and Parker were. Addy had been on the ship—god, hopefully alive—but if Kate got herself back there, what could she really accomplish? They'd certainly have the engineer under guard, especially now, and Kate was painfully aware she was not an invincible action hero who could take out trained mercenaries with her bare hands.

She should try and find Parker first. She'd feel a lot more confident about odds of survival and ass-kicking with some muscle on her side. Then they could figure out how to rescue Addy and Sam.

Sam. Mac must have done something to her before he had sedated them. Maybe even before they had left the pirate base. She shouldn't have let a closed door deter her, she should have—

Kate bit down on the inside of her cheek and pushed the thoughts aside. No time for that now; it wouldn't help anything. Neither would staying put. She had to move.

Getting out of the narrow space took more effort than getting in, mostly because her adrenaline had worn off and the pipes were hot.

But with only a few superficial burns, she managed to worm her way out into the empty corridor. Looked to the left, then to the right. Both directions were clear, but neither pinged her memory. She thought back to the first dive behind the pipes. She had twisted... to the left, pushing her right arm and shoulder through first. So, she'd been coming from what was now her right.

Kate hesitated. Did she *want* to head back that way, toward the ship? It had to be guarded, but it was familiar. And better yet, it was the point of intersection. No matter where the others were now, they had all started there.

She began walking; she couldn't quite manage a normal gait and ended up in what she thought was a skulk.

Skulking around a space station was not as easy as one might assume. Part of the trouble might have been the fact Kate had never once in her life assumed she would be skulking around a space station. She didn't think she had ever skulked in her entire life. As a bonus, she thought she was a bit loopy from the burnout of adrenaline. Thankfully, she couldn't feel any residual effects of the drugs Mac had given them, other than an acrid taste in her mouth.

It did not take long at all to return to the docking bay—less than five minutes. It had felt like twice that, but maybe that was how time felt when you were expecting blaster rounds in the back.

The space between her shoulders twitched and she couldn't help glance behind her. The hallway was still empty.

Kate turned as the door to the hangar slid open. She jumped back around the corner, feeling her heart leap into her throat, even as she peeked out.

It was Mac. Her breath held as she registered that he was engrossed by the tablet in his hands. He took two steps in her direction, then stopped. She could see his features twist—eyebrows drawing down and mouth tightening—and he pivoted, hurrying away.

She followed, her earlier fears shoved aside in favor of... revenge? Knowledge? Kate wasn't sure which desire was currently pushing its way to the forefront of her brain. She was confident, though, that Mac would know where the others were. He'd tell her, willingly or unwillingly.

For some reason, at that exact moment, Kate flashed back to standing on the hull of the ship, with the end of a rusted pipe pressed into Sam's back. How easily Sam had twisted and disarmed her before she had even had a chance to blink.

Maybe she'd simply keep doing what she was doing until a *viable* idea came into her head.

By the time she reached the hall opening, Mac was far ahead.

His head was bent, and she thought he was speaking into the tablet, though she was too far away to hear what he was saying.

He turned, and she pressed up against the wall of the corridor, expecting him to look back. Without so much as a glance her way, he passed through a door and out of sight. She hurried to follow, nipping through the doors before they slid shut behind her. The room she slipped into was partitioned in two with tall panels of clear glass separating one side from the other, closing in an office. Kate hung back and kept track of Mac's movements beyond the windows. He strode around a wide desk, setting the tablet down. A massive screen behind the desk blinked on, and the smooth face that she had seen only once before filled it.

Being digital did not diminish Floodwater's presence. Kate felt a curdling in her stomach as he glowered out from the screen. She inched back from the window as far as she could without losing her view into the room.

"Have you recovered the files?" Floodwater's voice seemed to curl around the corner, as if he were speaking right beside her ear. Her shoulders drew up to make herself smaller. Invisible.

Mac shook his head. "No. There was nothing on the ship."

Floodwater's eyes narrowed, his displeasure magnified on the screen. "And the woman who escaped? Have you located her?" he asked, a faint edge to his otherwise calm tone.

From the stiffness in Mac's posture, Kate could tell he heard it, too.

"No. They're still searching for her."

"Wonderful. I'm delighted for you to explain to our benefactors that you lost a potential because of a cat. Now, if you haven't managed these two minor tasks, then what exactly is it that you are contacting me about?"

"There are two ships approaching out of jump space. One is the HEXOR flagship."

Irritation rippled across Floodwater's features, and he glanced offscreen. Kate wished she could see what or who had captured his notice. There was nothing she could see that gave any sort of hint as to where he was. Apparently, a cubicle number was too much to ask for. "The CXO is early. Have someone from the research department meet and delay him. I want those files found before we speak. And the other ship?"

"It hasn't come within identification range yet."

"Probably the CXO's sycophants. See that they're confined. And find me those files."

The conversation was over if the coldness on Floodwater's face was any indication. His lips moved ever so slightly before the screen went black. Mac waved a hand angrily at it and shoved away to stare down at a different console nearby. Kate watched him, trying to steady her racing mind.

A foot or so inside the room was a small canister. Metal. Possibly heavy? She contemplated her chances. Briefly, she considered what Sam might do. Or Addy. Or Parker.

Well. She *knew* what Parker would do.

Every second she stood there debating was another second Mac could turn around and see her peeping in. Pressed up against the wall wasn't exactly the best hiding space and *oh, what the fuck—*?

Kate leapt forward, ducking low to grab the canister. She swung out as Mac began to rotate, and both heard and felt the thud as the canister connected with the back of his head.

He crumpled to the floor.

Kate stood over him, canister still in hand, and blinked down at his motionless form. "It worked," she uttered to herself with quiet amazement. She shook off the feeling and concentrated on the console Mac had been working at. In her head, she had visions of swiping through station blueprints and video feeds until she came across some giant, obvious marker highlighting Sam's location. A view into a cell or a transfer communication detailing her whereabouts. Maybe she'd be able to pick up Addy and Parker the same way.

The reality was, when she looked down at the screen, all she saw was a mess of charts and graphs, an open document full of chemical formulas surrounded by blocks of text filled with words containing more consonants than she thought possible. Frowning, she dragged the open windows around, searching for the system's main directory and anything else that did not look like a boardroom presentation.

Judging from his discussion with Floodwater, it seemed like an unusual time for Mac to be working on a slide deck, but maybe he was one of those people that liked to multitask?

One of the open folders had a series of videos; she clicked on the first in case everything she had ever seen on television wasn't complete bullshit.

It was evident after the first few seconds that what she was seeing was not useful to her current predicament. Neither Sam, Addy, nor Parker could be seen, and for that Kate was incredibly grateful. Because it was also clear that what was playing on the screen was something she never wanted to see again.

Screams were just coming through the system's speakers as she scrambled to close the file. They echoed in her ears even as silence returned to the room.

Kate stared at the console, suddenly parched. From the naming conventions on the remaining files she could tell the contents had been taking place there on Dravanol. What the hell was going on in that place?

She brought back the windows she had minimized. The graphs and formulas still didn't make any sense, but she recalled her conversation with Iris. Iris thought Floodwater had been looking for files regarding experiments done to the mining colonists. It looked like he was already running his own.

Kate fumbled around the desk, pulling open drawers. This was evidence they could take to the UNE. Violations of the Genetic Accord wouldn't, *couldn't*, be swept aside or hidden.

She hoped.

With a huff of frustration, she slammed a drawer shut. Of course. Sitting in front of a mountain of damning proof that could literally save the galaxy from the grips of a madman, and not one fucking memory stick to be found. What the hell kind of office manager did they have on this station? It's not like her *word* was going to be enough.

Frankly, a memory stick probably wouldn't even be all that

useful. All she'd need to do was to lose it or get captured, and poof! Conspiracy suppressed. What she needed was to get the information out immediately and someplace secure. She took half a second to lament the fact she'd never curried favor with some strong-willed, righteous officer of the law or hard-nose reporter type. Well, there was always Alan in IT. Shit, she couldn't remember his comm address.

Kate paused and considered. Sending it to her personal communications box was most likely a terrible idea, but there was one other place she could think of that might work.

As long as her credentials were valid.

She navigated through the communication portal, engaged in the upload and transfer of the files. In her ears, her heartbeat thrummed.

There was a sharp prick at her ankle and she looked down in time to see Mac pressing an injector against her leg.

Two figures dressed in dark jumpsuits and both carrying long barrel blaster rifles marched almost in file, disappearing into the room labeled "Security." The single door swooshed closed behind them. Three others had entered before.

"Five," Addy counted under her breath.

Hunched beside her in the small alcove, she could feel Parker twisting to eye the empty passageway behind them. She was banking on it remaining empty for at least a little while longer because she didn't know exactly what Parker thought she could do if the stillness was broken before they had vacated their current position.

"Addy," Parker muttered, out of the corner of her mouth, "You cannot seriously be considering this." Her fingers tightened on the handle of her stolen blaster.

Addy continued to watch the door, some 30 feet or so ahead of them. "We have to find Sam and Kate. The best way to do that, without searching the entire station, is to get access to the security feeds. Best place to do that is in the security room," she explained for the fourth time.

Not that she was counting.

"Right. The security room, which has five armed mercs in it."

"Six," Addy corrected, watching as another blaster carrier passed through the door. Fleetingly, she caught a glimpse into the room and the hint of motion within.

Then the door closed again.

"Six?" Parker echoed in dismay, swinging around so she could stare hard over Addy's shoulder. As if she could dispute the number with the strength of her scowl.

"Yup. And that's assuming this is the only entrance. I didn't really get a good look the last time we were here."

Parker scowled. "How did you get a look at all?"

"Not really important. Have you got a better idea?"

"Yeah, and it's the same as before. We get the hell off this station and come back better prepared."

Addy's face tightened as she faced Parker. Gone was any trace or hint of amusement or ease. In its place was a look that did not invite disagreement.

"Look Parker. I like you. I like you a lot. I think we could maybe have something. But for the last time, I'm not going to abandon my friends to a space mobster and his lackeys.

"Now, I completely understand if you don't want to risk your life. That's your choice. And I'm not saying risking your life is a prerequisite to a relationship, but if you are going to leave, don't bother calling."

With that, Addy reoriented herself toward the door, bending slightly and bouncing up to the balls of her feet. She figured at a run she could close the distance to the door in a few seconds. Bursting through had to give the element of surprise. But if she went slow, tried to sneak forward, she might get the chance for a little more recon on the inner activity.

Or, she could get spotted and captured, the least desired outcome.

"So, it *is* a prerequisite," Parker protested, still behind her.

Addy shook her head as she vacillated between her two choices. "No, actually, I just don't have a dedicated comm line." She flashed a grin over her shoulder. "Besides, are you telling me that you can't take down six mercs?"

Parker stared down at her for a long moment. Finally, reaching forward, she slid one arm in front of Addy and pushed the smaller woman back.

"Stay behind me."

"You know, you could always give me that stunner. That would even things up a bit."

"Yeah, for them. Now be quiet."

Addy frowned at the command, but Parker was moving before she could offer up any sort of retort. She tucked one away for later, when they were in considerably less dire circumstances.

She figured Parker for the bash and smash type and was taken aback when the mercenary adopted a brisk but easy pace, just fast enough that Addy had to stretch her legs to keep up, but not so quick as to appear as if she were running. The closer they got to the door, the more foolish she began to feel, tagging along without any means of offense or defense. She was determined to not let Parker take all the risks, but what exactly was she going to do against armed guards?

It made her earlier plans to assault the security room herself somewhat blusterous. That was obvious now.

They were going to have to revisit the whole *you-don't-get-a-weapon dynamic.*

Sam imagined it was feasible she had been in a worse position. The time they had been boarded and the entire cargo had been stolen, the one that absolutely couldn't be stolen. The time just seconds before the middle and ring fingers of her right hand had been removed. The time Jonah had insisted, *no, he could definitely fix it.*

But, if she was perfectly honest with herself, being strapped down on what might have been a surgical table, woozy from whatever drugs had been pumped into her, and having Miles Floodwater lording over her head, not even looking at her—that seemed like it might take the cake.

She racked her brain for some poetic or even half-witty final words, but all she zeroed in on was the fact the inside of her mouth felt and tasted like dirty socks.

Above her came a heavy, drawn-out exhale. *Please just let him kill me before he tells me his tragic tale of woe*, she thought, feeling tired in ways she never had before.

"I am disappointed in you, Sam."

Oh, go fuck yourself, was what she wanted to say, but her tongue was heavy and thick in her mouth.

"After all, it was an easy enough job."

Sure, easy. Yep. Go find something, I won't tell you exactly what it is, but someone you knew told me they had it. They didn't tell you, but you knew where they were, so you probably knew where it was, too. Oh, and "it" happens to be a bunch of files showing how I am, literally, the worst person in the universe.

"Did you ever wonder why I sold you your ship? For such a paltry sum?"

Her eyebrows drew together at the bizarre shift in topic. *What the—*

As if sensing her confusion, he patted her shoulder, still not looking at her. "Did you know I knew your father?" Without waiting for an answer, he continued, "Actually, he saved my life when I was a young man. That terrible explosion. He was a good man, your father. A hero."

Yeah, I know.

"Of course, I suppose you didn't get the chance to know him at all. Or your mother. So much loss in your life. Everyone that knows you seems to end up dead. Do you ever wonder about *that*, Sam?"

Sam tried to swallow the dryness in her throat.

"Is there... any chance... you... could just go ahead... and kill me now? Without talking anymore?"

His hand tightened on her shoulder. "I'd almost forgotten how unpleasant a conversationalist you are, Sam. It's one of your worst traits."

"And here I thought... I had... such a... sunny personality."

She took some small satisfaction in his huff of irritation. In the grand scheme of things, she wasn't much more than a gnat to him, but boy did she enjoy annoying the shit out of him.

"So flippant, even now. All that trouble to find what I asked of you... you could have brought it to me and been free to go."

The chuckle escaped her unexpectedly; she hadn't had any strength to hold it back. The clarity of the small laugh surprised her, and it seemed to startle Floodwater as well. He glanced down, eyes cold. One hand rested against the thin sliver of shiny, wrinkled skin showing between his chin and the top of his high collared shirt.

"You... weren't going to let us live," she managed to rasp out, the words slurring together.

His fingers pinched together underneath his chin, and he nodded. "You? No."

The door to the room swept open and Mac entered, the motionless form of Kate slung over one shoulder.

"But this one? We have something else in mind for her."

Oblivious to Addy's inner musing, Parker strode forward, muscles unconsciously tensing and un-tensing with each step. She was focused on the security door, but the rest of the hallway remained in view. If anyone else were to suddenly appear, they'd be in trouble. If the door opened before they reached it, they'd be in trouble. Hell, once they got to the door, they'd definitely be in trouble, but they had already gone that far. Might as well follow all the way through.

In her head, Parker tried to see beyond the door, to imagine what the setup might be behind it. Six guards. Separate stations. Shift change? A couple could be grouped together, un-alert. At least one or two were probably searching the video cameras for signs of Kate, eyes fixed. Reactions slower.

She lifted the blaster and the stun-rod to chest level a second before she breached the door.

Directly in front of Parker were two guards, one on either side of a half row of terminals. She ignored the one with his back to her, fired a blast into the chest of the one facing her even as his eyes were widening. To the right, further into the room, were the two guards who had entered minutes before. Parker fired twice more, striking the first in the abdomen and the second in the chest. At the same time, she struck out with the stun-rod, catching the guard behind her in the side of the head and sending him crashing to the ground.

On the far side of the room, in front of a wall of monitors, another man had grabbed hold of a blaster rifle, but Parker nailed him mid-body before he could even lift it to shoulder height.

She was cursing as she was turning, her battlefield calculations coming up one short. But rather than the searing pain of laser fire or the numbing punch of a stun blaster, she heard a strangled grunt. As she completed her turn, she saw the crumbled form of a woman sprawled out behind her, a laser pistol still clutched in one hand.

Addy motioned to the band around her wrist, twisting it to retract the conductors. "What do you know? It had another charge." She tapped an index finger against it thoughtfully. "You know, my mother gave me this the first time I went out on a job. I was sixteen. I'm kind of amazed it still works." Her lips twisted slightly before she added, "I don't think we should try for three though."

Parker paused, considered, and then wordlessly handed over the stun-rod.

Eyes lighting up, Addy took hold of the weapon and made a quick swipe through the air. "You're welcome."

Already regretting the decision, Parker knelt, prying the pistol from the unconscious woman's fingers.

"Just try not to do anything to get yourself, or me, killed."

Addy's grin was quick. "It's my daily mantra," she quipped before sliding over to the computers.

Parker went to work restraining the fallen foes, a task made considerably easier since nearly all of them carried security manacles. Five out of the six at least. For the sixth, she had to improvise. It had been a while since she had any need to tie a binding knot, but she was confident in the result, especially considering the cables and duct tape she had to work with.

Just to be safe, she kept that one propped in front of the others so she could keep her eye on him while she looked over Addy's shoulder.

"Find our friends?"

"Aww, did you just admit to having friends?"

Parker lifted one brow and remained silent.

"Don't worry, we'll keep it between us. To answer your question, no. There are 400-plus cameras in this place. It's going to take a couple of minutes."

"We'll be lucky if we get a couple of minutes," Parker warned, glaring down at the screens and watching the scenes flip past. On a separate console, a map of the station was displayed, and from the icons, Parker figured it was a readout of the camera locations. She could see Addy's steady, methodical search as each icon blinked once the engineer accessed it.

Parker zeroed in on a section of the map curiously devoid of icons.

"Why would one level not have any cameras?"

Addy didn't look up from her search. "It's got something somebody doesn't want other people looking in on," was her suggestion.

Parker nodded, her lips pressing together firmly. "Yeah, and I bet that's where they took Sam. That's where Floodwater is."

"Great, that's 50% of the mystery solved. Now, let me figure out the other half."

Parker shook her head. "Look, Kate's not stupid. She's going to stay off camera if she can. We could look for hours and not find her."

"Better idea?"

"We go after Floodwater."

That pulled Addy away from the screens. Shock stretched every line of her face.

"You want to go after Floodwater?" she repeated incredulously.

"Sam was taken to Floodwater; we know that much. We find him, neutralize him, then we have control of the station. We'll be off camera. Anyone tries to contact him, we'll know about it. Maybe then we can figure out a way to get word to Kate, to let her know where to meet us to exit."

"That's assuming we're not horribly killed in the attempt."

Parker made an impatient gesture with one hand. "Obviously."

Addy pushed back from the console. "Well, I love it. Let's do it. One question though; why the change of heart? I thought you wanted more firepower before we took on Floodwater."

Reaching forward, Parker punched in a few commands on the console. One of the screens flipped to a view of the docking bay. Drawn up beside the kraken were two additional ships, sleek and shiny compared to the curvy, brassy exterior of Sam's vessel. While the kraken was a large class spaceship, it was dwarfed by just one of the new crafts.

Spilling out from wide bay doors in neat, ordered lines of five were uniformed figures: an orderly procession of troops.

"We're about to have a lot more company. Those are corporate flagship shuttles. They can carry a thousand, easy."

Addy rubbed a hand over her mouth. "They said Floodwater had allies high up."

"We have to figure out how to get on Floodwater's secret level, find Sam and Kate, and get the hell out of here before they finish deploying."

"Tell me it'll take them a while to finish deploying."

"It won't."

Grimacing, Addy turned to look at the station map. "Great. So, the main elevator bank doesn't go to that level. There's a personal one here," she motioned to the screen, "but I'm willing to bet that it's pass-coded or locked somehow. Probably guarded. Floodwater seems like the paranoid type."

"If we got past the guards, could you break through the security?"

Addy laughed. "I doubt it. I'm an engineer, not a security expert. I could try and guess his code, but I'm assuming it's not going to be 1234 or 'password.'"

Parker bore down on the wave of frustration that passed through her, recognizing it as the opposite of helpful. Still, she couldn't help but bite out, "So what do we do then?"

Leaning closer, Addy continued to study the blueprints, fingers tracing along the clusters of intersecting and parallel lines. She was quiet, engaged in her investigation for so long that Parker started to repeat her question.

But then Addy tapped the screen and straightened, lifting one finger into the air beside her head, her eyes far away. Then they snapped over to meet Parker's impatient gaze.

"I have an idea."

twenty-two

Sam watched as Mac deposited Kate on a table similar to the one she was on, wincing at the way the other woman's body sprawled lifelessly. Her eyes shifted, suddenly more interested in the room than she had been before. It contained some of the apparatuses of a med-bay, albeit one mixed with a laboratory and crossed with a conference room. There was medical equipment she recognized, scanners and instruments, along with strange machines, beakers, and tubes she did not. Tools that did not look at all like they were meant to stitch flesh back together. Near the back of the room, before a wide bay of windows facing out into space, was a table surrounded by high-backed chairs.

The only other figure she could see was Benny, sentry still near the door Mac had entered through. The moon-faced muscle was motionless, save for the sluggish blink of his eyes, but Sam had no doubt he was following Floodwater's every movement. Not difficult since Floodwater was hardly moving.

"So… what, I guess that means you have some… kinda horrible torture in mind?" Sam asked, pushing past the numbness in her mouth. She tried to wiggle the arm furthest from him, hidden by her body, to see how tightly the straps were secured.

Her arm remained limp, only the tips of her fingers twitching slightly.

Wonderful.

The corners of Floodwater's lips rose. "Oh, no. Well. I suppose it depends how you look at it. You could say that I'm about to give you and the entire universe a great gift. One that will vastly push the bounds of science further than it's ever gone."

Sam waited. "So. Horrible torture, then?" she repeated.

Floodwater didn't reply. He gave his attention to Mac as the doctor finished securing Kate's feet to the table. Sam had yet to see the other woman make any kind of movement of her own. Maybe she was already dead. Biting the inside of her lip, Sam tried again to twist her wrist.

Again, her fingers fluttered uselessly.

"Well? Did you find the files?" Floodwater's voice was heavy with impatience yet tinged with nervousness. It prickled Sam's ears even as she started at Kate; tried to ascertain if she was breathing. Mac stiffened and half-turned toward Floodwater, his eyes averted.

"No. As I said, they weren't anywhere on the ship."

"You also said she told you she'd seen them. That she knew everything. So, they must be somewhere."

Mac shrugged, a seemingly careless movement of his shoulders. But Sam recognized it for what it was. Jonah had done the same thing whenever he felt backed into the corner in an argument. "Maybe she was lying."

"*Maybe?*" Floodwater hissed. The same mirror of rage from back on Icarus 3 bulged in his eyes, warping his typically flat countenance. "That is the answer you want to take to—"

Spinning all the way around, Mac slashed through the air with one hand. "Look, I told you, I checked the ship's logs. There's no record those files were viewed. And she's not savvy enough to have gotten around my programs."

Floodwater sneered, leaning forward on his cane. "Clearly, she *is* savvy enough, considering you haven't found them. What about a personal tablet, a comm device?"

Mac shook his head. "They're all linked to the ship's logs. The only way she might have been able to see it is if she—" Mac stopped in midsentence, his forehead wrinkling in thought. He lifted his eyes to Sam, head skewing. She sent a strongly worded mental message to her arm to move.

Twitch.

Stalking forward, Mac reached Sam's side in four long steps. His hand shot out, tugging up the sleeve of her shirt and revealing her wrist unit.

"Of course. Always the last place you look," he murmured, with a sneer. His fingers felt like spider legs against her wrist as he removed the accessory. She ignored the feelings of revulsion his touch inspired and concentrated on the nerve points registering.

"I wouldn't mess with it," she warned, struggling for airy nonchalance. Between her paralysis and the aridness in her throat, she was sure it came out more like a dying croak. It was enough to make Mac pause and squint, first at her, then at the unit, and then back at her.

"And why not?"

She wondered if he was truly curious or just humoring her.

"Because Addy fixed it for me. Made some upgrades."

His eyes narrowed further even as his smirk widened. "And what? You think she put a failsafe on it?"

Sam wanted to shrug; only managed to jostle one shoulder. No doubt it looked more like a convulsion, but sometimes you had to work with what you had.

"She's pretty crazy."

Mac regarded the unit once more and nodded, appearing thoughtful. Then he bent down and spoke close to her ear. "She *was* pretty crazy," he corrected unkindly.

Sam absorbed the blow with barely a flinch, grateful for the weakness in her muscles. If she could have, she would have wiped the smile from his face, no matter how much it shortened her lifespan.

He started to straighten. "So, what are you going to do? Blast us out the airlock?" she asked, hoping to keep him near and distracted. Mac appeared almost remorseful, but the emotion was jostled away with a quick shake of his head.

"No. Nothing like that."

"Think of yourself as having the opportunity to be part of scientific and medical breakthroughs," Floodwater stated, his voice fading as he moved away from the table and out of Sam's view.

"Mr. Floodwater?" Benny's low intonation cut across the room.

"Not now, Benny."

Sam kept her eyes on Mac. "What does that mean?"

Mac opened his mouth but didn't get the chance to speak.

"It means that, since you were so interested, we're going to give you the chance to take part in our experiments," Floodwater answered instead.

"Uh, Mr. Floodwater?"

"Not *now*, Benny."

Sam rolled her head and barely managed to glimpse the back of Floodwater as he looked out the wide windows.

"First off, though, we need to ensure you meet the parameters of the subjects currently involved in the project. You see, right now, you're missing a very important piece."

Sam's gaze cut back to Mac; again, she thought she saw regret flash across his face.

"And what is that?"

Floodwater chuckled, mirthlessly. Without warning, he was craning over her once more. "Madness," he replied simply, acting for all the world like he was afflicted himself.

"At the moment, we're still not entirely sure what causes temporal catatonia. The concoction Dr. Whent will be injecting you with is simply our best guess. You will either become another candidate for our little program or you'll... well, we're not actually quite sure *what* you might become, but it won't be pleasant."

Sam could think of nothing to say, nothing to spit back at him, nothing that could push past the fear slowly taking over the defiance in her body. She just glared back and hoped the implied *fuck you* was discernible.

Floodwater set an almost gentle hand on her shoulder and bent his head. "I would tell you this won't hurt a bit but... I have a feeling it's going to hurt quite a lot."

"Mr. Floodwater!"

Irritation and anger twisted Floodwater's face and he uncurled with a nearly audible snap.

"What is it?" he barked, raising his head toward Benny.

The goon was pointing one hand in their direction. "Is she supposed to be doing that?" he asked, dully.

Both Floodwater and Mac spun. Mac's body jerked, and as he twisted, Kate was revealed, holding an auto-injector in one hand. She held it out in front of her like a weapon.

"Is this the scary vial of the tempers you mentioned?" she threatened, innocently.

Parker eyed the frankly *unimpressive* elevator with a heavy dose of skepticism. She let it color her voice as she asked, "This is Floodwater's private elevator?"

Addy looked up from the access panel she had all but crawled inside. "No, this is one of the auxiliary service elevators."

"I thought you said none of the other elevators access the level we think is Floodwater's," Parker recalled, brows knitting together in confusion.

"They don't. But this unit is multi-directional. Most elevators are in space stations and satellites. It makes construction a whole lot easier. Once the outside is complete and the station is online, they re-configure the lift paths. But all the shafts and bays are still in place and connected. Usually."

The *usually* came out muffled as Addy ducked her head inside the panel. Parker wasn't sure what she was doing or what she was doing it with, since the only "tools" the engineer had were a couple of stylus-like objects she had taken from the security room.

"What do you mean, *usually*?"

Some clanking noises came from inside the panel, followed by what sounded like the snap of a spark, and then Addy emerged again, patting at her pockets.

"Well, there is the remote possibility one of the shafts has been disconnected or blocked off. Sometimes stations turn them into storage spaces."

Parker eyed the elevator warily. "And how do we know if the shaft we're in has been blocked?"

Dropping her hands, Addy squinted up at her. "I imagine the loud bang will be a good indicator. You don't happen to have a laser drill on you, do you?"

Reaching up to her waist, Parker tugged free one of four laser pistols she had relieved the guards of. She pushed it into Addy's hand. Addy studied it, considered, and then squeezed her shoulders back inside the panel. "Might work."

Parker cast a worried look down the short corridor. They seemed to be out of the way of a major junction, but they were still exposed.

"You think this is a better idea than trying to guess Floodwater's passcode?" she asked, trying not to imagine what the impact of crashing an elevator would feel like.

More clanks and cranks sounded, along with a few high-pitched whines. A small billow of smoke poured forth, followed by Addy coughing slightly. She held the laser pistol out. When Parker took it, she saw the handle had been partially melted. Rather than ask, the mercenary simply tossed it aside.

"Look at it this way. Floodwater's elevator has got to be guarded, right? We try and assault that, we'll probably be killed. We do this, *maybe* we'll be killed."

"You're saying it's a difference of probably and maybe?"

Addy nodded, sliding forward into the elevator itself. The control panel hung out from the wall. A small tablet, also courtesy of one of the guards, was hooked into the circuitry. The entire setup looked the furthest thing from safe, and Parker could not fathom why in hell she was even considering getting into it. "It's at least a 30% difference. If that helps."

Parker reluctantly got into the car. "It doesn't. Are there any other potential disasters I should know about?"

Lifting the tablet, Addy began entering the sequence she had previously stated would get them where they wanted to go.

"There is also the potential we might strike another car if one is running within one of the shafts that we bisect."

Parker sighed as the elevator doors slid shut. "I wish you hadn't told me that."

"Well, just in case."

"Just in case what—" Parker's question was cut off when Addy reached up, grabbed hold of her neck with both hands and tugged her down into a long searing kiss.

And then, just as abruptly, she pushed the mercenary back. "So, you want to date after this or what?"

There were a dozen or so things that leapt into Parker's mind. What they were attempting to do was crazy. She, in all probability, was going to die. They wouldn't get the chance to date because Addy would be dead, too. She was sorry about everything. She'd trade herself to Floodwater for Addy's safety if she thought for a second she could trust him. Because she was pretty sure she was in I—

Parker shook the last thought away before it could finish and returned Addy's steely-eyed, if somewhat misty, glare.

"Yes. Yes, I do," she affirmed.

Addy nodded. As one, they turned and faced the elevator doors.

And waited.

Mac grabbed at his shoulder with one hand and lunged for Kate with the other. His body gave a second, more powerful shudder, and with an inhumane cry, he crashed to the floor. Kate crossed the gap between their tables without even glancing at him, pointing the injector at Floodwater, and clicking the dosage reload. Floodwater reared back from it as if it were a plasma rifle.

"Benny! Get down here!" he screamed as Kate fumbled with the restraints on Sam's left arm. She wrestled it free from the strap as Benny lumbered toward her, swinging his massive hands. Kate ducked away from his outstretched arms and scrambled backwards, trying to put space between them.

Move, damn you! Sam shouted mentally and finally managed to fling her free arm across her body. Her left hand landed limply near the binding on her right wrist, but her fingers could only paw at it. Baring her teeth, Sam persisted, digging her nails into the leather because fuck all if she was going to die lying down.

She forced her head up, trying to keep track of the motion in the room. Kate led Benny on a chase, sliding across tables and ducking through the small spaces between the equipment to keep her distance. Benny simply barged through any obstacles, smashing glass, plastics, and whatever else without pause.

"Kill her!" Floodwater shouted, edging himself around the room toward the door. His eyes locked on Mac's spasming body as if he expected some odious beast to emerge from the shaking form. The thought had Sam clawing harder, feeling some measure of dexterity returning to her fingertips. She managed to slip the strap off the metal binding and wrenched her hand free. Her vision swam; all her limbs were feeble with exhaustion and the lingering effects of the drugs. Still, she successfully rolled onto one side in time to see Floodwater inching toward escape. Then Kate was flying toward her, Benny hot on her heels.

Before she could even consider her next action, the doors to the room swished open. Floodwater cried out in triumph and dove at them, only to pull up short when Addy and Parker passed through.

"How did you—" he began. His words cut off abruptly; Addy's fist shot forward and connected with his jaw. Eyes rolling, he fell backwards into a heap. At nearly the same time, Benny's forward motion suddenly halted as he seized up. When his body crashed to the ground, Sam could see Parker with her arm out, stunner in hand.

Kate didn't stop until she reached Sam and then, to Sam's shock, embarrassment, and—though she'd never admit it—pleasure, threw her arms around her. Sam nearly fell back onto the table and grunted from the force of the squeeze. After a second, she lifted one hand and patted it awkwardly against Kate's back and listened to the other woman sigh with relief into her shoulder.

Addy took in the room, the fallen bodies, and embracing figures. She flexed her fingers, grimacing.

"Let's never do this again," she announced, motioning to the scene before her.

Parker's long strides ate up the distance between the door and Sam. She gave a brief, almost disinterested look at Mac's crumpled, quivering form before moving to undo the remaining bindings at Sam's ankles.

"We have to get out of here. Now. Can you walk?"

With Kate's help, Sam lurched up into a sitting position. She glanced down at the floor and considered putting her feet down onto it. "I—" she began and realized her legs felt more like bio-gel than support structures. "—don't think so. He must have given me some kind of paralytic." Grunting, she lightly punched the side of her left leg and felt no response from the cybernetic nerves. "Did something to my prosthetic, too, the asshole."

"Can you carry her, Parker?" Kate asked, still gripping tightly to Sam's arm, as if she thought Sam was going to wander off. Sam saw the white of her knuckles and figured it wasn't the right time to say anything. Then the question registered.

"Carry me? What? Why?"

Parker began rooting through the drawers underneath the med-bench Sam was on. "If I have to. It'll be better if she can walk."

Sam shook her head. "What's the hurry? I don't think any of these guys are going to waking up soon."

Addy motioned down at Mac. "Yeah, what happened to him?"

Sam and Kate exchanged looks. "Far as we can tell, he was infected with the tempers. Or whatever they cooked up to simulate the symptoms," Kate answered, her voice tight.

Addy took a long, cautious step away from the body. And then another. "Sounds fun. Anyway, to answer your question, two corporate flagship shuttles just docked, and it looks like a couple squads of corps are unloading. We probably want to be out before they get here."

"Shit," Sam and Kate cursed at the same time.

Sam felt something press against the side of her neck. She twisted toward it. "What the hell—"

"Hold still," Parker ordered.

There was a click and a jab against Sam's skin. Even as she opened her mouth to protest, what felt like an electric shock zapped through her entire body. Every muscle jerked in response. Gasping, she all but fell forward off the table. She had a split second to consider bracing herself for hitting the floor when her left leg caught her. A second, smaller shock wave coursed through her: her body jolted again.

Her eyes widened like they were being stretched open by invisible fingers as she looked at Parker. "What the hell was that?"

Parker tossed aside the injector. "Stimulant. Don't know how long it'll last, so let's get moving." She stepped over Mac's form without a second look.

"Should we take any of these guys with us?" Addy questioned, reaching out to take hold of Sam's other arm. Sam waved her off; Kate's grip was enough to keep her steady, even if the other woman's fingers were like a brand.

"We could just take them out," Parker said, from beside the door. "Do the universe a favor."

Floodwater lay there, motionless and completely vulnerable. She thought of Triss and Ollie. Of Jonah. She thought of the dead bodies the pirates had found on her shuttle. She thought of the files she had found that Jonah had hidden away. She wondered how many crews, how many lives, had been destroyed by one man.

Sam shook her head. "No. There's a better way to beat him." Though she hardly felt in control of them, her legs shuffled her over to the console Mac had been working on. Kate's hand remained firm and supportive on her arm. With fingers still slightly numb, Sam ejected the small memory card and tucked it away in a pocket.

"Let's get the hell out of here."

"There's more."

Sam narrowed her eyes at her. Kate wasn't entirely sure that it was on purpose, or just another twitch.

"What do you mean, more?"

Kate took a deep breath. "I saw some files Mac was working on. Floodwater has been running his own experiments, here on the station. They weren't trying to cure temporal catatonia here. They were using it for something else."

Sam's jaw clenched. "Yeah, I kind of figured that from his 'contributions to science' speech. Doesn't sound like we'll have time to go digging for anything."

"I might have sent a comm out with some files."

At Sam's surprised look, Kate lifted her shoulders. "I sent it to my old workspace link. Hopefully they haven't deleted my account yet."

Sam let out an impressed chuckle as the door to the room slid open. A tall man in a fitted suit entered, several heavily armed uniformed men on either side of him. Parker retreated from the door, raising her blaster. Addy joined her, holding out the stun-rod. Sam wasn't sure how she felt about the fact the two of them had neatly placed themselves in front of both her and Kate. Even Kate had subtly shifted so Sam was a step behind her.

The armed men lifted their own rifles in response to Parker and Addy's movements, but the suited man remained relaxed, hands at his sides. They slid into his pockets while he took in the room, from the four of them, to the scattered debris, to the bodies on the ground.

Sam shook off Kate's grip and pushed forward, setting one hand on Parker's arm and another on Addy's. She had to apply considerably more pressure on Parker's arm to get her to lower her weapon, but the mercenary acquiesced.

The man zeroed in on her.

"It seems you've already taken care of things for us," he noted, mildly.

"Who's us?" Sam demanded.

The guards shuffled, moving aside, and another tall figure emerged, familiar, with long hair tied back from a sharp face.

"Iris!" Kate exclaimed. "What are you doing here?"

Iris offered her measured smile. "I told you we had powerful friends." She turned to Sam. "I know you didn't actually accept our offer of help, but we decided to come anyway."

Scowling, Sam opened her mouth to speak. Her body gave a sudden, violent twitch, her eyes rolled back into her head, and she pitched forward, collapsing to the ground. Crying out, Kate dropped down beside her, her fingers going immediately to Sam's neck.

"Pulse is there," she breathed as one of the men came to join her, a scanner already in hand. He ran it along Sam's body, nodding to himself.

"Vitals are good. Some high levels of nerve suppressants, but nothing approaching toxic levels. We should get her to a med-bay though."

Addy glanced over at Parker. "Guess those stimulants didn't last long at all."

Parker rolled her eyes. "Floodwater is a cheap ass."

twenty-three

"And in the latest update regarding business magnate Miles Floodwater, additional charges have been brought against the man some are calling the most dangerous crime boss in history. Three months ago, Floodwater was arrested on suspicions of violating the Fundamental Agreement Against Genetic Manipulation. That arrest has since led to a massive investigation into all of Floodwater's business holdings."

Kate's eyes lifted from the expense report she had been reviewing and drifted to the wall screen set to the Universal News Channel. Even after ninety days of nonstop coverage, it was still strange to hear Floodwater's name bandied about without a fumble or stutter. To hear it spoken with as much banality as "John Smith." Seeing his face in the corner of the screen, glass green eyes staring out from the flat, expressionless face, hardly even inspired any feelings of fear or trepidation. Looking at the mug shot, she felt a small measure of pride knowing that she had helped put him where he was probably going.

Of course, she was *also* thankful that her name and actions were not part of the official capture report. No need to borrow trouble if anyone was out looking for revenge. Not that it seemed likely anyone *would*. Every day and every news story seemed to highlight another informant who had stepped forward to offer further evidence of a vast laundry list of crimes. Years of weapons and drug trafficking, racketeering, loan sharking, torture, and murder had been enough to ensure silence but slicing and dicing the genetic code of hundreds of helpless CT victims apparently was the bridge too far.

Thinking of Dravanol, Kate was reminded that she hadn't responded to the comm from Addy she'd received that morning, the one mentioning she and Parker would be in the area and maybe they could do lunch. Kate had every intention of saying yes because she was dying to know how Parker, who she had last seen in the custody of UNE officers, had avoided prosecution as a known associate of Floodwater. And if the engineer had updates about certain others, it would be appreciated as well.

The story onscreen switched as Kate took a sip from her mug, tasting bitter tea mellowed by vanilla. Pirates becoming incorporated, speculation around if one of the Big Five was to be relegated to a lower tier and which it might be. Noise about territory rights and rules of governance, talk of moving or abolishing the Secession border. Idly she recalled another conversation—felt like ages ago—over corporate expansion. The TISAD / Chester merger hadn't come to pass, which was why relegation was currently on the table.

I think it'll never happen.

Kate deliberately avoided wondering what the opinion would be now.

She spied Iris on screen, moving among a sea of reporters, answering questions in her stately, even voice, looking perfectly poised and unrushed despite the crowd. In Kate's mind she saw the pirate leader outside the medical unit of the TISAD flagship, still dignified but with a slightly chagrin expression on her face.

How did you know to come here? Kate had asked.

A moment's hesitation. *I was… concerned that something like what happened with Jonah would happen again. So. I had the ship bugged.*

Oh. Well, that doesn't bother me at all, actually.

Good. Another pause. Best not to mention it to Sam, though.

Yeah, Kate had said, glancing toward the med unit. *Probably not.*

The camera panned and centered on a tall man in a fitted suit with dark hair tightly coiled to his head. The CXO of the TISAD Group, the largest in the universe, de facto leader of the Big Five, was announcing their support of pirate incorporation and looking forward to cooperation for the betterment of humanity. She wondered what the pirates thought, having once been cast to the very edges of known space, about being once more connected to the web of civilization. How long before they found the new boundaries too restrictive or the welcoming masses no longer welcoming?

She turned the screen off. He had been nice enough on the station for the ten seconds they had spoken, but she wasn't sure she was ready to vote him supreme leader of the universe.

There were certainly worse choices.

Sitting back in her chair, she swiveled to face the wall of windows behind her desk. Her new office overlooked one of the service yards for ships and she found she liked to watch the different sized vehicles as they came and went. There were even two kraken class transporters currently on their roster of vendors: the sight of the stretching tendrils of engine gave her a little pang in her chest.

Hadn't had the need to step foot in either of them though, and she wasn't sure if she was disappointed or grateful for the fact.

She stood up, needing to move.

Her last time on a kraken had been a few days after the confrontation with Floodwater. It had taken Sam that long to recover from the drugs Mac—and then Parker—had injected her with. An unlucky consequence of the combined doses. Standing in the corridor had been the first time Kate had seen her out of bed.

"You look... not dead," was the best Kate could come up with. She winced.

It was true. Sam stood on her own two feet, awake and moving. That was pretty much the extent of the positives. Her face was ashy and sweaty, dark circles marred the skin under her eyes, and a livid bruise marked the right side of her forehead where she'd hit it after collapsing.

Sam touched her fingertips to it in an absent gesture and flinched. "I feel... not dead," she agreed.

The conversation that followed had been short, since a transport had been waiting to take Kate back home, and she couldn't quite remember what was said.

It was so strange; she could recall so many of their conversations with startling clarity—but not that one. Instead, it was hazy and vague, like she had been watching it unfold from 30 feet away rather than being a part of it. She couldn't seem to separate what she had said from what she had wanted to say, and so it all mushed together in an incomprehensible static.

She had wanted to talk about everything that happened, to offer her gratitude for everything Sam had done, to ask about the future and if there was any chance of their—

God, it all sounded so stilted, even in her own head. She should be grateful for the fuzziness.

Those last words, though, she did remember. Spoken so casually.

This'll probably take a while; feels like everyone and their mother wants to talk to me. You should take the transport. I'll check in when they shake me loose.

And then nothing.

She felt a stirring of regret; she had gone on a tremendous journey, faced evil, escaped death, and returned safely, but had let slip through her fingers the very thing she had gone looking for.

Connection.

Now she was back on planet; safe, secure, and enjoying her spreadsheets once more. But she had to admit, if just to herself, that she missed that cranky grump of a spaceship captain. And maybe, if she looked around, she could find whatever it was they had been building again, perhaps with someone closer and more open to *any* kind of communication.

But she didn't want to.

Kate turned back toward her desk, intending to respond to Addy's message—surely the engineer had some idea of Sam's whereabouts—when her comm app flashed on screen. It displayed the name of her department head and a moment later the woman's round and slightly harried face blinked into a frame.

"Kate. I was hoping I would catch you."

Kate lifted her eyebrows. "Is something wrong, Reneé?" she asked, already mentally flipping through her active projects.

Reneé waved a hand dismissively. "No, no. Not at all. It's just that we've hired a new vendor, and the representatives are here a bit earlier than expected. Ian is next in the queue for onboarding, but the captain has specifically asked for you. Probably heard that you were our best. I was hoping you would have some time before the conference call?"

Frowning a little at the request—why did good work always seem to lead to *more* work—Kate switched from her projects to her calendar and glanced at the clock. She estimated the time for onboarding, juggled the other minor tasks she had flagged for the morning, and subtracted the scheduled time for the call.

"Yes, it shouldn't be a problem," she replied, nodding. "They're already here?"

"Yes, they're on service pad seven, I believe." Reneé's gaze shifted and after a second, she nodded. "Yes, seven. You'll find the information you need for the onboarding in your access folder. And thank you."

"No problem."

The comm window blinked closed and Kate stepped around her desk, snatching her tablet up as she moved. She considered grabbing her jacket from off the back of the guest chair but decided against it. Service pad seven was near enough to the waiting lounge that they could do the onboarding there if the temperature outside was uncomfortable. The elevators were only a little ways down the hall from her office and still she managed to catch a handful of greetings in the short walk.

There was no one in the elevator car when it arrived, and no one joined her as she stepped in and programmed the route to the service pads. As the elevator shifted, she busied herself with the pre-check data on her tablet. The vendor was a transport specialist, rated for both on- and off-planet. Kate read over system specs and cargo capacity, felt that familiar pinch in her chest when she read the ship classification, *kraken*. She skimmed across to the identification column and rolled her eyes at the text filling the space listed for the ship's secondary identification. Sam's voice echoed in her head—*I haven't ever thought of anything that seemed to fit.*

Well, whoever the ship owner was, he wasn't very inventive.

The elevator halted and the doors slid open to the cavernous opening of the service bay. Filling a large portion of the space was the expected kraken class transport ship. Her throat became suddenly dry.

The cargo ramp was extended, a lone figure standing at the base of it, looking up into the ship. Kate began walking forward, her heartbeat quickening with each step. When she got within a few feet, the figure turned.

The corner of Sam's lip lifted slightly, the start of that reluctant grin Kate hadn't been able to completely push from her mind. As if the captain wasn't completely sure it was appropriate.

"Hi. I wasn't—"

Kate reached out, grabbed hold of her jacket—new, she noted—and tugged the other woman close. She could feel Sam's surprise in the slackness of her mouth, in the seconds it took for the kiss to become a kiss. As she pulled back and felt their lips release with a quiet sound, she simultaneously heard and felt Sam's slow exhale.

When she opened her eyes, she saw Sam gaping at her. "What... what was that for?" Sam asked, voice shaky.

Kate swallowed the laugh that wanted to escape but let the smile stretch her lips. "To take your mind off the pain."

Sam's forehead furrowed in confusion. "What pain?"

And that was when Kate did what she hadn't even realized she had been waiting nearly three months to do; she reared back and kicked Sam directly in the left leg.

"Fuck!" Sam shouted, leaping backwards and grabbing for her shin with both hands. "What the hell—"

Kate punched her solidly in the shoulder. "Three months? You don't send one word to me in three months? Are you kidding me? Do you have any idea what I... What makes you think that I... I can't believe you just show up here like..." She pressed her lips together and raised her index fingers to her mouth, trying to force her thoughts into a single, comprehensive line.

"Where the hell have you been?" she demanded, finally.

Sam rubbed her shin. She opened her mouth and then closed it, clearly reconsidering what she had been about to say. An entire fleet of emotions seemed to work their way across her face and Kate waited, interested to see what would win out.

"The UNE questioned me pretty extensively about Floodwater and the files that we—that Jonah found. They wanted to know how he had gotten them, where they had come from, who had supplied them. There wasn't a whole lot I could tell them, but then the UNE forces have never been known for their sharp minds. Luckily, Iris finally intervened and was able to give them more information, I guess." Sam paused and jerked a thumb back toward the ship. "Then I had to get Parker out of their lockup. It took quite a bit to convince them she wasn't one of Floodwater's accomplices."

Kate glanced over at the ramp, expecting to see the mercenary leaning against one of the struts. "Parker's on board?"

Sam shook her head. "No. She and Addy are picking up a few things at the market station two blocks over. Damn cat needs more food."

At that, Kate's hands dropped to her sides. She'd have a few things to say to Addy the next time she saw the engineer. "And you couldn't send a message? Not one, single little message? Not even a *word*?"

The hand that had been rubbing her shin went behind Sam's neck. "I wasn't sure I would be coming back," she admitted.

"What do you mean?"

Sam glanced off to the side. "I started thinking. About Floodwater and his experiments. And the experiments that had been run on the pirates. And it didn't really make sense."

"What didn't make sense?"

"I read some of the files. And Iris told me a bit the couple times she came by the med-bay. The pirates were set up in that system over *two hundred years ago*. How did Floodwater even know about them?"

Kate frowned. "Maybe he didn't. Maybe whoever stole them offered to sell them to him?"

"How would someone know that Floodwater would be interested in them?"

"Maybe it was a matter of, 'I found some evil shit, who's the evilest person I know?'"

Sam shrugged. "Maybe. Seems like a pretty big coincidence someone finds these files about experiments that are pretty close to the experiments Floodwater himself was running. I started thinking there had to be more to it. There had to be something else. So, I started looking. Hit a couple places I knew were his." She smiled faintly. "Parker was pretty helpful on that front."

"What did you find?"

"Nothing. I didn't find anything. I kept looking and finding nothing and eventually I just..."

"You just what?"

"I didn't want to look anymore. I wanted... something else."

Kate curled her hands into fists and took a deep breath. "What?"

"You."

She felt her breath punch out of her. Sam was looking at her apologetically.

"I'm not good at this," Sam stated.

Kate shook her head. "Sam, you are fucking terrible at this," she corrected, despite the fact she felt a giddiness rising up inside her like charged particles in an engine core. She struggled to school her face into a mask of seriousness.

"I mean, I don't even really know that much about you," she pointed out.

Nodding, Sam jammed her hands into the pockets of her jacket, and there was that charming half- smirk.

"What do you want to know?"

Clearing her throat, Kate glanced down at her tablet. "Well for starters, do you have your SOW-4, your vessel license and are both up to date?"

Sam blinked. "What?"

"Your SOW-4 for employment and vessel license for—" Kate motioned toward the kraken, "proof of ownership or lease? Oh, and a preferred account for direct payments."

When Sam continued to stare, Kate gave her best innocent expression. "You did want to work for us, yes? Or was this all just an elaborate ruse to see me again?"

Sam blew out a long breath. "I mean, I wouldn't call it elaborate... oh," she stated when Kate burst out laughing. "You're fucking with me."

Nearly overwhelmed with fondness, Kate just barely resisted reaching out to tweak the other woman's nose as it crinkled adorably.

"Well, I will need those files if you do actually want to work for us—" she glanced down at the tablet again, "*Sameev*?"

A muscle in Sam's cheek twitched. "Technically."

Still reading, Kate continued with, "Hero. Oh, are you related—"

"Yeah. He was my father."

"That explains so much," Kate mused, shaking her head in bemusement.

Sam appeared affronted. "How do you figure? It's not like I ever threw myself on an exploding hatch."

"What do you call flying to the edge of the galaxy for a woman you've known twenty-four hours?" Holding up one finger, Kate added, "Think very carefully about what you're about to say."

In an undoubtedly wise move, Sam merely held out her hands. "What else do you want to know?"

Turning, Kate looked at the ship instead, folding her arms across her chest. "You named it."

"I did."

"Couldn't think of anything better?"

Sam tipped her head back slightly. "I think it's got a nice ring to it. *The Ship*. Says everything you need it to say."

The door slid open and light from the corridor cut in like a wide blade, illuminating the tall back of a chair over which only the top of a head could be seen. Steel gray hair glinted.

"Madame, we were unable to retrieve the files."

There was silence and then the chair turned slightly, enough to reveal the hint of a profile in the shadows beyond the light. In the open doorway, the man that had spoken trembled.

"Is that so?" The voice that replied was smoky and full, betraying neither disappointment nor irritation. He could only assume she felt both.

Swallowing, he nodded jerkily. "Yes. I'm afraid the UNE seems to have completely disposed of both the digital and the—"

A hand shot up and the man immediately fell silent. Silence stretched out but he knew better than to leave.

"And what of our captain? Sam?"

"We still have her under surveillance."

"Still? You make it almost sound like you didn't lose track of her, allowing her to make contact with the experiments on HRC16."

He swallowed the words of defense, of protest. It wouldn't matter. Another span of silence. He could hear his heartbeat pounding in his ears. Could feel his pulse jumping in his neck. Still, he stood in place, waiting.

Finally, "Did she find anything?"

"Nothing," he swore vehemently, straining to regain favor, even though he knew, knew it was pointless. "We were careful."

The next words were a cold reminder of that. "If you had been careful, we would have the files."

"We—"

The hand, still raised, flicked in an obvious sign of dismissal. The man gave a low bow and beat a hasty retreat, the door swishing shut a moment later.

The chair shifted again so its occupant faced a massive screen that stretched the entire length of a wall. In the upper left corner of the screen, a window showed a man, seated on a cot in a small room. He stared vacantly ahead, not a muscle in his body moving. In the upper right, numbers and formulas were displayed. A third window in the bottom left showed a handful of figures in lab coats buzzing about like worker bees. In the bottom right, simply a row of faces, darkened by shadows, watching.

Leaning forward, the glow from the screen chased some of the darkness back from her face. There was more, lurking in the depths of her eyes, that no amount of light could dispel. Those eyes remained fixed on the man as she spoke into a small microphone.

"Doctors, let's begin again."

Acknowledgments

First I have to thank my wonderful wife, Nicole DeGennaro, for being such an important part of my life. Thank you for always helping lift me up when things feel hard and making me smile every day.

I would like to thank Ana Giovinazzo for reading this over twice and helping me edit it down to a manageable size. Thank you so much for all the incredible feedback and for always answering my random questions about which version of a paragraph you liked best. About a million times.

To CJ Moore, for being such a fantastic friend and advanced reader. I really appreciate all your enthusiasm and encouragement that you shared with me.

To R Teschner, and Eri Cesar for catching a host of possibly embarrassing mistakes and giving some very excellent suggestions on how to correct them.

And thank you so much to everyone for reading.